PSYCHIC

*Nowhere
to hide...*

1863

1994

1973

F. P. DORCHAK

Also by F. P. Dorchak

Novels

Sleepwalkers (2001)
The Uninvited (2013)
ERO (2013)

Anthologies

"Tail Gunner":
The You Belong Collective—Writing and Illustrations by Longmont Area Residents (2012)

"*Psychic*...is a page turner...full of mind-numbing worry and questions..."

Madelon Rose Logue
Editor/Publisher *The Black Sheep*

F. P. Dorchak, author of *Sleepwalkers*, has upped the game. His new novel, *Psychic*, is a ground-breaking, reality bending, mind expanding metaphysical mystery and action thriller that had me hooked from the very beginning. There are passages in the work that describe the nature of existence as beautifully as those in the Seth material, but are uniquely his own. I loved *Sleepwalkers*...*Psychic* blew me away.

Joyce Combs
Creator of the *Seth Deck*

Copyright 2014 by F. P. Dorchak
Published by Wailing Loon, 2014
Cover design by **Duvall Design**
Print formatting by **A Thirsty Mind Book Design**

ISBN-13: 978-0692261811
ISBN-10: 0692261818

WAILING
LOON

Thanks to John "Chief" Keith, U.S. Navy (OTC, ret.), Jerry Johnston, U.S. Army (Warrant Officer 3, ret.; ex-Huey and Blackhawk pilot), Dave Lirette, Cherry Weiner, the online John F. Kennedy Presidential Library and Museum, Karen Lin, Janet Fogg, Betsy Dornbusch, and Deb Coleman. Thanks to Joseph McMoneagle, Jim Schnabel, Dale E. Graff, and David Morehouse for their works documenting the fascinating world of remote viewing. I did my best trying to adhere to the official protocol, but of course ran down rabbit holes of my own making. A *huge* thanks to Joyce Combs and Mandy Pratt for their copyediting and proofreading! To Duvall Design for the cover! Thanks to my wife for always being there and putting up with my "writer's mind." Thanks to the Seth material, Jane Roberts, and Robert Butts. To anyone else I may have missed, it was not intentional, but thank you! Also...thanks to *Starbucks* for never throwing me out when I didn't buy a damned thing and just needed a corner in which to write....

FPD

Always, for Laura

What Do You Believe?

Ring around the rosie,
A pocketful of posies,
Ashes! Ashes!
We all fall down....

Chapter One

Out of the moonlit darkness, worn, black combat boots fell silently to earth, quickly followed by black, uniform-clad shins, hips, and upper body.

The man collapsed gracefully onto the ground, completing a perfect "parachute landing fall." In one effortless, flowing movement, he rolled across his back, thumbed release of his chute, then shot back to his feet. He swiftly collected his collapsing canopy while scanning his silvery surroundings. Hands and face blackened, weaponry barely rattling about him, the Bravo Force operator bunched up his canopy into a tight ball and glanced skyward, eyeing the other shadows descending behind him. He quickly dug a large hole among the Socorro cactus, using a portable shovel, threw his chute and harness into it, then checked his Starlight Scoped CAR-15; he adjusted its strap about his elbow and forearm. Listened to the soft thuds of his comrades as they landed around him, ever scanning the moonlit plains. With silent approval, he noted the tight grouping of his team's landing. Took a compass bearing. Each man then stowed his chute in the bury pit he created, performed his own equipment and weapon's check, then also scanned the darkness with his Starlight Scope.

The Bravo Force leader led his face-darkened team forward.

Like specters flying across a ghostly landscape, the team advanced swiftly through the darkness, their objective a lone set of buildings set against the moonlit eastern plains of Colorado, no more than a hundred yards ahead. Reassembling his men, the leader switched weapons to a Beretta .22, as did two other team members. The routine had been well-practiced, but as they pushed forward, the leader experienced sudden, acute anxiety.

Would they make it? Could they complete their mission? Were they biting off more than they could chew?

Signaling the predetermined team of two toward the rear of the house, the Bravo Force leader signaled the others to fan out into position around the building. He took up his own position about fifty feet out from the front door. Looked to his radium-illuminated watch—and its trembling arm. He shook the arm, fingers splayed apart, and internally commanded the jerking still. All trembling ceased.

What was the matter with him? He was a hardened, tested, professional—a goddamned government-trained killer, for Chrissakes. This was *bullshit*.

Clenching his hand into a tight fist, he narrowed his focus to his watch crystal.

Time...watch the *time*.

The dog...it would pick them up soon. 0210 hours. Mentally counting, he closed his eyes and steeled himself, burying his growing anxiety.

Where the hell was this shit coming *from?*

The leader raised his Beretta in both hands before him as if in silent prayer...then smacked himself in the forehead with it. Shaking his head, he quietly grunted as he readied and coiled his superbly trained body...

And charged the door.

He shot out across the darkness, taking note of the position of his team and their targets—those inside the building and unaware of their presence—but as he burst across open space, another resurgence of oppressiveness grabbed hold of his insides like grappling hooks. His breathing, normally calm and relaxed, was now labored and short. The intense sense of dread continued building and now filled every crevice within him. He felt like he was again jumping out of that C-123 into the moonlit night—*but this time without a parachute.*

As he gained on the door, he once more eyed his targets through the curtain-draped windows, reaffirming their positions. Three of them. He saw the food on their table—as had been briefed—a table full of it.

Who ate like that at two in the fucking morning?

His anxiety increased ten-fold.

Shoulders and upper back painfully bunched into taut, constricting knots, his chest tightened, and it became even more difficult to breathe.

No! Do not *do this!* a little voice sounded off inside. *Abort! ABORT!*

But he had no choice in the matter; had signed away any such control long ago. This was a job—*his* job—one that had to get done at all costs. Whether or not he or his team were killed in the process…didn't matter…just as long as all three targets in that house were neutralized.

Where was that goddamned dog?

Two seconds from the door and still sprinting, the leader again sighted his target—the man at the head of the table—but he also glimpsed, in his heightened state of awareness and through curtains, a picture of forty-six-year-old President John F. Kennedy, displayed on a hutch by the window. Beside that was a book, the title of which he couldn't quite make out, but *knew*, in some strange, fucked-up and hyperaware manner, to be *The Prophecies of Nostradamus.*

The *what?*

Something wasn't right, his voices again pleaded, *Get out!*

Focus.

He reaffirmed his grip on the Beretta. The other two he'd sent inside should already be in position.

Were they also having second thoughts?

Had the dog already sniffed them out?

Without breaking stride, the team leader reached the door and kicked it in. It flew wide and loud, in a hail of splinters and metal, bouncing off the inside wall with a deafening crack and reverberation. He stood, inside the doorway, Beretta swung to and locked on his target's forehead. Sweat coated the Bravo Force leader's body.

What the hell were they doing?

What the hell were they thinking?

How many more times could they cheat death?

This was nuts—*crazy*—*you didn't just off an entire* family!

Hesitating, the leader shot a look to his other two operatives, also positioned within the room, their weapons similarly trained on their targets.

He saw it in their eyes.

That same apprehension. *Fear.* Both were nervous, their focused, hardened demeanor all but drained from their faces. He saw, instead, sweat and uncertainty...eyes that silently pleaded with him.

What were they supposed to do—where was that damned dog?

The leader turned back to the man, still, amazingly, seated at the head of the table, staring back blankly at him. In fact, they all stared blankly at them, as if they'd just been sitting there...

Waiting.

Why hadn't he moved?

Why'd they all just sit *there,* staring *at them?*

Why the hell were they goddamned eating a banquet at two in the fucking morning?

Run, you idiots, run, *or you goddamned well deserve to die!*

Years passed in their mental landscapes as the three assassins all stood poised, uncertainly, before the family at the two a.m. banquet table, President John F. Kennedy and Nostradamus silently observing from their hutch-side perches.

Why was Kennedy staring at them so accusingly?

The leader's upper back balled up tighter, thick rivulets of sweat cascading down his back, armpits, and face, stinging his eyes. *Focus— that damned dog—focus—where the hell was that frigging animal, and why hadn't they pulled their triggers?*

That was when he heard the deep, throaty growl emerge from underneath the table.

The dog emerged in a savage and unreal slow motion from beneath a table covered in a red-and-white-checkered tablecloth, upon which were napkins, green beans, mashed potatoes, salad, and a hunk of beef that looked and smelled like a roast his mom used to make. By the dark color of the liquid in their glasses—with ice—the leader surmised iced tea (and why did *that* bother him?).

All this he took in in the instant before he and his team executed their mission.

Through a sheer force of will he was barely able to muster (*what would his mom think of him, now?*), the leader squeezed his trigger with a clammy, slippery trigger finger—a finger he'd used countless times to point, scratch his nose, or excite his latest one-nighter—and now he was again using it to kill...a family of three. To do...*a job.*

It was at that moment that the dog, that damned, demon-growling hundred-pound beast, already out from under the table in that slow, deliberate advance that meant business, had coiled its powerful hind quarters to spring into the air like a surface-to-air missile.

They shouldn't be *here!* The lead Bravo Force operator's inner voices insisted.

This was wrong! All wrong!, his men's glares accused, *We can still* leave!

They never knew what hit them.

As the dog left the ground, all three assassins were suddenly and forcefully thrown back against the walls—

The lead Bravo Force operator shook his head, sending large beads of sweat everywhere. Blinked stinging eyes.

What the hell just happened?

Nothing.

Not a damned thing.

They had *not* been knocked back against any wall—they all remained poised and standing where they were, their targets untouched....

But he'd *felt*...

He looked to the other two, who looked similarly confused.

What the hell was going on?

No more bullshit.

Each assassin squeezed his trigger.

Three .22 rounds found their marks with deadly accuracy, one into each head. The man slammed back in his chair, his wife fell sideways to the floor, and the boy, shot on an angle from behind, slumped forward onto the table.

The German Shepard was now airborne. It headed directly for the leader. With cool precision the Bravo Force leader twisted, aimed and again fired...and removed the dog from consideration. It flew past and thumped lifelessly beyond him.

Each man lowered his weapon and approached his victim.

The leader grabbed the man's body, ensured no exit wound, as did the others to the woman and boy. No exit wounds. Soft rounds. Each team member grabbed his target and quickly and callously pulled them from the house, just as the remaining team members stormed the building. The support team looked to the shooters, each of whom nodded to a successful operation, and immediately set about cleaning up what minimum amounts of blood had sprayed the table, chairs, or leaked out onto the floor. One of the team members removed the dog, ripping up the floor boards that had become soaked with the canine's blood. Bloody floor boards where the woman had fallen were also ripped up. The bloodied table cloth was quickly ripped from the table, noisily upsetting the untouched feast. Still somewhat confused, but feeling all his internal fear quickly drain away, the leader collected all of their spent round casings. Four. One for each target, one for the dog.

As the Bravo Force leader dragged his target outside, he looked to the other two who had been inside with him, but they did not return his look. The Bravo Force leader wiped sweaty palms on black uniformed pants, just as all the lights around them went dark.

What had just happened? Why was he sweating?

Off in the darkness came the sound of rapidly approaching vehicles, vehicles that quickly surrounded the house and assaulted them with the glare of headlights. The leader and his men waited for the covered flatbed that quickly slammed to a stop before them, kicking up a flurry of silvery moonlit dust. Two men exited the truck and silently assisted the three with tossing the corpses onto the flat bed, quickly covered them with a tarp, then closed the truck's rear flap. The two men jumped back into the cab of the truck and sped off into the night.

Other vehicles, including two heavy-equipment transporters carrying bulldozers, pulled up behind the house and barn and immediately set about unloading. An empty troop carrier swung around before the Bravo Force, coming to a stop. Before the Bravo Force leader and his team piled into it, the leader paused to look to the surreal images before them, played out beneath the watchful Cyclops eye of the full moon. He furrowed his brow, narrowed his gaze, and cocked his head ever-so-slightly, bringing a blackened hand to his blackened forehead. Closing his eyes, he forcefully massaged his forehead and temples.

Something just wasn't *right*.

Reopening his eyes, he saw to it that his men had loaded into the rear of the truck and hopped up into the cab's passenger seat....

The vehicle hadn't driven fifty feet, when a blizzard of quiet weapons' blasts erupted from within.

It continued to drive off into the darkness.

Another dark vehicle, a Jeep, pulled up on a short rise nearby. Out of it stepped another figure, in similar uniform to the Bravo Force operators, who looked to his radium-illuminated watch then up to the house; to the two additional bulldozers unloading before him, and those set up before the barn. From behind the house the man heard the work already two minutes into completion. Confidently, he surveyed the task and watched as the International Harvester, Ford truck, and a Chrysler parked alongside the house were all loaded onto larger vehicle silhouettes, then quickly covered and removed. Oversaw the telephone poles to the property as they were yanked down, pulled from the ground, then reduced to pieces. Heard the pitch of the diesel engines change behind the house. Again looked to his watch. Observed the dozers as they plunged into the house. Heard the crunch of wood, shatter of glass, and burst of pipes. Utilities had been cut off exactly three minutes ago, and all records of this family expunged from any public and not-so-public departments three hours ago. Water sprayed up from torn pipes, only to fizzle out as the house was quickly and efficiently razed to the ground. To his right the same happened to the barn. Each building was demolished into a heap, then pushed into the hastily dug ditches that had been gouged out behind them. The cut telephone poles, all outbuildings, fences, and wood piles were summarily plowed and scraped into the ditches, then quickly and efficiently covered with earth. In the distance came the on-time approach of helicopters. The dozers completed their tasks and withdrew to their transports, where they were loaded back up. The bulldozer flatbeds quickly departed back into the night. Four choppers now hovered above the graves of the house, barn, and shacks, pausing with their shadowy extensions swinging lazily beneath them. One after the other then made their well-practiced sweeps of the area, depositing eastern-Colorado-specific top soil across the scars below. Completed, they, too, departed back into the silvery night. After the dirt had settled, a handful of men in a pickup truck dashed out and hurriedly planted Socorro cactus throughout the area. When done, they jumped into the back of the pickup and departed.

The lone observer surveyed the nearly completed task with his Starlight Scope. Now, the sweepers pulled up to the dirt driveway, which was the only remaining sign that anyone had ever inhabited this spot of earth, and began erasing all signs of its existence as they drove over and erased any last vestige of human activity. They, too, sped off when complete.

Satisfied after making another Starlight Scope pass, the man turned to reenter his Jeep—when he spun around.

"Who the fuck are *you?*" he asked the intruder, raised his nine millimeter, and fired....

Chapter Two

1

One Tree, Colorado
July 11th
2358 hours

"Will zat be VISA or MasterCard?" asked Lizzie Gordon, in her best faux-Romani accent, stroking her Calico cat, Lucy, all curled up and purring in her lap. How Lizzie kept from laughing at her fake accent was a mystery to her...but maybe it was because she'd been doing it for so long, or that if she laughed it would be her undoing, and she wouldn't be able to help those who so desperately needed her assistance. Lizzie adjusted her headphones.

"MasterCard?" the caller replied.

"Your number?"

Lizzie glanced to her trailer's clock and jotted down "11:58 p.m." in her log, next to the date.

"Hmmm, almost ze witching hour," Lizzie said, absentmindedly.

The caller chuckled briefly and uncomfortably, then gave Lizzie her credit card number. Lizzie read back the number for verification, then got the card's expiration date and caller's name (as it appeared on the card). She entered that data into the credit card terminal.

"Thank you, Sher-i. Zorry about zuch trivialities," Lizzie said, continuing with her faux accent. "Now...what would you azk Madame Nostradameus?"

Lizzie kicked away a toy ball that had come rolling under the table, bumping off her bare feet.

"'Nostradamus?' Like that prophet?'"

"'Nostra*dame*us'—it iz pronounced with a 'dame,' az in I am a woman, and Nostra*dam*us wuz a man."

Lizzie grew more annoyed with this name than she'd expected. When she'd first created the identity she'd thought it cute, but after having to constantly correct its unwieldy articulation, it had grown quite tiresome.

"Oh," the caller said. "Well, it's about my boyfriend."

Lizzie nodded like a bobble-headed doll, and again adjusted her headset. She looked down to Lucy, still nestled in her lap, purring. The questions were always the same, whether from men or women.

When will I find true and lasting love?

Is s/he cheating on me?

Will I be successful, or rich and famous at (fill in the blank)?

Should I invest in (fill in the blank)?

Though Lizzie felt for each caller, since they were calling—most of them, anyway—honestly thinking they were going to get some bit of useful advice. There were also those who called just to test her, to play the "for entertainment purposes only" portion of the advertisement. Why people called these numbers to waste their money amazed her…though she understood. Everyone wanted to find some genuine, life-changing event to affect their lives for the better, something to transcend the mundaneness of everyday life, and this saddened her even more. They obviously never read the disclaimer at the bottom of their television screens, nor put trust into their own lives and direction. But, yes…everyone needed help now and then. She knew that even the jesters hoped—deep down—she'd say something insightful even they could take away with them. As much as humans loved to prove others wrong…they also loved to be pleasantly surprised. It was human nature, plain and simple. Lizzie reached down and scratched her exposed upper calf; took another sip of Mountain Dew.

Oh, and another reason she loved the job—no dress code.

"I know…you want to know if he haz been true to you, yes?"

"Um…yeaaah. I feel bad abou—"

"Eez okay, Sher-i, I understand…."

It was here, while stroking Lucy, that Lizzie tuned in to Sheri's question.

Lizzie psychically split herself apart, so to speak, from the *talking* her…dissociating herself from the call on the one hand, yet keeping Sheri occupied in polite conversation on the other. Lizzie suddenly felt that familiar extrasensory ride she'd grown accustomed to all of her life. That feeling of expansion and contraction, of slipping away from her "physical package," and sliding into another, nonphysical, one. She rode Sheri's intent and psychically met her boyfriend. She experienced several things at once: her boyfriend's genuine and (pardon the pun) unadulterated love for her; the fact that though he loved her, he did occasionally look at other women (and even chided himself for doing that); and, thirdly, how he really, *really* loved mountain biking. Lizzie smiled. There was nothing wrong with this guy nor their relationship. He was a normal, twenty-two-year-old dude in love with his twenty-one-year-old chick. Lizzie returned to the call.

"Sher-i, I am picking up on…your man…he eez active, hmm?"

"Yeah…"

"Where are you calling from—Boulder?"

"How'd you—"

"You both love to ride bikes in ze mountains, I zee, he eez very good, but you feel intimidated by theez, yes?"

"How did you—oh, my God—um, well," Sheri said, surprised, "I am pretty good myself, but he's *so* much better—"

"Just be yourself, leetle one. You are doing fine. He does not look down upon you nor your ability, but eez pleasantly amused and gratified you keep up weeth him when you go out together. There eez nothing to worry about—but I digress. I see…I see that theez man truly loves you, my dear. You have nothing to worry about…and Madame Nostra*dame*us means for you to believe her. Your man eez quite in love weeth you, but you know theez…"

"But I catch him—"

Lizzie chuckled her faux-Romani laugh. "Looking at other women? Eez that eet?"

How long could she continue with this ridiculous accent?

"I do not mean to laugh at you, my dear, but have no worries. Your man eez just that—a man—and as such, men are—how shall I put theez?—much more…ummm, *visually* stimulated…than weemen. It is in their nature to *look*. After all, eez that not how he found you?"

"Well, uh…"

"Does he not continue to find *you* attracteev?"

"Sure, I mean…I *guess*, but…"

"Then you do yourself a great deez-serveez to compare yourself against others! You are beautiful yourself—he loves your auburn hair, your large brown eyes—"

"How do you know this stuff?"

Lizzie chuckled. "Am I not Madame Nostra*dame*us?"

"But I thou—"

"You thought me a fake? Ack! Eez all right! There are many charlatans out there—Madame Nostradameus knows *all!* Your man, though he eez a *man*, and though he may occasionally look at other weemen, knows what he has, knows heez love for *you.* Just as he appreciates the beauty and majesty of the mountains and trails, he alzo appreciates the beauty of weemen. You know each other's hearts…be not afraid, my dear. He eez true to you."

Sheri paused, and Lizzie heard—felt—her relief at the other end of the phone. *Just don't cry*, she thought, *just don't…*

"Thank you, Madame Nostra…*dame*us…for everything," Sheri sniffled, "You don't know how much this means to me—"

"Ah, but I do, my sweet!," Lizzie said, smiling, "now go—call heem—but go in peace…and love."

Lizzie disconnected from the call and sat back, staring at the muted TV screen across the room from her. She wiped away her own tears. Damn them when they cried! She took another swig of Mountain Dew, focusing on the muted television, which was set to the SCI FI channel, and on which there just so happened to be a commercial for her *1-900-PsiKick hotline—call* now! Lizzie needed a break and called in to disconnect. She removed the headset and slowly came to her feet, allowing Lucy time to leap off her lap. As she took her first step toward the kitchen, she kicked aside a green-colored plastic donut from a children's Rock-a-Stack rings set. She opened the refrigerator, but nothing hit her fancy. She didn't have to be psychic to know what she really wanted.

To the freezer, she redirected.

Dreyer's.

Yeah, baby—Vanilla Bean. *That* was what she needed. As she dug into the container, her mind's eye filled with the happy, smiling faces of hundreds, *thousands* of playful children….

2

Travis Norton pulled off Nellysford, Virginia's Highway 151, down another short stretch of road, then onto the crushed-stone driveway that led up alongside his small, two-story clapboard house.

He shut off the Jeep Cherokee and sat staring out into the whispering trees; the calm, cool serenity of the nearby woods and early morning breezes.

Always there, always comforting.

Hardwoods and softwoods...the soft, hushing carpet and deep woodsy scent of forest humus. Wildlife coming and going. Chirping birds. The grounding, relaxing scent of pine and moist air. What had this area witnessed across the centuries, whether or not it had been an open plain or its current treed forest? Storms? Battles? The growth of civilization? How had this spot of ground changed?

What did the woods know?

He'd read in metaphysical texts that trees were supposed to have lives of their own (beyond just growing and bearing leaves or needles)—as well as an actual perception of human beings. That they were able to see the human equivalent of fifty years into the future *and* past. What did they see about him?

He'd have to look into that someday.

But Travis couldn't delay his enthusiasm—right now he was absolutely *ecstatic*.

For the first time *ever*, he'd actually had a good feeling returning home from a mission. Usually his tasks were all doom and gloom, peeking in on drug traffickers, terrorism, or other intelligence targets, but this one...this one had been *fun*—left him with a light, airy, downright optimistic feeling. He'd picked up on a group of young children dancing and playing about in a street, singing nursery rhymes...in front of a home. A home that had been the epitome of *normal*...yet somehow also had an indefinable element of *strange* to it...and to which he had been totally unable to penetrate. There had been an incredible overall feeling of giddiness and *love* to these kids and their play, and it not only permeated his mission, but instantly and thoroughly permeated *him*. It had been so intense; he had felt it long before "seeing" it. There had been levity on levels he simply couldn't begin to explain, a joy that had been more intense than anything he'd ever known. Never before had he experienced such an intense concept of the word. It had simply been out of this world—totally and lovingly enveloped his soul—as if he'd been enwrapped in thick down comforters on a cold winter's night. It had been his first mission as a remote viewer that actually had him feeling *good*—not only about the target...but himself.

Travis exited the Jeep and went to the porch, which was in dire need of a good sweep and coat of paint. The front door was similarly challenged. Fishing out his keys, he unlocked the door—and stopped. Furrowing his brow, he turned back around to again face the woods.

Nothing but woods and road…the sound of birds. The smell of fresh air, the hush of a light breeze through the trees, and the shiny glint of sunlight off their twitching leaves….

He felt…*watched.*

Travis squinted into the distance as if he would actually see something.

Was he actually being tracked, or was it just an aftereffect from a hard night's taskings?

The feeling immediately dissipated.

He continued on into the house.

A smile on his face, Travis went to the refrigerator for a beer, then changed his mind and pulled out an AriZona iced tea, instead. He popped open the tall can on his way into his home office and took a sip, swallowing the sweet raspberry tang. He went right for the closet. Opening it, he reached in for the only item that always made him feel good about at least *part* of himself—the last (unofficial) part of his own, personal, operative protocol about which he never told anyone—but (no doubt) his superiors already knew. He was a long way from that boy who'd built this plastic model, a long way in more than years from that boy of twelve, who'd found the somewhat beat-up model kit at a garage sale. It was the flying saucer from the sixties television show, *The Invaders*, starring Roy Thinnes. He'd never seen it in its original telecast, of course, but once he'd found the model, he searched the show out and found the series still in occasional reruns on late-night TV on the SCI FI channel, and, of course, on DVDs. He wasn't exactly sure what it was about this model that so captivated him, except that it was absolutely *cool* looking, but home he'd run with his newly discovered kit as that twelve year old, and immediately set about putting it together. Maybe it was the basic, smooth lines of the finished craft, or the fantastic imagery it represented, but whatever it was, this was the neatest version of a flying saucer he'd ever seen (well, next to that *Forbidden Planet* spaceship). He was quite disappointed to later discover that that spaceship actually belonged to The Bad Guys, the aliens who were always out to get us. Roy Thinnes had been The Good Guy and had been trying to warn everyone *about* The Bad Guys….

Travis took his UFO and iced tea and sat down, placing the craft on the desk before him. He stared at it. He had to admit, he'd done a superb job in putting the thing together. Its near featureless, gray plastic surface had only a small rectangular, indented view-screen near the top raised dome of the craft, and above that were the small, elongated and rectangular red running lights he'd painted himself. Underneath the six-and-a-half-inch diameter saucer-body circumference were five translucent red bubbles around a painted-orange center grill. He may not have known what had attracted him to the model all those years ago, but what he knew now was that this one model, perhaps no longer made, reminded him of the childhood naïveté he'd all-too-quickly lost and wished dearly to regain. Of his boyhood *purity*, now so far—light years, in fact—removed from his adulthood *filthiness*. God, how he wished he could return to that pure state and do things over again. Pick another line of work. As that twelve year old he wasn't divorced, and wasn't poking his nose around in everyone else's shithole business. He was constantly sticking his nose into (and inhaling *deeply*) the underbelly of the world's most scum-sucking bottom-dwellers. This ability to see what others did was so powerful, so wondrous an ability…yet he had to be wallowing in the parochial and shortsighted end of things.

But, that's what covert government psychics did.

He wanted to be engaged in its use in more peaceful methods. In more Humanity advancing endeavors. He wanted to use it as it was meant to be used—to change things *before* they turned rancid. He knew there were other units doing that kind of work, but somehow, over the years, he'd gotten stuck in the garbage-sifting end of the business. He wanted to see into the future and change world paradigms…end global warming, the burgeoning global drought, or any other declining environmental or financial issues…or just find a fricking cure for *cancer*, for crying out loud. That's what Kennedy'd intended, they all knew that—hell, they were *psychics*—they saw past the bullshit they were fed by superiors, but when it came right down to it, it was a job…and what were ya gonna do?

Travis set down his tea.

Hell, maybe they *were* using it as designed, and he and the others just weren't aware of it. After all, it's not like remote viewers had answers for everything. There was only so much an individual could process, do in a day, even a *psychic*. The human organism still got physically, mentally, even psychically exhausted, and could only handle so much. And besides—Big Question: just who would be deciding what would and wouldn't be changed?

Changed to *what?*

One solution would bring up a thousand more questions. What we needed, Travis mused, would be a whole new race of people gifted in this ability. People who were just a level or two above the standard human. Saints, aliens, or a demigod or two. Maybe that was what they needed...a demigod or two walking among us...

Or maybe humans just weren't meant to dick around with life quite so directly, and on that scale.

Travis picked up the gray spacecraft and removed the lid. Inside were five compartmentalized sections of the spacecraft, complete with eight miniature figurines, all glued into place.

Compartmentalized.

Just like his life. His job. The person in the next office—sometimes standing right beside you—couldn't tell you what they were working on.

And wasn't that just the irony?

They were *psychics.* Government trained. Trained to ferret out just that kind of information.

Three of the figurines were in the model's main control room, one sitting in the "captain's chair," with the other figures standing to either side; all were before the main view screen, which was behind the inside portion of the indented view port on the outside of the ship. Travis had long ago painted the four interior screens black. Of the three control-room figurines, one was an anatomically correct space babe. Okay, for a one-inch-tall figurine, she *was* stacked. Travis smiled, he'd painted her hair silver, and as he looked closer...saw there was a gossamer strand of what had to be twenty-two-year-old glue linking the silver-haired space babe to the seated pilot.

In the port-side compartment stood two other guys, observing another, painted-black observation screen. Directly across from these two, on the starboard side of the ship in another compartment, was a single guy attending to storage lockers. And to the aft of the ship, in yet another compartment, were two more men glued into their eternal positions in two of the three "accelerator tubes," as they were called.

As Travis looked closer, he noticed something he'd never noticed before as he played with the angle of the ship. In the singular guy's locker room he saw a strand of thick white hair sticking up from the floor, caught and glued under a section of gray plastic bulkhead. *How interesting,* he thought—had that always been there? It had to be a piece of hair from "Crackers," one of his family's dogs, a mixed Dalmatian that had long-since departed. He missed her. Thumped several times by cars, and, in later years arthritic, she kept on going until one winter, while home on vacation, he and Crackers had gone for a walk on crusty snow in a field of theirs in upstate New York. Crackers had run up ahead and gotten caught in a section of snow where brush had poked up through the crusty surface. She'd fallen through and couldn't pull her hind legs out. She looked up to him, helpless. Travis, his heart breaking, rushed to her, lifted her out of the hole she'd made for herself, and had taken her away to where the snow wouldn't break from her weight. He knew he wouldn't see her that next year...and hadn't. His dad had had to put her down. Her arthritis had been far too advanced, she'd had a loss of bowel control, and there had been all her whining and groaning at night in her sleep. It was too much even for his father, a tough upstate New York State Trooper. Crackers had had one last summer before she'd met her Maker.

We all have to die sometime of something.

Travis sat back and continued to admire his preteen handiwork. He placed the gray plastic lid back on top of the spaceship, making sure that the notch cut into the underside of the lid rested perfectly on its associated tab on the body of the craft, and settled back in his chair.

Wasn't life weird?

Once he'd been this wide-eyed, naïve kid, and now he wasn't— but he could still relive the memories, the *feelings*, and remember what it was like to be that boy. It was amazing how we all changed as life marched inevitably on. He was far and away from those naïve days, far and away....

But, there was something else about last night's target, something he hadn't drawn, described to his superiors, nor put into his report. There had been another...*feeling*....

Caution.

A feeling that there had been much more where he had been peeking into—but *wasn't* (if there had been, he would've seen it, right)? But the overwhelming feeling was that he *wasn't supposed to talk about it*...even *think* about it.

Still carrying the gray UFO, Travis left the office for his small living room and turned on the stereo.

He suddenly really missed Annabel.

Wished she were here.

He picked up a CD of mixed love songs. She'd given it to him, just months ago, on his thirty-second birthday. Better days. He took out the CD, inserted it, hit play; kicked back in the recliner and listened to the sad, bluesy melody of Elton John's "Blue Eyes."

They had been so playful, those children he'd encountered. Where did all our playfulness go as we aged? Was it that difficult to keep the fire lit? Where did youthful naïveté disappear to?

Travis rubbed a hand over the model's smooth surface, as if it were his own Genie Bottle. He imagined the glued-to-the-floor occupants inside, busying about in their duties. He looked to the red translucent bubble lights and orange grill he'd painted, and tipped the saucer for flying effect.

Could naïveté ever be reclaimed? *Should* it?

Not the bad kind, where you really hadn't a clue about anything, but the kind where you knew, but just didn't "participate in" the bad, because it never touched you—only *other* people. Where you were able to just focus in on what was going on in your own life…*now, this very moment*…that you were playing, yes *playing*, and enjoying it. Where you plain forgot about all the ill going on elsewhere in the world—all that had gone on in the past and all that would yet occur in the future. Sure, in the back—the *very* back—of your mind, you knew there were evil people out there, but for now you weren't out saving the world, you were here, right here, playing with your toys or watching that late night show you'd been trying to catch for three years. Actually reading a *book*. No one was sending you on missions, no one had your phone number, your address—your *mind*.

You were truly—100%—*free*.

Travis loved the solid, hollow feel of the model in his hands.

Or, he thought, smile disappearing, you were in the arms of the one you loved and had pledged your life to for all eternity. *Til death do us part*. What a crock. No death, but we'd sure parted. And it wasn't even because of anything he'd done…instead, it had been about what he *hadn't*.

The life of a psychic spy.

I'm not really a loving husband, but I play one in real life.

Travis set down the model just as the tears exploded. No…he had never been that loving husband. Probably never would be. He was a psychic government spy, that's what he was, on call 24/7. His body wasn't his own and neither was his mind. His outlook on life forever tainted by his work. He was merely the government's little gray *Invaders* toy.…

3

"Okay, Ryan, tell me what you see," the task monitor asked.

Hidden away in the clandestine bowels of the remote-viewer tasking unit in central Virginia, Ryan Dunham was seated in the "RoboRecliner" or "RoboChair"—RV-slang for their huge, comfortable, leather-bound recliner specially built for their psychic operations. Neither he nor any of the other remote viewers knew what their assignments were. Those were sealed within double envelopes by "taskers" who had no contact with them nor their monitors. The remote viewers simply *focused* upon their objective—the double-sealed envelopes—and were psychically transported to whatever their unseen tasks directed. It was a double-blind operation that provided extraordinary results. Results they were never made privy to…yet "they" kept coming back for more….

"I'm just not getting much…blackness, is all.…"

"Take your time," the monitor coached.

Ryan sat motionless, his breathing slow and deep.

"It's not so much the target…but I'm still in that feeling…my body is tilted…spinning…it's taking a while.…"

"Go with the feeling, Ryan."

Ryan remained still for several more minutes.

"Okay," Ryan finally said, "I'm there…in…a boardroom. A meeting. Decisions…and plans. There are men…ten of them. American and Asian. Five are drinking coffee, two Cokes—no, three. Two aren't drinking anything. Tension—lots of tension. A major decision…war—they're talking about war."

"Go on."

"There's a map. Political and physical boundaries discussed. Weaponry. An overthrow. It's 196—"

Ryan suddenly paused, wrinkling his brow. "Something…something's not.…"

"Go on," his monitor said, also pausing his pen on his notebook. He looked up. "What else do you see?"

"Something's not right…don't know how to explain it. Something's really off…*wrong*—"

"Explain."

Ryan shook his head. "Seems like I should be able to, but…I can't. It's about…this whole thing…this-this meeting…those men. I get the sense of large amounts of money being exchanged—made—but something's still not *right*...."

"Okay, that's good enough, Ryan. Calmly back away...relax...bring yourself back."

Ryan did as instructed. Physical eyes closed, Ryan now mentally closed his nonphysical ones, shutting out the images. Events that made little sense to him and also made him quite uneasy. Events he couldn't explain, but which were centered around a war—a "police action"?—somewhere in southeast Asia. A "conflict" that felt contradictory. That didn't really exist...not in his reality.

Ryan came out of his trance and back to reality, and as he and his monitor debriefed the task, Ryan couldn't shake the uneasiness. There had been another feeling he had had and hadn't mentioned, an even worse feeling than the uneasiness.

Ryan felt *dirty*.

Chapter Three

1

Seventeen-year-old Mel Roberts awoke—and literally—leapt out of his bed before realizing he'd been dreaming.

He stood before his bed in his shorts, shaking and tingling, trying to recall what the dream had been about and why all his nerves were on *fire*....

He looked to his bedside clock. Two a.m. Two a.m., and here he was standing in the middle of his bedroom in nothing but his skivvies. Confused and running a hand through tousled hair, he left the bedroom and made his way down into the semi-darkness of the nightlight-illuminated hallway and steps. He tried to avoid the second and third steps and their loud creaking, as he descended to the next landing, down into the kitchen. Didn't wanna wake the parents.

Mel stood in the middle of the kitchen in his bare feet, lights off. Listened to the sounds of a settling house, the ventilation system; the "kinking" of ventilation ducks as the air-conditioning clicked off and something, somewhere "popped."

His eyes darted to the closed-curtained window above the sink.

The kitchen window.

Window.

He yawned, stretched open his eyes wide, rubbed them, then scanned the kitchen.

He loved this time of night.

No one was up and all was quiet...still. Dark. There was a spiritual quality to these hours, the early, early morning hours, he loved.

In the kitchen, without turning on the kitchen light, and mulling over the events of his still-unremembered dream, he explored the refrigerator. Inside, he found it utterly bare, except for a lone, green can of Vernors Ginger Soda. He grabbed it.

Hadn't his mom gone shopping this week?

He did the standard, cursory check of the freezer. Nearly empty as well, including the ice maker. He took his soda to the nearby dining table and sat, opened it, and downed a tingling gulp. Stray, powerful effervescence scrambled up into and tickled the hell out of his nasal cavities.

Dang it, now he'd have to brush his teeth again before going back to bed.

Mel set the soda on the table and stretched his arms out before him, slumping his head forward. A business card sat before him. He closed his eyes.

What the hell had he dreamed about that had caused him to leap out of bed like that?

Wait a minute...his mother *had* gone shopping.

Mel shot to the refrigerator. One hand holding open the door, he stood before it, bathed in its spray of soft light.

There, before him, *presented a stocked refrigerator...*

An interior jam-packed with food and drink.

Mel reached in and touched an eighteen-egg family pack that sat under the mid-level chiller compartment drawer...crammed with lunch meat...ham, turkey, and cheese.

Looked to the six-pack-minus-one of Vernors (*Barrel Aged, Bold Taste!*) soda that sat above it. To the apples, oranges, and nectarines nestled in the smoked, see-through crisper bins at the bottom.

"What the *hell?*"

He closed the refrigerator.

Stepping back, arms to his sides, he just stared at the appliance.

Reached down and calmly opened the freezer.

Of course.

Stocked.

Packed with meat, vegetables, and bread—even a filled-to-capacity ice-maker.

Mel closed the freezer, backed up to the table, and sat back down.

But *when* had she gone shopping?

When had his mother supposedly had the time to have done all this? Something still wasn't right. There was something about—

A birthday.

Hadn't he just had a birthday—and hadn't she gone to the store the day before?

When had that been? This *week?*

Why was it so difficult to remember!

It had been his own birthday, for crying out loud—*no one forgets their own birthday.*

Why, it had been yesterday, of course—*yesterday*—and his mother had—

Mel spun around to the table.

The remains of a birthday cake, housed within a glass cake protector—there, in the middle of the table. Right next to the business card.

Coconut frosting. Not a chocolate cake, nor a raspberry cake, but a full-on *white* cake, with *coconut* frosting. The best kind. And—

Where were all the cards?

If he'd just had a birthday, where were all the cards? The gifts? No one puts up cards for one day and takes them down.

And the gifts—*where were all the gifts?* Not that he was greedy, but people always—

People?

Who'd come to his party? *Who'd* been invited?

Good Lord, what was wrong with him?

Why couldn't he recall who had come to his birthday party? Why weren't there any cards, and where were his—

Mel rushed down another short flight of stairs into the lower-level family room. It was unfinished (which only mildly disturbed him), but, without turning on any lights, he rushed into what was supposed to be his...(c'mon, pull it out, maaan)...*hobby*...room? Where he hung out away from his parents to read, play games, and meditate (*Meditate?* Who the hell *meditates?*), and (*why why* why *was he having so much damned difficulty with all this?*)....

Mel flipped on the light.

Empty.

The room, white and bare-walled, was totally and utterly, devoid of furniture, books...*anything.* He spun around. Except for a card table and some folding chairs, the entire family room was frigging empty. Even the unfinished walls looked oddly—no, *weirdly*—unfinished. He wasn't an expert (and had he ever really seen exposed sheetrock before? "Sheetrock"...what *is* sheetrock?), but everything looked...*two-dimensional.*

Not all there.

He went up to a wall; inspected it up *über* close. Brought his face right up to it...touched it with a tentative hand as he peered insanely close to it, nose nearly touching its surface.

He could barely feel it.

What was going on?

No longer merely amused, Mel backed away from the wall. He suddenly felt unsteady, didn't feel at all like himself. Felt...out of control.

Was *he* all there?

He sat in one of the folding chairs.

Was all this a dream? Was he still *dreaming?*

Had to be...he was still in bed...sound asleep...underneath comforters and blankets, dreaming...

But was he?

Or was he having one of those, what was it called—out-of-body experiences? And if he was, could he get back to his bed, and would he find himself still asleep there?

What would happen if he did?

Mel slowly made his way back up the two flights of stairs. As he passed the kitchen, he curiously noted all the birthday cards and opened presents scattered across the kitchen counter, one card tipped over. He continued on to the bedroom. Images of him and a small group of people crossed his mind. But, as he fixed his sights on his still-open bedroom door, he knew what he'd find, knew it in his bones. In that darkened space, he'd find messed-up bed sheets and blankets. An alarm-clock radio...

An empty bed.

Who was he kidding?

And he'd peek into his parents' room and find his parents' room empty. He knew it would be, and it'd be empty because he *wasn't* dreaming.

It'd be empty because they weren't *there*.

He knew the difference between dreaming and consciousness, and *he wasn't dreaming.* He didn't need to check the bedroom.

But, of course, he did.

Mel poked his head inside his room and flicked on the light; found exactly what he knew he'd (not) find.

An empty bed.

In a bedroom that wasn't quite as empty as the downstairs family room, but not far from it. There was only a bed, a nightstand, and that expected clock. No dresser, chest of drawers, books, posters, or a stereo (and how did he know he had, or was supposed to have had, any of these things?). Knew there'd be nothing in his closets, either. No clothes, no shoes, no sneakers.

Nothing.

He also knew what he'd find next. He didn't know how or why, just knew it as he knew he was awake and not dreaming. Mel Roberts did an about-face and went across the hall to his parents' door, the closed door to which he reached out and turned the doorknob; felt like Dead Man Walking. But, open the door he did, and feel around the inside wall for the light switch, he did. Even before he switched it on, his heart sank. There was no denying it. The light that clicked on only confirmed what he already knew.

There wasn't a single stick of furniture in the entire room.

Not a board.

Not a toothpick.

Not even a *body*.

Nothing.

2

Lizzie Gordon sat with her feet up on her trailer's coffee table, all lights off except for the television. She'd hit the "mute" switch on the remote, as a commercial narrated by an overly excited woman played on about a set of children's songs for only twenty-four dollars.

Ring around the rosie
A pocketful of posies
Ashes, ashes
We all fall...

Lucy silently padded out of the darkness and jumped into Lizzie's lap. She purred loudly as she massaged Lizzie's thighs with her forepaws before nestling in. Lizzie turned the volume back on as *Village of the Damned* returned, the original black-and-white, 1960 version. Though the children were definitely creepy, their presence was a hard-to-explain comfort to her.

Lizzie took a sip of Mountain Dew; glanced to the empty cereal bowl nearby. She watched as the children intensified their takeover of the small English town. As the children talked, Lizzie heard whispers of her own at the edges of her awareness. She knew better than to ignore them, but just remained aware of them for now…content to let them build their own momentum. She didn't have much of a sense of things, yet, though there was a swirl of colors. The feeling was shaping up to be something huge. It buzzed around just outside her grasp…taunting her like a fly to a cat, but Lizzie kept her focus on the movie…trying to fight off sleep…when, finally, it hit her.

She leapt off the couch (Lucy flying from her lap) and headed for the kitchen counter.

(*cards? presents?*)

She reached for a pencil from the pen-and-pencil jar that sat beside the microwave—

No pen-and-pencil jar sat beside the microwave.

Oopsy, she thought, and went to a kitchen drawer. She removed a pencil and a small yellow notepad and immediately set about writing down her impressions…

Huge motorcade.

Major city.

Southern part of the country—Texas—Dallas, specifically.

People lining streets.

Famous man.

A man, though admired by many, hated—no, perhaps *feared* was better—by others, including…

Lizzie stared off into space.

The motorcade wound through the town, as this man—she found it hard to focus on just who this man was—sat in the back of a long car…or not really long, but *felt* long…a convertible? He sat in the back of this convertible, on the right, his wife to his left. Two others sat in the front. Famous Man was happy, though a part of him, an unconscious part, actually knew…considered…what was about to happen…

Images of a young Indian—*east* Indian—a beggar boy—

Images of another…very close to Mr. Famous Man…traveling through Dallas…

A brother.

Killed earlier in life.

Blackness…something about a very dark, very *evil*…

Blackness.

Black. Black, black, *black*….

Lizzie shivered.

The convertible and its procession rounded a bend. It's a beautiful, *gorgeous* day…Famous Man waves to the crowd. He's extremely charismatic...happy where he is...how he'd gotten there. Thoughts for the future race through his mind...social reforms...racial equality...global peace...

The number five comes to mind.

Five.

Weird perspectives of the motorcade scene superimpose themselves upon her...something's...*changing?*

Yes, it's almost as if—it *is*—the scene was changing before her very eyes...

"Five," again makes itself known.

Popping sounds.

A street drain.

Flashes of great pain.

Books. Top floor.

...a *knoll*...

It happens.

Lizzie jerks.

Eyes closed, it's as if she's sitting beside Famous Man—yes, *she is*. She's pulled from her living room, barefoot, in her White Stag "hearts" over shirt, and is holding a child in her lap, sitting beside this man of fatal distinction, in the open air of a top-down convertible driving through a town.

Now, she recognizes him.

Thirty-fifth president of the United States.

They're riding together through Dealey Plaza on this fine, fine Dallas morning. Her husband, John Fitzgerald Kennedy—is actually holding her hand, and there's a bouquet of red roses in the seat between them.

Red.

She can feel it, though, and the number five...that "five"...and impending blackness...*black.*

Black, black, *black!*

No!, she screams, but her mouth doesn't work...and again...

(*East-Indian beggar boy*)

Lizzie turns to JFK, to force words—any words—from her mouth, anything to tell the president to *get down!*, *to* hide!—*don't you feel it? Don't you know you're going to be—*

But nothing.

Smells exhaust.

See flashbulbs burst.

Hears shouts and calls and motorcade noise.

Crowd noise.

Knows that her perspective, that what everyone around her sees in this image of hers is that of *Jackie*, JFK's wife, not the barefoot hearts-shirt-clad woman with unkempt dirty-blonde hair, an infant cradled in her lap.

She turns.

Murder screams through her head.

It's not her angst-ridden, desperate face that JFK and the public sees, but the calm, placid face of Jackie Kennedy.

Pleasantly smiling face.

Calmly twisting wave of a white-gloved hand. Hair…hat?

Pink.

Pink, pink, pink…outfit?

A kind of "coatdress"—pink…pink hat.

Red roses.

Red.

Pretty, red, *thorny.*

Pink.

She can still feel it, the threat—it wasn't supposed to be this way—but it's still there—she can *feel* it like an oncoming

(Blaaack…black, *black*….)

shockwave that has already happened.

Unstoppable.

Pink, red, thorny, *black.*

Please, Mister President, you have to get down!

Too late, it's too late. Hot

(*red*)

splatters her pink face, pink body, pink life…not once, but twice…

Pink, pink, pink…

…husband bowls over…collapses into her…before a black

(*black black black…*)

terror drowns out her soul—

Lizzie Gordon.

Trailer.

Kitchen table.

Lizzie is staring at the table top and a pencil. The pencil is jammed into and through many yellow pages on her paper tablet, its lead wickedly shattered. She studies the broken tip and its pieces that litter the pad before her. Flickering light from her television dances about the walls around her.

She stared at her paper.

Village of the Damned.

Dallas.

This made absolutely no sense. None at all.

3

Mel Roberts stared into the empty room, dumbfounded.

What the hell was going on?

What did he mean he had no parents.

No *parents?*

The words reverberated in his head like a pounding kettle drum.

How could he have no parents? Everyone had parents! His had to be gone, somewhere, on a vacation—a trip—*something.*

But there was no furniture.

No bed.

Clothes.

He flew into the room and flung open the closet doors—

Clothes.

Their closet was now filled?

"This just can't be...."

Mel stared at the attire. He turned to leave, but, his knees ran smack into a queen-sized bed, complete with pillows and fluffy comforter. He doubled over onto it, rebounding back against the closet.

A bed that hadn't been there moments before.

"Oh, come *on...*"

He looked to the immaculately made-up bed, to the two indentations his hands had just made in the royal blue comforter. To the nightstands on either side of the bed...the hope chest at the foot of the bed...the lamp and pictures on the nightstands and dressers.

Mel snatched up one of the pictures. It was of a couple, a man and a woman, arms around each other. Smiling.

He felt acute familiarity. Longing.

Yes, these were his parents!

It was all coming back!

Mel sat on the bed, riveted by the picture.

How could he have forgotten?

The accident. There had been a terrible accident...twisted metal. Bodies. Out on...on...Route 20...good *Lord*—

He closed his eyes.

Yes, it all came back...he'd been at a party—parents out on a date. Late night. Drunk driver. Two-lane road. You're supposed to drive *through* the deer...but this was no deer...a '75 Ford flatbed—replete with whiskey dents and hair and blood from a dog earlier in the evening—its driver passed out forty seconds ago...happened to be there...swerving...taking up the entire road....

You can only do so much...and sometimes...sometimes...*enough* just wasn't—

A connection was made.

Metal screamed. Gasoline belched. Bodies consumed.

On a dark, lonely stretch of country highway, a fire quietly popped and sizzled.

Wiping away tears, Mel carefully replaced the picture on the nightstand.

Of course, it all made sense, now, didn't it? He didn't remember any of this, because...because he didn't *want* to. The rooms, they hadn't been empty—he just hadn't *wanted* to remember...to see...the truth. To relive....

But as he withdrew his hand, he paused, looking to another picture. Grabbed it. Brought it in. It was of a large group of kids lined up in five rows. All smiling. The intensity of their smiles and faces and eyes *unnerved*—he *knew* these kids...they were familiar to him.

A baseball team?

Summer camp?

Everyone he'd followed through the school system?

He turned the picture over—no markings. Opened the back of the frame and removed the picture—still no markings, no dates. Just young, smiling, insanely happy faces.

What was wrong with him? Why was he having such a hard time remembering things? Why was everything so familiar...yet not?

He put the picture back into its frame and returned it to the nightstand. Mel lay back on the bed, spreading out across the bed as if to touch the memory of his parents, then swung his legs up.

He stared into the ceiling.

An automobile accident.

His parents…killed.
Dead.
Alone. Weird pictures. The vibrancy of those kids' faces staring back at him…murderous nightmares…and it was (he looked to the clock) a spooky time of night to be up and all alone, in a creepy state of mind.…

4

Lizzie pushed her cart down the aisles of Safeway, pausing only long enough to pull a box of Honey Nut Cheerios from the shelf and toss it into her basket. Okay, there was some nutritional value to the stuff, and it did claim to help kill bad cholesterol and all, but what she was really getting it for was the comfort factor. It brought back warm, cathartic memories of childhood, of late nights up watching horror movies with her dad. It was her *fun* food. Just enough to settle her stomach from the late-night hungries, while simultaneously satisfying her soul's need for cozy, endearing, solace.

Her dad had been a great man up until the accident, and, she knew…beyond. He was one of those rarities who was great while try-ing not to be. Wanted no part of greatness other than to be part of a family. Her mom, though she'd had her moments, was the strong, si-lent type. Lizzie was aware of the stereotyping, but that was just how she was. *They* were. Her mom stood her ground when necessary, but normally rode an even keel. Both her parents were strong willed, and while powerful individuals in their own right, devoted their lives to their family. Frederick Parker (not Freddie, Fred, or any other curt de-rivative) was a lineman for the state of Colorado, and Libby Parker an occasional stringer for the One Tree Gazette. She seemed to have had a nose for news, always just "happening to be there" before—or soon after—an event had lit up the landscape. She used to say that she never had to search out news, the news found *her.* And if there was a time where no news was good news, Libby worked her hand at editorials and essays. "Musings from far afield," she called them. Lizzie remem-bered her mom always writing, her father always working the lines, but both parents were always there for each other and their only daughter. It would have been daughter *and* son, but Henry had died prematurely of a nervous system failure. Had never left the Denver hospital. Her baby brother had died a baby. Lizzie knew that episode had so disturbed her mother that she never wanted another after that. The pain had been too great. Her mom, Lizzie had later discovered, had always been haunted by images of giving birth to a still-born.

Frederick Parker had been a large, powerful man. His father before him had been a lineman and had frequently brought her father along to learn the ropes, so it was only natural that her father had followed in his father's footsteps. Something virtually unheard of today. His knack for pinpointing trouble spots before they occurred was legendary. Father Frederick attributed it to all those years apprenticing with his dad that he could smell trouble a mile away. He'd also managed to avoid several near-life-ending accidents by pure Providence. One day while taking over for another who'd been working a hot wire, a cable had swung loose and his way. He'd never seen it coming. Fortunately for him, he'd dropped a tool and had bent over to pick it up, when the cable swung past and instead struck a coworker.

Instantly electrocuted.

Frederick barely got out of the way as the cable swung back. He knew when it was your time to go, you went, but to have had such a direct part in another's passing, well, that had been just a little much to handle at the time.

Unlike many of his day, he never cursed God. Never blamed Whomever was in control of life. *People came into this world…lived, worked…and left,* he used to tell Lizzie during those late-night weekend horror movie marathons (he also used to tell her that monsters and ghosts weren't real, but made for great stories), and if no one ever died, then the world would be a sorry place to live in. We all have a limited time on this earth, and it was our job to do and make the best of it— *then move on.* Clear the way for others. *It was our duty,* he said, that life would get pretty boring and stagnant otherwise, not to mention severely overpopulated, if no one left.

It was the cycle of life.

All one had to do was to observe nature, he would explain, how things came and went. Frederick used to tell her that it was nonsense how folks blamed God for deaths, forever lamenting and cursing God about taking away a human life "in their prime." Frederick didn't believe in "untimely" death. And just what *would* be timely, he posited? No one ever seemed to define that. Just like in the fields he worked in every day, life came and it went, but there was always…*life.* If it came and went, it had to come and go from and to *somewhere.* That was where God came in, he told her. God *allowed* us our lives, and when it was time for us to go, allowed us our *deaths*. Gory or not, he would reiterate, we all had to die sometime of something.

It was our obligation.

And when asked whether or not we ever came back, he was just as philosophical. Her father had said that life was so full of, well, *everything*...that he was hard-pressed to believe a soul could experience all it needed to experience in just one, meager, existence. Like the seasons, Father Frederick said, just as he was sure there were continuous winters, there had to be continuous springs.

And it was philosophies like that, watching those late-night weekend horror movies, and eating Honey Nut Cheerios, that Lizzie treasured most. And nearly every time she went shopping, and reached for that tall golden box, the same memories flooded back, and she'd smile.

Yes, Honey Nut Cheerios was her comfort food, and boy, did she miss her folks.

Chapter Four

1

Lizzie pushed open the trailer door, grocery bags in hand, and lightly kicked the package at her entrance way along the floor before her. After greeting Lizzie at the door with several urgent meows, Lucy gingerly stepped along, heading toward the kitchen, trying to avoid being struck by the kicked-along package. Lizzie deposited her bags on the kitchen table, as Lucy wove in and out of the legs of the table and chairs. The package at her feet was small and brown, with UPS markings. Excitedly, she picked it up and placed it on the counter. She was unable to take her eyes off of it, as she returned to her groceries, removing eggs and milk from the grocery bag and into the refrigerator, cheese and deli meat, fruit and soda. When she was done stowing perishables, she used a paring knife, and—smile on her face—sliced open the package. She pulled out the first of several books she'd been expecting. She held a child's six-page "Touch-and-Feel-Home" book. It had a Teddy bear, toy clown, choo-choo, and a kitty on the front cover. Lizzie smiled, glancing down to Lucy, now sprawled on the linoleum floor like a cocky Lounge Lizard, her tail tripping out. The Teddy bear's fur stomach was exposed through a hole in the cover. Lizzie rubbed her fingers along the fake fur, and smiled. Opened the book.

Let's explore the house with Chloe the kitten!, it said on an inside page.

On another it said, *Tickle Teddy bear's FLUFFY tummy!*

On that page was an identical Teddy bear from the cover, only this one's entire stomach had the fluffy, furry fur she'd been petting. Lizzie turned the page and found *Lift the SOFT cottony curtain!* on a page with Chloe the kitten sitting beside a vase of black-eyed Susans. Lizzie looked down to Lucy, who just so happened to be looking up to her with a whiskered expression of "Yeah, so?" Lizzie smiled and returned to her book. On the opposite page a loose piece of material flapped free. She moved it and found it covered a fake window, more

(*people at a table?*)

flowers behind the fake curtain.

Lizzie closed the book and looked back into the box. There were Touch-and-Feel books on farm animals, wild animals, and baby animals. A book on ponies and one on shapes that kinda looked interesting. Lizzie took out the book on shapes. An orange, gold star, and a cube were on the front. She opened it and flipped through it, checking out the BUMPY orange, SILKY cushion, and FLUFFY pencil case...

Images of children.

Thousands of them?

Millions...

In her head...they all stood in a field that stretched out as far as her mind's eye could see. All smiling, all happy.

Lizzie turned the next page to find SMOOTH sunglasses...and mentally zoomed in on the crowd of children. She psychically giggled and laughed with the energy that radiated from the boys and girls in her image—when someone, way in the back and who stood out from the crowd, caught her attention. This person stood head, shoulders, and torso above the children.

Turning the page, Lizzie came upon a SHINY magic wand.

She stared at the word "magic."

Zoomed in on the person standing above the children in her mental image.

Lizzie touched the book's shiny magic wand and closed her eyes. She knew this guy, and now she saw him...smiling...standing between two children, one hand resting lightly on a girl's head, the other on a boy's. There were incredible amounts of energy swirling—arcing—about the images. Lizzie found it harder to focus. She heard the distant-yet-joyous laughter of the children. Felt their excitement....

When are we coming home, Mommy? one of the children, the boy, asked, still under the smiling man's hand.

When, Mommy? the girl asked.

Lizzie couldn't answer. Too much emotion, too much energy.

Vapor locked.

I...I don't know, she was finally able to get out. *Mommy wishes she knew...you know how Mommy misses you. Every day.*

The two children smiled. Lizzie looked back to the smiling man. Compassion radiated from him, not only for the children, but for her. Specific emotionally charged energy purposely directed toward *her*.

Then it was gone. Children, field, the smiling man.

Lizzie gasped, flung open her eyes and jerked, sending the children's book across the room.

Slowly inhaling, she again closed her eyes; centered herself.

Lizzie exhaled slowly and deliberately, then got up and retrieved the surprisingly undamaged book, placing it back in the box. Picking up the package, she took it into the hallway and placed it before a closed door to a bedroom. A crooked sign was tacked up on the door that read "*No Grownups Allowed!*" It was written in multicolored crayon, with the "G" and "e" written backward. Lizzie stared at the sign. She stared at it for a long, long time before she left the door....

2

Mel didn't know how long he'd been awake. He just lay there in his parents' bed, staring into the ceiling. Bright light now filtered in from between closed drapes. It made absolutely no sense he had no parents. He had a car (had he checked this?), money in his wallet (or this?), a stocked refrigerator, and a house full of furniture (though he *swore* when he'd first awoken there'd been *nothing*).

Mel sat up. It felt as if, though he *had* slept, he *hadn't*. Not really.

Mel swung out of bed and padded along on bare feet over carpeted floor, into the hallway. He descended to the family room on the middle landing; pulled open the drapes and looked out the picture window. The sun was indeed shining (at least *that* hadn't changed), birds chirped, and it was still high summer. Somewhere in the neighborhood he heard someone mowing their lawn. He looked to his.

Mowed.

In fact, it was so fresh, there were still clippings scattered across the sidewalk and steps that lead up to the front door (the house sat on a small rise, up from a culvert full of flowing water). Opening a window, he could smell the fresh-cut grass and hear the calming flow of water through the culvert. In fact, the lawn was still wet from early morning dew. Across the culvert Mrs. Cole walked her dog.

Mrs. Cole?

He knew her?

Of course he did. This is where he lived.

Right?

Of course. His parents...the accident...school...did he have a job? Why couldn't he remember much about school (but who did, or wanted to, anyway, during summer)?

Okay, ignore school.

Did he have a job?

God, it was beautiful out! Absolutely *gorgeous*.

Mel left the window and went to the bookcase. A huge oak one that covered most of a wall.

Did anything here ring a bell?

There were all kinds of science fiction, history, and travel books. "Weird" books on dreaming, ghosts, and other paranormal stuff, as well as something called remote viewing. Books on JFK grabbed his attention, one simply titled *Kennedy*. He reached for it...when the doorbell rang. Mel pushed the book back into its slot on the shelf and answered the door. A mail carrier stood before him.

"Morning!" the carrier said.

"Good morning," Mel answered back, cautiously. There was something about the guy...he seemed *too* there, anything but two-dimensional. He was dressed as your standard-issue mail carrier, and was certainly friendly enough, blue-gray shorts and all.

"Mail call, my young sir!" the carrier exclaimed, eyes wide and attentive. He handed over a fistful of mail. "Here you go!"

As the carrier extended his hand, Mel looked to the bundle without taking it. It should have been a normal gesture, a transfer of mail from an agent of the United States Government to Mr. Private Citizen, but there was something more to this transfer. Something...different...*out of the ordinary*. He studied the outstretched hand, the fistful of letters, and what looked like a catalog or two.

Was there any mail in there for his parents? His *dead* parents?

"Go on, take it—it's for you."

Take it.

Mel noticed that the look in the mail carrier's eyes had somehow changed—for just a fraction of a second—from the happy, no-care appearance, to...something else. It had been so fleeting that Mel wondered if it had even happened at all.

It's for you...

"Me?"

He continued to study the outstretched mail stupidly, as if afraid to touch it, then looked back to the man, who continued to smile back at him—now, unsettlingly so. *Pleadingly* so. The carrier's eyes burrowing into him. Dark, deep eyes.

Intense.

"Yes, for you. Of course for you. *You.* Who else *you?*"

"But—"

Mel thought about protesting, *but what of his parents?*

Why couldn't the mail also be for his folks, and how would he have known they had died (and why had he felt so little remorse for them now?), but it was at that moment that the mail man began to grow more than a little agitated.

"Please, son, *take* it, I—" the carrier said, "I have to continue my rounds. *Here,*" he said, shaking the handful of mail in the air between them.

Mel took the delivery.

The carrier smiled (why was his smile so electric, so *penetrating?*). Mel saw an intense sense of relief flood over the man.

"Now…you go out and have yourself a wonderful day, young man!" the carrier said, back to his cheery self. "It's a beautiful one, isn't it?" he said, turning and looking up into the sky.

The minor wave of stress that had temporarily washed over the carrier was as if never there. He turned to leave, but remained on the stoop, continuing to admire the day.

"I say, it's such a waste, being cooped up inside on such a wonderfully *gorgeous* day like this, don't you think?" He turned back to Mel. "*Don't you?* A great day for a walk! Why, a young man like yourself could walk just about anywhere, on a day like this. *Anywhere!*"

"Yeah, sure," Mel replied. "Thanks…for the mail," he said, raising the bundle in a parting gesture.

Again that smile. The mailman stepped off the stoop, and walked out to the sidewalk. Mel watched him for a few moments, before closing the door.

"Weird little man," Mel said, and tossed the mail onto the coffee table.

3

A mailman.
A boy—a teenager.

Lizzie jerked awake on her couch.

A tall black scarecrow….

Lizzie again closed her eyes; rubbed them.

What had she been doing?

She'd put away her groceries…putzed about the place a little…then sat down—apparently ending up in an unplanned nap.

Was there something about her parents?

Lizzie sat up, rubbed her hands, and realized she'd left her rings—her wedding bands—in the bathroom. She went to the bathroom by way of the bedroom, and directly to the sink. She opened the third drawer down, where she always kept her rings…but didn't see the radiant-cut, one-carat diamond engagement ring and wedding band she'd expected to find there. Rummaging around in the drawer, she hastily moved things around. Still nothing.

"*Damn it,*" she said, "where *are* they?"

Lizzie removed everything from the drawer—old Ziploc bags, toothbrushes, Clearasil, an extra toilet-paper roller, a brown plastic bottle of iodine and a box of bandages—but still no rings. She stepped back. Jammed her hands to her hips.

"*I* do *own a wedding ring, don't I?*"

Lizzie closed her eyes. Tried to remember.

She'd been married…yes, that was still the same…his name had been Joe, and he'd worked in One Tree…also still the same…and his *death*…yes, his death had been an accident. That, too, unfortunately, also remained the same.

Lizzie opened her eyes; directed her gaze about the room as if trying to secretly detect something not meant for her to see.

Yes…it all continued to ring true, she grimaced…so, *where the heck were her rings?*

Lizzie again looked down to the drawer.

Nothing had changed.

She pulled out the other drawers, rummaged through all their contents, but still found no rings.

They were gone, plain and simple.

Lizzie replaced everything she'd taken out of the drawers, and began a methodical search of the bathroom itself, of the storage space and cabinets beneath and above the sink.

The room was suddenly filled with the laughter of children.

"Not now, please—I'm not in the mood," she said sternly.

All laughter ceased.

Images of the earlier Kennedy scenes returned to her, but she also brushed them aside. Lizzie headed for the bathroom closet.

Mommy!

Lizzie whipped around.

No one.

Lizzie again closed her eyes and leaned into the closet door. Arms crossed, she slowed her breathing…and listened.

Nothing else…no other pleas for attention. In her mind, she shouted, *Ridiculous! This is absolutely ridiculous! Not this! I refuse to allow this to be! I want my rings back, and now, goddammit!*

4

Mel sat in the blue swivel chair, paging through a book entitled, *JFK: His Life and Times*. He thumbed through sections of JFK's WWII experience with the Japanese *Amagiri*, and its ramming of his Navy PT 109 patrol boat, on August 2, 1943, in the waters of Blackett Strait, off the south Pacific's New Georgia. He glanced at a section describing his 1953 marriage to Jacqueline Bouvier. Glanced at sections detailing his dual-term presidency, including the Cuban Missile Crisis, African-American Rights, and something that gave him cause for pause.

Remote viewing?

This was the second time he'd encountered that term this morning. Mel settled in, reading the section on psychic research, and what had come to be known as "remote viewing." John Fitzgerald Kennedy, the book had begun, created the ultra-secret program back in 1962—at least the initial research into it. The book went on to say how it had met with much resistance, even from his closest advisors (one was quoted on record as saying "I wouldn't believe in it even if it were true"). The entire program had originally been highly classified, the book reported, but in the early nineties, when industry began to openly use it, portions of the program had been declassified. Though only a year of research had begun in 1962, actual operational work (called "tasks," or "taskings") had begun in earnest in 1963, and was instrumental in averting the Vietnam Crisis. The power of the remote-viewing program had not only proven itself with Vietnam, the book continued, but also in fighting crime through the powerful and insightful stewardship of JFK's brother, Robert F. Kennedy, who continued its use into his own two terms as president, immediately following his brother. A section was devoted to how the Kennedy brothers were the only sibling presidents, made even more eventful because they had served back-to-back presidencies, having had an unprecedented sixteen years in which to reform and shape the country under one unique vision shared by both men. In March of 1963, the book said, during his first term, JFK created the John F. Kennedy Center, or "The Center," against the beauty of the Blue Ridge Mountains of north-central Virginia. "RV-ing," as it was now called, was quickly applied to many applications beyond national security and global terrorism. Much less violent uses had also been applied, such as historical research, future predictions for various industries, population growth, economic catastrophes, global warming and other environmental issues. Though government use of psychics had been secretly used as far back as governments existed, JFK had single-handedly begun the focused modernization of its application—and had been determined to bring it out of the shadows and into controlled public use. Kennedy believed in secrecy when needed, but also believed that in making this particular tool known, it would prove to be its own deterrent. In fact, there were several declassified sessions in which remote viewers, while working tasks, had become suddenly aware of becoming tasks themselves, when Russian and Chinese counterparts (it was discovered) peeked in on them with their own programs. There had been much opposition to JFK's point of view, but he and his brother had ultimately prevailed, and now the paranormal had become accepted as just another application in humanity's toolbox, proclaimed the book.

Not that that had stopped the 1-900-numbers, Mel thought.

Something clicked.

Mel got up and went to the kitchen table. The gray business card was still there, beside the rest of his unremembered birthday cake:

Madame Nostradameus
1-900-PSI-KICK

Where had this card come from? He certainly hadn't remembered picking it up anywhere, and his parents—

Mel took the card with him back to his swivel chair, trying to remember where it had come from—when the doorbell again chimed. Mel got up and went to the door. A man's back greeted him, as he opened the door. A dark-haired man dressed in a dark suit coat, well over six feet tall, had just shouted something to the handful of kids running about on the sidewalk in front of the house, and though he hadn't made out what he'd said, the tone was unmistakably harsh and dismissive. The man had also just thrown a ball back to the children, but Mel watched as it arced high above their heads and into the culvert behind them, carried swiftly downstream.

The man spun around to greet him in what seemed an impossibly quick movement.

He paused for a moment. A smile unnaturally

(*painfully?*)

crept across his face.

Dreams.

Darkness.

An evil scarecrow?

A really *baaad* feeling....

"Good morning," the man said, extending a large hand. "I'm Black. From the FBI. We're investigating a kidnapping...and I understand the suspect frequents this neighborhood."

Black produced a picture from within his jacket, uncomfortably working his left shoulder as he handed it over to Mel.

Large hands, Mel noticed. *What had those hands—*

"Seen him?"

Mel examined the picture—a sketch; looked back to Black and his forced smile. Looked back to the picture (of a man in his forties or fifties, maybe even late thirties).

"Nope," Mel replied, "haven't." He attempted to return the sketch, but Black held up a hand.

"Keep it. My card," he added, handing him a card with only his name and number on it. "If you should hear of anything, please be good enough to call."

Mel nodded.

"Thank you for your time, Mr. Roberts."

Mel closed the door. He turned away, still examining both the card and picture—

He shot back to the door and whipped it open.

Black was gone.

Mel rushed out onto the sidewalk and daylight. The kids were once again playing with a ball, but Black was nowhere to be found.

Mr. Black, from the FBI...who had somehow, and for some unknown reason, during a *casual*, neighborhood canvassing, known his name without him having given it.

Chapter Five

1

Lizzie switched off the ignition to her '80, baby blue Chevy LUV, and stepped out into the parking lot of the Waffle House restaurant.

Her craving for waffles was not to be denied.

She entered the tiny "yellow-hatted" building and took a seat toward the rear of the restaurant, at a table that hadn't yet had its previous customer's place setting cleaned and replaced.

"Sorry," the server apologized, appearing tableside, "Guess we weren't quite ready for you, were we?" she said with a smile. "Been slammed today!" She left Lizzie a menu and unceremoniously removed the mess and tip. Lizzie smiled politely. The server disappeared into the back of the restaurant, only to quickly return with a wash cloth, new table setting, and a pitcher of water. She poured water into a fresh glass.

Lizzie smiled. "Thank you."

The server asked, "Juice or coffee?"

"Just some milk and orange juice, please."

"Okay, I'll be right back, hon. My name's Viv."

Lizzie nodded and opened her menu. The hustle and bustle of the place felt good, especially after having been alone at home and so confined to the inside of her head. Waffles were what she wanted. Big ones she didn't have to make herself. Food just tasted better when someone else made it.

As Lizzie scanned the menu, she glanced up at the sound of children-being-children at the opposite end of the eatery. Unexpectedly emotional, she brought a hand to her mouth then wiped at the corners of both eyes. Bringing her hand back to her mouth she turned to the half-wall beside her and tried to recompose herself. She checked to see if any of the restaurant staff on the other side of the half-wall had caught her.

Nope. She was safe.

Lizzie observed an older

(tall black scarecrow)

gentleman enter the restaurant and immediately got the creeps…she wanted to ignore him, but couldn't help track him as he took a seat at the counter. He had a face Lizzie could only explain as never having smiled in its lifetime, yes, the tall, lanky frame of scarecrow, and a sense about him that he had never known any real joy (she winced as the next feeling overcame her)—*short of through the control and manipulation of others.*

But, most of all, she sensed in this man…*fear.*

Lizzie watched as the man picked up his menu and casually glanced in her direction, but before their eyes could meet Lizzie looked away, bringing her menu up before her. She closed her eyes—squeezed them tight—and tried to block out the wave upon wave of unpleasant, nauseating feelings that barraged her.

And she knew he was still looking at her.

Did he sense her sensing him?

That would not be uncommon in her line of work, but this time it scared her. Something wasn't right, and she wished she'd picked any other day to have had her waffle craving.

"Ready to order, ma'am?" Viv asked, holding a glass of milk and orange juice. Lizzie jumped, upsetting her water.

"Oh! Sorry!" she said, embarrassed, lowering her menu. Lizzie quickly glanced back to the dark man at the counter—but he was gone. Momentarily unnerved, and still sensing things weren't quite right, she darted her gaze about the restaurant's small-but-cozy interior.

"I'm sorry—guess I just stepped out to Hawai'i for a moment!" Lizzie immediately set about soaking up her spilled water with a hand full of napkins.

"No, I'm sorry—I shouldn't have snuck up on you like that," Viv said, setting down Lizzie's milk and juice. "I'll get another glass and clean this up," she said, as she took over clean up. "Ready to order?"

Lizzie's images of the dark man began to drain away—not entirely, but enough so she could refocus on the reason she'd come here in the first place.

"Yes, I'll have the pecan waffle."

"Very good. I'll have it right up." Viv leaned in to her, and in a lowered voice, said, "I'll bring two—the second one's on me." She winked and left, making one last swipe of the table with a dish rag.

Up ahead, the children continued their spirited cacophony, but now actually began to dart about and among the patrons and their tables. It seemed very odd and rude public behavior to be allowed by any parent. They should be better controlled—

Viv returned with Lizzie's replacement water and quickly left. Lizzie took a sip of the juice. As she set the glass back down, she was suddenly bumped into, causing her to nearly spill the glass's contents. It was a bump that actually felt like a *burn*, and she shot a hand to her shoulder where the contact had been made. In a grimace of pain, she looked up.

"Pardon me," the man said, in a gruff, cold voice, and continued forward, working his left shoulder.

The man from the counter.

Lizzie looked behind her. She sat before the restrooms.

How had he gotten past her?

Lizzie watched in stunned silence, rubbing her arm. The man took his seat at the counter. He never looked back to her, nor seemed to give her a second thought. She watched as he gave the server his order. Watched as glasses of milk and orange juice were also placed on the counter before him, and from which he immediately took a sip of *his* orange juice.

Lizzie looked away; checked her "burned" arm. Of course, there was nothing wrong with it. The stinging and searing sensations had also passed.

She shivered, briskly rubbing her arms.

There was no other place to sit to avoid her direct line-of-sight view of the man, so, in an effort to get her mind off the guy, she grabbed an unused newspaper from a nearby table. But, as she sat back down, she was again bumped, this time by one of the children, children who were becoming increasingly boisterous, and had, apparently, found their way down to her end of the restaurant.

"*Excuse me*," came out of her before she realized it, and in a tone that'd surprised her for its annoyed severity.

The child, an adorable chestnut-haired beauty of about five, she guessed, stopped. The girl-child turned to Lizzie, and in a most genuine and apologetic tone said, "*I'm sorry.*"

"Oh, well...*thank you*."

The girl smiled warmly to Lizzie, then returned to chasing her sister (she surmised) down the narrow restaurant to the opposite end. Their activity seemed to grow continually nosier, and Lizzie couldn't fathom such odd public behavior. Who and *where* were their parents?

Lizzie returned her attention to her new-found paper; again glanced behind her.

How were all these people getting behind her without her seeing them—and why were they all ramming into her? Did she have a "kick me!" sign pinned to her back?

Lizzie grabbed her orange juice to take another sip—saw the man at the counter drink from his—and changed her mind, picking up her milk, instead.

From the already warm temperature outside, so early this morning, it was definitely going to be a hot one....

The waffles had been great.

Lizzie took a sip of water and wiped her mouth with a napkin. She loved the rich smell and taste of real maple syrup, and loved that it came directly from trees. Such a pure food! Sap tapped from a tree boiled down to get rid of the water to the desired flavor. That's all it was. Pure and simple—until someone figured out a cheaper way to make it using flavored mixes and corn syrup. Took all the mystique out of it; the in-touch-with-nature part.

Lizzie sighed in stuffed relief; again checked on the dark man at the counter. She'd noticed he'd also finished his breakfast and was actually in the process of paying. Reading the paper had been a good distraction from the man; sometimes her ability could be such a burden, especially when she'd "locked onto" unsavory situations or individuals and couldn't disentangle herself from them.

It was like a bad taste in your mouth you couldn't rid yourself of.

But she actually felt better, now, and, she also noted, the kids were still here, but no longer as noisy and rambunctious. Good. Guess the parent or parents had finally stepped in.

"Is there anything else?" Viv asked, again standing beside her table. "A piece of breakfast pie, maybe?"

"Pie? Oh, no—"

"Sure?" Viv playfully insisted, scribbling on her ticket and eyeing her.

Lizzie nodded in the affirmative, "I'm sure—thank you."

"Okay." Viv deposited the check on the table. "Have a great day!"

"Oh, and one thing, if I may," Lizzie said, as Viv began to leave, "those children…down there—have they bothered any of the other customers?"

Viv looked down the length of the restaurant then back to Lizzie. "No…did they bother you?"

Lizzie opened her mouth to say something, when she noticed that the group seemed to have thinned out considerably. No longer was there the large crowd of screaming kids she'd earlier observed. In fact, she didn't even see the child who'd earlier apologized.

"Huh. Well, no, I guess not." Lizzie narrowed her gaze and cocked her head, somewhat confused. "Guess they left."

"Sorry, I've been so busy I hadn't noticed. Sorry if they'd upset you," Viv said, "kids'll be kids, won't they? I have two of my own, so, sometimes—noisy or not—I tend to tune out noisy levels at work. But I'll keep an eye out for them. You have a good day, ma'am!" Viv departed.

Lizzie reached for her pocketbook inside her booth. When she turned to leave, the little girl who'd earlier bumped into her and apologized stood quietly before her, eyes big and wide.

"We're sorry, ma'am. We didn't mean to be so noisy."

Lizzie again looked around. Patrons at nearby tables eyed her. Lizzie cleared her throat.

"Well…you and your siblings did get a little out of control, you know," she said in her most motherly sounding manner.

"I know. We do that sometimes. We were just having fun."

"Fun is okay, honey, but when you're out in public you need to be mindful of others, so you don't annoy them."

"We only annoyed one person," the girl said simply, still staring at Lizzie with her wide-eyed and deep, all-consuming gaze.

Lizzie removed her pocketbook and counted out her money, still looking to the sweet little girl. "But, had you been more mindful you wouldn't have annoyed *anyone*. Where are your parents?"

The little girl smiled. It was a big smile, a radiant smile, one that filled Lizzie with goose bumps. Suddenly the girl's eyes were all Lizzie knew…eyes…deep, dark…comfortable. Without moving her lips, the girl replied, *But Mommy, you know the answer to* that!

And was gone.

Lizzie gasped and fell back into her booth. She laughed loudly and unabashedly, and nearby patrons continued to glare at her.

"Sorry! I'm so sorry!" she apologized to those around her.

No matter how many times this happened to her, it still never failed to—occasionally—catch her off-guard…especially when she wasn't thinking straight, or was so focused on having to have her damned waffles….

2

Lizzie closed the door to her trailer behind her. After running errands and meeting with a couple friends for a walk, if felt good getting out of the heat. She picked up the little yellow ducky toy on the floor at her feet, and tossed it over toward the door that read "No Grownups Allowed." Lucy chased after it. With a deft mid-air paw swipe, she knocked it back to the floor. Lizzie then entered the kitchen for a glass of lemonade. It was a hot one out there, had to easily be in the nineties. The air conditioner was sweet relief, and she was thankful she'd closed all her curtains before going out. She brought the glass of lemonade across her forehead and cheeks, then took a deep drink…when the image of a smiling man holding a condensation-covered glass of iced tea filled her mind.

She looked to the refrigerator.

"But, I don't have any…"

Lizzie went back to the freezer to add additional ice to her glass, sipping more lemonade to make room. Returning to the living room, she collapsed into her favorite recliner. The image of the smiling man remained strong.

She closed her eyes.

Who are *you?* she asked, mentally.

The man smiled.

No name?

I have no name, he replied.

Why not?

No need.

What do people call you?

Whatever they wish. I don't bother many folk.

Are you bothering me? she asked, mentally smiling.

This bother you?

No, she said, and laughed aloud. *I just find you…curious. Who are you, why are you contacting me?*

Whether or not you know it, you already know me. I'm interested in the same things you are.

Okay…

Children.

A knock at her door jarred her back to the present.

She shot to her feet.

Bad vibe. *Baaad* vibe….

Lizzie stood holding her upset glass of lemonade. Half of it had spilled onto her lap and the carpet.

The knock continued.

Dark vibe…

Chiding herself, she went to the door and peeked through the peephole.

And dropped the glass altogether.

It was the tall dark man from the Waffle House.

Dark man.

Black. Black, *blaaack…*

(*red!*)

The knock continued.

"Missus Gordon? Victor Black, FBI," the man called through her door. "I need to speak with you."

Dear God, she thought, *FBI? What have I done?*

"Missus Gordon?"

Lizzie stood, frozen, before the door.

Did he know she was home?

Of course he did; he'd obviously followed her. Had seen her enter her trailer.

She tuned in to him; still sensed that earlier "bad vibe"…along with another feeling, one she could only describe as…*evil*….

"Just a minute!" she shouted back, and picked up her glass. She rushed back into the kitchen and grabbed a towel, and her gaze fell upon a box of tea bags on the counter, back by the toaster. She looked to them questioningly on her return trip to the living room. She hastily began sopping up lemonade from the carpet.

"Just a minute!" she again shouted to Mr. Black-from-the-FBI.

She dropped the towel to the stain and stood on it for several antsy, uncomfortable moments. Retrieving the soaked towel, she rushed back into the kitchen, tossed it into the sink, and, on the way back in, grabbed the tea-bag box. Examined it. It was real all right. On her counter.

She knew she hadn't had any tea bags—yet here they were.

She tossed them back onto the counter and returned to the door. Catching her breath and straightening herself out, she opened it. Mr. Black stood on the other side of the screen door. She quickly clicked on the lock to the screen-door handle.

"Is everything all right?" Black asked.

"Everything's fine—sorry," she said, wiping away loose hair behind an ear. "I'd just spilled a glass of lemonade and was in the middle of cleaning it up, as you can see," she said, wringing wet hands to her sides and drawing attention to her damp lap. Black remained expressionless.

"What can I do for you, mister—"

"Black. Victor Black. FBI." He showed his badge.

"How do I know you're really who you say you are?"

"You don't. Just have to take my word for it. Or call the district office. May I come in—"

"To be perfectly honest, sir, I don't feel entirely comfortable with that. I'd like to know why you're following me, and how you know my name. I saw you at the restaurant."

Black cracked an awkward—pained?—smile.

"Ma'am, I work for the government, and I intentionally sought you out. I'm following you, as you put it, because I need to talk with you about a sensitive matter. May I?" Black tucked away his badge.

Did she let him into her life, behind the closed doors and drawn curtains of her trailer, like some horror-movie vampire, or did she say no-thank-you and take her chances with whatever law she might be breaking?

"Mrs. Gordon, I understand your hesitation. I'll stand right here—won't move—and you can call the Denver office. I see a phone back there. Give them a call—the number's most likely on the very front page of the phone book—and give them my badge number," he said, again pulling his badge from his jacket and holding it out to her.

Lizzie unlocked the screen door and quickly grabbed the badge. She then closed and locked the main door.

She hefted the badge uncertainly, as she picked up the phone book and went to her phone. Finding the FBI number, indeed, on the "Emergency" page at the very front of the book, she dialed it. As the phone rang, horrific images of a vampire-like Black, crawling in through the screen door overwhelmed her, and she shot a look back to the door.

Still closed.

Still locked.

Still *evil.*

An official-sounding voice answered, and Lizzie got right to the point.

"I don't mean to sound hysterical or anything, but I live in One Tree, Colorado, and have a guy, here, who claims to work for you people—a Victor Black? Can you verify him for me, and what his business with me might be?"

"Do you have a badge number?"

"Yes," Lizzie replied, and gave it.

There was a pause at the other end, and the person came back to say yes, they did have a Victor Black at their bureau, verified his badge number, and told her he was scheduled to interview an "Elizabeth Gordon." The individual then verified her address. Not entirely satisfied, Lizzie described Black to the person on the phone—which was also corroborated—right down to his awkward smile and trick shoulder.

"Thank you," Lizzie said, not sure if she was pissed off or relieved, and hung up. But before returning to the front door, she unlocked and opened the back door and opened all curtains in the place. She then returned to the main door and—reluctantly—unlocked the screen and main doors. Handed Black back his badge.

"Well, it seems today is my day for embarrassment."

Unaffected, Black slid his badge back into his jacket, favoring his left shoulder.

"Come on in," she said, "I'm sorry, but I'm sure you understand my caution."

Lizzie stepped aside, afraid to touch him. As Black passed by, she shuddered to a sudden chill—and noticed he hadn't broken a sweat in his tie and jacket. In this heat. Lizzie positioned herself before the now-opened picture-window, feeling the assault of the mid-day swelter.

"Nice place," he said.

"It's not much, but it's all I—"

"Since your husband's death?"

Black turned to her. His presence seemed to *consume* the room, all *life* in the room....

Lizzie crossed her arms. "Have I done something wrong? What is it you want?"

Black absentmindedly smirked, then turned back around to examine the interior. Spotted the package and toy by the "No Grownups Allowed" door.

"Children?"

"Look, sir, I don't mean to be rude, but I really must insist—"

"May I?" he asked, directing their attention to the couch.

Lizzie motioned him on.

"Would you like something to drink?" she asked, wiping perspiration from her forehead.

"Iced tea is fine," he said, taking his seat and opening up a folder he held.

Lizzie stared at him.

Black never looked up, but added, "or lemonade."

He sat on the couch, carefully working his left shoulder as he unbuttoned his jacket. She looked to the folder he carried. A black folder.

"I'll check to see if I have any," she said, and left for the kitchen.

In the kitchen, she gripped the refrigerator door handle and paused before opening it.

"Okay…let me guess…," she whispered to herself before opening the door.

Inside she found a pitcher of freshly brewed iced tea already made, already cold, and sitting on the top shelf. She shot a glance toward the glass she'd just held and spilled and saw the remnants of iced tea—*not lemonade*—in it.

And on her hands.

"Of course."

Lizzie returned to the living room to find Black reviewing his black folder. She placed the *black* tea on a coaster on the coffee table, then took a seat in a glider rocker opposite him.

"So, what's so important you feel you have to stalk me?"

Black closed the folder and tapped it on a leg. "Mrs. Gordon…we know a lot about you. We'd like to enlist your assistance."

"What on earth for?"

"We've been trying to locate this man," Black said, handing her an artist-sketched picture from the folder. "We can't go into detail, but suffice it to say that the least of his crimes are kidnapping and child molestation."

He stared at her.

Lizzie examined the picture.

She knew this man.

It was the same guy from her vision.

The one who'd been holding the iced tea. She definitely did *not* get those kinds of vibes from this guy at all.

She looked to Black.

She did, however, get those feelings from Mr. FBI sitting before her…behind closed doors…and those feelings were much stronger now. There was something not right about him. If she tried to make a run for it, she knew—*knew*—this man would be all over her like sharks on chum—and before she could even *consider* screaming. Before she could kick him in the balls or jab out his eyes, he'd be on her and that would be that. This she picked up as easily as others breathed air. This man was totally and utterly dangerous, and she had to watch what she told him—or radiated *to* him. He'd made no overt moves on her and had even been verified by the Denver FBI. But that didn't mean a thing. She wasn't stupid. He might not have killed the real Agent Black and taken his badge and identity, but he could very well be working for some other government agency, and all this had been carefully orchestrated…arranged….which she did try to tune into, but felt…*distracted*…

(deflected?)

(…unable to properly focus…)

But…why *her?*

No, she'd have to play this one extremely close to home. There were too many contradictions about this guy.

She suddenly noticed him eyeing her eyeing *him*.

"Child molestation, huh," she said, "how come I haven't heard of this before—like on *America's Most Wanted?*"

Black again performed a forced, pained smile.

"For other reasons I cannot disclose, we're keeping a low profile. For now. That's why we want you. We know of your abilities."

Black's gaze burned into her.

"Just what abilities do you think I have that could possibly be of benefit to the mighty and far-reaching arm of the FBI?"

"Madame Nostra*dame*us, if I may use your professional *nom de plume*, please don't make this any more difficult than it has to be—"

("*has to* be"?)

"How do you know about me?" she said, jumping to her feet. She walked over to, and stood before, the picture window.

"I'm just a cheap phone psychic—'for entertainment purposes on-ly'—ever read those disclaimers? How in the hell could you guys possibly know anything about me? *Why* would you?"

"Mrs. Gordon…again, I am not at liberty to discuss this with you, only that we presently require your assistance. Your *country* requires your assistance. This man…has done certain crimes against national security, not to mention the heinous nature of child abuse…."

Was it getting hotter in here?

Lizzie nervously changed her stance several times, while remaining exposed before the window. This man definitely wasn't telling the truth, the whole truth, and nothing but the truth, yet she did pick up that this man "they" were searching for really did pose some kind of threat to him or those he worked for. Why was it so hard for her to pick up any other specifics? She was far better than this—*why wasn't she seeing the whole picture?*

And did all this mean this other man posed a threat to anyone *else?* Was a legitimate bureau interest?

Now, that was the question, wasn't it?

And if this guy was FBI, why did she feel like she was being violated in her own home? He was sizing her up as they talked, just as she was doing with him—only on a psychic level. He was stronger than most she'd met—was he trying to block her?

No, "blocking" was wrong.

Misdirect.

If she'd learned anything about her ability, it was that you could pretty much pick up on anything you were sensitive to. Nothing could be blocked if you were sensitive enough…things might be *misinterpreted*…but never *blocked.* But what was it about him that she couldn't penetrate? He didn't seem interested in her, in that most men she met—heterosexuals, anyway—she could pick up on an unspoken sexual attraction, but she felt no such stirrings in this guy…though she did feel a powerful sexual energy *about* him. He had a totally different—and focused—agenda, one that seemed to pose a dire threat to his very existence.

A curious thing.

And it wasn't just about him, which was even odder; it affected others. This man was definitely a mixed bag of impressions. And there was something odd about that left shoulder of his.

"Can we expect some form of assistance?" he asked.

"If you know me as well as you think you do, then you know I am in no way comfortable with any of this. Whatever ability you feel I have, and you feel I should use it *for*, I am *not* comfortable with you knowing whatever you *think* you know. I need some time to consider this—what I should or shouldn't lend in this matter, Mr. Black."

Lizzie stood firm, inching closer to the window (she could launch herself through it, she was certain) and staring back at Black, who didn't bat an eye. He was good, she'd give him that. And creepy.

Black looked down to his folder and closed it; came to his feet.

Lizzie remained at the window.

"Certainly. The Bureau in no way wants you to feel coerced into this matter."

He again reached into his jacket.

"Here's my card. You can reach me at any time of the day. Take your time, but know that the longer you delay, the longer this man remains at large. It *is* a matter of national security."

Lizzie took the card.

"Thank you for your hospitality—and *iced tea*."

Lizzie couldn't open the front door fast enough, and opened it to the sound of chirping birds, crickets, and withering heat. Suddenly, the heat didn't seem so bad any more, as Black walked past her and onto her stoop. She looked past him to his, of course, big, *black* car....

"Have a good day," Black said, without turning back. He got into his car and left.

Why did she feel as if she'd just been raped?

Chapter Six

1

Seventy-seven-year-old former president John Fitzgerald Kennedy awoke sweaty and anxious. Bolt upright in bed, hyper alert and aware, he stared out across the darkness of his Hyannis Port bedroom. Looked to the empty space in bed beside him.

Jackie.

Good Lord, he missed her.

Jackie's long gone, a little voice inside reminded, *gone of non-Hodgkin's lymphoma. 1980. Gone after twenty-seven years of marriage.*

Yet he was still going strong.

Fourteen years, and every so often it just hit him wrong. Usually during the wee hours of the night.

Kennedy closed his eyes, opened them, shook his head, and looked to the bedside clock.

One-seventeen a.m.

He again shook his head. Didn't quite feel "all there." Like he was still dreaming—*in* a dream.

What was his last memory?

All he remembered was an intense feeling of anxiety—nothing else, just the *feeling* of the dream...its intensity....

He lifted his hands in the darkness and looked to them. He felt electrified...tingling...*he actually felt as if he didn't belong here*...now...in this bed—this *time*.

Again, looked to the clock.

One-eighteen.

Okay, Time was ticking away.

But, something was wrong, dreadfully wrong. Out of place.

Kennedy brought both hands to his face and pressed; rubbed. Tossing the blankets off, he got up and made his way along the wood floor to the bathroom to relieve himself. Upon his return, he diverted to a window and pushed aside the curtains. Looked out over the dark expanse of sea. Cracked open the window…listened to the roar of its crashing breakers.

Alone…he was alone.

No Jackie and a confused sense of identity…*place*.

Turning around, he wrinkled his brow as he desperately tried to sense something, *anything*, about this room, his place in it, his loss of Jackie…life in general.

He returned to the window…inhaled the sea air and allowed the crash of the ocean to wash over him. All anxiety slowly began to drain away, as he listened to the most comforting sound in the world…a sound that had defined his very existence…from learning to swim at thirteen in New Milford, to his time as the swim-team captain at Harvard…his Navy years…his design and creation of the Navy's swiftest, stealthiest Littoral Combat Ship….

But it was that night in 1943 when his PT boat had been rammed by the Japanese in Blackett Straight that he thought about most (was he sure about this?).

He shuddered.

Had that really been him all those years ago?

It seemed so distant, now, and in more than just years. That twenty-six year old seemed like an entirely different person—an entirely different *life*.

Had he and all those other men really been dumped out into the black, open ocean, as the *Amagiri* plowed right on through them?

Had they really swum all those miles across open, South Pacific Ocean, or had it, too, been just another dream?

He closed his eyes and leaned into the window sill, desperately trying to discern fact from fiction.

Had that really been something *he*—the *him* who now stood before this late-night window—would do? *Could* do?

Of course not, he was no longer that young, tough, twenty-six year old. Those had been different times and extraordinary circumstances. But still, he *had* done it, he couldn't shake that memory, but he couldn't quite believe *something* about it….

Wasn't it odd—heinous even—how healthy, strong bodies

changed and deteriorated over the course of a lifetime? A short life-time, really; just how long was seventy-seven years, anyway? Seventy-seven was nothing to the entire timespan of history or geology.

And he was so safe and secure now, and, yes, still relatively healthy at his age. Excellent genes from a long-lived family, from a father who had lived to be ninety-six, to a mother who was still kicking it up at one-hundred-and-four. He swam every day, took one-to-two-hour-long walks, and even worked out with weights. He remained active in the global community and world politics, had written many books, and organized many charities, his favorite being the Children Are Our World, or CHOW

He was engaged in life.

Yes, he'd lived a full life, but still had something out there he had yet to accomplish…*needed* to do. There was still something he couldn't quite put his finger on before he'd had enough and called it quits from this existence. No regrets. He believed in more than one life, and had had the dreams and psychic experiences over his lifetime to prove it enough to himself (or at least had the *feeling* he had, the strongest of which being dual-Civil War personalities of being a soldier in a Federal brigade and a direct connection with Lincoln himself, which totally confused him, and the other about being an impoverished kid in India or somewhere…), even if no one else believed it. He wasn't afraid of dying. He just wanted to make sure he'd done all he was supposed to have done before moving on. Never let it be said a Kennedy never completed what he or she'd set out to do. Enough power, money, or influence, and you could do just about anything.

He didn't ask for much.

He just wanted to change the world.

2

Shit, what the hell am I supposed to do, now?

Lizzie'd been asking herself this question all night.

Two a.m., and she'd had a busy night. The activity had helped keep her mind off her problems and on other peoples' problems instead, but now she found dead air between phone calls, and her predicament filtered back.

Christ, show a little psychic ability, and the whole world wanted your soul.

What was she going to do?

She sure as hell didn't want to work for that man, FBI, national security, or otherwise, but felt inexplicably tied to him, and *that* caused her great distress. How could she be tied to so evil an individual? It actually upset her stomach, and she felt the onset of a headache. And, in dealing with the headache, she kept losing focus and returning to that evil feeling back at the Waffle House. That feeling of deepest darkest *blackness*.

His name totally fit him.

She couldn't stand it any longer. Removing her headset, she went to the bathroom, where she spilled out a couple Gelcaps, and greedily gulped them down with mouthfuls of water straight from the tap. She splashed water onto her face, shut off the faucet, and grabbed a towel. As she looked in the mirror, drying off, she noticed a pimple forming on her forehead.

"*No!*"

Lizzie re-racked the towel and examined the pimple closer in the mirror. She always got these things whenever she worried too much about something. Of course they never formed on some hidden part of her body, like her butt. Always the face.

Grumbling, she opened a drawer to pull out some Clearasil—when she heard a light metallic tinkling sound, as something fell to the linoleum. Unscrewing the tube, she looked down.

Her engagement ring sat on the floor beside her bare feet.

Emitting a joyous shriek, she snatched it up. She looked inside the drawer, replaced the Clearasil—and found the wedding band. She again shrieked as she lifted the rings into the light for better inspection. They were, indeed, *her* rings. She slid them back onto her finger and examined them in their rightful place.

"*That's* more like it!"

She'd searched those drawers inside and *out*.

They had *not* been there.

Lizzie caught a flash of a reflection in the mirror, and looked out the bathroom door.

Heard distant laughter.

All she'd caught was the briefest glimpse of bare feet.

Nothing like the pitter-patter of—

Her phone rang and Lizzie realized she'd all-but-forgotten she was still on duty. Rushing back into the kitchen, she kicked aside another stray toy.

* * *

It was slightly after four a.m. when Lizzie finally hung up the headset for the night, brushed her teeth, and got herself to bed, Lucy following her around the house. Lizzie fingered her wedding bands.

In sickness or in health.

Til death do us part.

Maybe that last line was good enough for most people, but what about those like her? What about those more sensitive to the afterlife?

She still felt Joe out there.

No, she wasn't pining away for him, hoping to meet him as soon as possible in some glowing, revolving tunnel of hereafter light, but she still *felt* him. Aspects of him. She knew he was fine, carrying on with the rest of his soul's journey in whatever way he was—but she also knew that he wasn't pining away for her, either. And that didn't bother her.

In sickness or in health...

Lizzie closed her eyes.

It had been an accident.

That was what bothered her—that she'd never seen it coming.

That she'd never seen it coming. He'd been the owner of his own construction company, and had been talking with his foremen. It had been a local job, a no-brainer he'd called it, just throw up another apartment complex, get in get out, collect a tidy sum, then move on to bigger fish: an industrial office complex on the outskirts of Parker, southeast of Denver. About halfway into the apartment project, he'd given his foremen their marching orders for the day, when, out of nowhere, it came. A one-ton I-beam soaring through the bright blue sky like a terrain-hugging cruise missile.

And Joe had just happened to be in its way.

There had been shouts, sure, even some of his foremen rushing in his direction, but with all the heavy machinery, their shouted conversation—and the use of ear protection—it was just another business day in the scheme of things. Joe's number had simply come up, was all, and that I-beam smashed into him like no tomorrow. He'd never looked up, never heard a sound, nor spied any peripheral movement. One moment he was alive and thinking...considering plans for the day, whether or not the project would be complete within the next year, whether or not to have a child, what to bring home for her as a surprise for-no-particular-reason gift, and how life was going so great for the both of them. And behind *those* thoughts had been the other ones, the thoughts that always seemed to quickly drift in and out, barely making themselves known before splitting, but leaving a backburnered portion of his mind always working on them…bills, and what to do about that Jeff Skopchek, whose wife had just left him and was suing him for everything he had…or his upcoming vacation time he'd been promising Lizzie, since he'd been working like a dog the past two years without a serious—more than three days off at a time—break….

Yes, one moment he'd been alive and functioning, and the next he was crumpled up in the dirt, his head…*gone.*

At least he hadn't seen it coming.

Jeff Skopchek, however, had not been so lucky. He'd been at the crane's controls that had swiveled that I-beam into Joe's direction; swiveled a little too fast for practice. Unfortunately for Joe, Jeff had just talked with his wife that previous night. His soon-to-be-ex-wife had told him just how much she was going to screw his ever-loving ass—and he better not have that little slut there with him now. And—by the way—did he think that little bitch would stay with him once he was living under a bridge? She'd better love booze and the great outdoors, cause after the loss of his money, house, and that classic red-hot Vette of his, that was all they were going to have in common.

So, good old Jeff came to work late in a less-than-optimal state of mind, and when he'd been told to move that pile of steel from here to there, Jeff Skopchek was only a quarter there in the Focus Department, and said steel I-beam took up its weighty trajectory through Joe Gordon's noggin.

What's the last thing to go through a bug's head when it hits a windshield?
Its asshole.
What was the last thing to go through Joe Gordon's head one sunny workday?
A one-ton steel girder.

Needless to say, Joe, who signed Jeff's check, didn't sign Jeff's—nor anyone else's—check that day, and Jeff found himself criminally liable, and, in one respect, no longer having to worry about living under a bridge anymore.

3

Lizzie stirred, groggily. Good Lord, just fall asleep only to immediately wake back up?

She looked to the clock, but all she saw was that it read four-something. The rest of the display was hidden behind a silhouette—

Of a head.

Someone tugged at Lizzie's elbow.

"*C'mon*, Mommy, it's time to *go!*" the little boy whispered urgently, tugging at her nightshirt sleeve. "*C'mon.*"

The boy darted to the doorway, where he turned back to her and waited.

Lizzie wiped her eyes and sat up. The boy stood against a night-light-backlit doorway.

"Okay, okay…I'm *coming.*"

Lizzie got out of bed and went to the boy.

"*C'mon*…everyone's waiting!"

Lizzie went to the boy, who took her hand, then excitedly rushed her out into the living room. She noticed Lucy curled up on the couch, watching the two of them as they walked past to the front door, which the boy opened. Lizzie stepped outside. She found herself standing on a wide-open plain, and as far as the eye could see…

Children.

"It's okay, Mommy, this is what you wanted."

"I know, I know, honey," Lizzie said, trying to swallow and finding it hard to do so.

"It's just kind of…overwhelming!" Lizzie brought a hand to her chest.

Gentle laughter bubbled around her. As Lizzie looked from face to face, she realized she knew each and every child. Their names didn't matter…but they were names that were so much more meaningful and full of depth that to utter them would never do them justice. It was the *sense* about them, the *feeling* that led her through various inner journeys of each individual that mattered. Like a buoy marker, it was used to identify each boy or girl, but it was so much more than that…there was an *inner* importance. A flowering of identities. She found she could get lost in trying to sort it all out, but the identifications had already been made, and additional focuses were already shifting in and out of awareness.…

The children's laughter washed over her, like a warm, gentle rain.

"Wow. I've never been with all of you at once before."

"You *have*, Mommy, you just don't remember," her son said.

"I miss you," Lizzie said. She went to her knees and hugged him.

"We *all* miss you!" the boy exclaimed. Tears ran down his face.

Lizzie backed away, wiping away her son's tears. She looked to the mass of children and saw they all cried tears of joy, each pair of eyes brimming with love and understanding.

"Don't cry," Lizzie said, "there's no reason to cr—"

But she was already well into her own bout of weeping.

"When can we come home?" the boy asked.

"Soon," Lizzie answered, wiping away tears, "soon! Mommy still has a lot of work to do, you know that."

The boy looked down. "I know. We just miss you. We miss you so much, Mommy. It's that bad man, isn't it."

Lizzie shot him a surprised look. She grabbed him firmly by his diminutive shoulders.

"*You know him?*"

He nodded.

"*How* do you know him? Tell me—*how do you know this man?*"

The boy looked behind her and pointed. Lizzie turned.

There stood the Smiling Man, cradling an infant that babbled contentedly to herself.

"Who *are* you?"

The man smiled.

When Lizzie got to her feet, the man no longer held the infant. She stared at him for a moment before turning back to the sea of children—but they were all gone.

"They're still there. We're inextricably linked," the man said, smiling. He took a sip of iced tea, then sat in a chair. Lizzie found she now stood on the nighttime porch of a small, cozy clapboard dwelling. The Smiling Man leaned back in his chair until it rested against the outside wall of the house.

"So…what can you tell me?" Lizzie asked.

"What do you want t'know?" the man replied, taking another sip of tea. "This is good stuff, you really oughta try it."

"Okay."

"Great!" The Smiling Man all but leapt out of his chair and disappeared into the interior of his house. While she waited, Lizzie went to the porch railing and looked out into the night; inhaled the fresh, cool air, and listened to chirping crickets.

"Don't you just love it?" the man asked, back with another glass of iced tea in hand, his glass refreshed.

Lizzie turned to him. "I do." Inhaling deeply, she smiled and sighed, then casually crossed her arms. "I really do. I always wanted to live out in the country like this."

"But, you already do."

"Yeah, but not *now*."

"Have a seat."

Lizzie took up the chair next to the Smiling Man, who again leaned back against the house. "Go on," he chided playfully, "there's no carpet to dig chair legs into, here."

Smiling, Lizzie tipped her chair back against the outside of the house.

"So, why have we met?"

"You know. You're just clouded by all that guilt."

Lizzie took a sip of iced tea.

"You know what I'm talking about—don't pretend otherwise," Smiling Man said.

"You smile too much, don't have a name, and cop an attitude."

"Most of what's occurring *is* in the journey, not the destination, and were I to give you blanket answers they'd take away from your journey, and you'd learn nothing. Just because you're so-called psychic doesn't mean you're perfect. To learn, you need to experience not only your answers, but the *questions*. Sometimes questions are more important than answers."

Lizzie took another sip of tea. "I'm not sure I want to find out."

The Man with No Name suddenly leapt off his chair, and the porch.

"Hey—let's do some weedin—and I'll tell you a story!"

Lizzie awoke, eyes wide and alert. Though tired, she felt good. She looked to her clock, but the display was partially obscured by a corner of pillow. She packed it down and saw that it was only four-forty-one. She lay back on her pillow, closed her eyes, and quickly fell back to sleep....

4

Victor Black opened the safe by the light of a penlight clutched between clenched teeth. He removed a specific handful of sealed envelopes, found the ones needed, and separated them from those he placed back into the safe. Then he took out identical envelopes hidden inside his jacket and held them side by side to the ones pulled. The type-written control numbers were identical. It was their contents that differed.

Black inserted the switched envelopes into the safe and closed the drawer, spinning the S&G combination dial. He yanked on the steel drawers to ensure the safe was, indeed, locked, then pocketed the re-placed documents. He briefly worked his left shoulder when done.

Black left the office and walked down the empty hallways like a well-practiced rat in a well-worn maze. He came to the dimly lit cafete-ria, and continued through it until he came to the large plate window at the opposite end. He stared out past his reflection at the few lights that showed through the black cherry, maple, and sweetgum trees. He sat down at the end of a table, then leaned over onto it with an elbow, as if in thought. Continuing to stare out the window, Black used his free hand to stealthily reach under the table…careful that the ceiling-mounted "bubble cameras" wouldn't see his actions. He felt around until he found the compact package that had been taped there mo-ments ago.

The digital disk of his intrusion into the "control safe" and office, where he'd just switched out documents….

Chapter Seven

1

Buddy LaRouque pinned Gina Massey's firm, squirming body against his front door as he passionately worked her mouth with his own. Gina pulled Buddy in and ran her hands over his short, crew-cut blond hair and French-Canadian features. Buddy pulled away, smiling, panting heavily.

"*God*, I love you," Gina whispered, breathlessly, her hands anchoring his face before her. She pulled him back in, devouring him some more, then pulled away. "I don't want to let you go…but I *really* have to get going…."

"I know," Buddy whispered back.

Both closed their eyes and leaned their foreheads into each other.

"Besides," Gina added, smiling, "we're not supposed to be fraternizing, *you* know—"

"Aw, fuck em all."

Gina pulled her head away from Buddy and they both looked to each other.

"How bout just me?" Gina said.

Buddy smiled.

"Blame me?"

"How could I? "Buddy said. "How could you resist the Buddy LaRouque Machine?"

"Can't—no way, no how," she whispered, chuckling. "That's why I gotta *go—now*," she whispered, gently pushing him away and wiggling free.

Buddy groaned. "Fine." He relinquished. "Thanks for stopping by. I always love your impromptu…visits."

"Oh, right, like you never know I'm coming."

"I can always tell by the screams and groans—"

Gina punched him. She grabbed up the material of his bathrobe in both hands; brought him back in.

"Hey, just cause we're government-trained-you-know-whats, don't mean I have to use it all the time."

"Then I'll see ya tomorrow."

"It's already tomorrow."

"Then I'll see ya…in a couple hours…"

"Let me walk you to your car—"

"I'm a big girl…a psychic big girl who sees no baddies out there—and you're in your bathrobe…."

Again they kissed.

"You make it hard not to be chivalrous."

"Thanks for the effort, knight." Gina smiled, eyeing every inch of his face.

"Then drive safe, me lady."

"Always. Bye, lover."

God, he could just *fuck* that smile of hers.

They kissed each other one last time.

Buddy reached around behind Gina and unlocked the deadbolt. Gina reached behind her and twisted the doorknob. Opening the door, but remaining as close to Buddy as long as possible, she slid out—maintaining focused eye contact. Buddy eased the door closed.

Sliding the deadbolt back into place, he stared into the door as Gina lingered just a moment before her side of the door; she actually touched the door with one hand, head tilted forward and eyes closed. Buddy closed his eyes and thudded his forehead against the door about where Gina's head was resting.

"Man, you drives me *nuts*…," he whispered.

I love you, Buddy, Gina thought back to him from her side of the door. She then lifted her head and left, cradling her arms close in to her, as she got into her car.

Buddy listened as Gina entered her car, closed its door, and started the engine.

Shivering for just a split second, he smiled.

I love you, too, he thought back to her.

Buddy left the door and returned to the interior of his house. A hallway light leading upstairs to the bedroom was still on, and he headed for the stairs—then stopped. Entered the kitchen instead. Standing in the darkness, he found himself drawn to the rear kitchen window. He looked out it into the dark woods beyond.

The smile left his face.

There was something about this window...*another* window....

A kitchen window and death. A horrible death.

A family.

He left the kitchen and went to the study. Leaving the lights off as he made his way through the house. He closed the study door behind him...hesitated—then locked it...pausing for another moment.

He just felt the need to close and lock that door.

Kitchen window.

Death.

Buddy went to the recliner in the far corner, facing the door. It wasn't the RoboChair at The Center, but it served quite nicely. He sat.

Something beckoned....

Something was up with this program, and he felt he was *close*....

Someone was misdirecting him, but it couldn't last forever. He'd get through—find out what was going on—what had never "felt" right from the day he'd reported in to this unit, about a year and a half ago. He hadn't wanted to bring any of the others in on any of this until he had better information.

Someone was messing with things. Now he was picking up something about a kitchen window and death. And this felt strong—close. *Real* close. He had to track it. The feeling was quite insistent.

Buddy smoothly reclined his seat back and closed his eyes. Already quite relaxed from his bedroom antics with Gina, he was under in no time, his hands and feet giving him that familiar expansive balloon feeling...his mental focus quickly departing the physical realm....

2

Ryan Dunham tossed about fitfully in bed. His partially opened windows allowed in an increasingly building storm's winds. Branches scraped away at the outside of his apartment windows.

"No...no...no, no—*NO!*"

He shot upright in bed.

"*What?*" he said, clearing his throat, shaking his head. "*No...*"

He blinked several times, wiped at his eyes. Scanned the bedroom's dark interior.

"Windows...*win—?*"

He looked to his windows. Listened to the scratching of the branches outside.

Ryan hopped out of bed and came to the windows. He peered outside and angled himself to better see what branches scratched the outside of the building.

"Huh," he said, examining the glass and window frames, "*what about windows?*"

More images.

A reflection in a window...death.

Something about *knives.*....

He backed up to the edge of his bed and sat, dropping his head into his hands, then rubbed his face.

Exhausted. He was flat-out *exhausted.*

The taskings at The Center had been nonstop the past month, and it was wearing them all out. Messing with their minds. All of them—Travis, Gina, Buddy, Cory, Ryan, and Lee. It was as if they could no longer tell fantasy from reality. Maybe "fantasy" was the wrong word—*supernatural from the natural.* As cool as some thought that might be—it wasn't. In order to live and function in this world, one had to be focused *within* it. If you constantly questioned whether or not you were walking down a street, or being tossed out of an airplane—well, *that* presented problems. Or if you were driving your car and you kept slipping in and out of Psychic Land, you had issues—*accidents.*

Images of a stabbing—in a bed....

Ryan jumped to his feet and spun away from the bed. Plastered back against a corner, he stared at the bed; jumped to the wall switch and flicked it on.

There was no one else in there with him.

He was alone.

He violently threw aside all the sheets and blankets...hurriedly went through them.

There were no stabs marks, holes, blood—nothing.

Ryan checked out the rest of his apartment, checked the deadbolt and flip lock, then returned to the bedroom. Flicking off the lights, he stared at the shadows that danced across the walls.

Yeah...some thought it cool that others with the psychic gift could dip into other realms, and made movies and wrote books about it, but the reality of it was that it really messed you up. At least the way they were using it. When your whole day was consumed with peeking in on assassinations, kidnappings, intelligence gathering, and drug shit—and you couldn't get those images out of your mind when you left work, or they assaulted you late at night—life took on a whole new tint, and it definitely wasn't

(*pink*)

(*red*)

rose-colored.

Something wasn't right, and he wasn't able to bring it in, wasn't able to focus on it at all.

The images were—

Ryan stared blankly into the dark, the storm wind hollering outside his window and walls.

Images? *What* images?

Again, he just stared blankly into the night.

Hadn't he just had a dream—a nightmare?

Maybe not.

Mind's constantly fucked up. Who knew what they *thought* they thought....

Yet a nagging feeling remained. A feeling that death was at his front door...

Or somebody's, anyway.

3

Grasping the arms of his recliner in a death grip, Buddy flung open his eyes—just in time to see a weapon pointed at his forehead and the explosion of white light that took away his life....

Chapter Eight

1

Lizzie wandered down the aisles of Babies R Us, pushing one of their partially loaded shopping carts ahead of her. In it were several toys. She only wanted one, but couldn't make up her mind about which one, so brought all of her choices along with her as she roamed the aisles. What she really wanted to check out was something called an "Incrediblock," but so far hadn't found it. One would think a psychic wouldn't have any such trouble....

But, perhaps the real reason she couldn't find what she was looking for—or make up her mind—was because she was consumed with Agent Black and his offer.

No matter how she dissected it, something about him just wasn't right, FBI or not. But every time she peeked into Black and his life, she found nothing—other than the line of work he was in, which she definitely picked up *was* government. But that was all...and it didn't sit well with her. She wouldn't feel this way for no reason...yet that was exactly what she was finding—*nothing*.

Why would he have searched her out?

For that matter, how did he even *know* her? Know *about* her?

Short of cooperating with the law, agencies like hers never gave out their psychics' real names. But, even beyond that, how and why would she ever stand out to anyone? She'd been very careful not to let too many know just how good she really was. Very careful. Sometimes intentionally not telling her clients anything at all, if it didn't matter. You didn't want to be too good. That attracted attention.

So, how had Black found her...and why?

Strange events had always been a part of her life, and she had, for the most part, grown accustomed to them, but

(*til death do us part*)

there was something downright scary—not right—about this man and what he'd proposed, and the fact that she couldn't pick up *anything* on him…well, nothing like this had ever happened to her before, except for—

Lizzie looked down to a little girl standing before her.

"Hello," Lizzie greeted.

"Hello," the freckled little redhead said. "Can you tell me where Hello Kitty is?"

Lizzie smiled. "Of course, dear, I saw it two aisles over. That way," she said, pointing.

"Thanks, Mommy," the girl said, cheerfully, and did a quick about-face. She sprinted off in the direction Lizzie had told her—then disappeared before turning the corner.

Lizzie smiled. Yes, she had gotten used to many bizarre things over the years, but this Mr. Black she never saw coming, and that was unacceptable. She should have been able to pick up on him, just like everything else she picked up on. *It just made no sense.*

*Hmmm, just like…*that little voice inside her head whispered…*Joe's "untimely" death? Why hadn't you picked up on that?*

His death would have been too much for me, so I had to unconsciously block it—

So, her conscience countered, *it* was *easier the way it happened?*

That's not what I meant—

What did you mean? If you're such a big-wig "sensitive," why hadn't you picked up on Joe's death and Black's arrival—or, for that matter, tuned into Black now? Find that stupid Incrediblock? Could it be that maybe you aren't *as hotshot as you thought?*

Lizzie paused at the end of the aisle, and reached out to a display shelf for support.

That wasn't fair. Wasn't fair at all.

Why couldn't she just leave well-enough alone?

Because she didn't *know*, that's why.

She had absolutely no idea why she hadn't been able to foresee Joe's death—not an inkling. Absolutely nothing—not a dream, not an itch—*zilch*.

Same with Black.

This totally malignant tumor enters her life, and she has no forewarning?

How could that be?

How could she see things in other people's lives, but when it came to her own, utter failure? And now she was being asked to actually *work* with the guy?

Maybe this was all a dream…a ghastly, wicked nightmare…and she was about to wake up any minute—

"Excuse me, ma'am…but are you all right?"

Lizzie looked up, embarrassed, and wiped her eyes. The clerk's nametag read "Melanie."

"No," she sniffled, "but I will be. Thank you."

"You sure? Is there anything I can get you—a glass of water? A quiet place?"

Lizzie stared at her for a moment. Eyes full of genuine concern, her short bob of stylistically unkempt blonde hair—with just a "jet" of pink

(…*pink-pink-pink*…)

in it—just perfect. *What was the biggest thing in* Melanie's *life?*

Finishing her degree.

Completing her degree in electrical engineering and starting her own consulting firm.

See—she could still pick up on others—*why the hell hadn't she picked up on Joe or Black?*

"Ma'am?" Melanie again asked.

Lizzie smiled and looked away, then returned to her. "Sorry. I was just reliving the loss of my husband. It tends to hit…at oddest of times."

Melanie reached out to her. "I'm *so* sorry…I-I can't even *imagine.* Do…do you…want to talk about it?"

"No…no, that's okay, but thanks for asking. He died in a construction accident." Lizzie choked off into silence, raising a hand before her. "I'll be all right."

"May I ask his name?"

"Joe. Joseph Gordon. Thanks."

"Well," Melanie began, "I'm sure wherever your husband is now…he's always thinking of you, too, wishing you the best. Looking after you." Melanie reached out and squeezed Lizzie's hand.

Lizzie looked up surprised.

"That's very sweet of you. *Thank* you."

Lizzie smiled, feeling renewed energy.

"It's been over a year, and I thought I was handling it— obviously I'm not," Lizzie said. "But…to change the subject—and I hope you don't mind nor take offense—but, I can tell you, because it's my business to know," Lizzie continued, "that you will have that firm you've been wanting. You'll have…a great life, an exciting one, and will travel the world."

Now it was Melanie who stared back in surprise.

"What—how'd—"

Lizzie completed wiping away her tears with the backs of her wrists and took hold of both of Melanie's hands.

"Because, my dear, it's what I *do*. You may not believe in it, but I'm a medium—a psychic. You don't even have to believe me, but it will happen—and isn't it better to believe and dream, than to do neither? You'll also do just fine in finishing your degree. EE, isn't it? Electrical engineering?"

Melanie nodded, flabbergasted.

"A three-point-four—no *five*—GPA? You'll break three-five," she added casually. "I have to go—but thanks. Enjoy your life, Melanie, and continue to be caring to all you meet. People—even psychics—need that every now and then. We're not perfect, you know," she said, smiling, "nobody is." Lizzie pushed her cart before her, and continued on down the aisle.

"Thank you," Melanie said, staring after her.

2

The Man With No Name stood before the safe Black had recently visited, and with a tug and a sturdy metallic click, pulled open its heavy steel door. The envelopes were filed as Black had left them, including those Black had swapped out. The Man With No Name unerringly reached in and removed the three envelopes he'd switched, and replaced them with three of his own. Grinning, he closed the safe.

Victor, you simply can't outsmart me.

3

"Mr. President," a Secret Service agent announced over her wire from her position outside the Hyannis Port home, "the Scorpion has arrived."

Victor Black's black Chrysler pulled to a stop before Kennedy's home. He exited the vehicle. It was early morning enough to still be dark as he approached the front door. Before Black could ring for access, the door opened, and he was greeted by another agent. The agent said nothing, but eyed him for a moment before allowing him entry.

Black entered the house, subtly rolling his left shoulder. He passed several other agents on his well-traveled route to the retired President's study. He was admitted into the study by another female agent, and as he entered the room, found two more agents positioned at opposite ends of the room, on either side of a desk. The high-backed chair was turned away from him, behind the desk, and in the chair Black was sure sat the former President.

"Good evening, Mr. President, or should I say 'morning,'" Black said, flatly.

"You should say 'good day, sir,' and, ah, make your way back to Virginia," Kennedy said, as he swiveled about in his chair to face Black. "And be bettah served to forevah leave old men like me alone."

The President folded his hands gravely before him on the desk.

"Now, what is it that you have need to disturb me at this ungodly owah and couldn't be done over the phone?"

Black, still working his left shoulder, addressed him squarely.

"I'm looking for someone. It's a matter of national security, or I wouldn't be here."

"I'm sureah it is, Victah. Get to the point."

"We've been tracking this man for years—"

"His name?"

Black paused. "You know who—and that we don't know it."

Kennedy burst into uproarious laughter so hard his agents momentarily started for their weapons.

"Oh, it's all right, gentlemen," Kennedy added with a tired wave of a hand. "You'll, ah, have to forgive me, Victah, but you, who have at your disposal the entiah national security resources of this and other countries, and you're telling me you *still* don't know this man's name?"

Black clenched his jaw.

"His real name"

Kennedy again laughed. "Well! Then you certainly have made it worth getting up—just to see that confounded look on that, ah, arrogant son-of-a-bitch face of yours!"

"Sir, I might add—"

"You might add *nothing*. You have the gall to awaken me at this insane owah, bahrge into my home, and make demands on me in the name of national security—and you haven't even *identified* the threat? And to think we put you where you ahr."

"Sir—"

Still chuckling, Kennedy again waved his hand. "Oh, go on, Victah."

"I need to know…anything," he said, again clenching his jaw, "anything you might remember all those years ago—about that meeting in the Rose Garden. We know you met someone—he can't be the same man, but he's most surely acting within an organization. The one from '62, the one who gave you the idea for Program One—"

All of Kennedy's mirth drained from his face. "Leave us," he curtly ordered his agents, who immediately departed the study. Kennedy rose from his seat and unflinchingly stared back at Black. Neither said a word as the study was cleared. Kennedy's words came out measured and thick.

"Let me make myself perfectly clear, Victah. I may be an old man," he said, "but as the, ah, second most powerful person in this room, you ahr at *my* mercy. You may be able to throw your powah around like a bad fahrt during a Mexican Siesta, but I can—and *will*—crush you like a bug if you evah get in my way, again. My dying doesn't scare me, Victah—but you, *you* dying—I know that scares the living hell outta you, or you wouldn't be hearah. You have used your prerogative for the last time, sir, and I will no longer entertain you—nor your requests. If I nevah see you again—in this or any othah life—it will be fahr to soon. I am sorry to have wasted your time. Good night."

Black paused before he turned to leave.

"And by the way, Victah," Kennedy said, "my ordah still stands, as I'm sure you're aware."

Black stopped, keeping his back to the President; again worked his shoulder.

"I've had at least two agents constantly trained on you evah since you entahed my home. Purely out of my own unadulterated hatred for who and what you ahr. Should you *evah* entah my circle of influence again, I shall entertain *my* prerogative. *Do I make myself cleah?*"

The study doors were opened, and Black silently disappeared through them.

"Fucking bastahd," Kennedy said as the doors closed.

Two agents with silencered weapons held at-the-ready emerged from their hidden wall recesses.

"Mr. President?" one massive, square-jawed agent asked, while the other checked in with the rest of the security detail on his wire.

Kennedy nodded. "I'm going back to bed," he said, and walked out from around the desk.

But, as he headed back to bed, a thought occurred to him:
Since when had Victor Black developed a trick shoulder?

Victor Black's anger boiled, as he returned to his awaiting jet. Even before airborne, he put in a call to the Virginia compound. True, there was no love lost between him and Kennedy, but the fact that he continued to work in an agency with that man's name on it got under his skin like no cancer ever could. Add to that at seventy-seven he still showed no signs of yet departing God's green Earth, and Victor Black's ulcers and headaches got no better. His shoulder felt worse. *And* he was no closer to getting any answers. It had been a calculated move—one that had failed miserably. He at least drew some measure of satisfaction in that he'd awoken Kennedy out of a sound sleep for this.

But, this was the last straw.

He would—somehow—get back at that man...and in a way that would forever tarnish his name, his reputation, his soul, his entire god-damned philanthropic and long-lived family. Every last one of them.

When the time was right.

Kennedy may have given him his job, controlled his paycheck, and groomed him into the man he had become, but embarrass him, then toss him away—*that* would be Kennedy's undoing. He'd put up with him long enough. It was time to put the old nag out to pasture and bring in new blood.

Yes, Kennedy would pay dearly for such a grave error in judgment.

4

Kennedy returned to bed, but ended up just lying on top of the blankets, eyes open.

He'd almost forgotten about that...the time he'd been contacted by that man in the White House gardens; had almost forgotten about him—or had he also just been part of another dream? In fact, for a while there, he would have *sworn* there had been no such meeting, out of which Program One had indeed been the result. Like so many other decisions he'd made, efforts he'd begun had been the result of him and his advisors working out solutions together.

Except Program One.

It had been 1962...May, mid-May of '62. It was oddly coming back...he'd taken a walk by himself through the gardens, and had been quite amazed at his position in life, that he was actually *President of the United States*—president of the most powerful nation on Earth. The highest honor ever bestowed upon anyone. He'd been walking along innocently enough, deep in thought...when the man approached, seemingly out of nowhere....

"Mr. President?"

Not-quite-forty-five-year-old President Kennedy spun around. Out from behind a hedge he came, thirty-something in appearance, well-groomed, in dark trousers and a pressed white shirt, sleeves rolled up—and an outrageous Dalmatian tie. The man was confident in his approach. Kennedy didn't recognize him—or did he?

How had he broached security?

"Who ahr you, sir, and how'd you get past—"

"Mr. President, begging your pardon, sir, I haven't much time," the man said. "*Please*, sir, we need to talk. It's about the present...and the world's *future*."

5

Lizzie Gordon lay on the couch in her trailer, drifting in and out of a troubled nap. Thinking about Joe had drained her. She *wanted* to think of him...but every time she did so, the same old demons resurfaced...the same guilt.

Why couldn't she just think about the good times and ignore her mistakes?

She was a *psychic*, for goodness sake, she's supposed to have just a little more control over her mental facilities than the average bear. Why couldn't she do what was needed *when* needed? What was wrong with her—

"Nuthin's wrong with you."

Lizzie sat up.

"You leave a door open and just about anybody can walk on

in...."

The Man With No Name sat in one of her living-room recliners. He got up and went to the refrigerator.

"Iced tea?" he said, calling out to her from the kitchen.

Lizzie stared at him, wiping her eyes.

"Who—*what?*"

"I asked, would you like some iced tea?"

Still groggy, Lizzie again wiped her eyes. "Wait a minute...no-no-no-no, I don't want any iced tea—what are you doing in my home?"

The Man With No Name came back and sat in the swivel chair, sipping iced tea. "Sorry, I don't mean to be rude, but I knew you had some, and, well, I just can't resist a tall cold glass of—"

"How did you...what's going on here? First the FBI—now *you?*"

The Man With No Name smiled. "Well, actually, I was 'here' first."

"And he had your picture!"

"My *picture?* The FBI?"

"Yes—"

"A *photograph?*"

"No, no—a *sketch*—a police sketch. Said you were a child molester and a security risk, or something."

"You believe him?"

"What he told me," she said, shaking her head, "just isn't what I'm picking up from you...but what he *didn't* tell me about himself, is definitely what I picked up from *him.*"

The Man With No Name smiled.

Lizzie dropped her head into her hands, bent over her knees, and groaned. "What *is* it about me all of a sudden that I'm the most important person in the world?" She sat back up.

"Utility. You're useful."

"What is that supposed to mean! I'm just living my life, trying to deal with my own issues—make a *new* life for myself—when suddenly, out of the woodwork, come you and this Black. One's a creep and the other doesn't have a name, and drinks *way* too much iced tea!"

"I did offer—"

"Could we get to the point, please?"

"There's nothing wrong with you—or me, for that matter. I'm no child molester. He just said that to get to you emotionally. Manipulate. He's extremely practiced at that. But, I also want to say...*you've* done nothing wrong. You shouldn't feel any guilt—"

Lizzie shot to her feet.

"How do you know—what do you know?"

"Christ! How does everyone seem to know so much about me? How do *you* know what guilt I'm feeling? What kind of a person I am? How does this Black?"

The Man With No Name calmly placed his glass on a coaster on the coffee table.

"Elizabeth—I know you prefer 'Lizzie'—but *Elizabeth*…listen to me. You've been through some trying times. You are a gifted person with much to offer the world—so much that you can't begin to imagine—"

"How do you know this? How can you say something like that? Look at me—*look* at me! I live in a trailer park and do psychic readings over the *telephone*, for God's sake! My husband's dead, and I'm racked with guilt over why I hadn't been able to pick up on it! Not one iota! Now, *you* tell *me* what the hell it is *I* have to offer the world that I couldn't offer my husband?"

The Man With No Name sat back in the recliner.

"That's what I thought," Lizzie said, pacing. "I don't know what kind of joke you guys are trying to pull, but—"

"It's no joke, Elizabeth—"

"'*Lizzie*,' dammit, only my mother calls me 'Elizabeth,' and she's gone."

The Man With No Name smiled. "When I came to you in your dream—"

"And that's another thing, how'd you do that? How'd you find me?"

"I need to tell you that some very nasty things are on the horizon…and that I need your help. Do not trust that man, Black, he's no good…and the less you know the better."

"Why? Is this supposed to be some super-secret cloak-and-dagger spy mission, and the less I know the longer I—"

"Yes."

Lizzie stopped pacing. "Well, that's the most direct, understandable thing I've heard from anyone so far."

"This ability of yours…you have what you have for a purpose, and that purpose is slowly being revealed as you become better equipped to handle it. Which is why I'm here. To help. I have this ability to enter dreams. There are things I need to show you, and you, in turn, can help me."

Lizzie looked at him.

"You're helping me now, whether or not you realize it." The Man With No Name picked up his glass and took another sip. "Mmmm—sure you don't want any? This stuff really is good!"

"I'm fine…," Lizzie said, "or like to think I am."

"Black is in charge of an ultra-covert government organization of remote viewers. Remote viewers are government spies who employ psychic abilities toward the world of espionage. But Black's twisting their purpose to suit his own ends. I found out about it, and now he's hunting me down."

"Oh, *great!*" she said, throwing her hands into the air. "He's probably watching us this very minute! Knows I know you!"

"He's not around, now, that I can guarantee. Doesn't even know I'm here. You're safe. At least for the moment."

"Right. This coming from a guy I don't know, talking about another I don't know, who's already been secretly stalking me—yeah, kind of like you, now, that I think about it."

The Man With No Name smirked.

Lizzie returned to the front of her couch and sat, shoulders slumped.

"Good God, I don't want any of this. All I ever wanted was a happy life. Didn't care what I did, as long as I had a husband and family—children—to raise and hopefully have them help the world along to a better place. Now I'm sucked into some secret sewer of espionage, all against my will. All this free will I believe in? Where's all that gone?"

The Man With No Name said, "Sometimes you realize a little better than most how good you are with it, free will, but other times, like now, feeling beaten down by the world, you lose sight of things."

"Look, I'm pretty wiped and would really like to get back to my nap before work tonight. Could we continue this another time?"

"Of course," the smiling man said. He stood up and brought his half-filled glass to the kitchen counter, placing it in the sink. "I'll find you when you're ready."

Lizzie only half-listened to the man, as she lay back down and lifted her legs back onto the couch. She was suddenly quite drowsy. The Man With No Name returned to the living room, picked up an afghan draped over the back of the couch, unfolded it, and draped it over Lizzie.

"Could you…lock the door on your way out?" Lizzie mumbled, already drifting off.

The Man With No Name smiled and nodded, and in a whisper, added, *"Be strong, Lizzie."* He touched her shoulder, then quietly left the trailer, locking the door behind him.

Chapter Nine

1

Mel Roberts stared outside into the beautiful, sunlit morning. Children continued to play up and down his block, while neighbors were out walking dogs, watering lawns, and washing cars. But it was mostly the kids running back and forth across the sidewalk that interested him.

Did they all still have *their* parents?

Mel left the window and returned his attention to his living room…looked to his coffee table; to the pile of mail that that slap-happy mail man had urged him, begged him—actually *pleaded*—for him to take.

"Well, I might as well see what was so danged important," he said, and reached for the pile.

Among the mail was a magazine subscription for a science fiction or paranormal magazine, and your typical *"Have You Seen Us?"* missing-persons mass-mailing, with a child's and a woman's face on it.

Mel took a closer look at the card.

The woman's face struck Mel as deep and passionate, most engaging. He stared at the woman's beautiful-yet-troubled face; looked into her darkly intense, halftone ink-and-paper eyes until he felt embarrassed and self-conscious and had to put it down. There were also bills and your standard junk mail. And then he came upon a plain white envelope with no return address, addressed to him. He tore it open and began reading—but was instantly disappointed. It was only a mass-marketing letter. He looked at it closer and saw that his name had been misspelled in the greeting. "Mell." He looked back to the envelope, and saw that his name had been misspelled the same way there, too, though he hadn't noticed that when he first picked it up. He returned to the letter. It was some stupid thing about *"What would you do to live in*

Hawai'i and live the Good Life?" It talked about living your life's dream and making a million bucks (in one year, no less!)...about buying that car and house of your dreams...about not worrying about how much things cost anymore, because...*you no longer* needed *to!*

But, then...an odd thing happened...as he continued on to the second page (and why couldn't he stop reading this tripe?)...

The lines on the paper began to blur.

He blinked and wiped his eyes...looked away to a far-off corner of the living room, to his hands—where everything looked fine—but every time he looked back to the letter, the lines blurred.

His mind felt *cheated.*

He was about to throw away the letter, but something urged him to continue reading...just a little more. What he found was that he was no longer reading the kitschy marketing come-on. He was now reading what seemed to be *another* letter...embedded within the first.

He found if he continued to focus on the "weirdness" of the letter, all he saw were blurry lines, fuzzy words, and his head hurt. A myriad of images barraged his mind...images he couldn't hold on to and that made him slightly dizzy. Images of him doing things...with unsmiling people in subterranean chambers...that made no sense...but once he allowed himself to go with the whole experience, like those "Can you see me?" digital posters (how'd he know about them and why was that even a question?)...he found an entirely different letter...and this one had his name correctly spelled:

Mel:

I'll get right to it, because I don't know how much time we have before we're discovered. You're being hunted. In fact, if you're reading this letter, chances are you've already been found and are currently under surveillance. This letter might even have led them to you, and for that, I do apologize, but it was a necessary and calculated risk. Things are not as they seem, and you have at your disposal resources you don't even yet realize. Be open to them, and keep an open mind about all you see, for there are worlds between the very spaces of these letters that are more real than the letters themselves. And beware of dark hues. The world is more than you see and not at all what you think. *I will contact you again.*

Now...

What would you *pay for such an opportunity? Is Hawai'i for* you? A Rolls Royce?

Mel blinked.

He was no longer reading a hidden communiqué, but was back to the come-on letter. He again blinked and shook his head, trying to get back into the hidden letter—but it was gone. He shook the papers, held them up to the light, even tried to peel the individual sheets apart, but it was no longer there.

People were tracking him?

"*Hunted*" was the word used. Good gravy, why would anyone hunt him? What had he done? He was…he was only—

How old was he?

A shiver ran through him.

"Oh, come *on*," he said aloud, "I have to know how friggin old I am! I'm alive, aren't I? I *exist!* I have to know my *age!*"

Mel sprinted upstairs to the bathroom and stood before the mirror. Stared at himself. There he was, big as day. Staring back. He touched the mirror, then his face. Nope, no illusion, he was actually staring back at himself, a person who really stood before a mirror and was actually casting a reflection. So, if this was the case, he actually existed and had to be *some* age.

Why couldn't he pull it out? Why couldn't he tell himself how old he was?

Mel sat on the edge of the tub, head in his hands, mulling over the events of the past few—

Hours?

Was that even right? Just how long had he been here? *Really?* And what was an "hour"?

What was going on with him?

Was he crazy? *Going* crazy?

First, he awakens to find himself alone, no parents—had even forgotten about the *loss* of them—then he begins seeing things and gets mail from some crazy-ass mail man, only to read a letter that *wasn't even there.*

What the hell was going on?

Regroup…take it easy—breathe deeply—what had that letter-that-hadn't-been-there told him? That he was being hunted? Under *surveillance?* Might have already been found?

By *whom?*

It also said something about things not being as they seem, that the spaces between letters were more real than the letters themselves…that he would be contacted again. There was the kicker.

Who had written that letter, and who had been trying to contact him—let alone hunt him down?

2

Mel stood out on the front stoop of the house. He didn't know if it was the letter-that-hadn't-been-there or what, but he found it extremely difficult to do anything—sit down, stand up, yell, read a book, go back to bed...or run away from this house and all its weirdness, as far and fast as he could. He stared past the playing children to the ditch behind them. Listened to its rushing water.

He could throw himself into all that water coursing through the culvert.

Mel flinched as cars sped past.

But those kids...playing out front...he found he felt at ease around *them*. They giggled and waved as they darted back and forth over the sidewalk. He didn't feel at home inside his house, but *did* with those kids. As he thought about this, one stopped directly in front of him. It was a little African-American girl. A tow-haired boy almost ran over her, and also stopped, giggling wildly. Then a red-headed, freckle-faced *Mädchen* joined them. They all stood before him, smiling. More children filed into the group, one or two, groups of three or more. Before he knew it, there was a small army gathered before him, out in the street and on his lawn.

"Good morning, Mel," they all greeted cheerfully, playfully, *"It's about time you woke up!"*

Mel Roberts bolted upright on his couch.

The television droned on into a late-night, darkened room. As Mel's senses cleared and returned to their more familiar settings, a commercial played on TV about a psychic hotline.

"1-900-PsiKick. Call us now," the large, curiously accented African-American*ish* lady implored. *"We can make a difference in your life."*

Mel shot off the couch and immediately rushed upstairs into the family room, flicked on the light switch, and looked for the pile of mail.

Nothing. There was no pile.

He rushed to the closed drapes, yanking them open.

It was dark outside. *Dark.*

What the hell?

Mel returned to the kitchen and found the empty Vernors can. It was still wet, almost cold. Can held in hand, he opened the refrigerator. There he found the same items he last remembered: milk, fruit, lunch meat, eggs, and more. All of it. He closed the door. Stared at it. This was also where he'd supposedly put that picture from Mr. FBI. In the dream. Of course, there was nothing there.

He was going crazy, plain and simple.

He'd lost his parents and was now losing his mind. A dream. It had all been a dream.

Mel went back down to the basement couch and sat before the flickering television. He still held onto the empty soda can.

"Do you have loved ones you're concerned about? Is there a message you feel you're trying to receive?" the psychic ad intoned. *"Give us a call! We can reach those who have passed. We can put your mind at ease. Our psychics are* real *and can give you that peace of mind you desperately crave. Are there unanswered questions to which you need answers? Call us…now…"*

Mel stared at her.

Call us.

Call us, now.

Mel pensively sloshed about the soda can.

Call us, Mel, we're waiting.

I don't know how much time we have…

You're being watched, hunted, *there's no time to lose!*

He did feel caged…not all there. He knew he was supposed to have parents, but, at the same time

(*unanswered questions*)

didn't feel he had *any.*

But the pictures…the *memories.…*

Mel set the can down on the end table and leaned forward, hands to his face.

C'mon, Mel, what are you waiting for! Call us!

Mel looked back to the screen.

The card. Back in the kitchen. On the table. The gray card with raised black lettering. Mel left the room and retrieved it, looking to it as he returned downstairs to the TV.

Madame Nostradameus
1-900-PSI-KICK

Mel looked to the number on the screen.

He picked up the phone.

3

Former President John F. Kennedy dreamed of the incident with the man in the garden, dreamed of how they'd talked about conspiracies, dreams, and grand schemes. Of the good in the world. Then he dreamed of how they talked about some of this stuff, and though he could see they were talking—in the dream—he couldn't hear the words, couldn't make out what was said. Recalled—again, in the dream—that it was actually like that when he remembered talking to this man all those many years ago. How he felt "beside" himself…outside his body…and while they'd been talking, there also seemed to be things he was saying *between* all the words…in-*between* the words and letters…but he couldn't quite focus on them. It was like a part of him was removed from the conversation, but, no, not entirely….

That's how intense that experience had been.

Kennedy remembered telling him about his own grand plan for world peace, about how he hoped to use the children of the world to help save adults from themselves. Children (he hoped) would be the saviors of the human race—if only they were properly guided. The mysterious man nodded, telling Kennedy that was actually a stellar idea, then questioned that wasn't Kennedy once a child himself? Weren't all adults once children? Where had all that childlike exuberance and spirit gone, and why hadn't *they* been able to save the world? Change it? Kennedy responded by saying that, at least from his point of view, he *was* trying to change the world. That he felt it was his destiny to do so. The problem with most people, Kennedy explained, was that they weren't properly guided. Kept getting diverted by life's daily issues. He, himself, had certainly felt that tug and pull, but had always kept his goal in mind—and being part of an incredibly wealthy and powerful family hadn't hurt. The mysterious man nodded and smiled. *Well, then, I guess,* boy, *do we have a job for you!*

Kennedy remembered, in this dream, that he had some questions fully in mind to ask—but never did. Questions such as: *who are* you *to task* me? *Who* are *you and how had you gotten in here?*

But, the questions had never been asked.

There was just this overwhelming feeling coming from this guy that he was here to help, and that—somehow—they'd met before.

Known each other?

For such a young man, he was quite full of wisdom. Wisdom beyond his years. Kennedy liked him, found himself drawn to him, and hoped he'd see him again—but never did. Not once in all those nearly thirty-two years since, and had all but forgot about him…until now.

And this dream.

4

Black stood behind the soundproofed and tinted window at the Virginia compound, watching and listening to the remote viewer on the other side during her tasking, who drew stick figures and skeleton buildings as she talked. He'd stood in on several sessions today, but not one of them had given him what he needed. The bastard had again tampered with him. Again—*somehow*—had intercepted his plans. *Damn* him!

But he was getting close.

He could feel him—even now—hovering about. Feeling him out. Watching. Probing. He had to stop him. Things were getting out of hand. He was close, he felt it in his bones. This guy's days were numbered, and he'd picked the wrong guy to fuck with.…

Victor Black closed the door to his sparse, Charlottesville apartment. Kennedy had been messing with his blood pressure for over twenty years, but recent events had roused his pressure like never before, and it was exhausting him. And to think he used to work for the guy. But over the years, something had happened. Since when did a president get a conscience? The job itself precluded presidents from having to worry about such things—they had advisors.

Victor entered the bathroom, eyeing everything as he walked through the barren apartment. Nothing looked or felt amiss. Out of place. Everything was as he'd left it. He switched on the bathroom light and stared into the aging, tanned visage that reflected back to him from the mirror. Wished his tan had come from a Caribbean cruise. He suddenly felt far older than his sixty-six years, and what years he wore were hard-earned. Looked to the unusually dark freckles that sparsely populated his forehead along his hairline. Flexed his forearms, twisted his neck, then worked his shoulder and back muscles. Everything was cramped and hurt, and he felt constantly nauseated. He examined his mouth, which he slowly opened and stretched, and saw the ever-so-slight bluish-black discoloration at its corners…that came and went…but were once again there. He could do what he did, yet he couldn't shake this damned disease. Something just wasn't right about that.

Black looked to his watch, grimaced, then reached into the medicine cabinet. Removing a prescription bottle of *prednisone*, he dumped out a prescription, then popped it into his mouth. Putting that bottle back, he removed another, one marked *fludrocortisone*, dumped out a tablet, and again quickly swallowed it. Closing the cabinet, he entered his small, ill-equipped kitchen (again noticing that nothing was out of place), and opened the refrigerator. Inside were rows of Gatorade. Nothing else. He grabbed one, chugging down several gulps of the lime-colored fluid before returning the bottle to its place inside the fridge. Facing forward, just so.

Black went to the kitchen table and sat, burying his face in his hands.

Not only did he curse Kennedy and his fucking family, but he cursed this damned disease. Kennedy should be the one with it, not him.

He looked around the empty kitchen, through the empty doorway into the empty apartment that mirrored an empty life. He didn't have a life…he peeked in on *others'* lives…interfered in *others'* lives. Messed with them. People were nothing but pawns. Life…was a game of chess.

And where had the time gone? Seemed like it was only yesterday he'd been twenty-two….

A knock came at the door.

He checked his watch. Time flew, and it just kept picking up speed.

Getting to his feet, Black smoothed back his hair, rotated his head and neck, and again loosened up his shoulders and back. Answered the door. An attractive, unsmiling woman in her forties, who looked as if she'd been around a block or two, awaited.

Black allowed her entry. He locked the door behind her. She removed her coat and placed it and her pocketbook on the couch and continued straight back into the bedroom. Black eyed her as she went before him. Eyed the professional swish of her hips, the long legs that ended in black, stiletto heels. For all his pain and nausea, he felt a powerful need to fuck. He had a lot of pent-up everything inside, and tonight he was going to take it all out on her. He was going to fuck her until she bled, and when he was done…do it again.…

He was going to make her—and the rest of humanity—pay.

Chapter Ten

1

Lizzie again stood on those deserted, moonlit plains, holding a child in her arms. Again she watched as the dark silhouettes quietly descended from above, collapsed their parachutes, then silently charged off into the night...and, again, she followed.

In advance of the Bravo Force operators, she stood before the same house, as pleasantly lit as before, its three occupants as naïvely unaware of their situation as the last time. The child cooed and gurgled in Lizzie's arms, a beautiful child.

She shivered at the kill team's approach, wishing for it all to just be over, so she could wake up and again put the scene behind her. But she knew that wasn't going to happen. For some reason she was meant to witness what was to take place—or had already taken place. She didn't know. She was usually able to determine an image's time frame, but this one didn't yet feel *set*. Lizzie remembered the last vision/dream, where some force had interrupted the events that were about to unfold. It had come out of nowhere, abruptly terminating the dream. It was a force that now, she realized, felt oddly familiar....

Like specters flurrying across a ghostly landscape, the Bravo Force team positioned around the house. Lizzie knew that two were already inside. She knew that they were all experiencing growing anxiety. In her mind's eye, she saw the Berettas. Felt the sweating and dry mouths of their owners. She knew little about the military, but figured these guys had probably seen plenty of "action," they liked to call it, so why were they always so nervous and uncertain in this dream?

Still cradling the child, Lizzie calmly stepped aside as the team leader positioned himself before her. Invisible to them, she sensed their fear as if it was its own entity. She watched the team leader glance to his watch, his arm shaking. *Stop it,* the man mentally commanded, and the arm stopped shaking. *What was the matter with him?* the man continued to chide himself. *He was a hardened, tested, professional—a goddamned government-trained* killer, *for Chrissakes. This was* bullshit.

Lizzie watched the man focus his attention back to the house and their task. Clenching his hand into a tight fist, the man narrowed his focus back to his watch crystal. *Time...watch the* time. *The dog...it would pick them up soon. 0210 hours.*

Mentally counting, the Bravo Force operator closed his eyes and steeled himself. Buried his growing anxiety. He raised his Beretta in both hands and smacked himself in the forehead with it. Shaking his head, and quietly grunting, he coiled his superbly trained body and charged.

Lizzie calmly followed behind, lightly bouncing the child in her arms.

The man shot out across the darkness, taking note of the position of his team and their targets, but as he burst across the open space, another resurgence of oppressiveness took hold of him. His breathing, normally calm and relaxed, was now labored and short. The intense sense of dread built and filled every mental, emotional crevice. He felt as if he was again jumping out of that cargo plane into that moonlit night sky—but this time without a parachute...

Such will power, Lizzie thought. As mortally terrified as these guys now were, they continued to push on. Too bad their discipline wasn't better utilized in more

(*construction*)

constructive efforts.

Lizzie could actually see the man's shoulders bunch up as his anxiety level soared. It was here that Lizzie swelled with emotion.

Whether or not they were to ever complete their mission, it was their *intent* to kill that overwhelmed her. Their *intent* to break in on a family's quiet, peaceful existence and eliminate them, coldly, calculatedly. Without prejudice.

Just following orders.

The man, she again noted, eyed his target, the father at the head of the table. Lizzie reached out to this man and found he had been a hard-working cattle rancher his entire life. A gentle and caring father. Firm.

Lizzie caught an image of the father punishing his son for lying about going out to visit his girlfriend down the road. The father had not been mad that his son had gone out to see the girl…only that he'd lied about it.

Then Lizzie's attention was diverted by the picture of President Kennedy, the one the Bravo Force team leader had also spotted. Lizzie focused on it. There was something not right about it…something different from last time. Lizzie followed the Bravo Force leader into the home, sidestepping around him and to his left to get a better look at the picture. There was a smudge on JFK's forehead, and the right backside of his head looked wrong. She stood before the photograph. Wiped at the spot on the picture. To her surprise, her actions wiped away sections of his head to expose a disgusting shot that clearly showed a section of Kennedy's head blown away.

Lizzie blinked.

It was gone.

Her gaze then fell upon the book, *The Prophesies of Nostradamus*. Carefully shifting the child in her arms, she picked it up. It felt comfortable. She opened it. Its yellowed and weary pages were full of nursery rhymes. Her gaze fell to one in particular:

Ring around the rosie,
A pocketful of posies;
Ashes, ashes,
We all fall down.

She smiled, gently bouncing her child as she turned the crinkly pages. As she read other passages, she heard distant, childlike laughter. She continued to flip through the book—until the shots came.

She dropped the book and turned. She was no longer holding the child. Instead, before her, stood Joe. He had a smudge on his forehead she knew to be three holes-in-one, so dead center they were hardly noticeable as distinct wounds. Joe had a surprised look on his face, hands to his side, palms open toward her.

"*Why*, honey," he pleaded, raising his hands up to her, "why *didn't you save me?*"

Lizzie opened her mouth, when out from stage right swung a one-ton I-beam. She looked to Joe's pleading bewildered look as the steel battering ram slammed into his head, popping it clean off. She burst into tears, lurching forward to help him, only to realize she was now cradling something that was no longer a child….

2

Lizzie's head snapped up, and her entire body shuddered violently. What had she been—

She had held *something.*

She sat before a table…holding a pencil, its point poised upon a piece of paper that looked…"official."

A call log? *Her* call log?

She had been

(*moonlight*)

(*running*)

penciling in her

(*1963*)

time? She'd been—a family. *That* family. That Bravo Force team *killing* that family. A book—and picture.

President Kennedy?

The first one. And there had been something else…something else that had brought about a momentary emotional reminiscence….

Gone. She'd lost it. Something to do with that family and those Bravo Force operators. It would return. It always did.

Lizzie sighed, and completed penciling in her time into her call log. She'd had five calls already, it wasn't yet midnight, and she'd had that vision in the space of what, three seconds? Busy and she still had managed to doze off. She pulled off her headset and sat back. Lucy immediately leapt into her lap. Lizzie stared at the 1932 black-and-white Boris Karloff movie, *The Mummy*, now playing on her muted TV, and took a sip of iced tea. It *was* good. Maybe that strange man without a name was onto something.

"Okay, girl," Lizzie said to Lucy, getting to her feet, "I'm hungry."

Lucy jumped out of her lap and padded ahead of her into the kitchen. Lizzie opened the refrigerator and pulled out a cold pan of leftover meatloaf, put it on the counter and undid its tinfoiled top. She sliced off a hunk and stuck it in the microwave, then leaned back against the counter, still watching Boris struttin his bad self back in the living room. The old black-and-white movies had atmosphere like nothing Hollywood put out today. Not always the best acting, but that didn't matter, it was the *nostalgia*, the overall feel and *atmosphere* of the films—and their short credits.

Lizzie watched as Boris's mummy-turned-museum-display-curator killed a museum guard off camera.

And no gratuitous anything. It was all about imagination...*story*.

The microwave dinged, and Lizzie removed her food. Fetching ketchup from the fridge, she took both with her into the living room. As she sat down, Lizzie had a fleeting image of a Civil War battle.

Gettysburg, Pennsylvania?

An Irish brigade charging across a field? Not discounting it, but shrugging it off, she dug into her food.

Did she really want to work for Black and his FBI? Did she have a choice? Did she feel safe in *doing* so? Did she trust the man, and if not the *man*...his agency—*supposedly* the FBI? Black had said this guy, this Man With No Name, was a child molester, but her meeting with him indicated otherwise.

Why the hell couldn't she figure this out?

Why the hell wasn't she able to pick up on whatever it was she *needed?*

It's okay, Mommy, the little girl beside her said. *Everything'll be all right. You'll see.*

The girl then skipped across the living room, toward the door with the "No Grownups Allowed" sign, and disappeared through it.

C'mon, Mommy, come play with me! It'll make you feel better!

"I can't honey," Lizzie said, "I'm working now. I will later, though—okay?"

Lizzie kicked away a red plastic doughnut-ring from her feet and finished her dinner. She then returned to the kitchen and her headset, and barely had time to inhale before the phone rang.

Clearing her throat, and in her best Romani accent, Lizzie said, "This eez Madame Nostradameus. How may I help you?"

"Uh, hello. I don't really know where to begin...I'm, uh, I'm a bit confused—"

"Eez okay, my dear, let's begin with your name."

"Mel—Mel Roberts."

"Okay Mel, that eez a start. Now, what eez it you are so confused about? Madame Nostradameus eez here to help...."

3

Kennedy sat back on his deck, late-morning sun shining, sipping a glass of milk—

Milk?

He blinked, looking to the glass. *Iced tea.* It was *iced tea.*

Kennedy looked to the glass, to the condensation on the outside of it. Listened to the clinking of the cubes within it as he gently shook it. Smeared a section of condensation with a thumb. Took another sip.

Nope, iced tea, all right.

Kennedy looked out over Nantucket Sound. A beautiful piece of ocean. Sun shining, kestrels and gulls soaring the ocean breezes. The coastal scents. A striking day! He smiled.

Amazing how life turned out, wasn't it? How it got away from you? He'd certainly regretted a couple actions over his lifetime, but never the gestalt outcome: how he and his family—right down to great-grandchildren, nieces, and nephews—had done some real good for the world. Even John, Jr. had finally decided to get into politics, as a New York State Senator (with global speculation of a future presidency). Talk about a family legacy. With all he and his family had done—and continued to do—it was extremely disappointing that his principal regret still walked the planet. The one blot upon the family name.

Victor Black.

How that had happened, he never quite understood. It wasn't like he'd ever gone after him. Not that he remembered, anyway. But as you grew older, you changed. Memory didn't always seem to work as well it used to. Or maybe it was just that you had *so many memories* it took a while to sift through them all…

He remembered actually selecting another man—a man he could no longer recall. Pathetic. However, he did remember he was going to let this individual take over a project in a position so powerful that it would (and did) end up changing the course of humanity—*and he could no longer remember the guy's name?*

Then *he* appeared.

One day. Victor No-Middle-Initial Black.

He'd arrived subtly enough as one of the remote viewers in the mid-sixties—1966. Kennedy recalled how he had had a bad feeling about him from the get-go, though he'd looked great on paper and had interviewed well. Black had done well in the program, exceedingly well—*scary* well. Excelled beyond every one of his peers, and against *Kennedy's* better judgment the council had begun to groom Black. In 1973 The Center's directorship opened up when the current director abruptly retired. Kennedy remembered preparing for the final interview of that director's replacement with that someone he no longer remembered…but who also—mysteriously—departed.

And in waltzed Black.

Kennedy'd always suspected Black of doing away with his original appointment though could never prove it, and this began over twenty years of Black constantly and relentlessly fucking-around-cat-and-mouse with his life and The Center's mission.

Inexplicably appointed as The Center's director.

His memory seemed quite clouded on this account, ever since.

What the hell had happened that day? *How had Black usurped that appointment?*

Black.

A man who stopped at nothing to get what he wanted, Kennedy later discovered, much to his distress—what *he* felt the world needed, through some warped, misguided sense of morality only Black understood. *How could a person like him even come to be?* How could a Supreme Being ever allow so dark a soul to exist? But history was fraught with examples, from Attila the Hun to Hitler to…Victor NMI Black.

At the beginning, Black certainly appeared harmless enough, performing the Council's directives, continuing the mission, building upon the firm groundwork that had been laid and shaped the ultra-secret government psi ops organization. He had established funding and gathered a core group of hand-picked, supremely talented individuals. But it had been over time that Kennedy had come to realize that there had been something dreadfully amiss with this man and his vision. He found that Black had had dreams that haunted him…someone chasing him down, for what, Kennedy never found out—and he doubted Black did either. But when Black discovered years later that Kennedy had been surveilling him…that had been where the two had overtly parted company. Kennedy directed background checks on him, but found nothing unusual, and very little, at that, except that he had had (and, of course, still did have) Addison's Disease. Not even any perceived Communist ties. It was easier to hide back then. It was as if Victor Black had simply materialized out of thin air….

Black had, however, certainly beefed up Program One and put it on the intel map.

He'd performed Kennedy's and the Council of Seven's ultra-classified operations, but when relations grew strained, Black had begun to divert. He'd begun conducting his own operations…killing and ruining many lives along the way, and it was that which Kennedy regretted most...the senseless and useless ruination of all those lives. That was when he'd attempted to reign him in, creating his very own *sub*-tasking, one in which a single remote viewer reported directly to him and him alone—not even the Council. Kennedy began psychically spying on Victor Black, and when Black found out about *that*, that viewer had also disappeared. Nothing could be proven, but the cards had been thrown down. It was near the end of Bobby's second term, and to the public things were looking great. A rare Camelot, indeed. He couldn't tell the Council what he'd done, for that would have exposed his subterfuge, burned many bridges, and wasn't at all conducive to the overall good the Council and his administration were doing. All he could do was watch. Keep an eye on him. In retrospect, he should have brought the Council in on his decision. He just wasn't sure who he could trust, and to have used the remote viewer to look in on who he could and couldn't trust would have added too many variables to an already stressed and urgent timeline.

Oddly enough, Black hadn't exploited that opportunity, either. That had always puzzled him. Black always continued to puzzle him in the most confounded ways.

Black had begun to use the remote viewers for his own ends, and he'd begun targeting Kennedy himself. It had become quite a rat's nest for a while, with Kennedy's life in constant peril—though, again, he could never prove it was *Black*, and curiously, Black had never made *that* an issue, either. Never leaked any information, lies *or* truths, that could have burned him. But he knew he knew. Never one to worry about bodyguards, Kennedy constantly rebuffed the need for personal security until the White House was forced to employ a permanent Secret Service detail on his behalf after several attempts had been overtly made on his life. Those attempts had ended up costing the lives of several agents. Kennedy had even been grazed by several rounds in one massive, several-shooter attempt in Texas. As a national resource, he no longer had any say in the matter and had since always been protected around the clock. And once Kennedy had left The Center and the political limelight and devoted his energies to altruistic causes...Black had backed off.

A constant puzzle, that man.

It was only a matter of time, Kennedy thought...and that man he'd met in the Rose Garden, a man who had looked professional enough, except that he had sported some outrageous black-and-white

Dalmatian tie and rolled-up sleeves—the man from whom he'd never gotten a name—told him that Black, at the time, anyway, wasn't a major concern. Black's time was limited, the man had informed him. Other issues were far more pressing. And, he'd added, he'd make sure nothing else happened to him. Kennedy, the Man With No Name said, would live a long and fruitful life—*not to worry*.

But now, at seventy-seven, Kennedy wondered when Black *would* become a major enough concern. He'd been running unchecked for a lifetime, and had managed to keep out of the public eye. But, Kennedy knew what lay in Black's heart: fear. A deep-seated, irrational fear that drove him in search of the source of that fear. Before he passed, Kennedy's remaining wish was to stop him. It was time he took matters into his own hands. But, short of anything drastic, what could be done? World peace shouldn't be gained through the spilling of blood...if at all possible. There had to be a way, somehow, to get rid of him that was ethically and morally sound.

Kennedy sighed and set aside his half-finished tea.

Camelot, indeed.

Maybe you just couldn't save the world.

Children, came an internal whisper. *Children....*

Though Black was in his sixties, he was affected by Addison's and had lived a hard life. To be honest, he was utterly surprised he had made it this long. But, he'd been loose for so long, did it really matter if he lived out the rest of his life continuing to do what he'd been doing for the past twenty? It was only a matter of time.

He just hoped he'd live to see it.

Ring around the rosie,
A pocketful of posies,
Ashes! Ashes!
We all fall down.
We all fall down.
We all fall down....

4

"...I don't know," Mel said, dragging out his words, "it just feels like, maybe...I'm living in a dream...."

Mel stared blankly at the television set flickering before him, in his darkened room. The *Twilight Zone* rerun "Where is Everybody?" played.

"Like I'm the only one actually living this dream—until I called you."

A commercial flashed up on the screen that said *"Life is what you make of it. Make something of it!"*

Lizzie found it hard to continue with the faux accent. She felt genuine sadness and confusion coming from the boy—but little else, which was unnerving. She just couldn't pick up anything else from him.

"Look," she said in faux-Romani, "So, you think your parents are dead, but that doesn't feel right to you—eez that what you're saying?"

"Yes, I-I think so. It's hard to explain, you know? Or maybe you don't—"

"I *do*," Lizzie said, mulling over his conversation. "Madame Nostradameus knows all...."

"I should probably go. I've taken up enough of your—"

"Your time eez my time, my dear." All the practiced phrases kept coming out without a second thought. There was something different about this boy...something she couldn't decipher and didn't want to get away from her. It was the same kind of unsettling impression she got from Black—only in a *good* way.

"I know, I know. I just wanted to talk to someone, is all—make sure I'm not the only one on the planet."

"Mel...Madame Nostr—*I*—really want to help. I know someone...why don't you take theez number down and give her a call. She might be able to help you...at least give you a shoulder to lean on."

There was a pause at the other end.

"Okay."

"She is someone you can talk to," Lizzie said, finding her faux Romani slip, "Maybe point you een the right direction."

"Okay."

Lizzie gave him her home phone number.

Chapter Eleven

1

Travis Norton settled into his "quiet place," as he lay back in The Center's RoboChair and opened his mind to the tasking. It was only him and his monitor in the room, but in the observation booth he knew there could be any number of observers—or the eminently spooky Mr. Black, himself. Travis wasn't alone in noticing that Black seemed to hang out around the place much more often the past few months, and that made everyone just a little edgy. They weren't supposed to talk among themselves, but who couldn't? It was bad enough they were all stuffed away in the bowels of the innocuously named John F. Kennedy Center, a highly classified compound in the foothills of Virginia's Blue Ridge Mountains, where almost every word or thought was compartmentalized, but come on, folks, we're talking government-trained *psychics* here. Who needed to talk when you could *sense?* And the combined sense was that something big was up, and bigger than anyone had ever before dealt with. There was more than the normal amount of whispering going on between viewers, and with Black around, that wasn't a good thing.

And Buddy LaRouque's disappearance last week?

Newcomers came and went all the time, but Buddy had been with the program for a year and a half and had just…disappeared. No forewarning. He was happy and joking around one day—and now it was as if he'd never been there. Even his house had been sold. One day he's living in it *and the next a family of* four?

It wasn't even like this family was still unpacking—*everything had already been unpacked and looked lived-in for* years.

The mailbox had their name on it.

The new family Rottweiler alertly napped inside a chain link fence that hadn't even *been* there yesterday.

And out in the back shed was a '57 Chevy being refinished by the new man of the house.

It was those kinds of facts that had Travis questioning his own sanity—had anything about "Buddy" been real, or had he just imagined it all?

Made him up?

Lost track of time?

Remote viewers knew that once they tapped into the power and world of remote viewing they couldn't just turn it off. Viewers routinely "zoned out" at the oddest of moments, and in the weirdest of ways, but, when Travis had asked his supervisor what was up, and the man just looked at him, didn't say a word—*just stared him right out of his office*—it didn't take a psychic to know something was going on. And, now, he found and felt people watching *him*.

So, like a good G.I., he'd backed off.

Who had Buddy been to him—really—anyway?

He'd just been a guy he'd worked with...had over for BBQs...hoisted a few together at the local watering hole—in fact with the whole *lot* of them had. Buddy'd even *dated* one of them, for God's sake—Gina Massey—the babe of the bunch. Newcomers came and went, getting whatever training they needed, then off to wherever they were assigned. Nobody asked questions. It weren't no big deal. They all lived in a highly classified, hidden existence, and they all knew that when they signed on *and* signed away their expendable little lives. For the good of the country and national security. No one had any issue with that. But, to go around sticking your nose into areas you didn't belong was just asking for trouble.

So Travis did what he was told, and reported to his current tasking. He'd felt uneasy from the beginning this morning, and the feeling just got worse the closer he got to his mission. And now, sitting in the all-too-familiar RoboChair, it was taking him longer to get settled and relaxed, a well-practiced process that normally took mere minutes. But, to not perform now after all the inquiries he'd made was not a good thing. He had to show he was still "with the program." That there were no problems on his part, so, he willed himself into a forced relaxation that belied a much deeper angst. Psychics couldn't hide from psychics—but psychics could definitely hide from your average

(*Joe....*)

"Okay, Travis, we need you to focus on the target, now," his monitor asked, carefully eyeing him. "What do you see?"

"Don't really see anything…but feel…"

"What?"

Travis wrinkled his brow. "Hard to describe…intense…dizzying imagery…angst?…I feel…*anger*…"

The monitor wrote down "anger."

"It's like…there's nothing *there*, yet—but, but…wait…"

Travis paused, willing himself to get more into the task. There was something very wrong here, he felt it chewing at him. Did he tell everything, or did he wait to feel things out a little more? It was like…when he tried to oppose those feelings of doubt…he felt *opposition*. And that made no sense. Travis decided to just go with the flow.

"What do you see now?" the monitor prodded.

"Still…lots of anger in the background…*angst*…lots of…*incompleteness*, I guess is the only way to describe it. Like things are not quite set, yet…but…but, there's something else—wait…dark…darkness…night—parachutes…covert ops. Bravo Force? Special operations operators parachuting through a night sky…"

The monitor jotted down notes.

"…they're making their way over the dark terrain of…barren plains—in the Southwest…southwest Colorado. I don't get a good fix on the date…maybe mid-to-late sixties?"

"Try to get a better bead."

Travis paused. "Still no better."

"Okay, move on. What next?"

"A house. I don't get a good feeling about this place. A farm house…isolated…in more ways than I can—"

"Are the operators tied to the house? Where are they?"

"The house. It's their objective."

"What are they doing now?"

Travis again furrowed his brow. "The leader—two are inside the house—having second thoughts. Not so much about killing, but about…the *mission*. Confused, they're highly confused—something's…clouding their minds…their *judgment*…

"These are experienced men…done this before…but something's interfering…making them question—"

Travis stopped talking. Images flooded his mind…images of another…a man whose face he recognized—*thought* he recognized—but couldn't bring into focus. Memories strobed on and off before him. A voice…"*no*," it said, and it echoed this word over and over and over, from a whisper to a more forceful, just short of a shout, voice. It came from this man who kept flickering on and off before him, like an old time, hand-cranked mutoscope. It was this man who was interfering with the Bravo Force operators. Travis saw this clearly, now...and he found that *he* now entered the picture...he, Travis, was part of the kill team...and now the unidentified man had turned to *him* and was trying to tell *him* something.

Why was it so hard to pick up on this shit?

Tension. There was a lot of tension...*conflict.* Travis tried to psychically shake off the tension, but it only grew. Now the man was moving his lips, but no sound came from them. The image continued to strobe crazily before him—

Then all the lights went out.

2

Lizzie hung up her headphones for the night and leaned forward, face in her hands. Exhausted...she was utterly *exhausted.* Tonight's session had drained her more than usual. Especially the call from that boy, Mel.

So, how many company policies—not to mention her own personal ones—had she violated by giving out her home number?

But there was something about that kid. What had he said? *Dreams?* Maybe that had struck a chord in her, what with her dream about Joe and the assassins. What if all of life *was* nothing more than a dream? Wouldn't that be an eye opener? If all this really was a dream, then she certainly didn't want to wake up to find out what reality was *really* all about.

"*Mommy, don't be sad,*" the little girl called out from behind the No-Grownups-Allowed door. "*Come in and see us...we need you, here...it'll make you feel much better.* Please, Mommy...."

"Mommy's tired, honey," Lizzie said, rubbing her eyes and kneading her temples and forehead.

"*Please, Mommy,*" the little voice continued to plead, "*it's been so long already...and you have our new books outside the door.* Please, *bring them in and read to us!*"

Lizzie got up and went to the door. She tiredly looked down to the books before the door, folded her arms across her chest, and sighed heavily. Leaned against the door.

*"Mommy, we know it hurts, but you always feel better in here...*please, *come in*...we're all waiting...."

Exhausted, Lizzie picked up the books and opened the door.

3

The phone call to the psychic had been good for Mel. It definitely meant he wasn't alone. That others *did* exist outside his empty little world and weren't just in his head. It had felt good talking to someone other than himself, listening to something other than his own voice, *including* the one in his head—communicating and getting it all out to someone else. Her accent, though, had slipped once or twice toward the end, there, but she seemed sincere enough and otherwise genuinely interested in him. He'd never called a psychic before (was he *sure?*), but the TV had all but screamed out to him to do so. Then she had given him *her* number.

How'd he know that?

He just did. Or would find out for sure, shortly, anyway.

And had he not been who he was, how did she know he wasn't some crazed caller? Wasn't she taking a huge chance? Well, she *was* supposed to be a real psychic, wasn't she? And he was just lonely and confused. Desperately in need of someone to talk to...

Should he call her? Now? Or wait? He didn't want to seem overly needy...but he was. It was pretty late...though she was on the late-night commercial. Would that be too much—calling her so soon?

Mel continued to stare at the TV. Another commercial popped up that simply stated *"Peace."*

Mel stared at it.

It was in a beautiful, elegant script, and there were all kinds of New Age-y sparkles flecking off and on all around it and in the back and foreground, but no voiceover. There were also low, New Age-y music playing in the background that suddenly made him cry.

Then the ad was gone.

The late-night horror movie *A Nightmare on Elm Street* returned.

Mel chuckled, wiping away his tears. "Now, *that's* funny!"

4

Travis sat on the front porch of a small house, in the middle of the night. In a rocking chair. Holding a glass of iced tea that sweat perspiration onto his hand.

"Okay…" Travis said, "what just happened?"

"You could say I just snuck you out of a bad situation," came the voice from the darkness before him.

Travis jumped to his feet, still holding the tea. He went to set down the glass…but not before taking a sip. His eyebrows rose in surprise at just how good it was, and took another quick sip before setting it down. Then he jumped down the two short porch steps, where he found the silhouette of a man hunched over in the darkness.

"*Excuse* me—and what the hell are you doing?"

"Yankin weeds. Haven't you ever seen anyone weed before? You just can't stay ahead of the damned things…."

"In the *dark?*"

"Don't have to worry about sunburn."

"Where the hell am I—and why am I arguing with you about pulling weeds in the middle of the night?"

Travis looked to his surroundings, but other than the outside of a dimly-illuminated house and the bent-over silhouette before him, there wasn't much to see. He had to be in some kind of *Twilight Zone* episode….

"You're right where you need to be, son—as for why you're arguing with me, that's your issue. Like the tea?" the man asked, standing up and tossing down a clump of weeds at Travis's feet. The man brushed his hands off on his pant legs.

"Yeah," Travis said, hesitantly, inhaling the musky smell of the dirt clump at his feet, "it was pretty good, but—"

"Well, then, let's have some more!" The silhouetted man rushed past for the porch, where he grabbed his own glass. The Man With No Name sat down in the rocker Travis had originally inhabited. "And, by the way, this is *my* chair, sonny. You pick one of the others."

Travis wrinkled his face. "Alright, one minute, I'm—"

"Snooping in on Bravo Force operators," the Man With No Name said.

"Yeah, that, and the next, I'm—"

"Here."

"Answers. I need answers."

"Take a load off, son. You're making me nervous with all your standing around and jawin."

"Making *you* nervous?"

"Don't get yourself all bunched up over it. I'm just trying to make you feel at ease and offer some of the best iced tea ever. Before we get started."

Travis returned to the porch. "Get started on what?"

"You're a big psychic warrior, figger it out." The man took a sip from his glass (where it had come from, Travis didn't know), ice clanking.

Travis retrieved his iced tea and sat in the chair next to the odd man. He didn't know what it was, but sitting in the chair just begged for him to tip it back against the house.

Which he did.

"Now, *that's* better! It's always better to smile and take a load off, ain't it?"

Travis shot him a look; realized he still couldn't quite make out his face, even in the porch light. He also recognized the smell of fresh-cut grass. "How can you—"

"Look, Travis—yes, I know your name—you're on the right track. Back where you're from, going it alone is gonna get you killed. Like your buddy…Buddy."

"How'd you—"

"It's my job. Sorry about Buddy…there was nothing I could do."

Travis stared at him.

The Man With No Name shrugged. "It's a long story that spans lifetimes—"

"I'm dreaming, is that it? I'm in a dream. All this talk of Buddy, other lifetimes—weeding at night—finding myself…here."

"It's the same kind of *medium* as dreams, but not really dreaming…*per se*—well, as you're used to it. Well, maybe *you* are, being a government-trained bad-ass and all, but, it's more like a layer cake."

"Layer cake."

"A layer cake—*our* layer cake—has many layers, and in between each layer are good-tastin fillins. We're *in between* some of those layers, like the filling. Like raspberry? Banana?"

"You're nuts."

"That may be, but banana or raspberry—"

Travis shot up out of the chair. "This is insane! I'm outta here—"

"You really wanna go back? Aren't you even remotely curious, pardon the pun, about why this has happened—where you are? You really wanna go back unarmed and unprepared?"

"Then quit jerking me around and get to the goddamned point."

"Fair enough." The Man With No Name nodded. "You are/were, indeed, between time. Time and consciousness, actually. I've kind of—how shall I put this?—*spliced* consciousness, and sort of…split you off from where you were and your points of reference for a 'space' of time, into mine. *My* 'space.' *My* point of reference, that is. By doing this, you have still not lost any so-called 'time' where you are, but are also where *I* am. An internal bi-location. You are, essentially, in two places at once, and no one's the wiser, cept you and me."

"How'd you do this…*why'd* you do it?"

"That's the hard part. That scene you were viewing? You felt it, didn't you?"

"The Bravo Force operators?"

"The tension?"

"You bet I did."

"That was me. I'm interrupting something that was going on—*trying* to go on. I'll explain as simply as I can.

"There are things going on back there at that compound of yours that are upsetting realities. When you interrogated your superior on your friend's departure, you placed him in quite the bind. He was given specific direction not to talk nor acknowledge anything about Buddy, and was told that he better *believe* it if he wanted to keep on breathin. But even more to the quick, he was suddenly caught in a reality-confusing situation. He swore that he'd dreamed this all up and had actually begun to question whether or not it had really been a dream at all—or if he was dreaming then, in your 'now'—when you confronted him. But he also had that directive still floatin around in the back of his mind—the 'you better believe this or die' directive, and didn't know if that had also been a dream or a *real* directive—but it *felt* real to him, and all *while* he felt he was dreamin. He felt it had actually been told to him by your Mr. Black. And, as we all know, everyone's afraid of that guy."

Travis remained silent. Looked out into the blackness.

"So, what had happened was that he couldn't answer your question on any grounds. He couldn't even acknowledge your queries with an answer, for to do so would put him at risk, and if it *was* a dream, and he questioned it, he still acknowledged your Buddy, which would still put him at risk. But if it *was* a dream then none of this was real to begin with, so, his action were the lesser of all evils for him, and he simply remained silent, hoping you never pressed the issue—which you didn't. But the really weird part will be when you return…you won't remember a thing about Buddy. It's part of your tasking."

"*What?*" Travis thudded his chair back down to the porch.

"Not many people are capable of noticing these, but we all have weird little warps that happen to us every day. Things changin…then are taken for granted without our notice. We take on the accepted changes without question, because they've insidiously become part of our lives, our realities…our *accepted* realities…and to do otherwise, to question, wouldn't make sense to us."

Travis blinked.

"Again, use your psychic experience to bear with me on this. Do you see that as we all go through life, we take different paths? That each and every decision we make changes our direction—the paths—we take?"

Travis nodded.

"Well, it's the same kind of thing that goes on nonphysically, beneath and between the surfaces of our lives, in the background. I won't go into what or how it happens, just now, but throughout the days and years and minutes things…*change*…and we never notice. That is, *most of us never do*. We go right on with our lives as if the changed events have always been a part of our lives, when, in reality, they haven't; *they'd literally changed that instant*."

"'That's nuts'…I was going to say," Travis said, "until I remembered…when I was a kid, I grew up out in the country. We lived on a small farm. Had gardens. So, my dad had me rototilling those gardens, and I loved doing that—especially as a young kid—doing work I associated with my dad. He'd taught me how to use it, and it was one of the chores I actually enjoyed doing. And I remember how neat it was to churn up all that dirt and make it silky smooth-looking and 'fluffy.' But a couple years ago, I was talking with him and talked about how I used to do this, and he swore up and down that he had never—*ever*—let me or showed me how to rototill. At first I thought he was fooling around, but I soon realized he'd been dead serious. In fact, he started to get kinda pissed about it when I pressed the issue. I began to wonder if he was just losing his memory—I mean, *I remember doing this like it was yesterday*. Then, a couple years later, he totally agreed with me."

"*That's* what I'm talking about."

Travis sat, pensively. "And there was this other time…there's this town in Australia—Woomera. All my life, I swear it was placed on maps way out in the very *center* of the country, in a No-Man's land, the Gibson Desert, I think it's called. Well, about a year ago, I was talking to someone about it, and this person told me it was just north of Adelaide, above Spencer Gulf, on the *coast*. I said, no way—but this person had actually been there. So we pulled out a map, and—"

"It was where your friend said it was, wasn't it?"

"How do you argue with something like that? With *facts?*"

"Facts change."

"But how? How can that *be?* Facts are facts, because, well, they're *facts.*"

The Man With No Name stared at him.

"Facts aren't supposed to change! That's the whole damned *point!*"

"Everything changes, friend, but, as I said, there are those of us who notice some of these changes, while most never do. Like Buddy. When you get home, *he will never have been.* And you will no longer remember him. It was part of your tasking. All the rest of it was obfuscation."

"How can someone make someone else so totally disappear that no one—I mean *no one*—is the wiser? *Who has that kind of power?*"

Chapter Twelve

1

The Man With No Name stood before the railing, set down his iced tea, and stared out into the night.

"All I can tell you—now—Travis, is that we're gonna meet again; you're not alone." He turned around. "You, and others like you at The Center, are noticing strangeness afoot, because something *is* going on. You don't know what to do about it, or what it's all about, but you *feel* it, smell it. You just can't put your finger on it. And you all know Black's behind it. It's a largely unconscious issue, but that's where I come in. My associates. We're here to help. Take control."

"Control of what?"

"Black. He's experimenting on all of you. Trying to change reality, at least as far as you and the rest of humanity understand it. And he's using you guys and gals as his unwitting tools. He's switching out official task orders with his own set...but I keep interfering...and it's pissing him off. To my extreme amusement, I must say," the Man With No Name said, grinning. "He just doesn't have a clue—well, that's not entirely true, either."

"He knows?"

"I've been tracking him for a long time. He can't figure out who is messin around with him, but he knows *someone* is. He's trying to hunt me down...thinks he's gotten close—"

"Has he?"

"In a manner of speaking...he's closer than he realizes. And there's so much more at stake than even he realizes. But on the other hand, it's not as big a deal as he thinks."

"Why is everything out of your mouth a contradiction?"

"It's the only way to fully communicate the issues. We have to use words, however limited in this environment, and this is their inner translation. But, it's time to return you to your world—"

"I thought we were outside of time?"

"It's not so much about 'Time,' as intensities."

"Okay...."

"And you won't remember any of this."

"How won't I?"

"I'm working at such an obtuse angle to your consciousness, I'm not in an area that'll be readily available to you. Okay, maybe some will *bleed* through, but—for the most part—as I've mentioned, I'm operating outside normal perceptions, even psychic ones. It's for your own good. Black has a knack of seeing through the best of you...hence, Buddy. But, as I started to say, there are more of you—not only at The Center—but elsewhere. I'm merely initiating contact...laying the foundation for our mission to put an end to Black and his efforts. I may be sarcastic and flippant in my delivery of this stuff, but this is deadly serious business."

The Man With No Name raised his glass before him, saluting Travis, then took a sip.

"The less you and the others know," the Man With No Name continued, "the better. Right now he's paranoid of his own shadow. I wanna keep it that way. But, let's get you back to where you belong, shall we?"

Travis cast him a sidelong glance. "Just keep me from getting killed, and we'll call it even. And—"

2

"...did I say they're feeling confused...as if something's clouding their minds, their judgment?" Travis asked the monitor.

"Yes," the monitor said flatly. "Is there anything else?"

Travis paused. An indistinct déjà vu overcame him.

"There's a great stress running among them, and—"

Travis was knocked out of the session, eyes open and stunned.

"Wow."

"What happened?" the monitor asked.

"I don't know...it was like I couldn't get past something— whatever 'it' was—it was kind of magnetic, like two opposing magnets. Knocked me right out of the session. That's exactly how it felt, like an intense magnetic—repelling—force. Never experienced anything like that before."

The monitor scribbled away on his notepad.

"Let me back in. I wanna give it another go—"

The monitor didn't look up as he continued scribbling. "No...not for now. That'll be all. We'll get back to you." The monitor stood and abruptly exited the room.

Travis knew better. No one ever got back to them. They were constantly left in the dark, but they were all used to that by now, and expected no less. It was all part of the game. If they hadn't been producing, they'd have been out of business a long time ago. Since they were all still employed, they all assumed they were doing *something* right.

Stone-faced, Travis followed the monitor out.

3

Lizzie closed the door behind her and was immediately overcome by tears. Setting down the children's books, she allowed herself to look about the small room she only rarely visited. Looked to all the scattered children's toys across the floor that appeared as if they'd all just been played with...to all the children's drawings taped up on the walls. To the hobby horse in the corner.

It's okay to cry, the little girl's voice whispered.

"I know, honey, but it's getting too painful."

Why?

"Because these things bring back to us—me—the way things were...can never be again. At least not in this life. It brings up all the possibilities we'd hoped to change...but couldn't. I never thought it'd be so hard. It's difficult to explain."

Lizzie wiped her eyes and went to a crayon drawing on the far wall. It showed the stick figures of a man and woman holding hands, standing amongst the many smaller stick figures of children. A yellow crayon-sun shone above, with thick green crayon-grass at their feet. One of the large stick figures had long hair, symbolized by large "S" curls to either side of its less-than-perfect-circle head. Beneath the entire scene were the words "We love you!" written in multicolored, upper-and-lower-cased, unmatched, crayon-letters.

We're sorry you're crying. We wish we could make you stop, the little-girl voice said.

"It's okay, I'll get over it soon enough. It's just hard coming in here anymore. I just don't understand...all this. Why things happened the way they did...."

Everything'll be all right, Mommy, you'll see.

Lizzie again wiped her nose. "I'm not so sure anymore, honey."

4

Kennedy lay wide awake, staring at the ceiling.

He wasn't alone.

He shot up in bed and looked to the Victorian chair in a corner of his bedroom. The silhouette of a man sat in it.

Kennedy went for the .357 in the nightstand drawer.

"It's only me, Mister President—nothing to worry about."

Kennedy paused. Squinted. That voice was familiar...*extremely* familiar...and hit a deep place within him.

The silhouetted man continued, "From the White House Rose Garden, back in '62? Pressed white shirt, whacky Dalmatian-spotted tie? Gave you the idea for you-know-what?"

"*What?*"

"Don't worry, this is all a dream."

"A *dream?*"

"Things are getting out of hand, sir."

"I, ah, remember, now...yes...the Rose Garden. Who *are* you?"

The silhouetted man sent a short burst of images through Kennedy's mind, images of wars and philosophies, men and women. A house that didn't exist in upstate New York.

Kennedy reeled. "What the hell?"

"Let's just keep matters simple and say I don't have an identity. Safer for all involved. You know who I am."

"I do," Kennedy said, sitting up and adjusting his back against the headboard. "What's, ah, gotten out of hand?"

"This mutual acquaintance of ours." The Man With No Name sent Black's image to Kennedy. "He's stirring things up again."

"That's nothing new, but how do you know him?"

"It's complicated. I know there's no love lost between you two, but I don't mean to be taking up all your time with small talk, Mister President. I've come because things are not working themselves out fast enough for my liking, and you're growing more troubled about how to handle him. I may have a solution. One you can live with. It's not immediate, and aspects of it may yet change, but you won't have to take him out and can look at yourself in the mirror in the morning."

"I'm listening."

5

Lizzie Parker and Joe Gordon had met when Lizzie was twenty-eight and Joe twenty-seven. Joe had only been in construction a couple years and hadn't yet established his own business. They'd both met at Lake Dillon, in Colorado's Summit County, during the spring of 1989—just like Lizzie knew they would. She'd first seen it in a dream a year before, seen it multiple times since, and it had been pure hell trying to be patient for that day to arrive. She hadn't been one to frequent Summit County, and wasn't sure if she really ever would...if it hadn't been for her dreams. She'd made one or two trips up during that year, not really expecting to find her husband-to-be, she kept telling herself, but was impatient, pure and simple, and was hoping she could speed things along a bit. Of course, that didn't happen.

She had been leisurely window shopping the day they were meant to meet, when she'd seen him walk out of Bentley's Restaurant. He'd left the restaurant and had turned away from her, heading back to the jobsite—and had never even noticed her. Aghast—he hadn't even *looked* at her!—she launched after him. She hadn't known what she was going to do or say, but had decided to let Fate and faith take over. As she closed the gap between the two of them, Joe had reached around to his rear pocket and found his wallet missing. It was then he'd hit the brakes and did an abrupt about face—right into the oncoming train of Lizzie Parker. Struck all but dumb, Lizzie now faced the situation of literally being face-to-face with the man of her dreams...dumbstruck. Joe still had his right hand on his rear pocket, thinking "wallet," and Lizzie had had her hands up in a knot before her, not thinking at all. The two had just stared at each other, as Lizzie realized she'd held her knotted-up hands pressed tightly against the man's fairly firm abs, braced for their collision.

Romancing took over, and the two began their courtship.

It hadn't been long before Joe had confessed to Lizzie that he'd also dreamed of her. He'd had several dreams in which he'd been walking away from the very same restaurant, turning around, then literally running into her. Everything was the same except he didn't have her name.

Lizzie unafraid of who she was, never blinked when she told him of her abilities, and how she'd also seen how they'd meet. Joe, who never gave much thought to dreams nor the paranormal, hadn't minded that his future wife was psychic and actually became quite proud of her ability. It came in quite handy when he'd asked her if she thought he should stay with his present company or move on. With whom he should or shouldn't trust when starting his own company, where to buy a house, that kind of thing. The only thing it hadn't been any kind of handy in had been in the hiring of Jeff Skopchek.

After moving to One Tree, Colorado, a friend-of-a-friend had approached Joe after work one long summer's day and asked if he could use another hand. This friend-of-a-friend had said Jeff was basically a good guy, but had been going through a rough patch. This friend-of-a-friend and Jeff had worked together for years in construction and he swore Jeff was an able-bodied hand. Jeff could really use the work, and really needed the money—he was going through a divorce. So, without consulting Lizzie, Joe thought he'd do a friend-of-a-friend a favor. Jeff really was likable enough, got along great with the rest of the crew, knew his trade—and was a skilled crane operator, which Joe needed. He did solid work, but when it came to women...this was Jeff's Achilles' Heel. He could never keep his eyes or hands to himself, which was what had brought about the divorce. He claimed to still love his wife—yeah, he wasn't perfect, but he'd explained to Joe one night after work that he just couldn't help himself and didn't know what to do about it. He used to think that if his wife hadn't settled into marital complacency that that would have been half the battle. But she was no longer the woman he'd married, claimed she was no longer interested in him, but nonetheless kept checking up on him when he had to stay late on jobs. The list just went on and on, he said. So, when other women gave him the time of day, "let's just say," Jeff told Joe, "it wasn't hard talking back." And there had been the excitement of it all. Before Jeffy knew what was going on, he'd been in...deep.

Fast forward: Jeff and the soon-to-be-ex-missus were undergoing divorce proceedings, and the missus, understandably hurt, had been ruthless and spared no quarter. Jeff didn't know what to do. He'd dropped the woman he'd been caught with, even offered to go through therapy, but it all fell upon deaf ears. Too little, too late, Melissa Skopchek had said. All Jeff wanted, he'd last told Joe, was a happy life with the right woman, and now he was at a loss over how things had gotten so rotten. He'd never meant to stray, but things had just…"happened." Joe, however, told Jeff "Things don't just 'happen' my friend; *we* make them happen." Jeff sat silently, sipping his brew. That had been the night before Joe's accident.

And Lizzie had not picked up on *any* of this. Not one iota.

Lizzie had never been one to need prompting in such matters; if the issue was important enough in her worldview, she'd always picked up on it, but this was the one strangely aberrant exception, and, unfortunately, it was the one exception that had cost her her husband.

The next day, Jeff showed up to work without a word to his fellow workers, donned his hard hat, and began moving steel around like Lincoln logs….

To Lizzie's credit, if the term be used, she'd awoken queasy that morning, actually sick to her stomach. The feeling remained with her throughout the morning. She didn't remember dreaming that night (she *always* dreamed and always *remembered* them). When that fateful phone call reached her around ten-fifteen that morning, her world fell apart.

Would her seeing it have prevented anything?

Could she have gotten to Joe in time?

Should she ever have met him in the first place?

The lawyers were more than supportive and helpful, and Lizzie did all the right things, though she did them all in a haze. No stranger to the paranormal and the fantastic, but all this was acutely unreal to her. She kept whispering to herself, when she was alone, that *none of this was supposed to have happened!* They were supposed to have lived their lives blissfully happily ever after, the vows and all the signs had *said* so. That she had never seen anything untoward happening to them, before or after they'd met. *None of this*, she continued to swear through her hot and copious tears, *was ever supposed to have happened!* The entire situation was *wrong!*

Lizzie painfully collected Joe's insurance, sold the house, and bought a manufactured home in a trailer park.

Why hadn't she been able to foresee any of this?

She'd retreated from as much human contact as possible, which, essentially, meant men. No one, she told herself, could ever replace

Joe, and even if there was someone out there remotely compatible—she never wanted to know.

And then there had been the other dreams, the dreams she'd had as long as she could remember.

The dreams about children.

Those had also made it especially difficult. She'd always had dreams about lots of children—scores, hundreds—and had always taken that to mean that they would have many of their own. But, for all their attempts and supposed premonitions and signs, she'd never become pregnant, and now, with Joe's death, she would never—*ever*—have that opportunity. So, to throw salt on the wound, she felt many times cheated.

Or, perhaps more to the point, short of memories and pictures, she would never have a physical reminder of Joe she could hold and love and hug.

So, it was with much confused pain that Lizzie created the room she now sat huddled in against a wall.

She continued to have her dreams, continued to have her visits from her "little people," but she also continued to remain child- and spouseless. The pain never went away. Some days she dealt with it better than others. She continued to buy her baby toys and books, and continued to keep this room alive. And on those days when she could better handle things—or when they actually called out to her, like now—she entered. But she usually ended up leaving the room in tears. There was no way to ever close the wounds, and she was not sure she wanted to. The pain made her feel good. The pain reminded her of Joe. The pain brought her closer to him. As much as she knew he was all right wherever he was, this made her feel...*comfortable*. She had never been able to contact him, but had, on occasion, *felt him around*. It was a never-ending source of frustration with her that, along with not even seeing his impending death, she could also never contact her husband after his death. But she could pretend he was still with her, that he was just late in getting home...and that they had their children running around their

(*house*)

trailer.

Of course, it didn't help that she actually had visits from ghost children she could never explain. Those who came to visit her, talk with her, and even seem to leave their toys lying around, and she could no more explain their ghostly presences than she could explain why,

why, why the *hell* she hadn't been able to foresee Joe's goddamned death.

Lizzie threw the books across the room, then, sobbing softly to herself, curled up into a tight little ball of pain....

Chapter Thirteen

1

Kennedy refused to believe it had anything to do with senility or hallucinations, but still had a hard time explaining the events of the previous night. Dreams of a mysterious man with no name—a man whom he'd met over thirty years ago, and had had no contact with until *now?*

Sixteen thousand feet over eastern Massachusetts, Kennedy peered out the port window of his Learjet, and checked his watch. He'd called an emergency board meeting in Boston with the Global Foundation for Peace, an organization he'd founded back in '69, but he still wasn't sure what he was supposed to do. He was just supposed to call an emergency board meeting and things were supposed to fall into place, the Man With No Name had said.

Right. Just like that.

Why couldn't he let him in on some details? *Because*, the Man With No Name'd equally insisted, *if you really knew what you were getting into, you wouldn't do it, and he* really *needed him in that boardroom. And in the world of dreams and psychics, sometimes the less you knew...the better.*

Kennedy sipped his orange juice and stared out the window, wondering what the hell he was getting into—but was also more than just a little excited. He hadn't had this kind of excitement since Peru, in '74....

2

A loud, obnoxious ringing assaulted Lizzie...would not go away. Filled her universe. It was more than just a sound, it was *evil*...a persistent and nasty evil, burrowing into the very depths of her being. She tried willing it away, but that only made it worse.

Lizzie snapped open her eyes and found herself still curled up on the floor of her children's room. And the noise...the noise was still there. It wasn't evil—it was only the doorbell.

Grudgingly getting to her feet and making her way to the door, she wiped at tired and tear-stained eyes and answered it. Unfortunately, she answered it without checking the peephole and immediately wished she'd remained curled up on that floor.

"Morning, Miss Gordon," Black said, more cheerfully than she ever would have expected from him, "I appear to have awoken you."

Victor Black stood before her in the early morning sunshine, like a black hole sucking up all the light.

The noise had been evil after all.

The look on Black's face was far too smug for words—as were the words she instantly knew were forthcoming. She definitely wasn't prepared to deal with him so early in the morning—if ever at all.

"What is it, Agent Black?," Lizzie asked, squinting in the early morning light and shielding her eyes. A part of her consciousness split off to experience the golden, early morning rays, but she was instantly angered that this man had disturbed and desecrated an otherwise gorgeous experience. How many other beautiful, soulful moments had he destroyed in other people's lives? "What can I do for you?"

"May I come in?"

Lizzie hesitated, swallowing nervously. She was just thirsty, she told herself. She still sensed no good in Black nor his purpose. He knew what she did for a living, and his calling on her so early was clearly an act of intimidation.

"No...you may not. And at the risk of appearing even more rude, what, may I ask, can I do for the FBI?"

Nonplussed, Black continued. "I'm calling on you about our discussion the other day. You have made a decision, I assume?"

Black inhaled deeply, his hands neatly clasped behind him, as he appeared to casually take in the morning...calm, confident. He still wore the same basic black attire as his last visit, but for some reason, looked decidedly more sinister, now, standing before her. And Lizzie wasn't in the mood, especially since he'd just corrupted what should have been an otherwise glorious sunrise.

"Yes, I have made one. I've decided against working for you—"

"But you wouldn't be working for me."

His response was just a little too quick.

"Wouldn't I? And how wouldn't I, Agent Black, of the FBI, or who or whatever it is you really work for? How would I *not* be working for you?"

Lizzie was suddenly bombarded by a myriad of images, all angry and spiteful. As calm and collected as he might appear before her, she knew he was absolutely seething inside; would have reached out and strangled her, probably, had she let him in. She suddenly grew extremely uncomfortable about what *could* have occurred had she invited him in....

Why the hell had he felt such an acute need for her?

"I'm afraid you don't truly grasp the extent of your—"

"I'm afraid I *do*."

"May I ask why?"

"You may."

They both stared at each other. As frightened as Lizzie was, she was also extremely pissed at this man's utter presumptuousness; that he and his kind felt they could enter any person's life—at *will*—and inflict their might. Offer them a choice that, indeed, never existed. There was never any choice involved when people like Black invaded your existence.

After a moment of an unflinching stare down, Black nodded, and said, "Sorry to have disturbed you." He calmly turned and returned to his car.

As Lizzie watched him go, his back to her, she found she'd unconsciously clenched her fists and was shaking with a barely contained rage. She still felt as if he continued to watch her. Eye her. *Curse* her existence. This wasn't over, and as angry as she was with him, she was more angry with herself. She was terrified of this man—her feelings continued to confirm that—but she also realized she'd just placed herself directly into harm's way and had never given *that* any real consideration.

Her hatred for Black burned even hotter.

After all, what could she have done?

She'd been inserted into a no-win situation. There was something dreadfully wrong about this man.

Had she made the right decision?

There were sure to be nasty consequences, and she was certain he would and could make her life quite difficult. Should she have just said she was going along with him...pretend to go along until she'd found out his true purpose, a better time to oppose him?

Then what?

What would a lowly, everyday person like herself do next?

She was screwed at every turn. This was a guy who lived to fuck up other people's lives, *trained* to do just that, she was sure of it, and had been no doubt doing it his entire adult life, and now, for some odd reason, had chosen to enter her life and disrupt any normalcy she might have enjoyed. She'd had no choice. He was playing with her. Toying with her. And she'd just sealed her fate.

Lizzie watched Black drive off without so much as a backward glance. She stepped outside and sat on the stoop, head heavy in her hands. Why had all this, suddenly, and out of the blue, happened to her? She wasn't some high-profile psychic, she shouldn't have ever even been *known* to him—nor anyone else of his kind. She'd just been trying to make a living, enjoy her life, and look what came in and shit all over it.

How had she come to his attention, and why couldn't she have seen it coming?

Lizzie looked up toward the sun, as it began to fully crest the tops of the Engelmann and Blue Spruce across the lot. She sighed. *Well, kiddo, enjoy the moment, because it's the last of them you'll probably see for a long, long time.*

If ever.

3

The Man With No Name stood in the center of a granite amphitheater with only the sound and light of a burning pyre against the backdrop of a bright, starry night. Upon the carved-out steps of the amphitheater sat hundreds of children. All silent, all attentive. Each and every one had chosen to be here, and the Man With No Name knew that. He'd hand-selected every one of them. They were ready to begin, if they weren't already too late. As planned as some things were, there was always room for the unexpected. And as knowledgeable as he was, he was far from all knowing. The unexpected—that was part of the game—the excitement of thinking on your feet and shooting from the hip. Giving it your best shot. As the Man With No Name scanned the faces that sat before him, he watched them wiggle in their seats. They sensed his excitement, and they were antsy for action.

Let the games begin.

4

Sunshine or not, Lizzie just couldn't stay awake, and ended up crawling back into bed. She'd drawn her bedroom blinds and curtains, found they didn't want to play together, and grabbed a clothespin to pin them closed. She'd lost her sleep mask, was exhausted, and felt as heavy as a millstone...that undeniably profound tiredness achieved only when awoken after having fallen into a deep slumber—then having been abruptly jarred awake. It actually felt as if she hadn't slept at all, though she'd been out for several hours. In the comfortable darkness of her bedroom, she slid in between her sheets, cool and inviting, and pulled the covers snugly over her. There was something about going back to bed that felt so deliciously hooky-ish, knowing everyone else out there was getting up and going about their business, but *you* weren't. *You* were shutting everyone out and declaring, night-night, Gracie!

Lizzie repositioned on her pillow and pulled the blankets up tighter about her chin. She was so exhausted she could cry. She let the heavy, already disturbed grogginess continue its takeover of her consciousness. Like that millstone, she sank deeper and deeper into the darkness of her unconsciousness...when the goddamned phone rang.

How could she have forgotten to turn that damned thing off?

She tried to shut it out of her mind, to ignore it, but it kept ringing (and why didn't that blasted answering machine pick up?).

Grumbling, she reached over, with every intention of lifting-then-replacing handset, when she found herself holding the receiver against an ear. For what seemed an eternity, she said nothing, heard nothing.

"Hello?" she finally asked.

"Um, hello...?" came the uncertain voice.

More silence. "Who is this?" Lizzie asked, annoyed. Unformed—dark—images flashed though her mind.

"Um, sorry to disturb you, but I was, uh...given your number by a Madame Nostra...Nostra*dame*us?"

Lizzie pushed herself up on her elbows. "Who is this?"

"I'm sorry, it's, ah, Mel—"

Instant wakefulness.

"Oh—yes! *Mel!* Hello! I'm so sorry...."

Lizzie quickly tried to shake the grogginess from her system. "Yes, um, Mel, I've been waiting for your call!"

"You were?"

Lizzie replayed (or tried to replay) her memories, but the sleepiness kept getting in the way. When had all this happened? Last night? The night before? Time had a way of blurring for her. Had it really just been last night? Wow, it seemed like so much had happened already....

"Yes, and I kind of have a confession to make—and I hope you won't be upset by what I have to say...but, *I'm* the one you talked with last night. I...I had to keep up my stage persona, if you know what I mean—"

"I'd wondered."

"Yes," she said, embarrassed. "I'm so sorry for all the shenanigans—me and that fake accent—all of it."

"So...what about the psychic part?"

"Oh, no-no-no, *that's* real, honey. It's the only part of all that that's real. I'm actually getting kind of tired of it, but it pays the bills and I get to help people. I really wanted to help you last night, but just couldn't, then."

Mel sighed. "It's okay—and you did help. I just didn't know where else to turn. I feel so, I don't know...alone."

Lizzie paused briefly, thinking of Joe, and momentarily re-experienced her own acute pangs of loss. Pulling herself together, she said, "Let me see if I remember things, and I certainly don't mean to upset you, but...you said you lost your parents to an auto accident, is that correct?"

"Yes."

"I'm so sorry, Mel, really I am. There're no words to ever take away that kind of loss. It's just something we all have to work through. Have you sought any therapy?"

"No. I think that's why I called. I have no one else. Don't want to see any shrinks. I was just watching TV, saw your commercial, and it seemed to, well, *speak* to me, so I thought—why not? It seemed like something different to do. To do something while not doing something, I guess. I don't know. I just wanted to talk to someone...."

"That's why I'm here, honey. I wanted to talk with you, too. I really did sense something was wrong, but, for some strange reason, couldn't get much. I'm kind of tired right now, so I'm not operating on all cylinders, but I am willing to talk, if you don't mind."

"Okay."

5

Jack Kennedy sat before the four members of his executive council. Was he *crazy?* Here was a seventy-seven-year-old man who'd hopped a jet to Boston, then found himself sitting before his executive board—all on the whim and fancy of what...a *dream?* He'd had the fates of nations resting in his hands, and now look what he was doing—following the apparent whims of pure fancy. Just what the hell had possessed him to make this trip? The members were sure to have him removed from the board, if not, committed.

"Well, Jack," Paul Stanford said, across the table from him as he sipped his latté. "You going to tell us why you've called us together on such short notice? I have beach plans, you know." Paul and the others chuckled.

Jack also chuckled, looking down to his spotted hands. Hands that had shaken the most powerful hands in the world, carved a rescue message in a remote island coconut, and delicately traced the outline of his now-deceased wife's loving face. Now he was fidgeting and unsure of himself.

"My, ah, apologies...I think I've made a grave errah—"

When Kennedy next looked up, however, he found everyone staring at him, wide-eyed. But upon second take, saw they actually stared *past* him.

Turning, Kennedy saw them.

The two of them stared back at him in the most understanding of ways that cut to the very quick of his soul. Once he saw them, he knew this had, indeed, been the right thing to do.

Behind former President Kennedy, and before the rest of the four-member board, stood two children—a boy and a girl, dressed like any other children of their age. They appeared to be five or six years of age, but both appeared far more intelligent...and aware...than the average five or six year old. They stared back at everyone, as if they were expected to be where they were, doing exactly what they were doing. Kennedy looked back to his board members and found, much to his surprise, that they were all smiling. He turned back to the two children, who were now looking directly at him.

"Hello," Kennedy said. "It appeeuhs we've been awaiting your arrival."

"We know," the girl said, sweetly. "And we, you."

Chapter Fourteen

1

Travis awoke, instantly alert.

Lying on his side and only moving his eyes, he scanned the darkness of his bedroom.

He wasn't alone.

Someone—some*thing*—was in the room with him. He could *feel* it.

As he scanned the darkness, his gaze came to rest at a far corner, by the window. He squinted. Gradually, a tall, extra-dark outline came into indistinct focus. Travis blinked; tried to refocus on the corner again, but the silhouette was gone—if it had ever really been there in the first place. Kneading the ridge over his eyes, he turned onto his back. Man, he was getting paranoid—

"You're fucked, and you better not forget it," an angry voice said.

Travis leapt out of bed like a firecracker, fists flying. His swings connected with air, air, and air. He rushed to the wall switch and flicked it on.

He stood there, alone and in his skivvies, blood pounding in his ears.

The bedroom was empty.

He checked the closet…underneath the bed.

Nothing.

He grabbed a baseball bat from the closet. His breathing rapid and shallow, he darted about the rest of the house, flicking on all the lights as he went.

Still nothing.

Tired, and coming down from his adrenaline high, he collapsed onto the living-room couch.

That hadn't been just any voice he'd heard. There had been a specific energy to it.

Black.

Things around or about that guy didn't just happen for no reason, and he was absolutely the last person you ever wanted to visit you—in dreams or otherwise. The first time he'd met him had been at The Center several years ago. He'd felt Black's penetrating gaze burning a hole through his soul like a laser before he'd even turned around to actually see him. As he was introduced to him and shook his hand, he couldn't help but wonder how many people he'd killed. His forced smiles were disarmingly unnerving, unnatural, and he always felt as if Black had already known the answers to every question he'd asked of anyone. And that was before Travis'd been trained as a psychic spy.

Oh, yeah, he was *fucked.*

2

Lizzie dreamed of blue and gray and blood and gore.

In her dream, a battalion of Civil War Federals were yelling and charging and rattling down a decline into Confederate forces.

As she watched the charge, her focus zoomed in on one soldier-in-blue, in particular. She didn't recognize the face, though she knew the essence of the man behind it. There was also another, a Confederate soldier, who stole her attention. A shudder ran through her. He, too, may have been wearing different skin, different clothes, and a different face, but she also knew him for who he was.

Victor Black.

Lizzie "pulled back" to observe the battle. The Federal charge rammed into Confederate lines, and the two men actually recognized each other's presence, though neither understood what or how they felt what they felt.

Lizzie also saw, in curious disbelief, a girl and boy, both about six, parachuting in under a full-moon night sky, though the battle took place in broad daylight. The girl and boy landed and observed the battle from the treeline at the edge of the field. She attempted to zoom in on them, but her attention was forcibly brought back to the first soldier she'd observed. Now in the thick of hand-to-hand combat, he was bayoneting a man who'd once killed him on another battlefield, centuries past, on far-away soil. They'd both worn armor then. His current opponent had worn the armor of the Roman army, while he'd worn that of barbarian leather. Lizzie returned to the current battle, and found this man to be John Fitzgerald Kennedy. The one-who-would-be-called JFK knew he was on a mission on this battlefield, knew there was something he was supposed to do, though he couldn't clarify it. He had other things presently occupying his full attention—like not getting killed.

Lizzie fast-forwarded to the next important moment during the battle, and saw the Civil War Black swinging around a busted-up musket in the hand-to-hand mêlée. Behind him was the JFK persona, still using his bayoneted musket—which had just been knocked from his hands. JFK sidestepped the attack and immediately lunged for his attacker with his bare hands, grabbing him by the throat. JFK channeled all his hate and fear and anger into killing this man—and broke his neck. Ducking another miscellaneous swing of weaponry, he picked up his musket, and turned—and came face to face with Black, also covered in blood and grime, also with his broken weapon poised before him. They stared at each other. Neither had ever before lain eyes on the other until this moment—in that life, that battle—but both had known they'd been searching each other out an entire lifetime. Or two. Unconsciously, both shared dreams each'd had of each other...of this battle, this place...of other times and other bodies, but always...*them.*

Before Black could react, JFK broke free from his trance first. Black was too far away for JFK to lunge after him with his rifle bayonet, so he shot a hand to a scabbard and withdrew a knife. In a blink of an eye, he flicked the blade at Black, who'd expertly caught it in his upper left chest. Black lunged for JFK, but before he could make contact, another soldier unintentionally intercepted Black's path, and Black's musket ended up hitting him instead. Black and JFK attempted to re-engage, but scores of fighting bodies quickly pressed in around them, and both had to deal with other attackers....

They would meet again, Lizzie knew. Had already.

Lizzie looked up to the contradictory full-moon night and sunny sky—and was pulled from the dream.

She found herself inserted into more mundane dreams, and was quickly whisked away into unconsciousness....

3

Travis hadn't been able to sleep once he'd gone back to bed, and hadn't been able to put aside the disembodied-voice incident. Somehow, he felt, it hadn't been a nightmare at all. Someone *had* been there, he was certain of it—and Black *had* been known to dabble in remote viewing himself, but it had been *years*.

Granted, dreams weren't in the technical sense *remote viewing*, but how far off were they, really? And what about RV *projection?* Like out-of-body projections? When Travis'd tried to zero in on the incident, all he got were weird sensations…like tasting color, hearing sight.

He looked to the clock (five a.m.) and decided to stay up and get in his morning run a little early. Dressed and ready to go, he grabbed his keys as he headed out the door, and again glanced at the time.

Four a.m.

Travis slammed to a stop, staring at the clock.

Four a.m.?

He went to the kitchen clock, then looked to his watch—to the curtained window. Dark.

Four a.m.—to be sure.

Okay, weird, but not entirely unheard of. This was one of his own, what he called, "Freaky Shit" experiences and it happened to all of his group from time to time, more often than any of them preferred. It came with the psychic territory they frequented. It wasn't just about time, there were other instances of Freaky Shit, everything from extremely elevated levels of déjà vu, to spontaneous and conscious out-of-body experiences, and usually, of course, at the most inappropriate of times. One classified report described one remote viewer as having had a spontaneous out-of-body projection while driving on the D.C-area Beltway. That remote viewer had died from injuries she'd sustained from the subsequent traffic accident she'd caused.

Not a big deal, Travis decided to continue with his run, anyway—which went uneventfully—but when he'd returned and cleaned up, the weird feelings returned, and he still hadn't quite felt "all there." Time continued to feel simultaneously elongated and compressed. He just wasn't quite synching up with reality. He didn't know if his nightmare had caused everything, or if the phenomenon itself had caused the *nightmare*. Whatever it was, it wasn't correcting itself. Things should have righted by now, especially with the run and focusing on things-physical. Though this was nothing new to him, the art and skill was in going along with things until they played themselves out—until you "reacclimatized" back into your current reality. Things always returned to normal—as long as you didn't kill yourself in a car crash—and it was weird that his reacclimatization was taking so long, but perhaps it was precisely *because* he was outside of the "time" he needed for things to take, for things to dampen back out and return to current reality, that things *seemed* so long in coming....

Travis cleaned up and left the house. A handful of miles down the road he pulled into Becky's Place, a local restaurant that served the best blueberry pancakes in Virginia. Becky McAllister, who owned and operated the restaurant, usually opened around six, but it was only five-forty. There were no customer vehicles parked in the parking lot, and though lights were on inside the restaurant, the "We Ain't Here" sign was still up. Travis pulled up into a slot directly before the entrance, and shut off the engine. Rubbing his eyes, he again mused at his timing. He'd sworn it was much closer to six. Placing his head back against the headrest, he again recalled the nightmare-shadow in his bedroom, and tilted his face to better see the early morning rays of the sun, as they began to peek up and over a nearby ridge. He closed his eyes. The sound of quiet was beautiful...the distant, quiet roar of early morning wind across the tops of acres and acres of hard and soft-woods...the smells of cooking...the laughter of children....

Travis opened his eyes.

The parking lot was filled with cars and trucks, even two eighteen-wheelers sat purring at the far end of the parking lot. He shot a glance to his watch.

Six-fifteen.

"*Damn* it."

Travis clambered out of the Jeep and made his way into the restaurant. Several patrons looked up as he entered. He nodded back to them.

"Morning, Trav," Edna, one of the two servers, greeted. Travis took a seat at a booth. As he looked toward the door, he saw two kids enter the place by themselves, casting him long glances.

When he blinked...they were gone.

Edna came over with a menu and a much-needed cup of coffee.

"Here ya go, hero. How ya doin this morning?"

"Not all there, 'mfraid." He picked up the coffee. "I *really* need this."

Travis took a sip, picked up the menu, and winced behind it, out of sight from Edna.

What the hell was the matter with him?

Two other patrons entered the restaurant.

"So...will it be the usual—or you need more time?"

Travis put down the menu. "I really don't know why I even bother to look at this thing anymore," he said. "Sure, usual, please."

Edna scribbled on her ticket. "One order of Blueberry Mountain, three eggs scrambled, no toast. You got it," she said, and departed.

Travis kicked back, took another sip of coffee, and acknowledged a wave from Becky herself, back behind the counter, busy with breakfast orders.

"Hey, Trav, great to see you!" Buddy LaRouque said, as he took up the booth seat across from him.

Travis shot up from his seat, but his legs rammed into the table's edge, forcing him back down and upsetting his table's contents—namely knocking over the sugar container.

"What the *hell?*" he said.

"What do you mean, 'What the hell?'" Buddy LaRouque said, grinning.

Confused, but all smiles, Travis reached out across to shake—

Nothing.

No Buddy LaRouque nowhere. No Buddy LaRouque hand to shake. All there was, was air—and lots of it—and Travis Norton reaching out across an empty table to shake a non-existent hand.

Travis stared at his hand. Brought it up before him. Saw Edna and some others looking to him from all the racket he'd caused slamming into the table. He smiled embarrassedly to no one in particular, shook his head, and had another sip of coffee.

Okay, he thought, *that was weird. Nothing like that had ever happened bef—*

He closed his eyes tight, then again looked up…and *again*…Buddy LaRouque sitting directly across the table from him, all wide-eyed and bushy-tailed.

"Hey, bud," Buddy said, "what's *up*, eh? You're supposed to be government trained, roll with this, would ya?"

Buddy's hand was still extended.

Flabbergasted, again the reflexes and instincts kicked in, because he saw—thought he saw, *swore* he saw—Buddy LaRouque sitting across from him, hand extended in a continued gesture of greeting. Human-American protocol dictated immediate extension of your own hand in return. So that's what he did, but as he reached out to shake hands, the image again disappeared, and Travis was once more left holding his hand out before him like an idiot.

"You okay, hero?" Edna asked, returning with his breakfast. She stood beside him, holding his order and ticket. Stood the sugar container back on its base and rearranged the jelly holder.

Travis looked up.

Where the hell was he?

What was he doing, and who *was* this?

"Um, sorry—I really don't...*Edna?*" He shook his head. "Sorry," he continued, "I'm having kind of a rough start."

Edna looked him over. "Well, if it's any consolation, you look fine." Then she cast a quick look to the rest of the room. "Can I ask a question, though?" she asked in a hushed tone, placing his food before him.

Travis massaged his brow, looking down at the table. Without looking up, he said, "Sure."

"We were all wondering," she said, clasping her hands together before her, "why do you keep reaching out in front of you? Should we be worried?"

Travis peered up from behind massaging fingers to her—past her to the rest of the customers, some of whom looked away as he made eye contact.

"No...I think..."

He glanced down to his plate, and saw his food partially eaten, and that he'd now—apparently—held a fork with pancake on it, ready for an apparent return-trip to his mouth. He smacked his lips together and tasted maple syrup and pancake. Smelled the rich maple syrup and pancake aroma coming up from the table before him, and even saw how he'd pushed off the butter to one side of the plate. There was even less coffee in his coffee cup. Yup, coffee taste was in there, too.

"Spasms."

"Excuse me?"

"Muscle spasms," Travis repeated. "I'm having really bad ones this morning. You know, like leg or eye twitches? I've always been prone to them," he lied, "but sometimes—like now—they get out of control, but thanks for asking."

Edna narrowed her gaze. "Never seen anything like *that* before...."

Edna turned to leave, then quickly returned to him. Eyeballed him. "You *sure* you're all right?"

Travis dropped his pancake-laden fork to his plate and smiled, reaching out to her. At least *she* was real.

"Really. I'm *fine*. But, thank you for your concern," he said.

Edna smiled, squeezed his hand, and cautiously moved on, occasionally glancing back in his direction as she worked her way across the restaurant.

Travis looked down to his partially eaten breakfast. Pancakes and eggs. Something was obviously and severely weird. *Why was he seeing Buddy LaRouque sitting before him when he really wasn't there?*

Or *was* he?

In fact—

Travis froze.

In fact what? What was it about Buddy?

Was there "anything" about him? Where'd he been? Didn't they normally have breakfast together, or...

Or *what?*

Nothing was making sense. Only that—

Without looking up, Travis saw a hand reach out from across the table and to his plate. In the hand was a down-turned fork. Buddy La-Rouque was again sitting before him, only this time cutting off a piece of his pancake. Travis stole side glances to his unintended audience.

"Look," Buddy casually began, "it's pretty hard having a conversation all by your lonesome, at least it is for me," he said, chuckling, "but if you don't eat these, *I* will!"

Travis saw him, clear as day. Across the table from him. Munching on pancake and smiling that big French-Canadian, shit-eating grin of his. Travis inhaled, then listened to all the normal breakfast-rich sounds and smells associated with restaurants; *they* seemed real...the smell of coffee and cooked meat...eggs and pancakes...the normal early morning rustle of subdued conversation and clanking of silverware and plates.

"Look, we gotta talk," Buddy said, reaching across for more. "I know we haven't seen much of each other lately," he said, eating Travis's pancake, "but things have been prit-tee busy, eh? Mind if I have some of your eggs?"

Travis looked around the room. Some continued to glance toward him, but, for the most part, most seemed to have lost interest and were back into their own little worlds and food. Travis looked back to Buddy, who, this time, remained there, still eating his food.

"Hey!," Buddy said, "you listening to me? Focus here, okay, pal?" he said, making a "V" with his index and middle fingers, alternating them between his and Travis's eyes. Then his voice lowered and he looked around. "I found oot some things...aboot The Cent—"

Then he was gone.

That was almost more of a shock than having had him show up in the first place. While he'd been sitting there, it was like he'd always been there, and now he just...disappeared...*while* he watched.

"You better start eating some of those before someone thinks we're dating," Buddy's disembodied voice said. Travis hurriedly looked around searched the booth before him, both above and below the table. No Buddy.

"What's going on here?" Travis whispered, trying to remain casual. "How come only I can see you?"

Buddy again reappeared, but this time had a plate of his own omelette and pancakes before him. Buddy was in the mid-action of sitting down with a bottle of Tabasco in hand. He immediately slathered it all over his Big Daddy Trucker Omelette. "Gotta love this stuff, eh?" he said, capping the bottle and placing it back on the table between them. "Man, if The Motherland had this stuff, it wouldn't be sew damned cold up there! Oooh-*wee!*"

Travis leaned forward, trying not to look crazy to the restaurant's patrons. He picked up and replaced the Tabasco bottle. He was also unable to avoid validating that Buddy LaRouque was—*indeed*—again, sitting before him and having breakfast—his own, this time.

"Look, I told you, *eat*—I'm not talking anymore until you eat. You're such a skinny shit, eh!"

Travis sat back, shot another glance around the room, and began poking at his food. Suddenly his appetite wasn't what it had been.

Buddy continued talking, but Travis was having a hard time paying attention. It was suddenly very hard to think...to focus. It was like...he was being stretched across some weird psychic canvases...two of them, one of which he wasn't supposed to be on. He felt his mind expand, his body tingled...vibrating in a deep, internally unnerving, way. He looked back to Buddy, but he was gone. As was Buddy's food, of course. The Tabasco sauce remained. Had probably always been there. Looking to other tables, he spotted several bottles of the stuff.

This time Travis caught on, and though he still cast a nervous glare around the room, he did so unobtrusively, and continued to pick at his food until Buddy returned.

"Well," Buddy said, fading back in, "that was great!" Buddy's cheery demeanor turned serious. "Okay, enough play," Buddy's tone got serious. "I've found oot aboot one of your former presidents—"

"Could you please get to the point? You keep fading out—"

"—but I'm not sure this is even the place to do it," Buddy said.

Buddy wiped his mouth with a napkin and set it aside. His form continued to fade in and out.

"*Buddy*," Travis insisted, whispering, but Buddy kept right on talking. Travis watched him. When he was sure no one was looking—or pretty confident, anyway—he slid a spoon across the table at him. Predictably, it slid right on through Buddy's image, hit the booth's seatback, and landed in the booth seat. Buddy hadn't moved an inch to react to it—or chide him about it. Travis tossed his knife at him. Same thing, only this time the utensil bounced off the seat and clattered to the floor. Travis acted as if it was an accident, as others again looked over to him.

"*Buddy*," Travis whispered, "I've been sleeping with Gina—"

Still nothing. Buddy was carrying on his own conversation, so, Travis began to eat…and listen. But, Buddy kept fading in and out. It was getting tiresome. Travis pushed away his plate and picked up the ticket Edna had deposited when she'd delivered his food.

"*C'mon, c'mon…*" he said, anxiously, "*come back….*"

But as he sat there, Buddy never rematerialized. In fact, Travis felt as if his entire presence was now…gone. And there was a nagging alarm going off about something *about* Buddy.

He sipped his coffee.

Still nothing.

Again, massaging his brow, Travis casually glanced about the room and found those two children he'd seen earlier staring at him. They stood against a wall on the far side of the room, alongside a table full of truckers and their glares. A "Liar's Table" sign hung above the table. He stared at the children and the truckers. *Hey, why not take a picture, it'll last longer*, one meaty stare from a trucker suggested. Travis looked away.

An involuntary spasm caused him to crush the receipt, and when he did that, it seemed to pull him outside of himself. He blinked, wiped his face, and blinked again. Okay, maybe he should just go. Get into work, and try to put this little episode behind him—or prepare for whatever was to happen next. But he really wanted to know what Buddy had to tell him about The Center, and what that nagging feeling about *Buddy* was in the first place.

Travis got up and pulled out his wallet, when he momentarily swore he was holding a double-blind tasking envelope. *Okay*, he thought, *let's get with the program*, and again forced his wallet back into his point of view. He pulled out a couple of bills, paused, then pulled out a five, leaving that for Edna. She more than deserved that for his public display of weirdness. Travis went to the register, paid his ticket, said a fond and uncomfortable "later" to both Becky and Edna…and departed. But once he got into his Jeep a realization struck that actually caused him to break out into a profuse and frigid sweat.

Who the hell was Buddy LaRouque?

Chapter Fifteen

1

Mel Roberts had another Vernors and sat back on the couch. He felt worlds better after having talked with Lizzie. It was amazing how much better a person could feel after having unloaded a heavily burdened mind; finally...*someone* to confide in—to...*talk* to....

But as he'd replayed the events of his life to Lizzie, well, somehow the recent events just hadn't seemed right. Something was missing. He knew the reality of the facts themselves, but something about them just didn't sit right. Yes, there *had been* a car crash—an accident—yes, his parents *had been* killed, and, yes, he *had been* left on his own, to forever fend for his parentless self, in his Family of One.

Was that so hard to believe?

So many others had survived on their own without adult guidance, and at younger ages...hadn't they? And had he absolutely no other kin—aunts, uncles, nor cousins?—to help raise him? He didn't know much about the law, but wouldn't the state...or some agency...appoint *someone* to oversee him? There was just something weird about *everything.*

And there was more.

He'd only just realized it after the phone call, and it was something that quite disturbed him. He felt—and this was hard to even admit to himself—but, about his parents, he actually felt...

Emotionless.

"How can I even *think* such a thing!" he said, shooting to his feet.

But the thought was there...and there, he'd said it. Put it out into the universe, as his mom would have said (would—had she—*really?*). After the initial outburst at finding the upstairs pictures, he'd found that all familial emotion (substitute "love"; there was no longer any need to distance himself from the facts) actually seemed to have waned.

And while talking to Lizzie he'd never said anything about "love" (it'd occurred to him during the course of their conversation), and he'd felt extremely awkward discussing—*using*—the word. *Feeling* the actual emotion.

"Love"…it just wasn't there.

How could he not *love his parents?*

Had they been evil? Deserved to die?

No. They'd been there his entire life, had been the best parents in the world, only to—one day—disappear. To forever be gone. Just like that.

How the hell could he not have any feelings toward them? About their abrupt departure from this world…from his life?

Mel stared at the television, his only family, now. Stared at the wall behind it…the walls surrounding him and the TV…the couch…the floor. Tried to let whatever intangibility might be drowning deep within him to bubble its way to the surface, where (he told himself) he could finally identify, grab, and categorize it. Make whatever it was that was wrong with him make sense.

Did he have any *feelings toward his parents?*

He sat in the flickering light of the television. Stared blankly through the television screen.

None. Nothing.

Not a damned thing.

2

John Fitzgerald Kennedy sat behind a high-end, highly polished, cherry conference table, with what looked like a dossier opened before him.

He felt on *fire*.

A clock ticked quietly in the background. To his right, on the table, was a partially emptied-but-still-damp-with-condensation glass of iced tea. He stared at it.

Diverting his attention to the pen he held, he thoughtfully rolled it about in his fingers, then looked to the hand itself. Bursting with incredible energy, and not at all sure why he did so, he tossed away the pen and shot to his feet, his entire body *electrified*.

My God, he thought, unsure of what to do with himself, as he paced a quick couple of steps back and forth. *What the hell is going on here?*

Kennedy looked about the room. It was familiar—the original conference room at The Center, circa 1970s. Kennedy rushed to the adjacent bathroom—to the mirror—and peered in at himself.

No. This can't be....

John Fitzgerald Kennedy stared into the mirror. At an image that couldn't possibly be—not in a million years. Kennedy alternately touched the mirror image and his physical face.

Blinked.

Stretched his mouth.

Felt and pushed about his nose and cheeks.

He was goddamned young *again!*

He took a step back, performed a confused and nervous two-step; emitted a surprised half-grunt, then again shoved his face before the mirror.

Touched.

Examined.

Flexed.

He looked around the bathroom, then slowly made his way back out into the richly paneled executive conference room.

Looked to his attire.

It was all as he remembered it—it had to be a dream—but it didn't *feel* like one...

Good Lord...he was really *young* again!

How young?

He looked for a calendar.

There, on a wall.

Tuesday, June 5, 1973.

He was fifty-six years old!

He wouldn't throw that outta bed. Definitely young enough for a previously seventy-seven-year-old man!

Back to the bathroom mirror.

As he again looked into that long-ago face he thought he'd never, ever see again, he suddenly grew short of breath in a microburst of hyperventilation and leaned over the sink. Momentarily closing his eyes, he managed to slow his breathing. Again looked back up into that long-lost visage.

As sure as he was breathing, the face staring back at him was his very own—that of a fifty-six-year-old man.

Time, it seems, had indeed—somehow—rolled back.

He flexed his arms, inhaled deeply, and stretched.

By God. It was real. *It was truly no-shit real!*

Kennedy returned to his desk; sat in the leather-bound chair. Stared into the open space of the empty and richly adorned-and-lit conference room. Not only was he young again, *but he was also back at The Center…*which could only mean one thing…

He slammed the palms of his hands down on the desk and chair.

Both felt solid and real enough.

Stomped his feet on the carpeted floor.

Also solid, real, and appropriately hushed.

Pinched himself—okay, that hurt.

Kennedy took in as much of his surroundings and mental state as possible.

Did this feel like a dream?

No…it felt like he was seventy-seven-suddenly-turned-fifty-six, *that's* what it damn well felt like.

Kennedy flexed and unflexed his hands, high on the energy of returned vigor electrifying his body and soul—even if vigor meant fifty-six versus twenty-six. Who was he to quibble? He was truly in his fifties—again—*truly* young again, but with all the knowledge and accumulation of his later years intact.

For what more could a person ask?

(*Jackie…*)

He felt like a *god*…when a sudden sobering wave of weariness hit him.

Did that also mean he had to re-live the entire past twenty-one years over again?

Kennedy's shoulders slumped.

He didn't think he had that kind of stamina—nor inclination—to do things over.

"Mister President?"

Kennedy looked up. Evelyn Lincoln—still his personal secretary—had poked her head into the room. She looked exactly as he remembered her, in *her* mid-sixties. And she hadn't noticed anything odd or unusual about him, so he really must appear as normal as he'd looked in '73.

"Mr. Sorensen to see you."

And, yes, Ted had stayed with him, as well! They'd been a well-oiled machine in those heady, adrenaline-fueled days.

Kennedy quickly retraced his thoughts. Ted Sorenson. Why would he be here to see him? What were the pressing issues of the day? He shot a look back to the papers back on the conference table.

Interviews.

June 5, 1973—*who were they interviewing?*

Kennedy headed back to that dossier.

"Mister President," Ted said, purposefully striding into the office and interrupting Kennedy's return to the dossier, "sorry to bother you, sir," he said, nodding in acknowledgement to Evelyn as she left, "but our candidate is here."

Program One. Okay, think…yes, they would have been discussing appointees about this time, whom to put in charge of—

Rosen. *Howard* Rosen. *Yes, they were supposed to interview one Howard Rosen.*

"Ah, yes…Howard Rosen—send him in—"

Sorenson looked to him strangely.

"Sir, there is no 'Howard Rosen.' It's Victor Black."

Jesus Christ, Victor Black was the front runner?

It was as if his memory had done a sudden about-face remove-and-replace, and a totally *new* memory supplanted. A cold sweat enveloped him.

Black had been the man he'd appointed in '73, and was the man he was apparently going to—or *supposed to*, anyway—re-appoint, now—*today.*

Shit!

Was he doomed to repeat history? Could he change things? Even if—in his mind—he knew he shouldn't appoint Victor Black, would history allow him to take a different route…to change its course? And if he did, who was to say he couldn't take over the program later, if not appointed now? He did have twenty years to do so….

"Sir?"

"Yes, Ted?"

"Black, sir? He's just outside." Ted looked to him, concerned. "Are you all right, sir?"

"Yes, yes, ah, I'm fine, Ted, nevah bettah, and really, you should start calling me 'Jack'…."

Kennedy had to watch how he reacted to things—especially regarding Black. He couldn't betray his thoughts, what he knew. If he was going to change history, he had to do so on the sly, watch *how* he was going to change it, and, he couldn't, by any means, ever show his hand—especially with Black waiting outside his office this very moment.

Black…the thought of meeting the man, here, *appointing* him, thoroughly disgusted him.

Whomever he was now—then—all those years ago—*now*, good Lord it was confusing—Kennedy knew what he would become and every fiber of his being revolted in its knowledge. Even if he'd meant well in '73, during these interviews, Kennedy knew he was going to turn into the most vile and corrupt set of genetics on the planet.

"Bring him in," Kennedy said, pensively folding his hands into a steeple on the desk before him.

Kennedy tried to recall all he knew of their encounter. What meeting would this be for them? First? Fourth? Damn, this was going to be tricky. He had a good memory, but, *Christ*, this was over twenty years ago!

"Mister President…Victor Black."

Kennedy approached Black in his usual, outgoing and stately manner, extending his hand in greeting. It was all he could do to keep from retching.

"Mistah Black—Victah—it is a pleazah," Kennedy said.

Victor Black, dressed in a dark conservative suit and a red power tie, extended his hand in return.

But, there was something decidedly different about him, from what Kennedy remembered…even way back then.

"Mr. President—it is an honor."

Their hands locked in a firm greeting, but as Kennedy looked into Black's penetrating gaze, he could have sworn there was more there than just first-meeting introductions. Maybe it was Kennedy's twenty years of experience and maturity since this event, but whatever it was—and whether or not he had recognized it on their first meeting all those years ago—Kennedy uneasily sensed that there was more to those deep, dark eyes—and they were dark—than belied the soft and respectful tones of their current encounter.

Black, it appeared, was also hiding something.

3

Well, that's simply insane, Mel thought, staring into the TV. How could he not have any feelings toward his parents?

He was simply in a state of shock. That had to be it. He'd been through hell...the flurry of the situation, the doctors, hospital, autopsies—the *funeral*. He was simply mentally and spiritually exhausted. That had to be it. It wasn't that he had no feelings toward his parents, but that he felt *so much* pain and loss that he was, plain and simply, *exhausted*. Shattered. It was bad enough to have your parents die, but to have them die in a violent car wreck...to imagine what they'd gone through in their final moments on earth...the pain, the agony...it just stretched the emotional limits of any family member.

And then to find yourself totally and utterly alone. On your own. Where previously there had been the constant hum and banter of activity throughout the house...now it was just you, kid. You, the TV, and a dark room. No one to talk to, talk at...no one with whom to eat dinner...watch TV, or play games.

No one to parent. To guide.

You expect to see or hear them at every turn, to hear them call out your name at any moment:

"Mel! Take out the trash!"

"Mel...did you finish your homework?"

"Mel—would you help with the dishes?"

But, no—none of that any more. Now, it was just...

Mel. And the SCI FI channel.

Mel sipped iced tea.

Iced tea?

He looked to the glass.

No, it was Vernors.

He lifted the soda and examined it. Grunted.

That was weird.

As he took another sip, he chuckled and rubbed at his nose, wiped at his cheeks as bubbles ran up inside his nostrils. Smiled. It felt good to smile. He set the soda down. Looked back to the television. *Something Wicked This Way Comes* played, but the movie was presently fading into a commercial. 1-900-*PsiKick*. Man, did they have a monopoly on this station, or what?

Come...call us, the New Age-y disembodied Caribbean dialect beckoned, *we have all the answers to* all *your problems* (complete with the "this is adult entertainment only" disclaimer at the bottom of the screen). The screen filled with neat looking stars and planets, and synthetic, New Age-y, music. *And with this special offer,* the commercial continued, *you now have your first reading absolutely* free! *We know psychic hotlines are a dime a dozen, that's why we're so convinced that once you try the* PsiKick *hotline, we'll make a believer out of you! We're giving you your first reading—* free—*in its entirety! For up to twenty minutes! No strings attached! Call our number now, 1-900-PsiKick! Our psychics are standing by!*

Then the commercial cut to shots of several individual (so-called) psychics, doing their thing, all complete with exotic accents. Mel wondered how many of them were faking it—not only their accents, but their abilities. He thought of Madame Nostradameus. *Lizzie.* Had she been faking her ability along with her accent? She'd said she was for real, had even profusely apologized for faking her Romani accent—but how much of that could he believe? If she lied about one thing—

He had to believe her. The feeling *he* picked up from her was that she had been telling the truth.

Was he in the habit of trusting his feelings?

God, it was like he had to totally relearn everything about himself!

He was so tired of questioning every little thought and deed…but she had given him her home phone. He'd never thought any of those people running across the screen of his TV set would ever do something like that with a caller. That had been gutsy on her part. She didn't know him from Adam—or maybe she did; she *was* supposed to be psychic—and had taken a chance, for which he was eternally grateful. It had felt so good to be able to talk with her, and he really wished he could call her again. She should be working,

(*our psychics are standing by!*)

shouldn't she?

As he watched the commercial fade out, another took its place…an odd little commercial. Simple white words on a black background said:

When was the last time you phoned a friend?

And was gone.

"Okay," Mel grunted, "I get the hint."

4

President Kennedy sat through the 1973 interview with Victor Black as if he'd just downed a gallon of pure, high-grade Columbian caffeine. The three of them sat around the conference room table.

Would everything play itself out exactly as it had already done? Could he really change the outcome? Did just the mere reemergence of his *presence* change things? He couldn't get around it, he owed it to history to change it—to at least *try*. Black was not someone he wanted in the history books, in principle nor footnote.

Sorensen had already indicated and Kennedy had concurred—at least in the original version—that Black was a virtual shoe-in. He had plenty of qualifications, a highly sensitive two-year CIA stint in the Asian theater, was an excellent, highly decorated remote viewer at The Center, had taken on increased responsibility in his remote viewer unit, and nailed the interview with insightful spot-on answers to each and every question. Almost too perfectly.

And there was that other thing that just wouldn't go away…what Kennedy had seen when Black'd first showed up "today," in this version of that "original" interview, anyway.

That look.

And whenever he cast a sidelong glance to Kennedy during *this* interview, and Black hadn't thought he was looking—or maybe he did and was just letting him know—his look screamed *Look pal, you're not the only one here for a second time. I know what's on your mind. Don't even think about changing things. Just fulfill your role like a good little historical pawn, and let things roll along like they already have…and we'll both be on our way….*

But, the more Kennedy sat before this man, the more fidgety and hot he grew.

He had a bad taste in his mouth.

These thoughts—his very *thoughts*—he knew, were not a part of the initial interview twenty-one years ago, because if they had been, he'd never have appointed Black to the position. So, new developments *could* emerge, things *could* change—in the past—his new behavior proved it. He was here, now…and his thoughts *were* different from those in '73.

So, maybe this was his chance.

And how had Black been so "knowledgeable" during that—this—

interview? He hadn't remembered that. *This Black was different from the original one*—he was certain of it.

So, Black was also—somehow—in on whatever was going on. If that was the case, then Kennedy had no choice. He simply could not afford to allow history to continue on as it had—or *would*.

God*damn*, this was maddening.

He had to change it, was *morally bound* to. There was, simply, no other option. He had to seize control.

As if suddenly awakened from a dream, Kennedy felt the wrongness of the situation in all its entirety; felt the wrongness of the situation in all its *philosophy*. Even if it cost him his own place in history—or his life—he knew what he had to do. Hell, he'd already been seventy-seven—had already lived a full life. Now, he was a seventy-seven year old in a fifty-six-year-old body. It wasn't a dream, it wasn't his imagination, *he was actually goddamned fifty-six years old, and was actually goddamned back in the original conference room at The Center, in 1973.* Tossing dialogue with Ted Sorensen and Victor Black—his future sworn enemy—and he had absolutely no idea how any of this had happened. He actually *felt* the chair against his butt, *felt* the fear constricting his chest…and the fact that he was very, very thirsty.

He cleared his throat.

Yeah, *thirsty*.

It didn't get any more real than this. This was in-his-face *real*. The air crackled with tension, the fate of the world's future—in very real terms—resting on his every move. He had to act *now* before things even had a hint of once more heading south. He remembered how the interview had ended. It had ended with Ted casting him a knowing look, as he and Black rose to their feet and came together around the conference table, Ted surreptitiously announcing that *Mr. Black, you have the appointment.* And it was about to happen at any moment.

Black quickly, casually, cast him another sidelong glance.

He knew, didn't he? The bastard actually fucking *knew*.

Kennedy shot to his feet.

As he did so, everything flew into slow motion. In his mind, Kennedy's thoughts raced, and he heard the words as they had been so casually uttered twenty years ago issuing from Ted's mouth, though the slow motion had slowed down Ted's lips and delivery. *Well, Victor, I think that about wraps it,* he was beginning to say. Kennedy desperately needed to interrupt those words, but felt his body was sprinting through a swamp. As Ted and Black got to their feet, Black looked to him, and in slow motion Kennedy saw Black smile a wicked, knowing grin.

An actual *sneer.*

Black then began to turn to him and slowly reached into his inside jacket pocket.

Kennedy knew that running through water or not, what he was reaching for inside his jacket meant him no-good. Just as Kennedy knew he had to risk not only history, but his life, Black had, apparently, already made that same decision. There was something inside that jacket with his name on it, and Kennedy knew it—and knew that Black *knew* he knew it—but was still willing to risk his life to keep history as it had already been.

But how could that happen, if Black ended up giving up his own life?

The questions hurt the mind to even consider, and he had no time to wax philosophical. Kennedy wished for something, *anything,* to interfere and upset Black's plans. He had no idea what to do—only that he had to *act.* He was changing history if he did anything differently, risking everything, considering the impact Program One had had on the world—

Especially if he was wrong.

Ted, totally oblivious to what was going on, was now in midsentence, half-way to the standing position, when Kennedy unceremoniously catapulted toward Black, who, still sneering, was also still reaching into his jacket lapel, eyes riveted on him as he approached Ted.

(Well, Victor, I think that about—)

As Kennedy launched into Black, images of Blackett Strait filled his mind, perhaps the last time he'd ever had to be a man of action—*physical* action—and he was not about to shy away from the challenge. During his lunge forward, Kennedy grabbed onto Black the way those drowning and injured men he'd rescued in that straight had latched on to the floating PT-109 debris—and he seized and openly embraced the presented opportunity.

No turning back now.

It was as if his body had had a mind of its own. Kennedy, jaw set and gaze burning into Black, willed himself to hurtle *fast* and *hard* into Black before he could pull whatever it was from inside that lapel pocket—prayed to God that he be allowed to set things *right* and in the least damaging of ways to history and its people. Even as the slow motion kept things at a manageable pace, Kennedy's mind continued to race, and he saw how Black had finally recognized his intentions. In that instant, Black's expression changed. Kennedy's only hope was that he got there first, and he prayed so hard he swore he popped a vein.

Fifty-six-year-old ex-President Kennedy landed squarely and forcefully into forty-five-year-old Victor Black, ramming into his left shoulder, forcing him backward into the table and chairs. The two then tumbled with a hefty *thud!* onto the carpeted floor. Kennedy heard a "pop" as he ground into Black's shoulder. With one hand, Kennedy forced Black's hand—the one part way into his jacket—away, and with the other deftly swept inside the lapel and went for whatever was there. But in order to do that he had to twist his body into a better, more commanding position, and in doing so (he internally smiled), ground harder into Black's shoulder. He felt and heard a distinct and sickening crunch and snap. Kennedy had one brief moment to stare into Black's eyes as he landed with his full weight on top of him. He could feel the venom Black willed into him, the tautness of his body, but ignored those as his hand found its target, wrapped around it, and in one swift-and-dexterous movement removed it from the pocket—barely in time to avoid Black's own attempt at thwarting his offensive. For a fraction of an instant Black and Kennedy eyed each other, frozen in time. Images of brutal hand-to-hand mêlée flashed through Kennedy's mind, one where he and Black were again combating each other....

But, in the end, it was Kennedy who'd gotten to the weapon first (in that mêlée—or this conference room?).

Black had tried another attempt to grab it back from Kennedy, but it was at this point that Ted Sorensen had sprung into action and was presently assisting the President to his feet. Kennedy quickly slid the purloined object into his own jacket pocket, as Sorenson's hands went to his shoulders. He didn't know if he'd actually sneered back to Black—but had felt as if he had…and it was a *good* feeling.

"Mr. President! *Sir!* Are you all right? *Sir?*" Ted begged, sizing him up.

As Kennedy was "righted" back to his feet, Black got to his, and backed away from the President, head down. Confused, Ted eyed both men, checking for injuries.

"I'm, ah, *fine*, Ted—"

"What happened?" Ted asked, "Are you all right, sir? Mr. Black?"

Black continued to back away, wincing as he straightened out, and briefly glared the hatred of Hell itself at Kennedy.

"Well," Kennedy began, and he found it quite amusing at how

easily he formed that smile on his face as he lied to Black, "I, ah, do apologize, Victah—Ted—but I had a sudden Chahlie Horse and, well, it goht the better of me—so, sorry, Victah—"

With heavy restraint and internally heightened amusement, Kennedy could see the barely contained rage that smoldered just beneath Black's equally benign façade. He was good, Black was very, very...*good.*

"My sincerest apologies," Kennedy finished, again, extending his hand to Black. "Hope I, ah, didn't *break* anything." Black hesitated but a fraction of a second—none of which Sorensen seemed to have noticed—but Kennedy did.

"Ah, Ted, Victah, I'm afraid this old wahr injury of mine begs attention." Kennedy turned to Black. "Victah, I hope I didn't injah you—we'll have ourah medical staff look you ovah."

Black worked his shoulder then abruptly halted the movement. The man was clearly in pain, Kennedy saw with measured satisfaction, but was also clearly no stranger to controlling it.

"I'm sure it's nothing," Black said, his countenance casual.

"Good. Then, we'll, ah, keep in touch and inform you of our decision," Kennedy said.

Without waiting for a response from either man, Kennedy abruptly departed the office...faking a limp.

He'd done it—he'd successfully interdicted Ted from outright giving Black the job, and removed the weapon Black had been intent on using on him. The fact that Black had even considered employing such overt means spoke volumes of him and his intentions. He had no qualms about fucking up either himself—or history. But Kennedy'd successfully diffused the situation and thrown the hugest of monkey wrenches into Black's schemes. He couldn't begin to wipe *that* smile off his face.

But, it wasn't over. Kennedy held no such illusions. If Black was able to go back in time to try to change things once (for that matter, both him *and* Black), who was to say it wouldn't happen again....

Chapter Sixteen

1

Travis's day had been just a hair short of boring. He'd had no taskings, and the paperwork had been more of the same old governmental B.S. So, he had had plenty of time to replay what had happened earlier in the day at the restaurant, portions of which he seemed to already be losing…like who the hell had been this "Le Rock" character? He knew no such "Le Rock," had even searched a couple of their databases for the name, but no one even remotely (pardon the pun) came close to that name. Sometimes the job really had them seeing weird shit—and there was nothing they could do about it; it was all part of the job, what happened when one spent too much time dipping into The Darkside, and the only way around it was to not freak out, to realize it for what it was and just deal with it. If it became too much, then that was why there were the White Coats with psych degrees. He'd known a few who'd gone that route…and had subsequently been removed from the program.

But if he hadn't known anyone with that name, then where had it come from?

What are ya gonna do?, his grandfather used to say. You just go on. If it was important enough, it'd come to him.

Travis left his desk, exited "the vault," where all their classified operations and administrative work took place, and leisurely made his way through the building and down stairwells, to the cafeteria. Nearly noon, the place was packed. And it smelled good, too. The quiet rustle of everyday needs and normalcy helped ground him, not to mention took him away from his largely administrative duties of the day. He entered the grilled-food line, picked up a cheeseburger and fries, then went on to pick up a Mountain Dew—then suddenly decided against the soda and grabbed an iced tea—two, in fact. Continuing on, he made his way to the cashier. As the girl totaled up his items, she looked to Travis, and asked, "*Have you heard the news?*"

Travis looked up. "No," he said, fishing out his wallet. He stood there, wallet opened, awaiting both an answer and a total.

"Excuse me," he asked, "what news?"

"I'm sorry?"

"You asked me a question…if I'd heard any 'news'?"

Smiling, she looked at him, confused. "No, sir…I'm sorry, but I didn't."

Travis looked behind him to those in line, hoping someone would confirm his end of the conversation, but no one did. He looked back to the cashier, decided not to push it at the rate his day had been going, and pulled a ten from his wallet. He handed it to the girl, who then mechanically counted back his change.

"Have a great day!" she said, still smiling.

Travis made his way toward his favorite table alongside a row of windows on the far side of the cafeteria. Windows to more normalcy—trees, blue skies, and birds.

News? What "news," and where had that question come from? He'd surely heard it, clear as day. He again glanced back to the cashier and the line. The girl was already handing back change to another customer.

Travis passed a newspaper someone held up. The headline declared, in big, bold, black print:

Children at Play!

Coming upon another table, a smiling bald guy with a big, bushy mustache and a gold earring, juggled and performed magic tricks for an intimate gathering of people.

Magic tricks?

Juggling—in the cafeteria?

Had he heard the news?

Travis arrived at his table and sat, half expecting that Le-Whatever person—what had been his name?—to be seated before him (and why *had* he?). He rubbed his eyes and forehead and looked out the window. His window to every day—*normal*—life.

What had been that guy's name? Lou? Leigh? *Lee*-something….

Travis broke open one of his iced teas and took a deep chug. Brief images of parachutes and full moons breezed through his mind. The bottle was cold and wet, the tea good. Travis turned his attention to his cheeseburger and found himself much hungrier than expected. The hot, dripping burger tasted better than any other burger he'd ever had. It was absolutely *incredible*…it was so good he didn't want to swallow…just wanted to continue chewing and chewing and chewing to culinary orgasm—the burger, the cheese…the onion and *relish!*

Man, what had they *done* to this thing?

Travis took another sip of tea and was almost overcome by the intensity of the slightly sweet, musky, bouquet of the beverage. It hadn't tasted like that a moment ago…had it mixed with the Olympian tastes of the burger? He could even *feel* the tea and burger traveling down his throat and into his stomach….

Okay, this wasn't normal. No one felt food heading into their stomach!

Travis put down the burger, sat back, and gripped the edge of the table. It was happening again, wasn't it?…things were getting *weird* again…

(*have you heard the news?*)

(*children at play!*)

(*magic!*)

There was a weightiness to this weirdness that felt different from this morning…like an ocean of water

(*Titanic*)

pressing down on him.

Something was wrong.

People were still walking about, talking, *eating*—

But, there was no longer any background chatter…that hubbub of constant noise and activity associated with rush-hour

(*restaurants*)

cafeterias, and people eating and talking and going about their lunch-hour business.

Was that guy still juggling?

The cashier still making change?

Were they even real?

Any of this?

He looked back out the windows.

For all he knew, there was nothing outside this haunting little microcosm of his…the table, tray, iced tea, and partially eaten cheeseburger (which he so desperately needed to get back to)…

Outside there were no taskings, compartmentalized vaults, rules, nor national interests. No secrecies. Only trees and shrubs. Dirt and rocks. Birds. Sun.

Reality.

Travis closed his eyes. It was like...a tsunami...it was coming, all right...subtle and deep...but the closer it got, the more power built up behind it, as it approached his shores. He couldn't put it off, couldn't...stop...it...

Please, oh please, *let there be nothing weird...let there still be a world, an existence, so when I open my eyes, I can finish the best damned cheeseburger in the world...*please, *make it so...*

Travis let out a huge, resigned, sigh, and opened his eyes.

Hundreds upon *hundreds* of children sat packed in the cafeteria.

Every one of them stared at him.

Gone were the juggler, the newspaper reader, the cashier. Gone were all the lunch-bunch eaters. In place of them were all these wide-eyed and smiling six year olds. Girls and boys.

On the floor before him was a poster, something he might see stapled to a telephone pole, perhaps. It proclaimed *Have You Heard The* News?, and had multiple worn staple holes and tears on it; was weathered, stained, and faded. Had a boot print on it.

Travis looked back to the children.

Still there.

Still smiling.

Out from somewhere to his left, and coming into his field of view, calmly strode a man of indeterminate age, dressed in an open flannel shirt over a black AC/DC T-shirt, jeans...and hiking

(*boot print*)

boots? He, too, was all smiles, and sat down directly across the table from him.

Did he know this guy?

The man reached across the table and grabbed the unopened tea.

"Travis—always good to see you. And thanks for picking this up for me."

The Man With No Name opened the tea and took a long swig. "Not as good as mine, but *damn* good just the same," he said with a satisfied sigh and a swipe of the mouth with the back of the hand still holding the bottle. He set down the bottle and looked between Travis and the kids. "Oh!," he said, chuckling, "you're probably wondering 'what the hell'! Lemme introduce you."

The Man With No Name stood, and with a carny like sweep of a hand before him from Travis to children, he said, "Children…meet Travis Norton, the government psychic I've been telling you so much about. Travis Norton…meet…*the New Breed*.…"

2

Lizzie Gordon tossed her Sonic Drive-In trash into the waste barrel, as she exited the drive-thru. She loved their bacon cheeseburgers and vanilla root beers. Joe had also loved them.

When he'd still walked this Earth.

They used to occasionally meet for lunch at Sonics throughout town. Now, all she had were memories.

Why was it that with all her so-called psychic prowess, prowess she'd had since birth, prowess she used so accurately and freely to solve so many other people's problems, little Lizzie Gordon couldn't seem to solve her *own*…little Lizzie Gordon (gave her lover forty whacks…) couldn't even contact her recently dead husband in the afterlife?

Just what the hell *was* her problem?

Lizzie took a right out of the parking lot, drove up the twenty-or-so feet to the intersection, then made a left at the light. She followed the street to another intersection, preparing to head uphill, when a billboard caught her eye:

"Love: it's not about Joe, Lizzie, it's about the New Breed."

Lizzie slammed on the brakes, skidding off onto the shoulder in a cloud of dust and gravel.

She twisted around in her seat to again catch the sign, but could no longer make it out from her angle. Swinging a U-turn, she raced back down the hill, then pulled another U-ey. Heart racing, Lizzie again looked up to the sign. This time she pulled off to the side of the road in a more controlled manner.

"Love: it's what New Life Church is all about. The New Breed of religion."

Okay…guilt about Joe…lunch where they used to eat…and the

recently added stress of the most unnerving and frightening scarecrow, Mr. Black.

Lizzie checked traffic and pulled back out onto the street.

You'd think being psychic solved a lot of one's ills, but with such super powers came super challenges. Somehow, Lizzie knew Joe was okay, but she was still human, and still in love with him. Time *does* heal all wounds, but it had only been a year since his death, and they'd had a deeper connection than most, given her (so-called) extraordinary abilities. She could safely say this because she'd dealt with so many relationship questions and issues in her job. Many people, it seemed to her, married for all the wrong reasons. Money, sex, loneliness (her mother had once told her you didn't marry everyone you loved), fairy tale fantasies...thinking they could change those they married from their evil ways. Then there were issues like mid-life crises...complacency and boredom...or those couples who really *did* adore and love each other at one point...only to become too damn busy in their daily lives and choose the "easy way" out. Trade in the old in-need-of-a-good-washing vehicle for something brand-spanking new without even bothering to give so much as a *little bit* of extra elbow grease and attention—or a car wash—to the current one. People wanted shiny and new, no effort. The Throw-away Society.

Or, perhaps, there was another reason, Lizzie thought: TV and the Internet. Computers. Short and flashy. And it wasn't so much the media, per se, but the minds and mindsets *behind* them. Those idiots, if she may use the term, only focused on one thing, and one thing only: money. Of course, if you focused in on the young, unattached, sex-starved and hormonally exploding demographic you were going to sell sex and flesh like no tomorrow. Heck, *any* demographic. The flood of such material into everything—the pure *availability* of it—was bound to have its effect on everyone—consciously or not. And this said nothing about cheapening the entire sexual experience itself. All the hype and flooding of the senses through sex and beautiful bodies was sure to affect many a relationship on one level or another, confusing the issues of many who were on the fence to begin with. People were just going to have to get tougher, more choosey. Learn that the grass was *not* always greener on the other side. Never, in the history of humanity, had people had so many choices. So many *perceived* options.

In her humble opinion and experience.

But, perhaps, what also affected Lizzie and her emotions, and certainly didn't help matters, was that being genuinely psychic she did still feel Joe out there…somewhere. There was no longer any such "Til death do us part" concept. She just couldn't *contact* him.

But, it was almost like *he* was trying to get in touch with *her*.

And that brought up all kinds of issues.

Like…was all this emotion hers—or *Joe's?*

For all her insight and advertised prowess, why was she having so much difficulty dealing with Joe's passing? She didn't miss him in the oh-we-have-but-one-life-to-live sense…all souls, she knew, live unimaginably *multiple* lives, and this life was just one of them—but she missed him in the sense that she missed his *presence*…and that she was only human and had *so* loved the man…that it had only been a year since his death—one tiny, insignificant historical barely-a-blink of an eye—and she still hadn't yet, apparently (psychic or not) gotten over that. According to her way of thinking, she should have. Moved on. But something kept her reliving the same old emotions, the same old tape….

Lizzie pulled into a parking lot and stopped.

Sheesh, get over *it, lady!*

Everything happens for a reason, and this might not have anything to do with you…maybe it's some issue in one of Joe's other lives that brought on his death. Just because you can't figure it out doesn't mean it doesn't exist. Maybe it was—

Lizzie gasped.

She'd found herself in absolutely the last place she'd ever wanted to be.

Her car sat idling in the parking lot of the last structure Joe had built—the very same lot where Jeff Skopchek had made a name for himself in the local news.

It may no longer have been the construction site as she'd known it…but it was Harbor Gardens Apartments…and it was here Joe had met his anything-but-graceful demise, one that should well have been prevented. A demise that should well have been foreseen by The World's Greatest Psychic.

Lizzie put the car in reverse and stepped on the accelerator—but it didn't move. The pedal wouldn't press to the floor. She looked into the foot well.

Something was wedged beneath the pedal.

A small plastic toy.

"Oh, *geez*…."

She tried to toe the toy out from under the pedal, but it wouldn't budge. Putting the car into park and gear into neutral, Lizzie again tried to free the annoying plastic obstacle. This time it came loose.

A large, yellow, rubber ducky.

Yellow.

Squeezing it once, she tossed it into the back seat. Grabbing the handle of the parking brake, Lizzie was ready to release it, when…

She was no longer at Harbor Gardens.

She now sat before a brand-new *construction* zone…complete with the grunt and grit of heavy equipment, construction workers, and the not-yet-complete apartment building.

Harbor Gardens—*to be*.

Lizzie couldn't think, couldn't move.

She was suddenly and inexplicably back at the old construction site, and there, a long stone's throw away, was none other than her husband, Joseph Michael Gordon…alive and well and vibrant…currently directing what had been his construction crew.

Lizzie tried to say—do—anything, but was frozen in place, one hand on the steering wheel, the other on the brake. All around were heavy equipment, girders, concrete, and men. Cranes lifting and moving and swinging steel about into the air. The smell and black puff of diesel exhaust from engines and trucks noisily backing up and hauling material about the job site. The occasional, indistinct shouts of men above construction din.

Lizzie didn't feel so great.

Joe was alive and real—in motion—before her. His gym-fed muscular frame supported by powerful legs. She watched him direct his men with a rolled-up set of construction plans.

Memories of his touch…his voice…those concerned little comical looks he used to give her—

Then she saw *him*.

Skopchek.

She didn't have to see him clearly through the crane's dirtied and scratched cabin windows…she *felt* him. He was operating the crane.

Whether or not the absolute love of her life was again alive and about to reenact his gruesome death, this was the first and only time Lizzie had ever had a visit or vision of him after his passing…and no matter how painful this was going to be, Lizzie couldn't and *wouldn't* look away. Watching Joe, Lizzie was surprised at how easy it was to fall back into the old ways. How easy it was to convince herself *he was still alive!* She'd always been proud of him, but it was indescribably weird how it actually felt like he was really there—*living and breathing again.*

That they were together again.

A short but hot spat of tears burst forth from a part of her soul that, for all her intellectualization, had apparently still not healed. Her pride in him had taken on a new depth. Scared her.

This had never happened before, not on this level.

One-ton I-beams were swung about above Joe's head, and he, she knew and watched, wasn't the least bit concerned about them. She looked to his bright yellow hard hat. All the years he'd worn that god-damned silly thing to protect that beautiful head of his had been a joke. A hideous, horrendous, joke. It wasn't like she'd expected it to save him from a falling girder, but, good *Christ*, lesser miracles had been known to happen. Why couldn't that hat had slid off his head at *just the right moment* with that screaming harbinger of death? Would that have been such a huge miracle to ask for?

Or, why not have had that damned steel missile fly into Skop-chek's head, instead? *He'd* been the one screwing around—the one whose life had been falling apart—not *Joe*, Joe's life had been great. Joe's life had been wonderful—perfect; Joe's life had been with *her*. Why had *Joe* been the one to get his Rockin Sockin block knocked the fuck off?

She couldn't turn away.

It was coming, and there was nothing she could do about it.

He stood there, her Joe, all proud and confident, performing the work he was meant to do, full of vibrant personality and energy.

Why hadn't she seen that huge chunk of steel in his future?

Why hadn't she felt his life and her world come crashing to an abrupt end—and stopped *it?*

Lizzie gripped the steering wheel with both hands, unable to stem the flood of emotion, knuckles white and clenched, beginning to hurt.

Stop this! Change, *dammit—take* me, *take* me!

But that wasn't to be. She knew what had already been…and this time…this time, she was going to be allowed to actually watch it happen—with her own eyes—not any imaginative mind's-eye projection, no psychic TV screen, which, up to now, had been all she'd had. No, now, for some reason, she was being given the rare opportunity—yea, *privilege*—to actually *see* her beloved cut down and killed before her very eyes…in all its Technicolor gory.

Lizzie could no longer sit still.

Her entire body trembling, her breathing short and shallow, she got out of the car and stood—trembling—hand to mouth watching her paranormal movie. Joe going about his work, oblivious to what lies in his immediate

(*minutes away!*)

future.

Had *he* had any feelings something was up before he died?

Lizzie watched as Joe laughed and joked with the crew. Watched as he finished showing the plans—or whatever had been rolled up—to another foreman, rolled them back up, then tucked them under an arm. Watched as he walked toward a stack of girders, all confident and happy with himself and his place in the world, and felt him inhale the mixture of diesel exhaust and dirt, hear that "beep-beep" of backing up front-end loaders. Joe then pulled out the plans, again, looking them over. He didn't see, nor care about, the I-beam that floated recklessly above…an I-beam, Lizzie noticed, that was curiously dark…an I-beam that—yes—actually looked *black*.

Dark black.

The others, she noticed, were reddish-brown, but this one was different. Black as coal. Black as death.

Black.

Black-black-black.

She watched as the steelwork swung about in the air above, like some perverse air-ballet, too fast for where it was headed. It looked unstable. She watched Skopchek, not all there at the controls of the crane. Felt the chaos swirling around within him and watched as he tried to do his job while his mind was consumed with hot confusion and emotion—not unlike her at this moment.

Lizzie watched Joe, the love of her life, take one of those moments to divert his thoughts to her, turning his back to the construction site. She watched as his face softened and he smiled, as he thought about her, about their upcoming vacation—about—

He was looking directly at her!

Lizzie gasped.

Backed up a step.

Both her hands involuntarily flew to her face, cupping her open mouth.

He actually met *her eyes!*

He actually seemed to recognize *her*—there, *now*, this very instant….

Look out!, Lizzie mentally screamed, coming forward a step or two, hands now thrown down before her, "*Oh*, please *God*, *no*, *not* again—

LOOK OUT?'

Joe smiled, warmly.

Of course, it was too late.

History had already made its decision, and Joe...Joe was already dead. Jeff Skopchek was already dead, having been divorced and racked with guilt for all he'd done, had taken his own life.

Yet, somehow, here it was—all of it—in living color, before her, and Dead Joe had managed to come back and thoughtfully replay the entire incident just for her. Just so she could see how it'd all gone down. Dead Joe was finally able to connect with Live Lizzie. And as Dead Joe made eye contact with his wife, he smiled, and it was a smile that melted away Lizzie's heart and caused her to lose control of her legs.

She collapsed against her car.

He was dead, but he'd made her forget he was dead.

A smile that had reached across the grave.

Her screams, as deep and terrible as they were, had again gotten caught in her throat. Her voice cracked.

Speechless.

Emotionally hamstrung.

Lizzie pulled herself along the car. They had finally connected—*connected*—and she didn't want to look away. It was just the two of them now, for all time, looking out across Time and Space, as defined by this surreal parking lot, from a construction site long since gone—happy and alive and vibrant, preparing for their *vacation...*

"*I love you,*" she whispered, her face hot and wet and swollen, *I love you* so *much...*

Joe's smile widened. He opened his mouth (in Lizzie's mind) to return the same words.

It was then that the evil, black, one-ton I-beam came sailing through the air and whacked off Joe's noggin.

Just like that.

Popped off as clean as if a blade'd been used.

No warning, no fanfare, and in an explosive, fine spray of crimson. Lucky for Lizzie she not only saw it in real time, but simultaneously saw it in exquisite, slow-motion detail, as the girder first connected with Joe's bright yellow hard hat that had been there to protect his head. She saw how the hard hat had actually popped off his head, the brim of it initially connecting with the girder. Dead Joe still had had that smile on his face, and his mouth had still been in the process of returning the "*I love you, too, honey,*" but was only at the "I" part, when Dead Joe realized something weird be afoot. Something…*touched his head.*

Hmmm, what could it be? the look on Dead Joe's face had queried.

And as Dead Joe turned his head, the smile departed his face, his hard hat popped off his head—

He almost started to laugh as he used to do a lot with the guys, thinking, *okay, what are the guys up to now?*, when—among other things—realization struck, and the sudden, stark reality (and cold steel) hit him that this thing was *way* heavy and felt like a friggin nuclear battering ram…

Lizzie read his thoughts…they had still been on his mind…their vacation—and the possibility of a *child?*…but as the tears streamed down her face, she knew he couldn't possibly have thought all this, done all this. Everything was happening—*had happened*—far too fast. It had been quick, out of nowhere. Unexpected. Her imagination had simply filled in the gaps with pure conjecture—trying to lengthen things out in her own adulterated and emotional attempt to stave off already occurred events; that maybe, if she did this *enough*—*hard* enough—she would, one day, wake up to find Joe still by her side….

But, meanwhile, Dead Joe's yellow hard hat had, indeed, popped clean off his head, and—lucky for it—shot off and out of the way of the black I-beam battering ram, which now, also, summarily popped off Joe's flesh-and-bone head.

As much as Lizzie wanted to watch as much of her dead husband as there was of him, when his head had separated from the rest of him—the very same body she had caressed, held, kissed, and made love to—she closed her eyes and looked away, collapsing over the hood of her car, sobbing. She heard the hollow clunking of that damned hard hat as it bounced off unknown objects when it hit the ground, continuing to bounce about like a hollow bucket. Then she heard (why—why-oh-*why* hadn't her filling-in-the-blanks stopped here?) the sickening, amplified thud of what sounded like fifteen pounds of so much meat hitting the ground and rolling to a stop…followed by the collapse of another two-hundred pounds of dead meat also thumping the ground….

Then, to add insult to injury, Lizzie saw something no one had ever told her about, no newspaper nor police report had ever mentioned: as that damned one-ton battering ram swung lazily back and forth above her now-decapitated husband—the cable snapped—and down it plummeted, the evil black girder, on top of Joe's body. There was a puff of dust and gravel, a concussioning jerk to Joe's muscular frame, and a deep, ground-pounding thud. When the dust cleared, Lucky Lizzie got to see her husband's body crazily sprawled out under the black, pitch-black, oh-so-*black* I-beam that lay atop him like a mother hen atop a nest egg. Joe was now a cartoon caricature from a Road Runner skit, to which Lizzie half-expected to hear that cursed "*beep-beep*"...his arms and legs spread out under the girder in a comical, distorted, "X."

Lizzie fainted.

Chapter Seventeen

1

Travis again became acutely aware of his surroundings, as he returned to the vault.

He stopped and looked behind him, confused. Looked before him.

Something was out of place.

What had just happened? Hadn't he just been at lunch?

Had he been so preoccupied in thought that he'd lost track of that much time?

And what time *was* it?

He looked at his watch.

Stopped.

He shook out his wrist a couple of times, but it still didn't restart. Time for a new one. Again.

Wasn't he supposed to be having one of those "Freaky-Shit" days? Why, yes, yes he was—then this all fit in perfectly.

Travis continued on to his office. Hoped that whatever he might have done while "out" wasn't so embarrassing he couldn't laugh it off.

The hairs on the back of his neck suddenly shot straight up.

A lone individual approached from the far end of the corridor.

Black.

Shit.

Blanking his mind and trying to appear as casual as possible, Travis nodded in acknowledgement (which was not reciprocated by Black) as they passed each other. Not a word was exchanged.

Black didn't do small talk.

Travis just needed to get past as quickly as possible.

Unscathed.

2

As Travis passed by him, Black paused and turned. He eyed Travis for a long moment.

Then continued on his way.

3

Mel waited patiently on the line, as he listened to the phone at the other end ring. His heart raced. He was excited—not only at the prospect of again talking with Lizzie, and that she'd become his source of the familiar—but also that he was going to be talking with a *girl*.

A real *female*.

He had no idea what she looked like, but loved the sound of her voice, the way her mind worked, and how she was so concerned about him.

Interested in him.

He hadn't had much experience in the girlfriend department…even wondered if he'd *had* one, since that memory also came up blank. But he also really didn't want to appear as being so needy. He just wanted to talk. To her. *Anyone*. And he really loved the sound of her voice….

When the ringing stopped he held his breath, and he had to consciously exhale when the expectant dead air after the ring (that seemed to last forever!) filled in with a voice—*her* voice.

"Hello?"

"Lizzie? Hi, it's me, Mel—"

"Oh, hi, Mel! How *are* you! I was just thinking about you! Hey, hold on, would you? Just a second…."

She'd just been *thinking* of him?

Mel sat back in the recliner and hit the mute button on the TV. Wow, someone he didn't know—outside this house and his weird little existence—had just been thinking about *him*.

Who was he that someone should be thinking of him?

Mel sat in the downstairs living room before the glare of the TV, on which was the *X-Files* episode, "The Field Where I Died." It was an episode involving Civil War past lives between Mulder and another character. It was presently cutting to a commercial, another weird one with no voice over, showing children skipping, laughing, and playing in a field. Mel leaned forward, almost forgetting he was on the phone. The commercial was eerie, but curiously playful.

One word filled the screen.

Play

"Mel?"

"Yes—I'm here!" he said, leaning back into the recliner.

The commercial ended.

"How've you been? I was just waiting on a caller, but they apparently hung up. Anyway, I put myself on break. I hope things are okay, since you are calling…"

"I guess they are. I've been having more weird feelings and all, but—"

"Weird feelings? How do you mean?"

"It's kinda hard to explain…but it's like, well, something's wrong—or gonna happen—but I can't put my finger on it. Or maybe that I'm not all there? You know, added to my normal, everyday Who-am-I-and-why-am-I-all-alone issues? And occasionally I see, well, these other images of me and some dark men. I'm awake when I'm asleep, or asleep when I'm awake…

"Does any of that make any sense?"

"Sure. I lost both my parents and my husband."

"Oh, right—sorry."

"Look, I know it's tough. You're probably having more going on inside your head than you care to admit—or can even sort out right now—but that's *okay*. It's only natural." Lizzie cleared her throat. "It's tough, but…"

Lizzie broke off.

"You okay?"

Lizzie inhaled deeply.

"Lizzie…I'm, um…sorry if I—"

"Oh, it's not you," she said, sniffling. "I had a rather weird experience of my own this afternoon."

"Would *you* like to talk about it?"

"It's not fair, since you called to talk with me, and I'm supposed to be giving *you* support and advice."

"I don't mind."

Another long, drawn-out inhale. Sniffling filled Mel's ear.

"Well...to make a long story short...I had a vision about the accident that took my husband's life."

"How'd it happen, if you don't mind my asking?"

"For some stupid reason, I drove by—well, actually pulled into—the parking lot...the very place where he'd died. It was a field when I knew it, but it's now an apartment complex and shopping center, and, well, I just saw everything unfold. Everything. It was the first time this'd ever happened to me—at least on this scale. It scared the crap out of me, and I got so emotional. I guess I'm still a little shaken up. So, it's not you, Mel, don't worry about that."

"Okay."

Mel listened as Lizzie continued to sniffle and quietly sob for another moment or two.

"I'm sorry," she said. "I think I'm better, now. Thanks for letting me, um, get that out."

"You sure you're okay?"

"Yes. Thank you."

"I have a question, then."

"Okay."

"How come you're all affected like this...and I'm not?"

"Excuse me?"

"My parents. It's really bugging me. I don't know if I mentioned anything about it before, but I've found that...that..."

"Go on...just say it..."

"That I don't seem to feel *anything* toward them. Not one thing. Isn't that strange? Isn't that...*evil?*"

"First off, my dear, sweet young man, don't ever compare yourself to anyone else about how you're 'supposed' to feel. Everyone handles grief differently, death...differently. Your situation just happened, right? It's recent?"

Mel chuckled. "As far as I know."

"Well, there you go. You're more than likely still in shock. I lost my parents a few years back, and my husband just over a year ago. I've already gone through what you're just beginning to experience. Not that it's anything to look forward to, but I'm sure you'll probably get to the crying-and-mourning stage sooner than you'll care to experience...

"But another thing," she said, continuing, "and maybe I won't quite explain this just right, since I'm not a psychologist, or anything, but I think—*me* anyway—I think that losing parents is different from losing husbands, wives, or girlfriends. It's not something I can adequately put into words, but though we love them all, it's a different kind of love and emotional attachment. Of course we'll mourn them when they do go, especially if it's under tragic circumstances like yours, but there's a different *kind* of closeness. One that also, I think, speaks to their having already been around for all our lives, and consciously or unconsciously, we *expect* them to go first, in whatever way they do go. Whether or not we admit it—we, their children—in a manner of speaking, know they've already lived their lives. We never want them to go, of course, but it's just the reality of it. We, and our spouses and mates, haven't really lived our lives *in that respect*. We're *younger*. I don't know…I guess it could all be thrown out the window, if you were really close to your folks, but that's kinda how I've been looking at it.

"Were you?"

"What?" Mel said.

"Close to your parents?"

Mel paused. "I guess we were, but I'm just not sure. Man, you must think I'm really bad, but I hardly seem to remember anything about them—"

"Again, Mel, please don't torture yourself over this. You're grief-stricken. You need time to work through this. You've been through a lot. Maybe this is how you react to traumatic events. Like I said, I'm sure you'll come out of it all right…and remember—when the time's *right*. Don't force anything. Right now, your mind, your emotions—your psyche—are all confused.

"How are you holding up otherwise?"

"Like the rest of this," Mel said, "as fine as can be expected, I guess, all things considered. I'm just feeling like I'm in a rut, is all, and needed to hear your voice. Thanks for talking to me, Lizzie. I'm sorry about your experience this afternoon, though, with your husband, and all."

"Well, there's actually a little more to it then I let on. A few days ago there was this guy—from the government, he claimed—who came nosing around. He actually followed me home from a restaurant. He said he was looking for someone and asked if I could help. But the more I thought about it, and tuned in, the more *nothing* felt right about it—*he* didn't feel right—so I turned him down—"

"Way to go!"

"I wish it were that simple. There was something bad about him I kept picking up on—and he did come back. I had to tell him no to his face, and it felt weird telling him that. He seemed...nonchalant enough...about it all, but I somehow feel that that isn't the end of it. He's very obsessed with tracking down this person, whomever it is, but never, or wouldn't, go into details. He was really quite creepy."

"How do you feel now? Are you able to pick up on anything?"

"I do pick up on a lot of—for lack of a better term, which I always hate to use—*evil*. It's interesting you used that word, earlier. I didn't trust him when we first met, and I still don't. He's looking for someone and isn't easily put off. I'm sure he's lied to me, though I'm pretty sure he *is* from the government. Just not the FBI. I really don't think that was the last of him—and it does have me a bit apprehensive."

"I'll protect ya!" Mel announced, proudly. He was kind of embarrassed after having said it, but he suddenly had a cause—something *else* to do—to attach himself to, rather than just mope around the house confused, getting all hung up in his head, and being glued to a television set.

"Oh, Mel, that's so sweet of you, but—"

"What's he look like?"

"Well...he's quite tall, well over six feet, large hands...dark, salt-and-pepper hair, heavy on the salt, and dark, penetrating eyes—"

"'Salt and pepper'?"

"Black hair going white...kind of speckled looking."

"And what's his name?"

"Black. Victor Black. Anyway, he always wears black, at least when I see him. His personality is quite intense. He bores right into you—even me. He's very scary. In his sixties or so, I'd say. But capable—*very* capable—of violence...and creepy. I really don't think there's much either of us could do, should he come for us, I mean, I doubt that's likely, but, thanks for your offer."

"You know," Mel continued, suddenly wishing he'd kept his mouth shut, "but I think I might know this guy—"

"Oh, don't tell me that, Mel, that isn't even remotely funny."

"Believe me, he scares me just from your description, but there's something about him that makes me think I really might have met him—"

"I did *not* need to hear that. Where? When?"

"Sorry, you know my memory. I seem to have blocked out much of my life, lately, but I do get the impression, once you started describing him, that we've met. And, now that I'm talking about it, he feels tied to those dark-men images I told you about. About being awake while asleep."

"Well, if that's true—stay clear of him. Be very wary. And above all, do not go *anywhere* with him. I picked up on some very bad vibes from the guy. He's not good news."

"'Delphi' just popped into my mind."

"*Delphi?*"

"Yes. It mean anything to you?"

"No."

"Do you pick up on anything else from him—Black—now?"

Lizzie paused. "No." She again cleared her throat, "I don't seem to…" Her response was flat. Frightened. "No…I'm not getting anything. I don't know what that means. But it's just not right. I always pick up on *something*. Don't know…not liking this trend."

"How about me?"

Lizzie again paused. "Okay, this is unnerving—same thing. I don't know…maybe all the stress has finally caught up to me. It was pretty intense, watching my husband—"

Lizzie again broke off.

"Sorry."

"It's okay…give me a moment…it was pretty intense, and it is harder for me to pick up on things when I'm stressed. When Joe died…it was hard for me to work—nearly impossible—and I had to take some time off until I could get it together. Maybe that's all this is."

"I'm sure that's all it is."

"Well, Mel, hate to do this to ya, but I still have to work, so I'm going to have to go."

"Okay."

"You can call me again, though, if you'd like."

"Really?"

Lizzie's tone then changed into one of total seriousness.

"And Mel…please, *please*, be careful out there—I mean it. Black is dangerous. Stay clear of him. I'm sure he's far more dangerous than either of us realize."

"I will. You too."

"I will. Take care, Mel."

Mel hung up and lay back in the recliner, eyes closed.

What a neat lady. He always felt better after talking with her. It's funny how talking with someone could ease a mind. Sometimes living in your head wasn't as good an idea as it sounded. You had to get out.

Interact. It was amazing what wonders talking did—what cheap therapy it was.

But there *was* something about that Black guy.

He was pretty sure he'd met him, though he wasn't sure if it was an actual memory, or something he'd made up.

Mel got out of the recliner and headed upstairs to the kitchen. At first he drifted about, not sure what he was looking for. He knew he'd know when he found it…a card, piece of scrap paper—a letter. But nothing caught his eye. He still had Lizzie's *Madame Nostradameus* card with him and took it out, placing it up before him like a target sighting as he surveyed the room. He scanned the room in this way, aiming over the stove, the countertops…the refrigerator…

…and stopped.

The refrigerator.

Mel stood before the fridge's door and lowered the card. Another card was stuck to the door, under a Pizza Hut magnet, along with a picture—a sketch, really, a police sketch, he guessed—of a guy he didn't know.

His blood ran cold.

There, on the card…Black's name.

His first reaction was to immediately call Lizzie back, but he couldn't. That would have been too namby-pamby, and she'd most likely be on another call.

Behind the card on the fridge was that sketch, which he pulled from the fridge. He left the business card under the Pizza Hut magnet. He really didn't want to touch it. The police sketch was of this guy Black said he'd been looking for—it all came back to him. He had come by the house, given him his card—and this sketch.

Some kind of kidnapping investigation?

But this guy…he didn't *look* like a kidnapper, not that Mel knew what a kidnapper was supposed to look like, but Mel definitely didn't get the feeling that this guy could do anything like that, in fact—

The doorbell rang.

The calm, monotonous tone, normally a pleasant one, was anything *but*, this time.

Who could possibly be stopping by at this hour?

Mel took the sketch with him as he went for the door. Through the vertical slice of glass in the front door, he saw a silhouette of a person lit up by the front porch's light. There was a screen door between him and whoever was outside, so, he unlocked and opened the door.

No sooner had he done that, than the door was forced inward and he was met with a well-placed and rock-hard haymaker that swung on down from above, like a ton of

(*steel*)

bricks.

Mel was unconscious before he hit the floor.

"Protected, in*deed*," Black said, as he casually stepped over Mel's unconscious body and entered the house.

4

Kennedy sat in his study, a book on the Battle of Gettysburg open in his lap. He stared blankly at its pages.

How old was he? Just how the hell old was he?

And how had it happened so goddamned fast?

Just yesterday he'd been a young, tough Navy Lieutenant, and not long following that, President of the most powerful nation on Earth…how had he ended up *here*, sitting in the dark of what was supposed to be his study, at who-knew-what-hour—in the body of an old man?

And *where* was he?

He'd been reading…unable to sleep, yes, that was it…but he'd also felt he'd been somewhere else…

Had it been a *dream*?

Was he really in bed, at home on leave from the Navy, and dreaming of a *future* him?

Kennedy shut the book with a solid *thwap*, and got to his feet. He paced the room, hand to his head in concentration…*why was he asking himself all these damned questions?*

Shouldn't he be in bed?

Kennedy stopped and looked to his attire. He was in sweats and slippers.

Good Lord, was *this* senility? Was this how it felt to lose your mind? To go off the deep end?

No, he'd just had a tough day, and was tired, was all.

What had he done to be so tired?

He'd been to Boston…had a meeting with the GFP…had lunch with Paul and Carol afterward. Visited his great-grandkids—

There'd been something else, though, hadn't there? Something...*odd*...what had happened at that board meeting?

Kennedy stood before his bay windows and opened them. He inhaled the sweet late-night breezes, as he stared out over the ocean, a section of which he'd privately decreed as his own.

What was going on out there, right this moment—what secrets lie beneath those darkened waters? What life-and-death struggles...what creatures enjoying the night?

And what secrets lie beneath his own darkened waters?

The Center's boardroom.

The boardroom?

What had that to do with anything?

He searched his memory. The boardroom...felt curiously familiar in a *proximity* sort of way...like he'd just been there....

And how was Sorensen these days? Hadn't talked with him in...

Damn, he was antsy! There was no way he was going back to bed.

Kennedy again inhaled deeply of the nocturnal salty breezes and thought—what the hell—why not? It was quiet and dark, and the calming effect of the ocean and breezes might relax him enough to get him back to bed....

Kennedy closed the window and retreated back into the bedroom, where he changed clothes and made his way out into the night, wondering, of all things (he was surprised to realize), what Black was up to....

Chapter Eighteen

1

Travis was in deep, focused on his target tasking, but something kept vying for his attention. He was picking up on another line of thought that seemed sandwiched in-between—*through*—the tasking. Whatever it was, there was a subtle "intent" nibbling at away at him....

Travis allowed himself to be whisked away in an extremely slight, tangential vector that took off like a bat outta hell, once he dedicated the slightest attention to it. He felt a portion—another "him," a probable *self?*—still performing his original, directed targeting...but also felt this "other him" heading off in this new direction....

Travis stood in an unfamiliar room, but one in which he felt was at The Center.

He stood before a barely illuminated desk, at which sat a man intent on something Travis couldn't make out. The man wasn't bothered by nor aware of his otherworldly presence. Travis moved around behind him.

The man was Victor Black.

Travis leaned over Black's shoulder. Black wrote on a piece of paper. It said:

Find Nightmare Man

Nightmare Man?
Black carefully folded the white sheet of paper in half and slid it into an envelope. He inscribed their remote-viewer coordinate protocol on it, then sealed it within another, larger envelope, also inscribing similar numbers on that envelope. Black then paused and looked up,

narrowing his gaze. His right hand slowly found its grip around the SIG 226 nine mil in his lap. Black cocked his head slightly, eyes alert, studying the room.

Stood up—

Both Travis and Black now stood in a different room. There were no lights on in this one, except for the tiny flashlight Black used as he made his way toward the five-drawer steel safe along the rear wall. In a choppy time jump, Black was now inside an unlocked and opened safe drawer, rapidly fingering through hundreds of similarly stored envelopes, like the one he carried. Finding the one he needed, Black removed it and inserted his new "Nightmare Man" one in its place....

Travis now stood on the dark plains of eastern Colorado, beneath a full moon. Off in the distance Bravo Force operators silently descended from the night sky.

They'd be here soon.

Ring around the rosie....

Travis spun around.

...a pocketful of posies...

Ashes! Ashes!

We all fall down.

Travis peered out into the eerie silvery shadows of the plains. No one. It was dark and empty—except for a ranch several hundred yards off to his right. But that children's tune continued to play in his head. It wasn't the high-pitched, lyrical tone normally associated with the rhyme, but a sullen, hollow timbre.

Sadness.

Boots.

Travis heard boots hurriedly rushing through Buffalo grass and Socorro cacti. The kill team rushed past him toward the ranch house....

Travis stood before the ranch house. It was surrounded, two Bravo Force operators inside.

The family—

Travis was inside the home.

On the floor lay the bodies of the husband, wife, and teenaged son. Each had single shots to their heads, small-caliber rounds, .22s. Travis spotted the framed picture of Kennedy on the cupboard mantle, its glass shattered. Beside it, Travis saw the book, *Prophecies of Nostradamus*, lying open. He read the exposed passage:

> *And the Maker shall dance*
> *Until the Great Darkness Descends*
> *Taking Everybody with it*

Travis turned and was

Outside the house.

He stood on the porch, facing the door. Alone, he examined the door's wood grains. How many blizzards and thunderstorms had it weathered? How long ago had it been built, and whose hands had worked it? Answers to all he had gotten, but none of which mattered. It would all soon be

(*oot*)

(*aboot*)

moot.

"Do you understand what you're seeing?" came the tiny, childlike whisper from behind.

In the silvery darkness and extending way back to the shadowy horizon, stood hundreds of *thousands* of children.

Do you? they mentally whispered.

"I'm not sure. I see…terrible events that seem to extend beyond…*through?*…time, but—"

*Ashes, ashes…*they all mentally whispered as one.

"Why do you keep singing that? What does it mean?"

We all fall down.

Travis was suddenly struck by an image of Black dancing around the house, his face ashen. Pockets full of posies. He skipped and danced about the place, pulling the posies from his pockets. Casually flung them about. When the flowers hit the dirt, they became bodies. Everywhere. And they, in turn, disintegrated into dust.

Travis looked back to the children. Gone. In their place stood men and women, equally as confused as he was. Among them…Buddy LaRouque.

"*Buddy?*" Travis asked, coming forward.

"Don't you get it, pal?" Buddy said, disgusted, but not at Travis. "Don't you *see?*"

Travis looked back to the house, which had begun to crumple inward.

"To tell you the truth, maybe I'm just thickheaded, but—"

"Black has to be stopped. He's gotten to some of us, but not everyone. Not you. But he ain't far off. He *knows.*"

"Knows what?"

The house choppily crumpled into a hole that opened up beneath it.

"*You,* buddy. He knows about *you.*"

Travis came to.

Stood in the RV lab. Beside the RoboChair.

Apparently the session was over. He didn't remember ending it. His monitor was just closing the door behind him on his way out, just having said something to him.

Travis winced.

He didn't remember a thing, not a damned thing.

Returning to his desk, more or less still in a haze, Travis made his way past other remote viewers at their desks, shuffling about paperwork. As soon as he sat down, he began to mindlessly shuffle about his own paperwork.

We all fall down...

We all fall down...

Ring around the rosie...a pocketful of...

Travis looked up. Squinted. That damned nursery rhyme was still in his head—

Still? As opposed to *what?*

Where had it come from? What'd it mean?

We all fall down.

We all fall down...

"Hey, Trav, you ok?" asked Don Rankin, the unit's ops director.

"I'm fine—why?"

"Well...you've been staring straight ahead for almost five minutes, now. No expression—nothing. Just a blank stare."

Travis looked at his desk. To the others, who were all looking at him.

Had it been that *long?* It'd only felt like a second or...

"Sorry...lost in thought, I guess. Today's been a weird-shit day."

"No problem," Rankin said and walked off. But, at that point, Travis looked to each of the other remote viewers. Was it just him, or were they all a little...preoccupied.

Travis watched Rankin walk down the center of the office, eyeing everyone on his way out. No, he didn't think it was just him. Down to the *person*, everyone seemed lethargic, elsewhere. Highly *off*. And there were no jokes flying about...no office banter. Whatever it was affected everyone. On a hunch, Travis passworded into his computer, brought up his e-mail, and typed:

Yo, all. Had a burst of inspiration—let's get together for a drink at Mel's—we hain't done that in a spell....

Then he entered the names of all those in the office—except Rankin's—and sent it. As he hit "Send" he eyed everyone. In no time various grunts and groans, a couple quick, furtive glances, and even one wadded-up ball of paper hit him in the shoulder.

What, you too lazy to talk to anyone in person?

You payin?

Pass; bad day.

Mel's? I'm in....

Travis assumed the flying wad of paper came from Mr. "Bad Day," Lee Everhart. But he curiously noticed no one responded back *out loud*—not even Ryan, who'd sent back the first reply. He also noticed how they seemed to look over their shoulders as they typed; glance out the corners of their eyes.

It wasn't *just him*.

Something was going on, and it affected every one of them.

Travis quickly sent: *It's on me.*

There was a louder collective grunt as the mails flooded back:

You're on, cowboy!

Now, we're talkin!

Rock and roll!

If you're paying, what the hell....

Another balled-up wad of paper beaned him dead center in the forehead.

He grinned back to its pitcher.

Travis typed in a time and sat back. Everyone, he noticed, glanced his way...and it was their looks that unnerved him. He could almost swear they were all silently pleading with him.

We need to get on this.

We need help.

Wasn't that the truth.

2

Five off-duty remote viewers all sat around two tables in Mel's Tavern, quietly picking at beer nuts and sipping colas and beer. No one spoke.

"How's everyone doin?" Travis asked.

"How d'you think?" Mr. Bad Day e-mailer, Lee, grunted.

"Well, if everyone's feeling like me," Travis offered, in as hushed a tone as he could muster in a packed and noisy bar, "then I pity ya...had a rough one, today—from what I remember, anyway. Don't even remember my last

(*Nostradamus*)

"task."

Travis stared down at the nuts—but noticed that everyone gave him that same thousand-yard stare.

"This happen to anyone else?" he asked.

Lee remained silent. Gina looked ready to say something, but didn't. Ryan looked to the others, saw the unrest, and said, "It ain't just you, bro."

Cory said, "Thought it was," then took another sip of beer.

"There ya go, thinking again," Lee said. "Apparently, it's all of us. Ain't that just fuckin hilarious."

"Don't really know," Travis said. "All I do know is that today's been the weirdest day of my life; I can't remember my sessions, or if I even had lunch."

"Yup," Ryan said.

"Me, neither," Gina said.

"And me," Cory said.

"And I feel as if I'm forgetting something...something really *big*," Gina added.

Lee nodded.

"Well, I guess it's unanimous, then…," Ryan said.

"And I'd had this really weird dream, too," Travis continued, "I could have *sworn*…" he said, lowering his voice even more, causing everyone to immediately lean in, "*he'd* been in my house. My *bedroom*," he whispered.

They all looked to each other and leaned back in their chairs.

"Okaaaay…can this *get* any weirder?" Ryan said.

"Keep talking," Lee said. "You ain't tellin us anything new."

Several others silently nodded, casting glances over their shoulders.

"You think we're being watched—drugged?" Cory asked.

"No," Lee said, "I think it's much more insidious than that."

"Agreed," Gina said. "And it's only been recently. Like in the past month or so…there's things I've wanted to say, but didn't know how to—or even if I—*we*—should."

"No place's safe," Ryan said

They all took sips from their drinks.

"Something's going on and it has to do with us, the job, or whoever's running things. I'm not even sure if Rankin's safe," Gina said. She stared off into space blankly for a moment. Ryan elbowed her, and she snapped out of it, eating a handful of beer nuts as if nothing'd happened.

"Agreed," Lee said, nodding and eyeing Gina.

"So…what do we do?" Ryan asked.

Pensive in his response, Travis smiled and rose his drink before him. With a mischievous grin, he said, looking to each of them, "We do…what we do *best*."

Chapter Nineteen

1

Mel's statement greatly bothered Lizzie.

He knew or *met* Black?

It was hard to get those thoughts out of her head as she worked to fulfill her *1-900-Psi-Kick* obligations. Whether it was worrying about Mel, or her afternoon vision, Lizzie was, again, unable to do her job. To *read* people. She couldn't fake it and never used Tarot cards, like other "psychic companies" did. Her ability simply wasn't working, and this was quickly becoming a trend. She'd tried two callers—even made things up—but just couldn't continue in this way. So what if she was wrong, she figured, no one really believed in the stuff anyway, even though she only made up *good* stuff—but still, it weighed heavily upon her. She'd hoped she could trick herself into getting into the groove, but it wasn't working, and she ended up calling it quits for the night.

And there had been more.

She'd almost forgotten about them, but she'd had those Bravo Force operator visions again. And every time they intruded, subtle things changed in them. But, that family...*it was like they were* meant *to die.*

Who were they?

Why were they murdered?

Vision or not, she kept coming back to what Mel had said.

He might have already met him. He might even know *him.*

Black.

Why would Black have anything to do with a young kid, like Mel? What could possibly be the connection between them? Maybe she should call him—

But, she'd never gotten his number.

Was that right?

He'd always called *her*.

Had it had never come up during their conversations?

Lizzie got up, almost tripped over some red, blue, and yellow wooden building blocks, and kicked them aside. Paced the living room.

Black.

He was obviously central to everything. He'd had contact with the both of them. Somehow, that had to make the three of them related, in some weird, scary way.

She shuddered, clasping her arms into her chest.

What could Black possibly want with a seventeen-year-old kid who'd just lost his parents, and a thirty-two-year-old psychic who'd lost her husband?

She had to—*somehow*—contact Mel.

Mel Roberts. She knew his name. Did he have a middle name? Did she know where he lived?

Somewhere in the Midwest.

That was all she knew?

Christ, she didn't even know his *parents'* names! Wasn't that just a little weird? What had they spent so much time talking about, for heaven's sake?

Lizzie sat down before her muted TV.

Why'd she always leave this damned thing on for, anyway?

You know why, Mommy, said the little girl who sat on the floor before her, playing with the wooden blocks. *Why do you always worry so much?*

"It's my nature, honey."

Do all adults worry so much?

"Yes, many do."

Why?

Lizzie folded her arms, frowning. "I don't know. Because we're insecure, I s'pose. Scared."

Oh, the little girl said, spelling out "Mel NMI Roberts" with the blocks on the floor. *He's a nice boy, isn't he?*

Lizzie nodded. "Yes, he is, and I'm very worried about him."

Why don't you go see him?

"I *can't*, honey," Lizzie said, getting to her feet. "I don't know where he lives!", she said, gesturing frustratedly. "And I have this *really* bad feeling about things—"

I thought that wasn't working.

The little girl now blocked out the name "Magic Man."

"Me, too. Interesting. Maybe I'm basing the feeling on what he said. He said he *thought* he met him. *That* scares me. He wouldn't say something like that if it hadn't actually happened."

He scares us, too.

"Black" was now spelled out. Lizzie saw the name on the floor.

"*What do* you *know of him?*"

He's trying to find us. Get rid of us. But, we're safe, for now.

"Murderer" was now spelled out.

"Oh, my God. This is…none of this makes any sense. How—"

You worry too much. Relax. Good night, Mommy.

As she disappeared, Lizzie grimaced and was about to turn away, when she again saw the blocks. This time they spelled out "relax."

Lizzie toed the blocks. They moved, but still spelled "relax."

"Yeah, right."

Lizzie sat back down on the couch, threw her head into her hands, then sat back and closed her eyes, letting out a long sigh.

Relax.

How?

She was a psychic prodigy who'd suddenly lost all her super powers, had ghost children giving her advice, and a strange "man in black" following her—asking *her* to work for *them*.

And why the hell hadn't she ever asked Mel where he lived? His *phone* number?

How could she have been so self-centered? Good God, what was her problem?

It wasn't like she could call the cops—all she had was Mel's name and a mysterious man who she felt could easily cover his tracks.

Would she really be able to bide her time and wait things out?

Lizzie looked to the clock. It was only midnight. Legs running in place a million miles an hour, she deactivated the TV's mute button. A commercial about peace flashed across the TV screen, which then returned to the movie, *The Terminator*. In less than an hour, Lizzie had nodded off into a troubled sleep, before the terrorizing cyborg killing machine and its glowing, red eye….

2

It was the sunlight boldly streaming in her windows that woke her. A *Voyage to the Bottom of the Sea* rerun played on the TV she'd left on.

Lizzie shot a glance down to the floor. The word "relax" was still there, a couple of its letters knocked out of place from where she'd toed the blocks. Lizzie grunted and sat up; rubbed her eyes. Her stomach rumbling, she got up and made her way toward the bathroom, but diverted to the front window. It was another positively *beautiful* morning. Should she make breakfast or head outside for a walk? When was the last time she'd gone for an early morning stroll?

Oh, yeah—Black.

Damn him, he was *still* harassing her, if only through her own thoughts constantly gravitating to him.

Lizzie watched the beautiful golden rays spray across the tops of the spruce trees. She left the window and hurried into the kitchen, grabbed an apple from the refrigerator, and filled a water bottle. She put her hair into a ponytail, threw on sweats, sneakers, a baseball cap, and sunglasses, and flew outside her trailer. She inhaled deeply of the cool morning mountain air, took a bite from her apple, and made her way out of the trailer park onto the back country road that skirted it. The sun's disk was just clearing the treetops.

Relax, the blocks had said, *relax*.

Sure, in a perfect world…before Joe had been ripped away. Before reliving his death yesterday.

Something inside her seemed to have changed. Her abilities had deserted her.

Why?

And how was she going to handle her renewed angst…her fears about Mel—and, above all, *why the hell was Black still on her mind?* She'd already given him her answer, and he'd taken it…and maybe that was the problem. He'd taken it *too* easily. Why he really wanted her, she didn't know, either, but he'd obviously put some serious time and effort into finding her. That scared her. She was a *nobody*…yet this government agent had put in all this time and energy to locate and track her down.

Why?

Finished with her apple, she flicked the core into a roadside bush, took another sip from her water bottle, and again looked to the sunrise.

Absolutely stunning.

It stopped her dead in her tracks.

With so much beauty in the world, how could there be so much evil?

Perhaps they balanced each other out on a global Zen level, but, for now, Lizzie was going to put—or try to, anyway—her problems behind her and complete the rest of her walk. In relative peace.

Enjoy the sunrise...

...easier said than done.

Problems didn't just go away when ignored.

On top of everything, she'd tried to figure out some way to contact Mel. A total bust, of course. She had nothing, not even Caller ID (apparently it had been blocked). She'd stopped several times to clear her head, soak up the sunlight, and bathe her face in the sunrise's glow...but thoughts of Joe (and everything else) nagged. Once or twice she even swore she'd felt Joe holding her hands.

Finally, he seemed to be making himself known.

If he'd decided to be with her, now, while she enjoyed the sunrise, then, better late than never.

But there was Black.

His face continually invading her warm-fuzzies.

She'd be all warm and cozy with thoughts of Joe, then—*BAM!*—in would pop Mr. FBI. Mr. Weird. Mr. Evil. Granted, it was easy to refocus back in on Joe and the glorious sunrise as it hung above the earth like a Biblical

(*Nostradamus*)

prophecy, but this—this man—always snuck back into her head.

Why had her life taken such a bad turn? She used to be so fervent in her beliefs, so sure of them and her life. That life would take her where she needed to go, that *good* things would fall into place—which, for the most part, they had.

It was Joe's death that had thrown things upside down.

Now, she asked herself, as the sun rose higher above the trees, what was she supposed to do?

What was life about, now? Why was she where she was?

There had to be more to life than met the eye, her livelihood was supposed to be proof enough of that, but, then, how could things go so terribly wrong with Joe's passing? And it wasn't even a case of looking at Joe's death as "bad"—we all have to die sometime of something—but she felt there was something more to all this.

And why now?

Why did Joe have to go before her, and in the *manner* he did?

Sheesh, die in your sleep, for Chrissake!

She believed we all, on some level, pick our time of passing, and maybe that's what bothered her the most.

Why had Joe decided to leave like that?

What could have possibly forced him into leaving when he had—and in the manner he'd chosen? Death wasn't the end and she knew (or at least *used* to believe she *knew...*) that, but, dammit, *why?* She still felt him out there, in the afterlife, but if he was allowing her to feel him now, *why wasn't he giving her more to work with?*

Once or twice she'd even heard the ghostly laughter of her children as they milled about, as she walked this empty road, and had even seen a group of them up ahead, playfully skipping and laughing and tussling with each other. So, her abilities hadn't totally deserted her. The children should have made her smile, but, truth be told, they only brought on another level of sadness and longing.

Joe and her were supposed to have had children...but they'd found a problem, hadn't they? She'd been tested...declared *"unable to bear."* Wonderful. No kids for you, but, hey, let's taunt you with visions of what you *could* have had, for the rest of your life....

Lizzie entered the trailer park, head down.

Defeated. Trailer trash, that's all she was.

A widowed ex-psychic. Nothing more than Colorada double-wide trailer trash.

So, why then did someone like Black need her? Why was she so damned important?

Keys out, Lizzie looked up as she approached her trailer—

Or what should have been her trailer.

She stood before the structure that *should have been* her home.

She looked about her.

No...she hadn't made any mistakes. This was the right spot.

But where her trailer *should have been*...now stood a completely different one in both design and paint.

In place of *her* trailer.

Impossible. This was *impossible!*

How could something like this happen?

Lizzie spun around and again examined her street and the neighboring trailers.

It was all right…all the other trailers she recognized were still there, the address was correct, *but, where there ought to be* her *trailer, was a different one.*

Knowing how warped life could be, she still tried the lock.

No go.

The key didn't fit.

She stepped back, grimacing, hands on her hips.

"What is going on *here?"*

She again looked to the other trailers.

"Okay, this makes absolutely no sense—"

Lizzie scratched her head and looked back to what was supposed to be her home. Again tried the key. Still no-go.

"What the—"

A large hand slipped around her neck, cupped her mouth, and a body

(Joe!)

pressed up behind her.

She swooned with excitement, tasted something sweet, but soon realized that the grip about her body was anything but pleasant, the hand cupping her mouth anything but amorous, and actually held a wad of material in it—material that smelled of ether and was forcefully shoved and held over her mouth and nose….

3

Victor Black quickly threw the slumped body of Lizzie Gordon over his shoulders and disappeared between and behind the trailers. A dark van sat idling, rear doors open. Quickly and well-practiced, Black deposited her unconscious form into it and closed the doors. He never looked back as he calmly entered the driver's side of the vehicle, undid the brake, and pulled out from behind the trailers, forever leaving behind the rest of One Tree, Colorado's trailer trash.

Chapter Twenty

1

Mel awoke on the floor of a room totally white and, apparently, without doors or windows.

He awoke to an extremely sore jaw, cheekbone, and left elbow, and lay within a dark puddle of what had to be his own blood; had a dried and crusty trail of same about his nose, mouth, and chin. His vision was cloudy—or merely overcome by the intense glare emanating from all surfaces of the totally empty room—which also brought on a spate of nauseating vertigo.

"*Where is he?*," came an angry voice. "*Where* is *he?*"

Mel shakily pushed himself upright.

"*Where is he?*"

Mel unsteadily got to his feet. His sense of balance was heavily impaired from the lack of solid, physical references. And *glare*.

"Where's *who?*" Mel asked, painfully working his jaw and shielding his squinting eyes. Both his elbow and face throbbed. Before he could ask anything else, he was struck hard from the left. Mel dropped like a sack of potatoes, and smashed his face into the blinding floor.

Calmer now, the same disembodied voice again asked, "Where...is...*he?*"

Mel opened his mouth, but the excruciating pain and the torrent of blood that freshly issued from his nose and mouth, mixed with a re-issuing of snot and tears, made it all but impossible. His jaw felt broken.

Mel looked up just as a barely discernible figure, covered head to toe in white, delivered a powerful kick to his stomach. The figure quickly retreated back into the white and glare. Mel lurched, more blood and snot ejecting from him and arcing its spray across the floor. He lay there, unable to move, staring into the ever-widening puddle of the only color in the room. Even his clothes were gone. He also wore a white—albeit blood-and-snot stained—overall of some kind, his hands, face, and feet exposed.

Where was he and how had he gotten here?

Something moved—flashed before him—and he felt a kick to his back. Kidneys.

None of this could possibly be real. Had *to be a nightmare!*

All he had to do was to outlast it all until he woke up...most probably on that downstairs couch before the TV. Maybe give Lizzie another call...*Lizzie....*

He didn't see the next kick coming, again delivered from behind, but, this time to his head. It shut down all the glare and light as neatly as if a light switch had been thrown...

...the next thing Mel experienced was the pain of opening his eyes. He remained imprisoned in the same pristine white room—but found himself...*standing.*

Yes...he vaguely remembered having been *helped* to his feet...

He looked down. Barefoot and hunched over, he was barely able to hold himself in this way. Yet, he still stood in a puddle of red, *his* red. A puddle of red that was smeared across sections of his blinding white overalls; stray blood, he could barely make out in all the glare, was what had to be darkly scattered across the walls. Tentacles of pain speared and throbbed throughout his body in sickening waves, as he forced himself upright. Checking his mouth and jaw, he found his wounds fresh and flared pain when he worked his jaw too much. He couldn't have been out more than a minute or two. His vision remained blurred and nauseatingly unsettled.

All he wanted to do...was *die.*

Mel coughed, and felt as if tiny knives lacerated his throat. He instantly doubled forward, back into that upright fetal position, and began to sob.

What the hell had happened to his life?

Two sets of hands reached out to him; gently supported him.

He started, staggering backward a step, and almost slipped in the blood-and-vomit puddle when the hands stabilized him.

White—everything was white—except for his hands and feet, his blood—and it were precisely these things that gave him the precious foothold of perspective he needed to orient himself and not go mad with vertigo. It was still hard to focus, but as he looked up, he saw a little girl holding one of his hands while she anchored an arm, a little boy holding the other. They couldn't have been more than six years old.

"Hello," the girl whispered, calmly, intently looking to him.

Mel coughed. "*What's happening?*" he said, wincing from his jaw injury.

"You *can* get out of this," the girl said. Mel saw tears running down her cheeks. Looking to the boy, he saw the same thing.

"*What's happening to me?*" Mel yelped, feeling and hearing broken jaw bones grind in his head. Keeping his jaw still, he gritted his teeth and focused on just moving his lips. "Why are they beating me up—what have I done...*what have I done?* Who *are* they?"

"We want to tell you," the boy said, "but it's *difficult.*"

"*He's* difficult," the girl added. "He knows we're here and isn't allowing it...or is trying not to..."

"*Who?* Allowing *what?*" Mel asked, wincing in another wave of pain.

"Us helping you. It's taking all we can just to be here like this," the girl said.

"*Why? Why* all this?"

"He thinks you know where *he* is. That man. He doesn't realize you don't," the boy said.

"He's going to kill you if you don't tell him," the girl said.

"We're trying to help you. Just hold on—*don't let go.*"

"It's going to get worse—just don't let go. Hold on to us—*no matter what.*"

"We'll be right by you," said the boy, "all the time—"

Mel lurched. He really needed to throw up.

"I don't feel good," Mel said, tears running down his face. "I don't understand—"

"*Hold on,*" the girl commanded, looking into his eyes.

"To *us,*" the boy reiterated. "*Us.*"

Mel again jerked. His stomach roiled like a train wreck.

"What's happening?"

"*Please,*" the little girl pleaded, "hold *on*—look at us. We're *trying....*"

"Oh, no," Mel said, again feeling the powerful impact of a locomotive ramming into his midsection, his back. "I don't think...I don't think I can...."

Something was wrong with his stomach, and it needed release. Moaning and groaning, Mel prepared for the inevitable. No longer able to speak, and a cold, clammy sweat running off his face and into his eyes in sheets, he squeezed the hands of the two six year olds in a death grip. They were full-on crying, pleading for Mel to stay with them—*to not let go*—their own faces swollen and puffy.

Mel seemed suddenly to be standing outside himself as he opened his mouth and turned his face away from the children, hoping not to spray either of them with his latest release of bloody vomit....

The torrent of vomit Mel unleashed did nothing to ease his pain. Something continued to assault him. He opened his eyes to partial slits, skin cold and clammy, and saw he was now restrained—but by two different individuals—the white-clad ghost figures from before. Another stood before him, wasting no time in again winding up and wielding what appeared to be a pure-white baseball bat.

BAM!

Into his stomach.

BAM!

Through barely open, semi-conscious eyes, Mel saw nothing but white glare, tasted the blood-and-vomit mixture in his mouth, and inhaled its revolting odor. There was also a warmth draining down his legs...and a bowel movement....

Yet, somehow, through his pathetic haze he noticed how all three ghostly figures had managed to avoid any contact with the spoils of their torture. It was getting harder to stay conscious...his attention wand—

BAM!

Following another delivery of the white bat came short strikes (and flashes of white light) to his head and face with the narrow end of the stick.

Hold on to us....

Had he dreamed up those children? Where were they...how could he look to them if they weren't here?

As Mel was continually pummeled...and the white baseball bat came crashing down upon his left arm with a brutal, distinctive snap that finally blacked him out in a blinding flash of white-hot pain...what were left of his thoughts drifted to the calm and peace and tranquility of what had been his home…to a mother and father he no longer had—nor remembered; to the birthday cake he'd found in the kitchen and which his mother *had* to have made; to the Vernors soda in the refrigerator…and to the warm and pleasant late-night conversations he'd had with Lizzie, in the comfort and safety of intimate familiarity…

If they were going to do him in…could they please get on with it, so he could finally meet his parents…he had *so* much to ask them.…

2

Travis awoke sweating, hyper alert, heart hammering away in his chest. It was shortly after one a.m.

Something wasn't right. He didn't feel well. *Why* didn't he feel well?

He lay back in bed, eyes open. Something to do with a dream? He had to bring it back, before—

BAM!

White!

BAM!

Red!

BAM!

Black.

A boy…*a boy was being beaten!*

Something about a kid getting the shit beat out of him? Pleas for help?

Travis's stomach revolted.

Queasy, he got out of bed and headed to the kitchen.

A glass of water.

But, nauseated and clammy, his legs wavered…and he lost it. He vomited into the sink—not once, but several times—until all he could do was grip the sink, repeatedly pumping out one dry heave after another and praying for the painful regurgitations to end.

Pale and weak, Travis clung to the sink. His vision blurry and wet, he unsteadily reached for a glass, filled it from the tap, then took a trembling sip, but ended up coughing it out; barely returned the glass to the counter without dropping it. He collapsed to the kitchen floor, gasping for air. Cradling his stomach, groaning and hunched over, he wiped his mouth.

The phone rang.

Still grunting in pain and unable to move any kind of fast, he let the answering machine get it.

"Travis…are you there? Travis? It's Gina. Pick *up*—we've got to talk—"

Travis crawled over to the phone, smearing vomit across the floor on his way over to the wall phone. He grabbed a broom that leaned against the wall and clumsily swiped at the handset until he knocked it free from its cradle. Travis then batted the handset about like a drunken cat, until he finally grabbed it.

"Gina—"

He again retched a dry heave.

"*Travis?*"

"Vomited…just vomited…feel I broke some ribs…"

Gina said nothing.

"Don't think they're actually broken…but this dream—"

"A boy…savagely beaten," Gina said.

Travis's response was another bout of dry heaves. Gina waited patiently until he could recompose himself.

"Any better?" she asked.

"About as much as anyone can be…like this."

"If it makes you feel any better, we all went through what you're going through. We've all had the same dream."

Travis said nothing, experiencing another set of *dry heaveus interruptus.*

"I've already talked with the others, Trav. We all had the exact same dream, the exact same reaction. Lee, Ryan, and Cory—everyone."

"Great, feel better already," he said, dryly. "White room, white figures…that fucking baseball bat?"

"That fucking baseball bat—all of it. Believe me, I've never had anything like this ever happen before. It scares me."

Travis took a couple deep, painful breaths—spit—then gritted his teeth.

"Right now, I guess I'm a little too sick to be scared."

"Is it a message?"

"Considering we're all getting it…I'd say so," Travis said, lying down on the floor. "Providing no one else is messing around with us."

"Agreed."

"Does anyone know who this is?"

"Nope. Who's 'Lizzie?'"

Travis grunted a "don't know."

"You thinking the same thing I'm—"

"We've got to. What about this call?"

"I checked it out before calling. No one's listening. I've been up for a while. I'm actually surprised you're only just getting this."

"Someone has to pull up the rear."

Gina chuckled. "This is pretty weird...but we gotta find this boy—and is this even real, or just a dream?"

Travis just continued groaning.

"But there's something odd about it..."

"You mean besides the men in white, doorless room, and two ghost kids? That fucking bat? We need to look into this—ourselves," Travis said.

"On our own?"

"Yes." Travis again grunted. "And, you're right, there is something 'wrong' with the whole thing...but we have to rule out The Center, first. Keep it among us."

"Travis...what am I thinking of right now?"

Travis continued to wince from waves of the continued aftereffects of his filling the kitchen sink. "Come on, Gina, not now—"

"*What am I thinking of?*" she insisted. "We have to see how in tune we are with each other. It's imperative—now, more than ever. You *know* what I'm thinking, don't you."

"Yes..."

"Tell me."

"It's not exactly the most appealing thing to me right now, given—"

"Oh, right, sorry. Okay—try now."

"You're thinking about some three-legged cat you saw crossing the highway the other day. With a field mouse in its mouth—no, a vole. Highway 29."

"*Damn*—"

Travis's stomach finally began to settle, making its weird little gurgling-and-groaning sounds.

"Your turn."

"Go."

"You're thinking...about a model you built as a kid? A, what was it called—*The Invaders*, television show?—you built a silver flying-saucer model when you were twelve. Red slits—*lights*."

"You got it. Too bad we'd never tried this before. Coulda helped me in my divorce."

"A couple of us played around with it, but were always too busy; we're always too busy."

"Maybe that's how they want it. Keeps us out of other people's knickers, if you know what I mean."

"Maybe whatever's happening—or going on with this kid—is somehow, I don't know…accelerating things. I mean, we've been doing this for *how* long, and are only now able to read each other's minds on *this* level? We were never able to read minds *this* good. There's something else going on, here."

"Or maybe all our work has finally paid off. This is what we do, Gina. We've just never bothered to check it out."

"True."

"Can you read, say, Cory's mind, right now?"

"Yeah, and so can you. I *know* you can."

"He's eating Cheerios."

"Honey-nut."

"So, I guess, nothing's sacred anymore," Travis said.

"This could get quite embarrassing."

"Yeah," Travis said, grunting.

"No time to waste. Don't know how much time he has."

Both fell silent.

"I'm remembering dreams," Travis said, "right now, as we speak."

"Dreams?"

"Yeah…I just had a flash of some dream classes…"

"Wow…it wasn't until you said that that I just recalled some of my own. I hadn't been sleeping very well, lately. Anyway, there's this guy in charge—"

"He doesn't have a name, does he?"

"Yeah—I mean, no," Gina exclaimed. "A large amphitheater? This man—oh, this is *sooo* weird…."

"We need to get together. ASAP. Home in on this kid and what's going on. *Who's* doing this. Whoever's doing this is somehow involved with us, I feel it. I can't nail down a face, but get the definite feeling he's—"

"Now, isn't *that* weird? Why can't we pick up on him?"

"Don't know. I'm sure we're being blocked—which makes no sense."

Gina went silent.

"I've got an idea," Travis said, "it's a little out there, but what the hell. We've played around with this before—why don't we all meet up in the dreamstate?"

"I like that."

"Yeah—and if it works, then we're just that much further along, and if it don't, we meet tomorrow? Before work." Travis glanced to the clock. "I guess that actually means this morning."

"Should I call the others?"

"No...at least, not the way you mean. Send out the call *mentally*. A request to meet each other after we go back to sleep. Let's see how far we can go with this. See if we can come up with anything in the morning.

"Man, my ribs really feel broken."

"Mine are still sore, too."

"Okay—after we hang up, put out the call, and we'll meet in a little bit."

"Hope this works."

"For his sake, I hope it works; I really don't think he has much time left, but I don't know where else to start. It makes me sick just thinking about it."

"Okay, then."

"Good night, Gina—and thanks. For calling."

Chapter Twenty-One

1

Kennedy again found himself sitting in the amphitheater, but this time not alone. In fact, it was packed with people, all talking and laughing and seemingly having a good old time. There was an infectious undercurrent of excitement running throughout the entire carved granite stadium's gathering. Kennedy turned to a group of men and women sitting beside him. "Hello," he said, "we must be dreaming."

"Yeah, we are," one woman returned. "I love dreams—everything's so much more *real!*" She returned to her conversation.

Kennedy knew her name to be Gina.

"Excuse me, but I know you, don't I?" JFK asked.

Gina focused her full attention on him. "I'm sorry, what were you saying? Oh, *yes*—you do," she said, touching his arm. "We all know you, too."

Kennedy nodded. It suddenly dawned on him that he also knew everyone else in the amphitheater.

It felt very comfortable here.

"Wow," Kennedy said, looking skyward, "it's absolutely *beautiful* tonight. The *stahs*…"

Gina looked up. A long sigh escaped her. "I wish every night could be like this…."

Kennedy reached out and put his arm around her. Gina, looking to Kennedy, smiled, and snuggled up beside him. Together they lay back on the granite steps and stared into the night sky.

"What do you think it all means?" Gina asked.

"Don't know. Nevah gave it much thought—I mean, we all give it *some* thought, ovah the years, but life usually gets in the way. I've just tried to, ah, live life the best way I knew. I've always felt destined forah something great—"

"You were president; have this incredible family."

Kennedy didn't immediately answer. "I guess so...and I had a lot of impact in the world. But I always felt therah was something...morah...still out therah. I thought bringing peace to the world would actually be my calling, to tell you the truth."

"You *are* doing that," Gina said, snuggling up closer.

Kennedy paused, as if suddenly remembering a forgotten memory. "Hm. Guess I am. That was weird. How could I have forgotten that?"

Gina smiled.

"It's pretty weird knowing you're dreaming, *while* you're dreaming," Kennedy said, "That happen to you a lot?"

"Yeah, actually; part of my job."

Kennedy nodded.

"Hey—and that's another great thing you did! You got *us* started!"

"Now, I *do* remember that! I was a little worried, at first, you know, that things would get out of hand, but it seems to have worked out quite well, hasn't it?"

"It has—we all love our work...except for one guy—"

"Black."

Gina sat up. "I just don't understand how people like him...well, you've taken care of that, anyway...."

Kennedy also straightened up on the granite step. "You mean it *worked?* Really *worked?*"

"You went back and changed things. You didn't hire him. You kept him out of the program for a long time."

"You say that as if—"

"Sorry, sir, but he did manage to sneak back in."

"Wait a minute, I'm confused...I thought you just said I'd taken care of him?"

"I'm sorry, sir, it is a dream...and sometime we say contradictory things. It's all about probabilities."

"*Damn!*" Kennedy said, shooting to his feet. "*How'd he do that?* How'd he get back in?"

"Not sure. Maybe that's why we're all here. All I know is that he's still involved with us, but how, I'm not entirely sure."

"You know, when I ran into him—back thereah—he did seem to know something was up. It was in his eyes. The way he looked at me. And I took this away from him," he said, bringing out the pen he'd snatched from Black back in The Center conference room.

"What is it?"

"Oh, it's an Agency-developed pen-gun. Quite ingenious those people. I wrestled it out from his jacket pocket. To think he was actually going to try to off me—right then and thereah—tells me how important all this is to him. In ways I probably can't even, ah, begin to imagine. All I know is that he's evil...a cataclysmic event waiting to happen, and I don't know how to stop him! *Damn* him," Kennedy again said, not knowing what to do with himself, but unable to pace the crowded stadium. "*This really pisses me off!*"

Gina stood and reached out to him. "Well, don't worry just yet, sir. You still have all of us, you know. It's not just your battle. Look around."

Kennedy did. All the talking and laughter had ceased. He looked to those in the amphitheater. Everyone—all the children, all the adults—looked to *him*; gave warm, understanding smiles. In his mind he heard: *Gina's right, we're all here for you, just as you're here for us. We're all in this together.* Remember *that!*

Everyone returned to their conversations, to the same level of excitement and noise prior to their diversion.

"We're all being taught here," Gina said, "Right now. You may not see it, but we are. He's very good."

"I've known him from way back. He gets around."

Gina laughed. "If you only knew how much!"

"I wish I knew how he did it."

"He's a very special guy. He's good at what he does, is all I know."

Kennedy and Gina sat back down, and again snuggled back up to each other. Together they again lay back to watch the stars....

2

In the dark of night, the Man With No Name took another sip of iced tea. He leaned back in his chair on his front porch.

"You did a great job, Mr. President. It may not seem like it—but you did."

Kennedy jerked forward, almost spilling his iced tea.

"Hey, now—careful there, sir! If you're not gonna drink the stuff, give it to me—I hate wasting a good beverage!"

"What—I was just—"

"I know. Not only does this illustrate how you are being trained,

216 | F.P. Dorchak

between layers of consciousness you may or may not be aware of, this is also my way of adding another layer of confusion to Black. He's a slippery bastard, as I'm sure you're aware. What Gina told you."

"Gina—wasn't I just talking with her?"

"Still are. I've just slipped in for a spell," he said, extending an angled hand into the night before him like a fighter pilot, "real tricky-like, so he doesn't know where we are. All he might possibly see are all of you in that dream together, and it'll frustrate the hell out of him, because he *knows* I'm around...somewhere...but he just can't nail me down!"

"How do you do all this?"

"Well, now, that's a trade secret, Mr. President. Can't tell you everything. Less you know, safer things are. Plausible deniability and all that."

"What 'things?'"

"Black's on a roll. You may have changed the outcome to whether or not you hired him, but he knew that was coming and prepared for it. It wasn't a big coup, what you did, but it was enough to monkey-wrench his plans and annoy the hell out of him."

"So he is still with us."

"Yeah." The Man With No Name took another sip. "Take a drink, Jack, see if you like it. It's my own special blend."

Kennedy took a sip, ice clanking about in the glass, and wiped spilled tea from the side of the glass and the back of his hand. "Thank you. It *is* good!"

"Oh, it's just a little something I whipped up. Now, you need to realize that you're not acting alone any more, like your friends said. I'm gonna have to get you all together sooner than I'd expected. Though you did delay Black, there's no contradiction when I say that that just caused him to accelerate matters."

Kennedy nodded. "So...what do we do?"

"Work as a team. Surround him, literally and figuratively. He's got a hostage, you know."

"A *hostage?*"

The Man With No Name took another sip, then got up out of the chair. He set his glass down on the railing before him. Stared out into the night.

"He's captured...and is torturing...a boy he thinks knows my whereabouts."

"*Does* he?" Kennedy asked as he also got to his feet. He heard the

Man With No Name inhale deeply and straighten up, as if his answer was gonna be painful.

"No...he doesn't. That's what makes all this worse. He's going to kill that kid to get him to give an answer he can't deliver. And it's all my fault. He's done this before."

"Why don't we just take him out? We have teams out thereah for just this kind of—"

The Man With No Name turned to him. "I wish it were that simple, sir, but just as we're working behind his back, he is working behind ours. If we were to just go in and do that, it would upset far more than it would alleviate. Believe me—I don't intend to let this boy die." He turned back to the darkness. "Not at all...."

"But, he's being *tortured.*"

The Man With No Name turned back around. "I know. And if we were to just charge on in there, with everything he has in place, far more would be destroyed. He knows this, he's not stupid. He's baiting us. This is exactly what he wants us to do, and we can't take the bait.

"If you knew you could save one life versus many what would you do—as President, Jack—how would you handle this scenario?"

The Man With No Name crossed his arms and leaned back against the railing.

"If I'd used all my options? If I'd already tried several times to rescue the one—and nothing worked?"

The Man With No Name nodded.

"Then, I'd have no choice. Go with the many—but, I'd still have a parallel task force working on the *one.*"

"Exactly. You'd do everything in your power to save that boy, but you'd also do all you could to save the world. That's what we're doing. But, to show our hand right now would do far more harm than good, and that kills me to have to admit, especially when it comes to an innocent.

"But we also can't put things off too much more," he continued, "because if we do...then our innocent dies. I will not allow that to happen.

"What we have to do, sir, is work together. You'll be working with Gina and her group, but on levels that may or may not be immediately clear—don't ask—it'll all play out as efforts solidify. I just wanted to let you know that we *are* close to our offensive, I guess you could say. Things change in an instant—"

The Man With No Name's face suddenly went slack.

218 | F.P. Dorchak

"What's the matter?" Kennedy asked.

"He's done it again!"

"Done what? Who?"

The Man With No Name paced the porch in quick, frustrated steps. "*He's got another!*"

"How do you know this?"

"I can't—Jack, just be ready. We're always in contact, just like I know what happened. Shit—this *again* changes things. I really didn't want to have to show our hand this soon!"

"Who's the other hostage?"

"A woman he thinks can also lead him to me—and he's much closer to the truth with her than he knows—but, not in the way he *thinks* he knows. Shit-shit-*shit!* He's been a pain in my ass for *lifetimes*...."

"Mr. President, I'm sorry, but I have to go. You have all you need for now, just be open and ready. Things are going to happen *fast*."

President Kennedy nodded. He was about to say something, when he found himself back in the amphitheater, talking with Gina. Still talking with her.

Had he always *been talking with her?*

Kennedy paused, as if suddenly remembering a forgotten memory. "Hm. Guess I am. That was weird. How could I have forgotten that?"

Gina smiled.

"It's pretty weird knowing you're dreaming, *while* you're dreaming," Kennedy said, "That happen to you a lot?"

"Yeah, actually; part of the job."

As Kennedy continued talking with Gina, he kept trying to pull whatever weird memory was way back in the depths of his mind...but it didn't budge. He didn't want to be rude to Gina, but it got to the point where he'd simply lost whatever the memory was, and had to let it go....

What had Gina just said?

"You say that as if—"

"Sorry, sir," Gina said, "but he did manage to sneak back in..."

"*Damn!*"

3

Black opened his eyes.

There *were* spies in his midst. He *knew* it.

Sitting behind his desk in his darkened office, he stared straight ahead at the wall. He didn't know who or how many, but that damned man from his nightmares was behind it all. First he'd been hunting him in his dreams, then he gets to Kennedy—and now The Center. Infiltrated them.

Time to drop the hammer.

If you wanted things done—and done right—you simply had to do them yourself.

No more fucking around.

He was just going to have to take matters more into his own hands—and now he had a little help. Too bad if things got messy. Wetwork *was* his specialty. And if he had to orchestrate a little world domination along the way, so be it. He would put an end to him forever—one way or the other. And Kennedy. Those two were inextricably linked. They were, in a manner of speaking, *history*....

Chapter Twenty-Two

1

Lizzie awoke, groggily.

Walking…she'd been taking a stroll…in the glorious sunrise…the air had smelled so sweet, so fresh and….

Then what'd happened?

Her trailer…*gone.*

Her trailer had simply up and left?

How had that been possible? How could her—

Slowly the haze burned off…she opened her eyes…made out her surroundings.

A blinding white room…

Upright. A high-backed chair. She tried to get up.

Unable to.

She looked down—tried to, anyway—but her head was anchored. She tried to move it back and forth, but was only able to move about a half-inch or so. Something was placed close to both sides of her head. Her awareness traveled down her body…to her chest, arms, wrists (*bound to something?*)…legs…to her ankles. All restrained. She wiggled and shifted against her bonds.

Not only was a shocking *why* in her head, but *who*….

Of course. There was only one "who" in her catalogue of individuals.

What had she gotten herself into?—or, more importantly, what had *Black* gotten her into?

She'd done nothing to attract any of this—except live. *Doing her own thing.* This was all Black's doing. *All* of it. She'd had no hand in it, hadn't stuck her nose into any areas it hadn't belonged…hadn't pissed off anyone. She'd kept to herself and out of everyone else's business—except where invited and accepted by both parties. *Black* had invited her to *his* party, and it had been an invitation she'd flatly rejected. Twice.

And now, where was she, and what had Black planned for her?

She closed her eyes and felt her fear expand like a rising bubble. She had to shut it down, nip it in the bud. Mustn't let him see her crack—even if she was a wreck inside.

But how tough was she? How much could she endure—physically or mentally? She'd read about people under torture. Those had been *other people. She* wasn't supposed to be one of them—she was supposed to be low-income, blue collar, living a comfortable, cozy existence undetected by *evil.*

This wasn't supposed to happen!

Once more, she'd failed herself, hadn't she?

Hadn't been able to predict Joe's death *and hadn't been able to detect her own abduction.* Not a *whisper.*

Lizzie went limp in her restraints.

Of what use was she, really?

Of what possible use was she to herself, Mel, Joe, or anyone else, for that matter, if she couldn't help herself? Was all her so-called psychic ability a *fraud?* A hoax? Had everything she'd ever told been *lies?* Good Lord—if there had been even *one* lie, *one* misstep—*had she screwed up her callers' lives just like she'd done to her own?*

She couldn't, and didn't, want to hold it back. If Black saw her cry, big fucking deal. Just get it over with. She wouldn't fight back—deserved whatever she got. She couldn't save her husband, couldn't help Mel, and now she was just as totally useless to herself.

What a waste of her parents' biology.

A world where evil was allowed to thrive and overtake good…

Lizzie choked out huge, hot tears that raced down her cheeks, chin, and neck. She felt their wetness run down and onto her chest, which would have tickled under normal circumstances, but now only served to further upset her.

She should have been able to wipe them away!

She should have been able to use her arms, her legs—her entire body—but was bound to this damned chair!

And where were her children—*where were they?* The ones she was never able to bear, yet played and taunted her every day? Left their toys all over the place?

Psychic.

The word made her sick.

She was a charlatan—a fraud—and had finally been found out.

Bring it on, Black, do your goddamn worst. Make it as painful as possible, because I *deserve* it! I've screwed up every life I've ever touched....

2

Like the snapping of a stick, Travis experienced a tremendous emotional release, as he parked his Jeep and made his way into The Center. He sat there, engine still running. He'd had more troubling dreams or images after having gone back to bed after Gina's call, most of which he couldn't remember. But when he'd awoken that second time (his ribs had no longer pained him, though there was still a dull reminder), he'd felt an unaccountable emotional weight, like an angry Ogre chomping at the bit and stomping about in the wings. It didn't feel like it was anything about *him*, but he'd been unable to pinpoint where or to whom it did apply. The longer he'd been awake, the more intense the feeling grew. It was difficult to show up for work—but he had to meet the others and see if things really were as he and Gina had talked about, develop a—

Of course they are, came a mental response.

Gina? *Am I just making this up, or—*

Come on up and you'll know.

You also feel all this...anguish?

We all do.

Sure do. It was Ryan.

Yeah, and it's fucking pissing me off, Lee chimed in.

I can't believe we're actually communicating like this, Travis thought.

Weird or not, we're doing it, and something's the matter. Somehow, we're supposed to deal with this thing...make it right, Gina thought.

I know, but it's so weird. *I've never heard or read of any kind of intense mental communication like this between anyone—let alone our kind. On* any *level. It's all science fiction—*

Get over it, Trav, Cory thought, *cause it's real and we're living it—and we have a job to do. We can isolate and study later.*

We've got to be careful, Travis continued, *remember*, no *looks*. No *grins. If we're caught—we're history—*

By who? Ryan asked.

Black. Has to be him. If we're suddenly able to psychically communicate like this, is it that far of a leap to assume he's not likewise or similarly affected?

Silence.

Just limit to emergency use for now. Try to sandwich our thoughts in with the intent of hiding our contact, our communications. It may not work…but it might. It's all we've got.

Agreed.

Agreed.

Sure.

And one more thing…we need to locate the source of all this misery…whoever gets the opportunity—okay?

Everyone agreed.

Travis shut off his vehicle and made his way into the building, past several layers of security and into the upstairs hallway to their office. There he met Gina, talking with Ryan.

"Morning, kids. How's everyone?"

"As well as can be expected," Ryan said, taking a sip of coffee, briefly eyeing him.

"*Believe?*" Gina uttered in a barely audible whisper, taking a sip from her *Mello Yellow*. She stealthily looked up from her can, and pinched him with her free hand, as she turned to follow Travis on his way to their office. Ryan winked, then acted as if he'd had something caught in his eye, fussing with it for a while.

"Back to another day in the grind," Ryan added, and turned to follow.

3

"You know," Black said, standing before Lizzie Gordon, "I once—twice—gave you the opportunity to assist me on your own. I could forcibly work on you, now—just for the hell of it—or you could still come around of your own free will."

Lizzie looked to Black, barely opening her eyes. She'd been out, out hard, and had had some kind of dream about *Joe*…but she'd been ripped away from that dream, and was now—again—dealing with Victor Black. FBI, he'd claimed. And was helpless. Her eyes were sandy and bothered by the intense white glare of the chamber. She tasted an extra saltiness to her lips from earlier tears, mixed with that sweet taste from before.

"What...do I have to do...with *any* of this? Why do you need *me?*" she asked, her voice hoarse.

Black paced the room around her, hands interlaced pensively before him. "To tell the truth, dear woman, I don't know. All I do know is that you and this person I seek are inextricably linked. Though I am curious of the link, I'm more interested in results. I need you to find this person for me."

"Why can't you find him?"

"I assure you, if I could, I wouldn't be wasting my time with a two-bit phone psychic."

"I'm no more psychic than you are."

Black laughed. "I'm not sure you truly comprehend the depth of that statement, Mrs. Gordon."

"I'm nothing but a fake."

Black made a pensive, teasing face. "That may be...it doesn't really concern me, because—as I've already stated—I'm more concerned with whatever *link* you and my target possess. *Results.* So, once again, I ask for your cooperation. Do I have it?"

"*Why do you need anything from me?* You can obviously take whatever you want."

"Yes, but where's the fun in that? I have my answer."

Black exited the room.

A low humming gradually increased beside Lizzie's ears. The sound came from what had to be mini-speakers placed on both sides of her head. It was an odd sound that made half her mind want to go one way, while the other half went another. Initially, she found it interestingly comfortable, but she knew no good would come of it. Not with Black involved. This was just the beginning....

4

Mel Roberts lay on the glaring white floor in his growing pool of blood and vomit, his left arm twisted underneath him at a crazy angle.

He'd been screaming—lots of screaming.

Even in his sleep the pain that fracture shoved into his consciousness was like a red-hot splinter underneath a fingernail. He tried repositioning, but the pain only worsened. He couldn't move, and when he inhaled, sucked in some of the blood and vomit before him.

And there was also a searing pain shooting up from his groin and stomach region.

It hurt to breathe. Hurt *not* to breathe.

He was still unable to see straight...unable to focus on anything in the glare of the white room. Until, that is, he saw the black shoes and pants standing before him like the Angel of Death. He painfully craned his neck, following the dark columns up, up...

"I'm glad to see you're a survivor."

Mel grunted, gagging up blood.

Black reached down and grasped Mel's wet, matted hair. Callously yanked his face up toward him. Mel howled.

"What if I were to tell you I could make this all go away?"

Mel sobbed. Black released his tangled hair, and Mel's face smashed back into the blood and vomit.

Black paced the room. "What if...I could take you away from all this? Take away all the pain, the hurt, the damage done to your fragile little body? Would you like that? Would you, perhaps, want to do something for *me?*

"Let's see...."

Black stopped pacing and Mel stopped crying—just like that.

Mel no longer inhaled blood or vomit.

Instinctively, he pulled in both arms and pushed himself up off the floor.

He shakily got to his knees, looking to Black.

"What—what's going on here?" Mel asked, as he examined his now undamaged left arm; shot a hand to his ribcage and stomach, his groin.

"Oh, let me assure you, dear boy, your parts are, indeed, all where they should be. Undamaged."

Mel shakily rearranged his stance.

"What have you done to me—*why? What have I done to you?*"

Mel's face now swelled with emotion instead of physical pain.

"What could I have possible done to deserve this?"

"This '*what*?'" Black mocked.

"This...*beating*. This—"

Black took on a look of surprise. "*Beating?* Why, I see no *beating*...nor do I see broken bones, vomit, or blood. I just see a scared, whiny little child before me."

Mel reexamined himself. He may no longer have had a broken arm, squashed testicles, and smashed ribs, but there was definitely something damaged *inside*....

"My dear boy, all I need—it's so terribly simple—is for you to tell me what I want…and off you go," he said, scooching him off with an "off-you-go" gesture. "It's that simple. I'm not a mean man…just a demanding one. I get what I want. Sooner or later. One way or the other.

"Now…will you concede? Give me what I want?"

"*But I don't know what you want!*" Mel bleated, a little whinier than intended. "*Please*, mister, let me *go!*"

Black was in Mel's face before he could blink.

"Oh, 'please, mister' me *nothing*. I do something good for you, and this is the respect I get? *Tell me where he is!*"

"Where *who* is? I really don't know who you're talking a—"

"*Tell me, you little fuck, or one by one, I swear, I'll gladly rip each limb from your body and peel the meat from your bones before your very own eyes.* Tell *me.*"

Mel again began to sob, and Black shoved him into a wall. Mel hit and collapsed, but Black was on him in an instant, lifting him up off the floor like a bundle of rags.

"Listen to me you little shit, don't you yet realize the unimaginable *pain* I can inflict? Quit fucking around and be a man! Tell me where he is!"

But all Mel could do was cry. He was thinking of his bed at home…the TV and his favorite late-night movies…iced tea…peace and quiet. He tried to say something, *anything*, but his mind was in knots, muddled, thick as molasses, and his body had long since failed him. *Nothing made sense.* "I…I…" was all that dribbled out of quivering lips.

"Very well," Black said, opening his hands.

In an instant, Mel was once more overwhelmed by waves upon waves of pure, exquisite, soul-searing agony and collapsed to the floor. He tried to get up, but his left arm was again broken, his groin, stomach, and ribs again all on fire.

"I'll be back. And I'll have my answers."

Black stepped over Mel, as Mel once again vomited dry heaves and again sucked in snot and blood into a smashed and bleeding mouth pressed into the floor….

Chapter Twenty-Three

1

Kennedy leisurely strolled his beachfront property, inhaling the cool, early morning sea breezes. He tossed bits of bread into the air for the diving seagulls playfully airborne

(full moon?)

(parachutes?)

above.

What if, his thought process had begun all those many years ago, *what if we spent as much time and energy on peace as we did on war? A* peace *special forces—special operations for* peace...*why not have the same aggressiveness...but toward non-violent—*peaceful—*solutions?*

That was how it'd all started out with The Center and the Global Foundation for Peace, but it wasn't exactly how The Center'd ended up.

And how far had either program progressed?

The idea had been pure, but once he'd put the dream into reality, things'd changed. They always did. Especially when government got involved.

There were budgetary and political considerations, not to mention entrenched paradigms near-impossible to overcome, political and otherwise. Though The Center had been created first, during his first term, in '63, it was actually the GFP that had been his first consideration...even before his presidency. But it had been several years before he'd see that inspiration come to fruition. And, now it had surpassed the Peace Corps.

He'd had to narrow his focus, and though that hadn't been difficult, it had still been a dilution of his original dream. The GFP focused mainly on peace and peaceful methods—anywhere it was needed—whether in feeding the hungry, clothing the poor, educating children, or fighting various forms of domestic abuse (at home or abroad), but it still fell short of the original goal of being a civilian peace special forces. And The Center was supposed to be the governmental arm of that, but, of course, once government got involved in anything it had been turned into a prosaic military spy training-and-operations center, and though they got much done from both the military and civilian fronts, it still wasn't what he'd intended both to be. He'd wanted to marry both organizations together. Psychics fighting violence. Oppression. Hunger. War.

A hand-picked select group of individuals who would never use violence, because they would never *need* to. They could walk into the midst of situations and extinguish them—but from a totally unique point of view. They would be as *saints*—Mother Teresas, if you will—and would be immediately recognized worldwide and *revered*. They would *think* differently, *act* differently than the rest of us, and would wield great power—*responsible* power. Unspoken to anyone but himself—and Jackie, before her death—Kennedy had secretly hoped that the remote viewer research would reveal things that could secretly and quietly be put to use in both organizations. Psychic things that could change paradigms and *lives*. World views. Kennedy doubted he was the only one with this on his mind (he did have Black on his trail), but he thought, *okay, we know we can see into the past, present, or future...now, why not use that information for peaceful, more human, developmentally strategic advantages and change things for the better?* But, to do all this would require such an incredibly advanced...a different *kind* of human...one the world had never seen before. *Christ-like near-deities.* Literal *saints* in an unsaintly world.

Was something like this even possible?

Were these kinds of people even out there?

Most people he knew could be, in some way, corrupted—intentionally or not. Hell, even he hadn't been immune. He'd had his own personal and professional...*challenges*...over the years, especially with what was needed to be done during his years in the White House, but to give such awesome power to humans was not only unthinkable, but unspeakably *frightening*.

But he'd always loved a good fight.

He'd secretly hoped that The Center would somehow be able to identify, screen, and school *just such individuals from birth*, and maybe one day...these gifted individuals would come public to help guide the human race toward improved growth and enlightenment.

That had been the goal.

Lofty. Idealistic. *Pure.*

He just figured that as Life took its course, these individuals would make themselves known, all his secret goals and desires would someday come to fruition, and he would be able to save himself the embarrassment and task of having to propose his insane ideas *first*, then look for the means of carrying out such idealistic efforts in a scoffing society.

That had been half a lifetime ago, and so far, no one had been identified. Instead, he'd had this renegade agent corrupting his efforts—a man he thought he'd been able to contain, control…but, instead, seemed to have *grown*. And he'd had—what was he going to call it, a *dream?*—an *experience?*—*where he'd actually gone back in* time?

Changed events?

Had all that been a daydream? A product of wishful thinking? *Or had he actually gone back?*

And thirty *years.*

How had they never been able to find capable souls to fulfill these roles in over thirty years? Not even *one?* The human race could not possibly be that dirty.

Time travel, changing the past, righting wrongs.

Powerful concepts, indeed, but he hardly believed one man—him—had done any such thing. It had to have been a daydream—wishful fantasy.

But…just the same…the thought was there, wasn't it? *Something* had to have happened….

Maybe his thoughts of changing the world weren't so farfetched…maybe they were attainable. Maybe all the crazy and dimly aware thoughts and dreams—of Black reemerging into his life after all these years—were signs of something big coming…that things *were* changing. Still, before he died, he wanted to leave a solid framework in place for his efforts to be continued far beyond his lifetime. He'd already laid everything out—even his most-secret agendas—in his will, which would only be read to and by certain individuals *not* of the government nor military. Individuals who would continue to monitor The Center and the world for just such an outcome—in utmost secrecy.

Hopefully, he could still find what was needed before he was done with this life.

It was definitely time for another trip to The Center.

230 | F.P. Dorchak

2

As Travis went about his day, he—and no doubt the others—had found it easier to remain focused on work more than expected. Running and monitoring taskings, reports and paperwork, overseeing training programs...had he forgotten he'd been paid for a job he'd been, up to recently, anyway, happy with? Sure, the occasional distasteful trash had to be taken out, but all jobs had their ups and downs, good and bad days. He'd usually been kept busier than could be worried about, and throughout the course of the day they'd all interacted as if nothing had happened last night. But, the day had gotten away from him—he'd not even eaten—and turned into night. He had to get away. Air out. Needed to think. Try to make sense out of what was going on, as risky as it was to just *think* about these things. But he also needed some time to search...to find out where this boy was and how to deal with things.

If someone was monitoring their thoughts, what could they do about it?

Nothing was sacred.

Thoughts, ideas, emotions. *Concepts*. Nothing could be hidden from a good operator. Perhaps the only consolation was that he was working with the best available team, and unless...and unless one of *them* was working for Black...now there was a thought, and quite an unpleasant one at that....

But, he trusted these people; had worked with some of them for many years. They were all good, solid people, not the kind of evil that sometimes made their way into The Center, like Black and his ilk—

Just the thought of the man sent shivers through him. Who'd he work for—or, perhaps, more likely, who worked for *him*. It was always a little fuzzy if he was directly associated with The Center or not. They'd tried, a couple of them, to find out whether or not he was, but got conflicting results. Some saw him attached, while others saw him not—some actually saw him dismissed during his appointment interview with the President. He was, *somehow*, attached to this place, that much was for certain, but in a way no one clearly understood.

Of course...intentional. There were no coincidences in this biz.

Black showed up when he did, did what he did, said little to nothing—at least to "the help"—then vanished. And while he was here they were all directed to avoid him like the plague. Not to ask questions. To do whatever they were told without fail or hesitancy. It was a very uncomfortable relationship, but one not uncommon in this industry. Certain individuals made their way here, individuals whose names were not their real ones, and whose organizations were never spoken of, and who, in all probability, actually ran this outfit, despite whatever was practiced—or on paper.

The world of covert operations.

Travis shuddered as he wound his way across the terrazzo's shadows outside his building. He headed for the nature path that wound through the surrounding grounds' wooded area. The terrazzo was lit, but the nature trail beyond wasn't.

Perfect.

So (he had tried to *subtly* convey), despite their fears at being outed…their new direction was to do the best they could until caught.

If Black—or whoever ran this outfit—really wanted to catch them, he would. It scared him, but they had little choice—they had to do what was right—and having the added benefit of being remote viewers, they could check in on themselves to make sure they were as safe as could reasonably be made. But, also being remote viewers, those more attuned to the psychic world, couldn't they also find some other tool at their disposal? Some way to send and receive that could, perhaps, *layer* their information in such a way as to confuse and confound those who might be peeking in? To…*sandwich* their information within other thoughts, other images? Technical intel did it with software, they had to be able to do it with *thoughts*. Feelings.

Travis carefully picked his way along the dark path and stepped on a stick that snapped rather loudly.

He stopped as if bitch-slapped and looked around. Was he being—

Magic?

No Name?

Children?

Travis felt unbalanced. Unable to any longer distinguish much in the darkness, the vertigo completely and swiftly overtook him. He flailed blindly for support, stumbled off the trail, and fell headlong into the brush, scrambling for anything to break his blind plummet. His fall wasn't as painful as anticipated. He lay there, inhaling dirt, when another image—

Layer cake?

Travis squeezed shut his eyes and tried to pull in the imagery.

Children and layer cake.

Some guy with no name.

Layer...cake. Lay-*er*...

He sat up.

He was no longer on The Center's nature trail.

No longer lying in bramble and brush.

He was sitting on the steps of an oddly familiar porch. It was dark, not even a porch light was on. From his left came ripping and tearing sounds. The words came out of his mouth without any thought.

"You weeding *again?*"

"Gotta," came the invisible response from beyond. "If you don't, your work gets overrun. Know what I mean?"

"I do...no, no I—what the *hell?*"

The Man With No Name emerged from the darkness. "So, I hear you're getting a might vexed."

Travis looked to the Man With No Name, at his dirtied hands and pants (he found he could make it out in all the darkness), and to the porch steps he sat on.

"Wasn't I just—"

"On the ground? Yeah. But, you had a good question, the opportunity was ripe, so I thought what better time to answer—"

"A question?"

"Layer cake. It was what we talked about when first we met. Kinda. About meeting. I mean—well, anyway, you can use the same principle where you are. Layering your information like I'm layering your training."

"Training?"

"Granted, it's not the traditional training you're used to, but, even now, there's training going on—*as we speak*. It's all done in metaphysical layers. It'll take some practice on your and your friends part, and I am doing my damned best trying to accelerate things, but it ain't easy. Most of what gets done appears to get done without your help or knowledge, but it *is* getting done, and *certainly* with your help and knowledge. I really wish I could give you more—in your terms—formal training, but circumstances dictate otherwise. What's of concern right now isn't the boy...it's the woman."

"Woman?"

"Elizabeth Gordon, or 'Lizzie,' as she prefers. You've dreamt of her. She's being held at your Center. I don't want her touched—in any way. Black is trying to play it cool, but can't. No longer has the patience. He's tired of playing games."

"How is this woman more important?"

"Time, in your case, is of the essence. Lizzie is being held in the depths of your compound, in Building 4250. In one of the subterranean rooms there. L5B03. She's...restrained. Undergoing..."

"How do you know all this?"

"*Stop wasting time and get to her. It's* imperative."

Travis was back in the bushes, sitting on the ground.

He looked around. He was alone again. That crazy spinning gone.

Groggily getting to his feet, he brushed himself off, then gingerly stepped back through the brush and scrub, onto the trail.

Flashes of a garden...weeding—at *night?* Images so strong, he felt as if he'd actually been there—wherever "there" was.

He checked his watch. No time had passed. He headed back toward the compound.

And this guy—a guy he'd apparently met before—knew of the woman he and the others had dreamed of.

As he made his way through the gently winding trail, he felt the familiarity of the man...yes, he *had* met him before, hadn't he? Where?

Building 4250.

I don't want her touched.

This Man With No Name knew all about her...asked him to find and free her.

Why didn't *he* do it?

Why'd they have to do it? They weren't versed in any kind of covert rescue—there were organizations specially trained for that kind of operation. They were just a bunch of hide-in-the-shadows government spooks....

Maybe it was because no one could be trusted. If Black was involved that was a sure bet. And of course, he was sure the Man With No Name was probably known too, if he knew where Lizzie was. Shit, just the same...how was he—*they*—supposed to rescue anyone? Just walk right on in and snatch her?

That was probably exactly what he had in mind.

3

Kennedy arrived at the Hyannis, Barnstable Municipal Airport tarmac, runway 06/24, where his Learjet awaited. All he'd been able to think about had been his lifelong pursuit of peace, and what little time he had left. He'd been unable to think about anything else—and to the point of a tension headache, no less. It was like getting a catchy tune stuck in your head.

So, why fight it?

He decided to pay a visit to the organization that bore his name, as well as the executors of his estate. He had to see if there was something The Center could do to get things moving.

His driver pulled up before the already whining engines of the jet, and before the ever-present Secret Service agent could get out to open his door, Kennedy was out. The pilot greeted him, and they all turned to enter the jet...but Kennedy lingered a moment longer outside. He closed his eyes and deeply inhaled the cool, humid, early morning coastal breezes. Looked to the scurrying ground fog that still hugged the terrain. This was beautiful country.

He smiled.

Entered the jet.

Kennedy took his seat and strapped in. After checking his buckle, and situating himself, he looked up—

The cabin was filled with children.

Silent. All staring at him.

"Morning, sir," the Man With No Name greeted, seated behind him.

Kennedy whipped around in his seat.

"It's time for a crash course for what you're getting into."

Chapter Twenty-Four

1

Lizzie lay in bed, eyes closed, arms wrapped tightly around Joe. She could feel his heart beating.

"God, I've *missed* you," she whispered, tears wet on her face. "I never want to leave you again."

Joe smiled. "It doesn't have to be this way,
(*bitch*)
"honey. You could come with me."

Lizzie squeezed Joe tighter.

Why didn't she reply? What was the matter? If she could go with him, why wouldn't *she?*

Joe shifted position. "What's wrong? You seem distracted?"

"I...I don't know. Something feels...strange...about all this—I mean, not about *you*, or us
(*was she lying?*)
"or what we just did
(*liar!*)
"...just...*something....*"

There *was* something strange about him *and* her....what they'd just done. There was something indefinably odd about everything...but something kept her from saying anything. Kept her from saying yes, *yes!*

(*oh, baby,* yeah!)

of course *I'll go with you—wherever you want, right this second—let's not wait a breath longer. Let's just get up and get the hell outta Dodge while we can! Before something...something*
(*what? WHAT?*)
happens!

"Let's do it, again," Joe whispered, squeezing her and kissing her forehead. Lizzie melted into the warmth and sweetness of his breath and embrace, the musky scent of his body. She wanted so desperately to feel him again inside her...but there was this growing uneasiness, this...psychic cold sweat. The first time they'd made love she'd felt that uneasiness—ignored it...denied it. She'd let him in, because she'd *wanted* him in.

But even while making love, something felt unaccountably dirty,

(*Oh, baby, God, how I....*)

and it was impossible to pinpoint.

Something around and *about* him felt...*off....*

But she'd convinced herself to ignore it, because he'd been gone...gone for so *long....*

And now he wanted it again—hell, who was she kidding, *she* wanted it again—*him* again. She wanted to make love with him for the rest of her life, and she didn't know what was so

(*bitch!*)

wrong about that, but the instant she turned to him and he made his move—

She pushed away and rolled out of bed.

Lizzie stood naked beside the bed, confused, a hand to the wall to steady herself. Joe looked to her.

"What's the matter?" he asked. "Something I did?"

(*BITCH!*)

Lizzie turned away, ashamed. Planted her forehead against a wall, and began to cry. Joe went to her, but as soon as he touched her, she twisted free. The grimace she knew graced her face surprised even her.

"Doesn't any of this feel *wrong* to you?" she asked, unable to look at him.

Joe, also naked and hands to his side, looked at her.

"No. Should it? I mean...I'm here with my wife—my *wife*—whom I haven't seen in over a *year*—"

"But doesn't that *bother* you? *Why* haven't we seen each other in a year—we're married for Heaven's sake! *Where have you been?*"

"Oh, honey, you're making a mountain out of a mole hill..."

"*Am I?* Will you look at us? *Me?* Why should I be having such a hard time with any of this? Why do I feel like something's dreadfully wrong?"

Joe made another attempt at making another go at things, when Lizzie whirled around and again slipped from his embrace.

"*No!* This isn't *right*...something...something about all of this

(*oh, you fucking* bitch!)

"*just isn't right*—"

"But you did it the first time—"

"*But I still felt it!* I'm not doing it again! *Please*...don't force me—"

Joe stared at her with a blank expression. Just looked at her. The entire experience suddenly felt flat, all of it. The guilt piled on like a one-ton

(*I-beam*)

weight.

"Oh, honey, I'm sorry," she said, reaching out to

Joe was gone.

Nothing.

The bed...gone.

The room—well, not entirely gone—she was still in *a* room...but it was a much different one, and she was

Strapped into a chair.

Restrained. Head to toe.

"*I could give you more of that,*" Black's voice said from somewhere around her. It was like sandpaper rubbed across a burn.

Lizzie searched the room with tearstained and gritty eyes. The glare was unbearable. She couldn't see clearly. A shadow—a man—emerged from the glare before her, dark in contrast to all the blinding brilliance.

"I could give you that all day, every day. Your Joe. All you have to do is work with me, Elizabeth. Give me what I want. It's that simple."

His last sentence had a creepy, casual lilt to it.

Black disappeared back into the glare.

Lizzie closed her eyes, fresh tears running down her face.

All she'd ever wanted was to live her life in peace and quiet with her husband. Now she had neither. Was at the mercy of a madman. A madman who thought she had some special powers. Even if she had, they were all gone, now, like everything else in her life. Even if she still had any, she wouldn't use them. She'd die first.

And would that be so horrible?

Depending on how things actually panned out in the afterlife, she could at least see Joe one more time—*be* with him.

But wouldn't Black be smart enough to know that?

He wouldn't let her die...no...he'd keep her around as long as possible, torturing her like he was now...creating Joe's images...them together...when all he was really doing was feeding upon the guilt that had already been smoldering deep within her. You didn't have to be psychic to pick up on what he was doing. This would go on forever and a day, until she really did go crazy, and that would be punishment enough, in Black's book, for her resistance and refusal. An insane asylum, or whatever they called them, now, for the rest of her physical existence.

But at least she would no longer have to deal with her guilt.

She'd be lost and unknown to herself...and others, like Black, would take of her until her body caught up with her mind.

She just wanted to die.

Get the remainder of this life out of the way. Start over. Was that so much to ask?

But again...Black would have none of that, would he?

And thanks to all his electrodes and technical wizardry, he was monitoring her brain, her mind, and her body.

Had anyone ever been able to will themselves to death?

Every time she'd try, Black would just adjust his equipment—her brainwave patterns—by whatever was coming out of those damned speakers against her ears. Like the hallucinations about Joe. She never realized they were hallucinations until well into them, so for a while she was always duped, trapped, except for those tiny inklings of

(*Bitch*)

evil she picked up in the background.

Maybe it didn't really matter if she knew or not...because, for a little while, anyway, a little while, she was happy...when she first met with him—real or not—she was happy that there was *some* form of hallucination called "Joe" that felt and sounded and acted like the Joe she knew, and it felt like they really *were* together. How Black managed all this, who knew, but she picked up on some things before he kept resetting her brain. Perhaps he was hypnotizing her, forcing her to recall memories....

And if so, how could she go wrong?

What would be so wrong with her going with him, as he'd asked her—or her *hallucination* of him had asked her? Black was never going to let her go—not after all this. Why not just succumb to the dream and never wake up? Have Black have his way with her—

The weird tones again started up....

2

We have to talk, Travis mentally sent out, as he hurried back to his office. He tried to psychically encrypt his mental outreach between multiple images of various current events, work-related issues, and images of his plastic *Invaders* model and other boyhood memories. *I hope you're getting this.*

I am, Gina responded. *I see where you are and am picking up on—*

This is urgent.

Understood.

The others?

In taskings.

I don't know how we're supposed to do this, but that Man With No Name said we had to get on it—ASAP. But, I haven't a clue about how we're supposed to do this.

He offered no help?

Just that we *had to get her and waste no time in doing so. I'm headed there now. See it?*

Travis sent an image of their objective.

Yes.

I need backup...someone to keep an eye out, help out.

I'm there. What about security?

Don't know. I'm...I don't know...filled with this incredible sense of urgency and can't seem to stop to think about any of this...it's...forcing...me there, like she might be killed at any moment.

Be careful, Trav, I'm on my way—just be careful. *I'll see what we can do.*

This shoves us out into the open. Nowhere to hide.

Be careful.

Travis hurried toward building 4250, at The Center's compound.

3

Lizzie was back in the bedroom with Joe, back beneath the sheets. Eyes closed, she still felt his warmth and fullness, even after he'd withdrawn from her. Inhaled his musky scent. She loved his smell. She reached out to him. Opened her eyes to find him staring at her.

"I love you," he whispered, gently squeezing her hand. "And I love making love with you. *Stay with me.*"

"Okay," she said without hesitation. "I'll stay." She squeezed his hand back.

Was that a floral scent she just picked up?

No…it was gone….

She smiled warmly, squashing that nagging little

(*bitch*)

voice. That niggling little voice that even now seemed to be, once more, clawing its way through her mind….

Joe smiled.

(*smiles…his smile…something about a* smile….)

"Good…then there's something else I want to show you," he said.

He hopped out of bed.

Lizzie watched as his beautiful naked body strode across the room. She wanted more of him. Much more. Forever. Joe walked out into the hall.

There it was *again*…that subtle floral scent….

Lizzie rose to an elbow, taking in the room.

Where were they?

If she was going to stay with him, it'd be nice to know. Where they'd made love. She lay back down, recalling Joe's powerful, rhythmic penetration of her body and soul. It all felt so right, being here, with him, now…like the old days….

Again, that flowery smell—where and what was that?

"Honey…," Joe said, returning, a huge

(*pained?*)

smile plastered across his face.

Out from behind the doorway stepped another woman.

A *naked* woman.

And along with her, an acrid, thick floral scent that filled the room. The smell burned Lizzie's nose and stung the back of her throat.

"Honey…I'd like you to meet Melissa. Remember Jeff Skopchek? This is his ex-wife."

Melissa smiled, lips slightly and seductively parted. "Hello, Lizzie," she purred, "So nice to finally meet you."

Before Lizzie could respond, before Lizzie could mentally switch gears from just having made love with her husband and him having told her how much he *loved* her—loved making *love* with her—before she could wrap her head around any of that, *Lizzie found her husband between* Melissa's *legs…pounding into her up against a wall!*

Melissa held Lizzie's gaze, her arms clutching at Lizzie's husband's muscular, working body. Melissa wrapped her legs around Joe's hips—grunting, groaning, *screeching*. The grunting Joe made was like shards of glass being ground into Lizzie's heart.

So this was what he looked like making love? was her surprising first thought. *This was what that magnificent body of his looked like while making love with* her? *Only this time the "her" wasn't* her, *was it, but someone else? Another "her." A "her" whose eyes began to dull and glaze over from the sex her husband was having with* her; *a* her *who was soon to be receiving the warm, explosive seed of* her *husband...as* she watched....

Lizzie couldn't turn away. Couldn't close her eyes. Couldn't scream. All bodily control was suddenly frozen.

Melissa closed her eyes. She clutched at Joe's hair, his shoulders, his back...her grunts becoming more and more high-pitched cries, screeches, and yelps.

Lizzie tried to yell, to leap out of bed and rip the two apart from each other—but was unable to move. She strained hard against the sheets, *but was simply unable to move.*

Joe's grunts and groans grew caustic, increasingly impassioned—mixed with Melissa's higher-pitched efforts. Lizzie tried to block them out, close her ears...but could not move her arms. Melissa was now shouting, *moaning...*

"Oh, baby, yeah...*like that, oh, yeah*...fuck *me, fuck me, baby...harder, yeah,* HARDER!"

Melissa looked to Lizzie. Burned her heady gaze into her.

Joe continued thrusting, a motion that at once excited and repulsed Lizzie. A motion she had just experienced not two minutes ago—between *her* legs.

"Oh, baby," Joe grunted, breathless, "God...*how I*...love *you*—"

"Yeah, baby...harder, pound me, *come on...yeah...yes...yes*...YES!"

Large, hot tears welled out from Lizzie's eyes, as Melissa let out a series of ever increasing wails. She couldn't turn away, couldn't close her eyes; she felt a rift tearing open within her, a chasm so deep and dark...and *black*—

Their screams reached a united crescendo, and Joe came powerfully into Melissa with deep, dark animal grunts, as he brutally slammed her, giggling and screaming in orgasm, against the wall. A picture crashed to the floor and another tilted lop-sided. Lizzie watched as Melissa's nails dug into Joe's back and drew blood. When they were done, each gasped for air like drowning victims.

Laughed.

She'd never drawn blood from her husband, but this bitch was doing it right now, before her eyes, and, apparently…apparently…he liked *it….*

Her husband never looked to her, instead tenderly touched Melissa's face and smoothed out her hair. Gazed deeply into Melissa's eyes. Melissa ran her hands over Joe's short-cropped hair.

"*More,* baby…more…*oh, God*…," Melissa begged, grabbing Joe's head

(*his* head!)

in both hands and leaning her head into his.

Joe and Melissa giggled and snorted—*snorted!*—and Lizzie knew—*knew!*—they were laughing at her.

Why was he doing this? Why didn't he stop…turn around and come back to her? *What had she done to deserve this?*

Joe backed up with Melissa still looped around his waist, her head now dropped to his shoulders. Lizzie noticed how her long, sweaty and messed-up hair was partially flung over Joe's shoulder, clinging against Joe's sweaty, flexing back. Joe gently deposited Melissa at the foot of the bed. Still crying, Lizzie watched as Joe then came around to his side of the bed—to *her,* now—and crawled back under the sheets beside her. Lizzie inhaled Melissa's sickly floral perfume all over him. Melissa turned to look to them, eyes droopy and heavy. She smiled a saccharine, closed-mouth smirk and repositioned herself on her elbows and stomach…

To watch.

No! Lizzie internally screamed, *Nooo!*

There was no stopping him.

Joe spooned right up against Lizzie. She couldn't fight it; was unable to even scream. Joe wrapped his arms and legs around her and whispered into her ear.

"*Oh, honey, how I love you….*"

Lizzie grit her teeth—*willed herself to die.*

And I was ready to go with him? Go with him where?

Joe forced himself atop her. Forced apart her legs.

No! Oh, please, God, no. No-no-no-NO!

Joe entered her, and as much as she fought—or thought she fought—she could do nothing. She tensed her entire body. Blood trickled out her nose.

Joe worked her callously—hard and brutal—like she was a mere receptacle for his animalistic urges, rather than…

His *wife*.

Someone else entered the room.

"Are you going to give me what I need? Are you now ready?"

Black. Victor Black. In a robe. Hands on his hips.

Grinning his painful grin.

He undid his robe.

4

Travis approached the entrance to 4250. He hid in the nighttime shadows as long as possible…when he came upon the young girl. She was perhaps six years old and sat on the steps of the building. She sat under the security lighting, smiling and humming to herself. When the girl saw him, she jumped to her feet.

"Come *on*, we haven't much time!" she said.

"Excuse me?" Travis said.

"*Hurry!*"

The girl led him into the building. When he saw the security guards at the front desk, his heart stopped—but the six year old continued to lead him along, past checkpoint personnel.

"But the—"

"They don't matter anymore. Just come with us!"

Travis looked up ahead to find a handful of other awaiting children. They'd been playing hopscotch in the hallway, singing "Ring Around the Rosie," a hopscotch grid drawn in chalk on the floor. But they dropped their chalk and stones and immediately joined in as they approached.

"*Hurry!*" they all chimed in, and together all funneled past the next security checkpoint, with its surveillance cameras and biometrics.

"But how—who *are* you?" Travis asked.

He was shushed.

The first little girl whispered, "Magic, it's all *magic*, maaan.…"

Stone-faced, Black stood behind the bank of computer equipment, monitoring Lizzie's experience. He had to kill those dreams, get rid of whomever had been tracking him all these years…preventing him from attaining his rightful place in history. And this woman was key. She could lead him to where this most persistent gnat was. Once and for all. But her brain wave activity wasn't looking promising. She was giving up, and he had to stave that off until she told him what he needed to cut this cancer out of his life. They all broke. It was only a matter of time. No one resisted forever.

Using his computer's mouse, Black upped the program's intensity. Into a microphone, he said, "Oh, baby, yeah…like that, oh, yeah…*fuck me, fuck me, baby*…harder, yeah, *HARDER*…."

He recited the words as if reading a newspaper article, both his face and voice emotionless. But he knew the effect his words had on her. He could see her responses on his displays…from the video feed of her face. She was falling for it. Hook, line, and dick.

She was his.

Cory Colbert wrapped up the remote viewing session with his monitor and went out to the hallway water fountain. As he bent over to take a sip, he mentally received:

Just that we had to get her. Waste no time. I'm headed there now. Need backup…someone to keep an eye out….

He bolted upright.

Another?

The next message hit: *What about security?*

Cory looked up and down the hallway. Empty.

Then came the final clip: *Shoves us out in the open…nowhere to hide. Be careful…*

Trav? Gina? Cory mentally asked.

We're here, Cory. It was Gina.

Both of us, Travis added.

What do you need?

To get into here. Travis sent a visual. *We don't know what we're doing, but we're going for it, anyway.* Travis sent along their sense of urgency.

Great. This is going to hurt—someone's going to die.

We need someone to divert Black, Travis sent. *Lizzie's being held. That Man With No Name feels her life is in grave danger. It's now or never.*

Okay.

Anyone else out?

Not yet.. I'm outta here, Cory sent, *I'll see what I can do.*

Good luck, Travis and Gina sent.

* * *

Cory entered the front doors to building 4250, and, to his amazement, found the security desk unmanned. That shouldn't be. He paused inside the entranceway, scanning the layout and cameras.

Highly uncomfortable. No alarms, no scurrying security. Something wasn't right—

Hurry, someone sent.

A *child?*

The same voice continued, *He's strong…needs distraction. In the booth. You* must *delay him.*

Okay, this was getting really weird. There were two security personnel, but, where *were* they? And the cameras…they still pointed toward the entrance…toward him.

Get moving! The little girl voice urged.

If they were on and manned, then he was already meat, and he had little time nor chance…but if those consoles were also absent, then perhaps he *did* have a chance—

Heart racing, Cory shot forward. At the next set of doors, and without thinking, he swiped his restricted area badge through the panel's slot, typed in his PIN, and scanned his retina. Why would his access clearance and biometrics work here? They shouldn't, but, before he could finish the thought, the light flashed green and he was in.

Blood continued to trickle from Lizzie's nose, as she continued to fight her physical paralysis and Joe's rape.

She was being raped by her husband!

With Black and another watching!

Why? How was this *possible?* This wasn't *Joe!* Not the man *she* knew!

Why had he had sex with that woman—*who continued to watch and please herself?*

Lizzie tried to scream, but nothing came out. Just blood and tears. Her mouth and throat burned from the goddamned perfume.

What had become of her husband?

The love of her life—turned evil? He toyed with her and she had no way to fight back.

She just wanted to die.…

But this…this couldn't *possibly* be her husband…Joe would never, *ever* do anything like this…he'd slit his own throat first—

Of course he wouldn't do anything like this.

What was going on?

He bit her—*he was* biting *her!*

This couldn't *be Joe!*

No—that wasn't possible.

This wasn't *her* Joe—*couldn't* be!

Joe would never, *ever*—in a *million* lifetimes—

Something was wrong!

This wasn't happening!

Lizzie renewed her efforts to free herself—to move. *Will* herself free. This was all a figment of her imagination—no, *Black's* imagination—*none* of it was real.

None of it!

Joe stopped.

Lizzie held her breath. Was still unable to move.

Two sets of hands then roughly grabbed her and spun her around; repositioned her, face down on the bed.

"*Oh, this is* real, *all right, my little princess,*" Melissa whispered into Lizzie's ear, as she repeatedly pressed her sweaty, floral-odored body into her, "*and we're going to show you just how fucking real it is....*"

Melissa backed away, and Lizzie heard and felt her shifting around, behind her. She was doing something...it sounded like she was *putting something on....*

What was she doing? *What was she doing?*

Lizzie found she could finally move and pushed herself up on all fours.

"*You should have given me what I wanted,*" Joe hissed, but it wasn't Joe's voice coming from Joe. It was another, blacker, voice. A voice Lizzie could never forget.

She lifted her head.

A naked Black positioned himself before her.

Melissa positioned herself behind her.

She was going to kill him.

She was going to rip his fucking black *heart* out...

Chapter Twenty-Five

1

The children hurried down the hallway and stairwells, leading Travis ever deeper into the dark, deserted recesses of building 4250. He'd lost track of how deep they'd gone, but it seemed three or four stories down. These kids apparently knew what they were doing and where they were going, and he dutifully followed. They finally spilled out into a hallway that spewed *noise*…like a TV or radio turned to an untuned station that showed nothing but snow, or spewed only white noise. His mind felt at odds with itself, as if one side of it was out of sync with the other.

He looked up.

Speakers.

There were speakers in the ceiling as well as set back into the topmost part of the hallway's walls—on both sides—spaced out above about every ten feet. He'd seen ceiling speakers before, but not speakers set into the tops of walls. Speakers used to drown out stray audible electronic emissions so personnel in the area couldn't pick up on whatever clandestine work was being carried on behind whatever doors these speakers guarded.

But what were these extra speakers set along the *tops* of walls?

Who put them there…what were their family lives like?

Were they overworked?

Tired?

Man, he could sleep for *years*—

Get your head back where it belongs!

Focus—*focus!*

Travis continued on. Thought back to the children. He finally remembered it…his previous association with them…sitting in the cafe-

248 | F.P. Dorchak

teria, eating lunch...then finding everyone in the cafeteria gone, replaced with these *überkindern*...

Recalled...*memories?*

He wasn't sure if these memories were his own...or another's...

...but, about a *trailer?*...about having to constantly pick up toys
scattered about the house...about talking to children in stores and restaurants that no one else could see...a room filled with children's
toys—*but no children.* These kids were helping them—*him*—out. Were
somehow tied to this Lizzie woman.....

Travis came upon a door.

Damn, it seemed so hard to focus!

It was your standard metal door at the end of a standard-looking
utility hallway that branched off the main hallway. The door was labeled L5B03 and was hidden by stacks of boxes, pallets, and other
camouflaging refuse, white noise also assaulting from above. A card
reader was to the right of the door at slightly below eye level. A tiny
green light glowed. But, Travis knew that on the other side of this door
was anything but standard. He was actually afraid of what he'd find,
though he knew this was his sole reason—his purpose—for being
here. He could *feel* the pain that radiated from the other side of this
door, was surprised by how it overcame him and actually brought
tears—*tears*—to his eyes. He paused until the wave of pain and emotion passed.

Focus.

Travis also picked up that this wasn't a standard room for what
was going on inside it. It was supposed to be a storage room—a storage room that had recently been converted. He was in a remote, subterranean section of this building, specifically selected for temporary
storage of

Elizabeth Gordon.

2

Cory wove his way throughout the maze of hallways and stairwells
on the heels of these ghost children. They faded in and out of view,
but lead him on they did. He'd never before been in this building,
knew he didn't have the required access, yet found himself within its
very bowels. And all the while he passed not one person. It was un-

bearably creepy. Maybe all the security aspects of this building hadn't yet been put into place...could be, it was new and still under

(*yellow hard hat...?*)

construction.

As he forged ahead, he picked up that the object of his mission was to run interference with a man who was the epitome of evil. Though he hurried and experienced a heightened sense of urgency, he wasn't exactly in a hurry to meet up with the guy. He didn't know how he was supposed to distract Black, didn't have a good feeling about any of this, but accepted his role.

In this building someone was being tortured...so, he had little choice.

Building 4250 appeared to be another setup for remote viewing like the one they—he, Gina, Travis and the rest—used, but newer and not yet completely populated with occupants nor offices. Above ground, it was smaller than their older, circa sixties building, but that didn't mean it was any less of a labyrinth. People at JFKC referred to these kinds of buildings as "icebergs." Not much above ground, but a world of secrets beneath.

But why and how was each security checkpoint deserted? How had he just been able to waltz on through each and every one of them?

None of this made any sense. But he followed his group's lead. He had to get to Black. Had to prevent him from—

Cory came to an abrupt halt before a control-room door. It had all the appropriate declarations that this was a secure area, proper authorizations were required—and that the use of deadly force was authorized.

Use of Deadly Force Authorized.

He looked up to the camera staring down at him. To the cipher lock and card reader to the right of the door. He reached out to the door...and quietly pulled it open. Cory registered the muted "click" the door's lock made as it disengaged for him.

The interior of the room was dimly lit, and though he recognized the basic layout, it did differ from the more-familiar control-room layout of their own remote-viewing compartments elsewhere on the compound. All lights were off except at the far end of the room, behind a glass—sound-proofed—enclosure that sectioned off the area he was in. It was there that he saw the dark silhouette seated at the console, back to him.

Black.

He had a unique "signature" when sensed—was hunched over and talking, quite probably into a microphone. Intent and focused on his actions.

Cory quietly closed the door behind him and immediately crouched down. He carefully navigated his way toward Black. As he wove closer, he still couldn't make out any words through the sound-proofed barrier. He tried to tune into him, but his mind seemed to constantly wonder...to mowing lawns...running high school track...his first lay...his second....

Black.

He was being misdirected.

So, just what the hell was he supposed to do, now?

Kill him?

He'd never killed anyone before, but at this stage of the game it appeared the logical conclusion.

Good Lord, what the hell *had they gotten themselves into?*

Had to remain focused. Something inside him edged him inexorably forward.

This man was secretly torturing another somewhere within this building, and that...*that* was *wrong*. Had to be stopped. Any hesitation on his part needed to be immediately squelched. He looked for anything that could be used as a weapon. Geez, not even a pair of scissors. In the low light, Cory's hand came down upon a three-hole punch on a console. Okay, not exactly James Bond, but...it was heavy and solid...and could easily pack a deadly wallop if wielded correctly.

Cory paused as he picked it up.

This was it.

Was he actually going to intentionally harm another?

That's what the government had trained into its soldiers and operatives.

A job.

This was no different.

Expendability.

It was just more *personal.* Though an ex-soldier, he'd killed from afar, sanctioned by his government. Here, there would be no such "distance"...no sending in of ordnance, no such sanctions.

This would be up close and personal. Hand to hand. The worst kind of fighting. The most brutal.

Cory was suddenly sick to his stomach.

He'd have to whack him from behind—if he was lucky. He was

sure it wasn't like anything portrayed in the movies, and wondered just how much force was actually needed to knock a man out—that was, after all, all he really *needed* to do—just knock him out. Intercept and interdict. *Stall.* Get him *off* that woman.

He just needed to take the spring out of this guy's step.

Cory inhaled deeply, hefted his three-hole punch...and advanced.

Willed himself to be healthy and strong. To—at all costs—get the job done.

The glass enclosure also had a door. Cory reached out for it. Damn. How was he supposed to—

He grabbed the handle...and it also opened soundlessly, *impossibly* quiet. Cory grimaced. This whole affair had an intense dream-like quality to it. How was any of this supposed to be possible? And, really, how could he possibly expect to have gotten this far...to be in here...with possibly the most dangerous man on the planet?

He had to stop thinking...and *act.* Needed to *focus.*

There it was...the opened door...the intently focused Black sitting at the console and speaking into a microphone. His back was to him and he was completely unaware of the fate that awaited him. Black's low-spoken voice was flat and unemotional. Lifeless, one could say. Cory entered the glass enclosure, three-hole punch at the ready. He was an easy fifteen feet from Black, who, in his still unemotional voice, continued speaking into the microphone: "*Oh, this is real, all right, my little princess, and we're going to show you just how fucking real it all is....*"

Black's words sent shivers down Cory's spine.

In a crouched position, hands shaking, Cory readied the three-hole punch. Steeled himself.

This was not going to end well.

Cory quietly stole up behind Black. As he stood there for just a moment, he noted a small pile of CDs on the console before Black. Six of them. Labeled. Gina's name was on top.

Just as Black uttered "*You should have given me what I wanted,*" and much to his own surprise, Cory sprang into action.

Black calmly spun around in his swivel chair.

As casually as reaching for coffee from the community coffee pot and to Cory's utter disbelief, Black swung around with an already positioned nine millimeter. The muzzle flashed just as Cory attacked. The round hit him square in the gut. It had a powerful kick—like a baseball bat to the belly—but he already had forward momentum. At the same time he was shot, Cory swung the three-hole punch...but Black had leaned back, away from the blow. Cory had only managed to clip Black's hand, instead, dislodging the SIG from his grip.

Cory fell into Black, and together they tumbled to the floor, but not before Cory had gotten a view of the console behind Black. Its displays and graphs were going wild. A video feed displayed the washed out features of a severely distraught woman. It was at that moment that Cory's boiling-point flared.

Failure was not an option!

He prayed to God that Travis and Gina would now be successful in getting this woman out of there.

Cory again wielded the three-hole punch. This time he felt a solid connection....

3

Travis entered the soundproofed room to the smell of excrement, urine, and sweat—and lots of terrified, strained *screaming*, which nearly drove him back out of the room. The room was brilliantly lit, so much so it hurt his eyes; he could barely keep them open. From what he could see, the room was devoid of all features except for what looked like a huge, modified version of their RoboChair in the center of the room...and into which was strapped a woman. Except you wouldn't have immediately known the person to be a woman from her crazed and matted appearance, eyes wide and wild, full of hurt, anger, and insanity. No matter how much he'd prepared himself...he wasn't.

The woman screamed a rage and hurt into the world that tore at his being.

Travis cursed himself for thinking this, *but was there even anything* left *to rescue?*

He sprinted into action.

In one swift and clean motion, he ripped away the wire-and-cable package that extended out the back of the RoboChair, from the speakers. Almost immediately, the screaming stopped. Travis came around to the front. He wiped his watering eyes and squinted in the intense glare.

Lizzie began crying, grunting, struggling against her restraints. It was almost like she was trying to talk, say something, but her mouth was paralyzed.

Travis reached out to her face with both hands—cupped it, holding it firmly—and quietly shushed her. She looked to him, and though at first it didn't appear she saw anything, she slowly began to focus her glazed-and-reddened eyes on him.

"Oh, dear, God," Travis whispered, "what has he done to you?"

Lizzie stopped.

Travis quickly undid her restraints, his own hands shaking and trembling. Saw and felt how her body continued to quiver uncontrollably. Her whole body sweat and strained, but as soon as he'd freed her, she collapsed into his arms.

"My name's Travis," Travis said, fighting back his own anger and emotion, "and there are a bunch of us here to help you—get you out. We're so...*sorry*...."

Fucking bastard, Travis thought. Fucking, *fucking* bastard, Black....

The woman mumbled and cried. Travis removed her limp form from the chair, positioning her across his shoulders in a Fireman's Carry.

Then he shot out of the room like a bat outta hell.

Cory struggled against Black's ironclad grip on his throat. His strength was quickly weakening from the gunshot to his belly. Throughout their struggle, the ability of Black to remain calm and detached struck fear in Cory. Black hadn't broken a sweat, and didn't appear to breathe hard—if at all—even at his age. Cory was clearly in way over his head, but was too far into things to just give up. He hoped he could outmaneuver the man just by being younger and stronger, but Black was clearly a skilled opponent—used to killing, a lifetime of killing, no doubt—and the bullet in his gut worsened by the second. Unless he got the upper hand—and soon—he hadn't a chance.

Black attempted a knee to Cory's groin, which only landed on his inner thigh, but which still inflicted a good deal of pain. Cory felt himself graying out...weakening further...but managed to

(*healthy and strong!*)

collect his focus and roll Black off of him. Black tumbled into the console's lower panels, bounced off and came right back at him. But, Cory (not knowing how he did it) was also up off the floor in a crouched position.

(*get the job done!*)

Coughing up blood.

254 | F.P. Dorchak

Spotting the nine mil, Cory dove for it...but Black kicked it away. Cory landed hard on empty floor and slid into another console panel, jarring his stomach wound. Weakening by the second and dizzy, he nearly threw up.

"You stupid boy," Black taunted, "I grew up in the killing fields. I do this for *fun*."

Black was calm, cool, collected—a robotic killing machine.

A real-life *Terminator*.

"Bring it on, boy...I ache for some physical activity."

Black allowed Cory to shakily get back to his feet. Cory spotted his stupid, insane weapon-of-a-three-hole punch across the floor from him, over by the wall. The nine mil was in the opposite direction, under a lip of console. There was no way he was going to get to the nine mil before Black would again be all over him.

"Feeling a little weak, are we? Losing a little blood? Woozy, maybe? Would it help to know that you're already too late—"

Black paused a moment, as if he'd caught wind of something...

"When I'm done with you," Black continued, collecting himself, "I'll do to your body what I did in the Asian jungles *years* ago—just for old time's sake. I look forward to fishing out your intestines for lunch."

And again that painful-looking grin—it was like his face wasn't meant to smile. It honestly looked like Black enjoyed whatever pain his smile *caused him*.

Cory went for the gun.

He definitely didn't have enough energy for another full-on go-around—but could always pull a trigger. The gun was his only, real, choice. As he lunged for the weapon, images of his life flashed before him...of swimming in Indian Lake...of his first kiss from Gabrielle Palermo...playing around in their backyard tree house...heading off to college...to *war*....

Never in his wildest dreams had he ever thought he'd be caught up in a futile life-and-death struggle with Evil Incarnate.

Never had he considered *dying*.

Unable to believe he was doing it, Cory wrapped his hand around the grip of the nine mil (images of all those killed with this weapon flew through his head), clumsily rolled across the floor, and unsteadily aimed the weapon at Black.

Gone.

Cory scanned the room, sluggishly directing the SIG SAUER

where his gaze went. He winced, almost dropping the weapon. It felt as heavy as an anchor.

It was a pained struggle to get back to his feet. He could feel his life leaving his body.

Black had slid out of the glassed-in enclosure, and was now in the adjacent support center through which he had entered. A brief probability of himself *not* having entered this lab room flashed through his mind.

Cory again winced, leaning against another console for support. He made his way to the doorway. As he slowly lifted his head, he looked up to see a chair sailing out from the darkness, one of its wheels twisting wildly.

The chair struck him, clipping his left shoulder.

Cory fired off a wild round, as he spun around from the impact. He collapsed against another console, yelping out in pain. Black charged out from the darkness. Cory had a sudden image of a huge, dark cloud enveloping him. He had nowhere to run and no energy left.

Cory's world spun before him. The gun grew so heavy in his hand he could no longer control it. He tried one last attempt at taking out Black, but only managed to get off several more, ill-placed, and ricocheted rounds.

Black just kept coming.

Nothing stopped the man.

Black descended upon him.

"Too bad you never saw this coming, remote viewer," Black said.

The last things Cory felt and heard, as he descended into a black void, were his screams and the jerking of his body as it was jaggedly torn open....

4

Lizzie continued trembling as Travis carried her over his shoulder.

But, as Travis made his way down the hallway, the hallway with the white noise speakers blaring out above and around him, he began to feel a little...off. Something was different about the hallway. Things felt...*weird*. Maybe it was all the glare and shit from that little Psycho Cell from Hell from which he'd freed this woman, but he definitely felt affected by something...

Disoriented.

Travis slowed his sprint down as he rounded a corner...and nearly ran into them.

Two of them.

Blocking his way.

He stopped.

Huffing, shaking his head, he looked up to the speakers—yes, that damned white noise continued to assault him. He felt sleepy...confused...just wanted to set Lizzie down and take a break....

"Mr. Norton," said one of the men, dressed in a conservative dark suit, "you really don't want to do this, do you?"

"You really ought to leave her behind," said the other, dressed in the same conservative suit.

There was an utter creepiness to both men...but Travis didn't care. He just wanted to stop. Take a breather. He swung his

(*oh, so heavy...*)

head up and looked down the hallway beyond the men...back around the corner he'd just rounded. His mind felt like a spinning top as he returned to the two men. Stumbled a step.

"You can't win," one said.

"There's no way out," said the other.

Travis stared at the two guys. They stared blankly back at him. Unmoving. Expressionless.

Travis blinked and shifted Lizzie's weight. She was growing heavier. Uncomfortable. He staggered.

"You're tired."

"Overworked."

"Your government needs you—"

"Your country—"

"This woman is the enemy—"

"Evil."

"Tried to kill you and the others."

"We had to do this...put her away."

"Evil."

"Put her down."

"On the floor."

"You're *tired*."

"Alone...."

Travis stumbled back against the wall. There was...something else...something tugging at the back of his mind...a memory, at once familiar and comforting, yet disturbing....

Where were those children? Why weren't they here, now, helping him?

Travis looked back to the two men. His eyes grew heavier. The two now slowly advanced on him. Together. In unison. Their faces expressionless and....

Why was this so familiar?

"Come back with us—"

"We can help you."

Travis shook his head. "No," weakly came out of his mouth. "This is wrong...something's...."

Travis's groggy mind worked. The men felt familiar...like he *knew* them...though he'd never seen them before. What was it...what *was* it about these guys....

There was something else niggling at him...something else was going on here. There was another sound in that damned white noise...its pure frequencies jarring, determined...sparks kept firing off in his mind....

Travis again shifted Lizzie across his shoulders, pressed harder into the wall behind him. It was so easy to close his eyes, to just go to sleep and slump onto the floor...right here, *now*...let these two men have what they wanted....

They were right.

Who was this woman to him, anyway?

Why should he risk his life for her?

He was so tired...

(Bark!)

Give her up...

Bark! Bark!

...to these gentlemen...

Invaders.

"*So, this is who you left me for?*," came the voice from before him. It was a different voice...soft and sweet, yet laced with

(...*familiar*...)

venom

Travis blinked burning eyes and looked up.

Bark!

"All those long hours, you said...all that *work*, you said...and this is the kind of 'work' I find you doing? The *person* I find you doing?"

Travis shook his head. It was so hard to lift his head and look up.

(growling)

"*A-A-Annabel?*"

Out from where the two men had been, she came. Just as he'd last remembered her, as she'd walked out their door that last time. A white blouse over blue jeans and some flats, he thought women called them. Her hair loose...her face angry...disappointed.

Sad.

"What...what are you—"

"Apparently catching you in the same old lies—"

"Lies? I never—"

Annabel came right up to him; stopped inches from his face. Travis could smell her perfume—"Red"—feel the arcing of sexual energy between their bodies so close after having been apart for so long...quaked under the intensity of her deep, dark scrutiny.

That damned white noise! Would somebody *please* make it—

"How can you—"

"Don't change the subject, you bastard," she said.

Travis found himself excited by her presence—her proximity—*wanting* her. Intensely attracted to her...in fact, never had he been so attracted to her as he felt right now. She stood so close he felt her breasts faintly brushing up against him. Felt her breath on the skin of his face...*swore* he also felt her deep need actually reaching out to him, the anger just a front...

Bark! BARK!

"Wait," Travis said, dizzy, confused, backing away, "What the hell? This...can't be..."

Annabel's tone softened.

"What do you mean, honey? I'm right here," she said, reaching out to him.

Travis again shifted Lizzie; straightened up a little.

"What the hell is that damned...*barking?*"

Annabel stared at him.

"No," Travis said, pushing away from the wall and reshouldering Lizzie. "There's—"

Bark!

"No way you could possibly *be* here—"

"Look, honey, I'm sorry...so sorry for running out on you like that. You did have a stressful job—I see that now—and if you needed another woman, that's fine, too. Let's do it now...right here...I don't mind. I *really* miss you," she said, continuing to come for him.

"No! *There's no way you could be here!*"

The next time Travis looked up, Annabel was naked.

"Don't you want this? Don't you miss me? I miss you."

"I...."

Did he miss her?

Did he want her?

Stupid questions, but what was even more stupid, Travis suddenly realized, was that she was here at *all*.

No way. There was no way any of this was possible. This *was* Mind Fuck Central.

Suddenly Travis heard the deep throaty growl, a growl that sounded like a two-hundred-pound Rottweiler, and it came from behind Annabel.

Travis looked up to the speakers in the ceiling and walls.

White noise.

Mind feeling out of sync.

RoboChair.

Looked to Annabel.

To the illusionary swell of her breasts, the intense, longing desire in her eyes. Her desperate, parted lips and outstretched hands....

Then he looked beyond Annabel, and spotted

Crackers!

He smiled.

Crackers again growled that deep, death-dealing growl. Crackers barked, and barked and barked...until Annabel disappeared.

Travis stared at where Annabel and the *Invaders* agents had been.

Gone. All of it.

"Thank you, girl," Travis said to Crackers, who barked once in acknowledgement, wagged her tail...then promptly vanished.

Travis looked up to the white noise speakers, reshouldered Lizzie, and sprinted as fast as he could down the hallway.

5

Breathing heavily, Travis and Lizzie wove their way up and out of 4250. But, he was slowing down. Throughout their getaway, Lizzie drooled and bled from her nose and mouth, mumbling incoherently. He tried to reassure her she was okay, that he wouldn't let anything else happen to her, and that they would soon be safe.

What had this woman been like before her abduction, before whatever it was Black had done to her?

Had she smiled a lot?

A sense of humor?

A significant other?

Would she now be forever scarred?

Was she mentally tough enough to endure?

Their passage had—again—continued to go undetected, and that confounded Travis. The children were now gone, and he seemed on his own, but even more disturbing, Travis felt a sudden and powerful loss. Something terrible had just happened—*and where had Black been all this time?* If Lizzie had currently been undergoing her torture session *with* him, where had Black *been?*

Surely, he must now know she'd been extracted. Enter, the hallway hallucinations.

Gina...are you out there? Travis called. *Gina?*

No answer.

Cory?

No answer.

Gina! he again tried.

Here, Trav.

Travis sensed heavy emotion. *Oh,* no—

Cory's gone, Gina answered.

What?

We haven't much time...dead. I tried reaching him...and got—look, we can't worry about him now...we need to get Lizzie out. I'm coming your way—*in a Jeep—open-top Wrangler. Be ready.*

Where are we to—

Outside.

The others?

Can't worry about them.

Don't like—

Neither do I. We knew the risks. Have to get her out—now.

Roger that.

We'll work on the details once we're moving—

Travis pushed open the door and bolted out of the building. Into the open darkness. He hadn't done this kind of activity in years and was quickly weakening.

Just left 4250, Travis sent, *starting to slow, so the quicker*—

Head east. Coming in from there. Can you make if?

Yes.

He's onto us. Knows we have her. Be on the lookout.

Travis acknowledged. East. Hoped she didn't get spotted by The Center's security patrols.

If Black knew—*shit*, that meant he could be anywhere.

Breathing heavily, Travis slowed, ducking into the shadow of the next available building. He leaned against the brick, keeping Lizzie on his shoulders. Again shifted her form.

"Lizzie," Travis whispered, his breathing labored, "we've got to keep moving. Speak to me—how are you?"

Lizzie barely opened her eyes.

"Let me…go…*leave* me…"

"No can do. Gettin you outta here."

"*Joe*," she said weakly, "…why…why'd you…."

"Sssshh," Travis soothed, "everything'll be all right. Whatever he did to you back there was all mental—*hallucinations*—"

A light, distant thud caught Travis's attention. A heavy door closing? He carefully poked his head around the corner. There, out the side of 4250, Travis saw the shadow of a man. The man scanned the area. Travis heard an approaching vehicle.

Gina.

"Time to go!" he whispered to Lizzie.

Still hugging the shadows, Travis watched for the open-top Wrangler and spotted it.

Travis—I'm—

See ya. We're over here, he thought, sending her an image. Travis saw her head turn, then the Jeep, as it whipped a U-turn. It pulled up alongside in no time.

"*Quickly!*" Gina said.

Travis lumbered up to Gina and the Jeep and quickly deposited Lizzie into the back. "He just exited the building!" he said, and jumped in alongside Gina. Gina looked to him—gave him a quick, nervous smile—then shot back into gear, spinning the wheels as she hit the accelerator. Travis checked on Lizzie. She continued mumbling, but the blood had finally stopped flowing. Travis heard a weird, muffled grunt and turned to Gina.

"I think she's—"

Gina lay slumped forward on the wheel, arms hanging limply to her sides. A bump in the road turned her face toward him.

Gone. It was just…*gone*.

He looked in their direction of travel and saw they headed toward a bend in the road. He knew there was a drop-off into a culvert at that bend. Travis grabbed the wheel. His grip initially slipped on gore, and he barely managed to avoid the unexpected detour over that drop off. Without the pressure of Gina's foot on the accelerator, the Jeep slowed. Travis checked behind him to see what he was sure was the same shadow he'd seen moments before. Yes, but he wasn't alone. Beside Black stood another, probably one of the building's security team, who still had the upraised assault rifle.

Take out the driver, Travis picked up from Black. *Do it.*

But just as he turned away, he saw Black casually raise his own weapon and take out the shooter with a bullet to the man's head.

"God*damn.*"

Travis looked back to Gina. He forced her back, away from the steering wheel and against her seat. He barely kept from retching, as he held her back against her seat and had to look through her brains and blood and bone debris splattered across the windshield.

Rolling to a stop, the Jeep harmlessly bumped the curb. Gina's body again slumped forward, and Travis again forced Gina back against her seat.

"Oh, God, Gina...."

He looked back to the shadow. It was now—*confidently*—striding toward them.

They had to keep moving!

"Sorry, girl," he said.

Travis set his jaw...and forced Gina out of the Jeep. Her feet got tangled in the foot well, but he kicked at them until she fell free. Gina thudded as she hit the ground, disappearing into the darkness below the vehicle. Travis jumped into the driver's seat and stomped on the gas. Spitting out gravel from beneath the tires, he heard a metallic *zing!*—the sound of a missed round pinging off the Jeep's roll bar.

Travis gunned the vehicle, weaving to avoid further hits. Glancing in the rearview, he no longer saw Black and sped off into the darkness ahead.

Chapter Twenty-Six

1

Travis drove out of the dimly lit side streets and onto the better-lit John F. Kennedy Boulevard, the compound's main drag. Wind whipping hair and face, he inhaled crisp night air and subtle floral scents…wished they were partaking of their nocturnal ride under seriously better circumstances. Travis twisted around to the back seat.

What was it about this woman that was so important torture and murder were necessary?

Travis glanced into his rearview. He still didn't see Black following—but, he could be anywhere. Up ahead, and far off to his right, came additional headlights heading perpendicular and toward JFK Boulevard.

What did this mean, now, for the rest of them?

A life on the run—which, with a remote-viewing program, was next to impossible? Would Black seek them all out and "neutralize" each of them, one by one? Was this what they all had to look forward to for the rest of their short existences?

Another pair of headlights popped up back in the distance in his rearview.

Black.

"Great," Travis muttered, eyeing the lights.

"Where am I?" came a weak whisper from behind.

"Miss Gordon?"

Travis again glanced back to her. She still lay as he'd left her, only this time her eyes were open. "How're you feeling?"

No response.

"I'm with a small group of people," he said. "We're trying to get you out of here."

Travis shifted his attention between the road and Lizzie.

"I'm—we're—very sorry...I wish we could offer more."

Lizzie remained quiet.

How were they going to get out of here? They still had to leave the compound, and he was certain Black would have already seen to it that gate checks were performed for all in-and-outgoing traffic. And they couldn't just drive off the compound and out into the fields, because of security fences.

Just where the hell did he think they were going?

"Joe...what about...." came weakly from behind.

"Excuse me?"

The lights behind them continued to follow, but kept their distance.

"I didn't see anyone else in there with you—"

Travis thought hard—*could he have* possibly *missed someone else in there, in all that glare?*

No. There'd only been her...

"...just you."

Travis again glanced back to Lizzie. As they passed under streetlights, he saw a damp face under hair tossing about in the cool night air. She'd closed her eyes and was squeezing them tightly. Travis reached back to her—but stopped. "I'm sorry...but there was no one else."

Travis tried to contact the others.

Lee? Anyone?

I'm here, Lee said. *You have her?*

Yes...but Black's on our tail.

Where?

On Kennedy. Travis passed a sign for the air strip, and sent the image.

I'll get there. Buy some time...weave in and out of buildings, streets—at normal speed—keep him guessing.

Roger.

Gina's dead?

Yes.

Travis immediately turned at the next intersection.

Lee?, Lizzie asked mentally, and Travis nearly swerved off the road.

He looked behind him, but Lizzie didn't look up. Even in the occasional streetlights they passed under, Travis could see she still looked beaten, raw, eyes still closed and swollen, as the light and shadows rolled across her face.

Since before you were born, Lizzie sent to his unasked query, *but, this is even new to me.*

Okay. Travis paused. *I work with him.*

Remote viewers. Two are dead?

Yes—

Because of me?

Travis made another turn.

"We need to get you out of here. That's all that matters," he shouted into the wind.

People are dying because of me.

Travis had nothing to say, but kept exchanging glances between the rearview and the road. He took another turn.

Don't worry, Lizzie sent, *they're fine.*

Travis shot her another look.

Gina and Cory. They want me to tell you they're—

"How can you—"

It's what I do. For the most part…I used to be pretty good at this stuff.

"How come I can't pick up on them?"

Lizzie mentally shrugged. *Don't know. Maybe because of your focus…stress? Don't know.*

"What else can you see—sorry…*are you all right?*"

Travis took another turn and looked into the rearview.

I mean—

I'm as fine as I can be. My children are with me—

"Who *are* they?"

Not quite sure. You'd think I would.

Lizzie sent images that showed how the children were attached to her in some vague metaphysical way that she'd never been able to figure out—how they'd helped her, given her support. How she used to think they were some probable children she and her husband were supposed to have had—but that there were far too many for that.

The room, the toys— Travis sent.

Yes, Lizzie returned. *And they've been with me since you got me out of….*

Since he'd removed her from hell.

People thought physical torture was the worst, but it's the psychological that was longest lasting…left the deepest scars. How would she—

I'll be okay, she sent.

Travis blushed. "Sorry, was just—"

No need. Thanks.

Travis glanced into the rearview and saw that the headlights kept their distance. Lizzie opened her eyes.

Your friend...he's here, she sent.

Another dark, open-topped Jeep pulled up alongside, flipping on his lights. Lee gave Travis a thumbs-up. Travis nodded.

Now let's play a little game of cat and mouses! Lee sent. *Let's whip in and out of each other to confuse things...then we peel off and go in different directions. Copy?*

Roger, copy, Travis sent.

Sorry we had to meet like this, Lee sent Lizzie.

Travis saw that in response to the extra Jeeps, Black had sped up. He was no doubt also calling in reinforcements, so whatever they were to do, had to be done quickly.

"Hold on!" Travis said to Lizzie, "you might wanna strap in!"

Lizzie felt around for the seat belt, buckled in, then grabbed the roll bar for stability. Travis and Lee began driving wildly about each other.

"And stay down!" Travis shouted.

The two Jeeps wove in and out of each other, tires skidding and skipping over pavement, kicking up dust and road debris. Black was quickly gaining on them.

Okay, Travis sent, *time to split!*

Lee nodded then peeled off, disappearing into the darkness. For the first time since this mission of theirs, Travis grinned as he glimpsed Black's car slamming to a confused halt.

Congratulations, boys, Lizzie sent, *just might work.*

Travis looked back to her.

"We're certainly not out of this yet."

Travis stepped on the gas.

Your companion Lee isn't so lucky, Lizzie sent. *Black just picked him as the vehicle to follow.*

Lee!

See him. Just get her the hell outta here!

"Shit," Travis muttered, "Don't know if I like this ability...."

2

"I don't know where else to go, but we seem to be coming up on our airstrip," Travis said.

Well, that's as good a place as any, since Black's back on our trail, Lizzie sent.

Travis twisted around in his seat.

As they passed a side street, he saw Black's car waiting for them, lights off. As soon as they passed, the lights flicked on and it again pulled out behind them.

"Crap!"

"*Go there,*" came a tiny voice from beside him. Travis jumped. *To the airstrip!* this new voice sent mentally.

The little girl who'd helped him find Lizzie was now sitting in the passenger seat, smiling, hands neatly folded in her lap. Her hair didn't move in the Jeep's windblast.

"Goddammit—there's too much ghost shit going on here!"

"Potty mouth," the girl said. "Just go right on through," she continued, "don't stop…do *not* stop."

Travis looked to her queerly. "Are you really there?" He looked in the rearview. "Can you see her?" he asked, looking back to Lizzie.

Course, Lizzie responded. *I'm more surprised* you *can—you're the first I know to be able to.*

Hello, dear, Lizzie greeted the child.

Hi, Mommy! the girl answered, cheerfully.

Mommy? Travis sent. "This is just too frigging weird," Travis said.

Travis forced the accelerator down.

The little girl looked back to Travis. "There's no need for that," the girl emphasized, "The guards won't see you."

"Oh, yes, there is. *I* need to do it."

Both the girl and Lizzie smiled.

Black sped up, keeping with them as they blasted past the open entry control point and its already lifted entry gate. The airstrip lay just beyond.

They were now out on open tarmac. Out of the corner of his eyes Travis saw a plane landing, its landing spots on bright as it touched down. But the lights in his rearview had disappeared. A glance to his left found Black speeding alongside and just a touch behind. The girl in Travis's passenger seat was gone.

Wish we could do that, he sent to Lizzie.

Zing!

Black was back in action. Another nine mil round was sent their way.

"Well, shit, shit, and *shit*," Travis said, zigzagging the tarmac.

Up ahead, Travis saw that the taxiing plane seemed to be heading straight for them.

Another shot, this time pinging off the roll bar above.

"God*dammit!* How the hell do we get out of this one?" Travis shouted into the windblast.

Lizzie remained quiet. Travis stole a peek. She seemed a little more *there*, now, sitting up at an angle while holding onto the roll bar, head low. She casually brushed away metallic roll-bar fragments from her face and hair.

Both vehicles were now in an all-out sprint. Black's vehicle was about a car length to the rear and left of Travis and Lizzie, which made it harder for Travis to keep an eye on what Black was doing.

Another *zing!*, and Travis saw a spark ricochet off the Jeep's hood. Again, Lizzie appeared unperturbed.

"Lizzie," Travis shouted, "could you *please* get down!"

Lizzie adjusted her position. At that point, another bullet screamed from the rear and punched a neat hole through the passenger-side windshield.

Then there was a loud *boom*, followed by the sound of screeching metal and tires and other commotion that quickly faded behind them. Twisting in his seat to his left, Travis saw Black's car spinning horizontally out of control, like a top. Travis slowed just a touch as he arced their Jeep around to see what'd happened.

An explosion.

Travis again pushed on the accelerator, redirecting their Jeep away. He didn't know where he was going, but figured he could cross the runway, ram the razor-wire fence, and hope the gods (or those children) had paved another way for them.

Lee rammed Black, Lizzie sent. *I fear he won't live to brag about it.*

"God*dammit*," Travis said. *Lee*, he sent, *Lee!*

No response.

He's unconscious, Lizzie sent. *His only saving grace.*

What do you—

The plane, Lizzie sent, *head toward the* plane.

What?

That's what we're meant to do. That's our way out. Now—before Black regains his advantage.

Travis gunned it for the Learjet.

Yes, Lizzie sent. *Just for us. Quickly….*

Travis quickly came up to the plane and whipped the Jeep around to the hatch side of the Learjet. The hatch opened as they pulled alongside. A figure emerged through the door and onto the hatch's steps. By the backlighting he saw the silhouette was waving frantically to them to hurry it the hell up. Travis pulled up beside the door and slammed to a side-skidding stop, jerking the both of them in their restraints, as the Jeep lifted then settled.

A nursery rhyme suddenly blasted through Travis's head, above the high-pitched whines of the Learjet's engines.

Ring around the rosie
A pocketful of posies,
Ashes, ashes!
We all fall down.

"What the *hell?*" he asked, but they were already in motion. The figure waving to them turned out to be an older gentleman with close-set, intense eyes. With the assistance of another, this gentleman was already helping Lizzie out the back of the Jeep.

"*Hurry,*" urged the gentleman with a thick Massachusetts accent. "We haven't much time!"

Travis jumped out of the vehicle, taking over the older gentleman's position with Lizzie. As Travis and the other man positioned Lizzie's arms across the backs of their shoulders, Travis and Lizzie's eyes met.

It was as if Lizzie looked right through him.

Unnerved, Travis stumbled. There was an intense mixture of hurt, appreciation, and…and that she had probed deep into him and had *found* something….

The two of them carefully positioned Lizzie though the hatch and into the Learjet's dimly lit interior. Travis then rushed inside as did the older gentleman and his assistant, who quickly pulled Lizzie the rest of the way in and locked shut the hatch. The Learjet kicked into action, its engines increasing in pitch. They were all slammed back into their seats as the aircraft lurched forward, spinning around hard and fast for the runway.

"Thanks," Travis said as they quickly settled Lizzie into her seat, buckled her in, and tried to keep from being tossed about within the cabin themselves.

"You're welcome," the gentleman returned. "Pleazah and honah to meet you, young man," Kennedy said, extending his hand to Travis.

"An honor to meet you, sir," Travis said, quite surprised to be shaking a President's hand.

"And this is Morris," Kennedy said, directing him to his body-guard. "One of my evah-present Guardian Angels. But we'rah not out of this yet," he added, and quickly strapped himself in. "I suggest you do the same."

The cabin lights blinked off, the jet's speed increased, and Travis slammed back into the seat beside Lizzie. All four went quiet as the jet picked up speed and lifted its nose.

"A friend of yours?" Kennedy asked, leaning forward and indicating out the port windows.

Travis looked outside. A body lay unmoving on the tarmac, a short throw from burning vehicles. Another figure approached the unmoving, prone figure. In the distance, lights from approaching security vehicles flickered.

"Yeah," Travis said, "one of them's a friend of mine. He bought us the time it took for you to get to us." Travis looked to Kennedy. "How'd you know?"

All of a sudden Lizzie grew agitated.

"No...*no!*"

Lizzie lurched forward and shot a look toward the window. Travis looked back as the jet passed the scene. From the glow of the burning vehicles, Travis and Lizzie watched as the upright silhouette extended an arm toward the prone figure.

The prone body jerked once. Twice.

The jet departed.

But what no one else had seen was that as the Learjet cleared the runway, the figure had then directed that outstretched arm toward the aircraft...and fired several more rounds.

Chapter Twenty-Seven

1

"I don't even know where to begin, Mr. President," Travis said, over the Learjet's quietly hissing air handlers.

Lizzie was out cold. They all remained belted into their seats, as they climbed through 20,000 feet at a steep angle.

"Call me 'Jack,'" Kennedy said. "Let me, ah, help you out—though I'm still a bit confused, myself," Kennedy continued. "I'd originally bahrded this plane with the intent to visit your Centah's directah, to discuss a project or two I'd, ah, had in mind…but as I entahed the plane, I was met by…children."

"*Children?*" Travis asked.

Kennedy nodded. "Cabin full of them. And thereah was anothah…a Man With No Name. A man I seem to know—somehow—from my past. I do, ah, have little memory of him, but thereah's something about the gentleman I just can't put my fingah on."

"Interesting." Travis studied Lizzie's face, which was now quiet and serene. He said, "I get the feeling I've met these children. That man."

"Indeed?"

"Yes, sir. But your story first."

Kennedy nodded, paused. "I was told my plans wereah about to change. That aside from another trip enroute, I was to meet you two, and that we wereah to then immediately take off. To take you two out of harm's way, and that we couldn't do it fast enough. That was heavily emphasized. I pray we're able to accomplish that."

Kennedy unbuckled, got up, and crossed over to Lizzie and Travis. Gently, he extended the back of a hand to Lizzie's face.

Though still unconscious, her face occasionally contracted into grimaces, and her body twitched.

"As for whatevah Black's done to her...I am so very sorry...and feel pahrtly to blame."

Kennedy took a different seat, across from and facing them.

"Some twenty years ago...I'd hired that man—Black—on my staff. Little did I know what I'd done. To make a long story short, and I'll try to better clarify lateah, but...somehow...and I know this sounds insane, believe me, sir, but *somehow...I'd gone back in time.* Thereah, I said it. First time I've said it out loud, even to myself. But, I'd tried to change my actions—and *thought* I'd succeeded—in changing my decision to appoint this man. I've come to find out, howevah, that I'd been unsuccessful—"

"*Back in* time?"

Kennedy raised a hand. "It's the only explanation—"

"With all due respect, Mr. President, are you sure it wasn't a dream? A hallucination?"

Kennedy shook his head. "Damned if I know. Don't really know what to believe any moreah. All I do know is that I'd felt I'd actually gone back to my days at The Center..."

Kennedy's gaze took on a momentary, far-away look.

"...back to the time of our interview with him, Teddy, Evelyn, and me—all thereah. I'd felt my office, my clothes, my *angah*. All thereah. But, it seems, as this mystery Man With No Name explained to me, Black is fahr more resourceful than we'd anticipated. It's a long story, but as a remote viewer, I'd have thought it wouldn't be such a reach forah the likes of one of your persuasion—"

"Again, with all due respect, sir, but it's not so much a matter of it being a 'reach'...as it is I've just never heard of anyone going back in time. Physically, I mean. And this mystery man—is he still onboard—"

"Mr. President," the cockpit intercom interrupted, "we have a situation."

2

Mel lay broken and battered on the blinding white floor in the blinding white room. The only other colors he saw were that of his blood and vomit. He wanted to move, wanted so desperately to run and cry and kill that bastard, but was drained. Physically, mental-ly…spiritually.

What did it all matter?

His parents had been killed and, now, someone he didn't even know was trying to do the same to him.

What was the point?

He just wanted to go home, drink iced tea, watch TV—and call and talk with Lizzie—Madame Nostra*dame*us…whatever her name. Wanted his parents back. His old life. Whatever he remembered of it was far better than where he was, now, and he'd never, *ever*, again complain about *anything*.

Mel jerked from another shooting stab of pain from his groin.

He winced, gritted his teeth.

He tried to move his left arm, which lay on the floor slightly ahead of and behind his head at a weird angle. His face was turned away from it and pressed into the floor. Any time he tried to move, he'd feel the pain shoot through his broken arm like a red-hot, twisting poker. He just couldn't get any leverage and felt little inclination to try any other movement. He'd probably get his other arm broken, anyway, so, again…what was the point?

Still the question haunted him: *why?* What had caused all this? What had brought this act of violence into his otherwise serene life? Who'd Black want him to admit knowing? Lizzie wasn't a man—and he did continue to insist he was specifically looking for a *male*—and no other man came to mind.

Except for his father.

Mel felt the dark presence first.

He looked up…or tried to. Dehydration, pain, and hopelessness pressed him into the floor as easily as any millstone.

Black stood above him. He slowly bent down, deliberately worked his fingers into Mel's hair, then yanked his head back, angling his beaten and sagging face upward.

"Have you decided on your course of action, my little friend?"

The tears came hard and fast. Mel squinted, blubbering through split lips, dried vomit, and snot.

"*I don't* know *anyone*…"

"Wrong answer, my friend."

Black pulled out his weapon, placed its muzzle hard into Mel's left temple…

And pulled the trigger.

3

Ryan wearily wandered into the office after a much-longer-than-planned, impromptu tasking. He flicked on a bank of florescent lights, then reconsidering, flipped them off. He liked the peace and quiet of the night. The rest of the department was long gone, but other departments in the building still had people sporadically inhabiting offices. Making his way through the administrative desks, he paused.

Something was different.

And he felt a little weird…beside himself.

He sat at Paula Harris's desk and dropped his head into his hands, rubbing his eyes and forehead; wearily stared into the blackness of the empty computer screen before him.

He reached out to the others.

Nothing.

Sighing, he again rubbed his eyes. If things were important enough, they'd contact him.

Looked to his watch. Good God, the hours flew by!

A handful of dark, face-blackened figures sprinted among the compound's buildings, hugging shadows. They paused, checked the intersection, performed silent hand signals between each other, then again sprinted across the streets.

Two buildings. One mission.

Ryan got back to his feet and stretched. He'd briefly nodded off at Paula's desk, but head-snapped wide awake to pictures of her daughter and her smiling at him from the Grand Canyon. Paula was great to work with, was cute in a freckled, "granola way," and recently divorced. No doubt this job had heavily contributed to that.

Parched, he dug into his pockets for change. Nothing. Pulling out his wallet, he found two singles, both rather worn, and one with a partial tear in it.

Trying to smooth out the wrinkled currency, he left the office and headed toward the soda machine, about mid-way down the now dark corridor. The machine looked comfortingly eerie under its own illumination, the hallway lights shut down for the night. Mountain Dew—that's what he wanted. Ryan approached the machine. The orange "empty" selection-indicator lights for his soda glowed steady for all of its regular and diet versions.

"Crap! No *Dew?*"

Forming one of the singles into a rigid and flattened, elongated "V," he considered his options. Pepsi, Pepsi, Slice, and diet Pepsi. He wasn't a Pepsi fan, and Slice just didn't do it for him. Smoothing out the bill, he inserted it into the slot. It didn't give that accepting, internal grinding sound he was expecting, paused mid-action, then spat it back out. Ryan snatched the bill and again tried. Still no go. Jokingly giving it a psychic "mind meld" with a turn of his head and narrowed eyes, Ryan again tried. This time it took, but he hadn't paid attention to which bill he'd inserted, and it'd been the one with the rip in it, and he didn't release it quickly enough. The bill tore in half.

"*Shit!*"

Two-man teams were simultaneously deployed to residences.

Dark SUVs quickly traveled to their destinations, turned off their lights, and quietly parked in dark, out-of-the-way shadows. Men silently ejected from vehicles, just as quietly hustled toward objectives.

One objective was Dr. Richard Haywood. "Dick" to his friends and coworkers.

Dick was The Center's Operations Director, was intimately involved in nearly every aspect of The Center's remote-viewing activities. Knew about both its covert and commercial applications. Created protocols and administered the projects with the apt assistance of Paula Harris, his head administrator. Dick had been watching a taped *X-Files* episode he'd missed, winding down from a long day, his family already in bed.

Dr. Haywood got up and stretched, then headed into the kitchen for a glass of water when the team found him. Standing at the rear window over the sink, Dick caught his own reflection in the window as he drank his last glass of water. It was a reflection that normally didn't have the silencered barrel of a .22 pointing in at him. The hissed round neatly punctured the window and Dr. Haywood's forehead.

His remaining family members were similarly dispatched in their sleep, then another dead body was brought in and placed in Dick's wife-of-twenty-one-years bedroom: Emily Frazier, formerly an administrator in one of Dick's many departments. A .22 handgun was placed in one of her bloodied hands, a crumpled note stuffed into the other. A note about how if she couldn't have Dick, no one else would. Several vicious stab wounds were applied to Dick's wife's body, the knife was flicked over Emily's body to create blood spatter, then tossed on the floor beside Emily, once her prints had been smeared all over it.

Amy Craig, Bruce McNeal, and Randy Forz were all sleeping in their beds when they were similarly hunted down by the two-man teams. Remote viewers for other departments were also similarly neutralized.

Ryan stood before the lit soda machine, silently cursing, holding one half of his ripped single. He fished out the remaining portion of the bill, as it was kicked back to him—but got it caught in the slot. Finally able to yank it free, he stuffed it into his pocket and paused.

He looked down one end of the hallway. There was a subtle commotion that had caught his attention. He looked to the other end.

Nothing.

This was nothing unusual, with pockets of individuals continuing to work late throughout the place. He fished out the other bill, straightened it out, then fed it into the slot. It was immediately accepted. Of the available choices, Ryan pressed one of the regular Pepsi selectors—and to his amazement, out tumbled a green, white, and red Mountain Dew can.

"Lucky day!" Ryan grabbed the can and popped it open.

Collecting his change, he headed back to his office—when alarm bells went off in his head.

Get out! Now! Move!

His warning was from another remote viewer he didn't know, from another department.

Ryan was overcome with images of dark-clad figures rushing about, guns, and *murder* taking place. He was filled with a paramount sense of urgency. His entire body tingled.

Get out now! the voice insisted.

Ryan immediately about-faced and peeked around the corner, back out into the hallway.

Again heard movement.

Closer, louder, and hurried this time...definitely on his floor and coming closer.

He tossed aside his soda and sprinted to the rear exit, putting his ear to the door. Muffled sounds quickly advanced up the stairwell.

He rushed back to the office and sprinted to a window. There were no vehicles outside he could see, but when he closed his eyes and directed his senses to the situation, he found himself across to their sister building and was met with images of murder and dead bodies. Unknown teams were literally killing their way through the buildings.

Everywhere.

"*Fuck!*"

The window!

Ryan flicked open the latches, his hands shaking. This couldn't be happening...it all had to be a figment of an overworked and tired mind....

"Goddammit!" he said, trying to open the stuck, early-sixties-vintage window, "*open*, for Chrissakes!" Suddenly, the window shot upward and slammed loudly into the upper casement. He froze. Great. He sensed the approaching team and that they'd also just paused, hearing his commotion. Quickly, he climbed up, making for the fire escape, but as he stepped through the window, felt a sharp pain in his upper left shoulder. It was accompanied by a low "*pop.*"

Had he just dislocated his shoulder?

He continued to climb through the window and glanced to his shoulder.

Blood.

Another hissing pop, and this time he lost all control of his body and fell backward.

Twisting as he fell, he found himself looking up into the darkened face and cold-steel stare of a twenty-four-year-old assassin. For a moment, it looked as if those eyes had also paused, and in that instant Ryan knew his assassin's name and life history, his training for this job.

Whom he actually worked for.

Then he looked back out the window toward the other building, but only saw blackness....

As his life ebbed from him, he thought about the coworkers across the way...about how his parents had been so proud he'd gotten his dream job. How happy and supportive they'd been of his ability— and desire—to help Humanity. And there had been one last thought that screamed through his mind just before the killing round screamed through his brain.

Why hadn't he foreseen any of this?
Why hadn't any of them?

Chapter Twenty-Eight

1

Deep in thought, the Man With No Name maneuvered his riding mower across the lawn…in the darkness…headlights illuminating his way.

He slammed on the brakes.

No!

This wasn't supposed to happen! What was Black doing?

The Man With No Name hopped off the mower, ran past his garden, and shot up onto the porch. He stopped and turned. Stared off into the darkness behind him.

Muffled "popping" sounds. All around him.

"My God…he just doesn't…he just doesn't *get* it…."

Sadly, he shook his head, turned around, and continued inside.

2

The Man With No Name calmly walked into Victor Black's low-lit and shadowy office. Black sat with his back to him, in a swivel chair behind an immaculately arranged desk. He was hunched over, working on something at a small safe. His SIG rested within arm's reach.

"I hear you've been looking for me," the Man With No Name calmly announced, standing before the desk, hands in his pockets.

Black whipped around.

The initial look on his face was of abject *fear*—unmistakable, shocked, and *primal*—but was quickly replaced by his usual cold, hard stare. Black shot to his feet, grabbing his SIG.

"How'd you—"

"You've been looking for me, have you not?"

"Don't toy with me—how'd you—" Black leveled his nine mil at the Man With No Name, carefully eyeing him as he circled around from behind the desk. Looked to his closed door. "You alone?"

"Is anybody—really?"

"Answer the goddamned question."

The Man With No Name sighed. "Yes...I'm *alone*..." He turned around to face Black, as he came from around the back of the desk, then leaned against the desk.

"Why now?," Black asked, narrowing his gaze at him. "Why now, after all these years, do you waltz in here, unannounced, and just...hand yourself over?"

"You mean besides the fact that you've gone crazy and killed off entire remote-viewing departments and their families?"

"Answer the question."

"You've performed wholesale slaughter on those who—even in *your* terms—have nothing to do with your problem."

"'Problem?'" Black repeated, standing with his back to a wall, his weapon still trained on the Man With No Name.

"You've been after me for a long time. And you're pissed you lost one...while the other simply never talked. So you just decided—hey, what the hell—why don't I just kill them all and let God sort em out? Maybe if I slaughter enough, he'll come to me."

"Was I not correct?"

"Would appear."

"I've wanted you off my back a long time. Now, with you handing yourself over to me like this...I feel I should make you bleed for as long as possible."

The Man With No Name chuckled.

"Think I'm kidding?"

"Oh, I know you're not, but, there's no cause for any of—"

"Once I'm done with you, there won't be any 'cause'...period."

The Man With No Name folded his arms, returning Black's stare.

"Why and how...do you know so much about me? Who do you work for, and why do you interfere in everything I do?"

The Man With No Name shook his head. "You're blind to the obvious. You can't hide in shadows forever."

"I would have found you eventually."

"Don't you get it? The dreams? The chase? All of it?"

Black returned to his desk, picked up his phone, and punched in a four-digit extension, still keeping his weapon trained on his guest—who turned to track him. "Get in here—*now*," he said, and hung up.

"I guess we'll see what makes you tick soon enough," Black said.

The Man With No Name again sighed. "Perhaps." The Man with No Name took in the office as he waited.

Within minutes, a four-man black-uniformed security detail rushed the office, armed with assault rifles and squawking radios. Two of the detail immediately and roughly restrained the Man With No Name.

"Is this really necessary?," the Man With No Name asked, as he was jostled about.

"You tell me," Black said. He came up alongside the Man With No Name and lowered his weapon; got right in the Man With No Name's face.

"Take him away."

3

Lizzie Gordon looked to the children who surrounded and tended to her. She was outside. It was night. The air was alive with the scent of pines and leaves riding wave upon wave of gentle breezes. She wasn't in the Learjet any more, and though tired, wasn't as exhausted as she thought she'd be. The torture, chase, and escape all seemed distant memories.

She'd returned to the amphitheater—and the children.

The pyre down in the center was lit, it's glow muted, less than what it should be. There was just a hint of charcoal in the air. She studied it—and the surrounding area. Children were everywhere, and those attending to her were busily washing and cleaning her wounds.

Wounds?

"There's been an accident," a little red-headed girl with freckles said to Lizzie.

"Is everybody all right?" Lizzie asked.

"The pilots died...but are with us, now, and are okay," said a dark-haired boy.

"Travis? The President?"

"They're over there," the boy answered, pointed, "also being attended to."

Lizzie saw them, down just a little way from where she sat on the cut granite steppes.

"I don't understand…what…what *happened?* Why are we—*how*—"

"Oh, he shot at the jet as you took off," said a girl. "The evil man. The pilots did their best."

"I need to know," Lizzie said, reaching out to the girl, "who *are* you? Why are you always around? How come I can never figure out—"

"You're our *mother*, Mom," a little brown-haired boy said, smiling.

"That can't be. I can't have kids, let alone *thousands*."

"Doesn't matter. You're still our mother. Children never forget their mother—even before they're born."

"I still don't—"

"You will."

"Who's your father?"

The children smiled. "You know that, *too*, Mommy."

They giggled.

"But, I don't. *Who's your father? Tell* me…."

"Mom, you know. You've always known. It's Dad. Your husband."

"Dammit, I don't have a husband, not—"

The children surrounding her giggled. The ones attending to her just gave reassuring smiles, as they tidied up what they'd been doing, then moved away, parting to show another who'd been sitting on the steps beside her, unnoticed.

"*Joe?*"

Joe smiled to her.

"Is that really *you?*"

"Of course it's me, honey—the *real* me, this time—but you know that, now, don't you? Really *know*."

Lizzie went to him, throwing her arms around him. "I'm so very, very *sorry!*"

"There's nothing to be sorry about," he said, tightly hugging her back.

"But I should have been able to foresee your death! *Prevented* it!"

"You did everything I could have ever wanted or needed. It had nothing to do with your abilities, hon. Black was the cause. It had *nothing* to do with you."

Lizzie pushed away.

"How could he have had anything to do with this? I only just—"

"Oh," Joe casually waved it off, "that has nothing to do with it. He'd engineered my death. He hasn't done it yet, but he will. And I agreed to it."

"*Why on earth would you ever agree to such a thing?*"

"I know it's a bit off center...but in another lifetime, I'd been...well, less than savory...took *his* life. This was my way of experiencing the other side of the coin, I suppose. I hold nothing against him, though I see how *you* would. I get it. Especially after what he'd just put you through."

"You *killed* him?"

Joe nodded. "Yeah...but *you* tortured him. Not that what I did was any less than what you did. You may not remember it, but back around 20 A.D., you were a Roman soldier. You didn't think much of Black even then. You tortured him for days, keeping him just barely alive throughout the entire ordeal. It was pretty gruesome."

"*What—why?*"

"Because of what he'd just done to you."

"That makes no—"

"—*linear* sense. Remember, honey, we're in-between Time, now."

"But why would I have done such a thing?"

"Don't you remember how you cursed him while he tortured you with images of Melissa and me? That one thought spun up that Roman experience. Once you leave physical experience, Time has no meaning, and emotions pack quite the wallop as they careen through the non-physical."

Memories of her torture flooded back—her impassioned oath.

"Oh, my *God*—"

"Honey, no one's perfect. It's all a learning experience, and, hopefully, we know what *not* to do next time around."

Lizzie sat, stunned.

"I thought...thought I was better than that."

"You mean, you honestly never had any idea?"

"I'd always thought—"

"Your actions then were so horrendous to you, you blocked them out in this life. Understandable. Not to mention, they wouldn't have made sense, since—"

"Since I hadn't yet gone through my—*that*—current experience. I'm so embarrassed."

"Don't be. You've spent *many* other lives more than 'making up' for that one—not that you ever needed to. I'm not saying what Black is doing is anything to be ignored—he has to be stopped. We need to set him straight, end all this. But at least, now—maybe—you can understand why he's doing what he's doing. He's an angry soul, and if things are not corrected—and quickly—he'll upset a lot more lives in ways that just don't need to be, nor should be. There are other ways to grow, other ways that are much more preferable to his current approach. But he has to be *stopped*."

"How are Travis and Jack?"

"They're getting similar attention."

"Will I ever see you again?"

"Of course you will! Don't let your emotions get the best of you, honey. I've never really been separated from you. You know all those times you questioned whether or not the emotions you were feeling were yours—or mine? They *were* mine. I kept trying to reach you, to reassure you I was okay, but Black kept redirecting my efforts. Messing with you. But emotions are powerful things, and they always get through. *Always*. There's a part of each other *in* each other. Forever. That can never be blocked. You did good, hon."

Lizzie teared up. Joe bear-hugged her.

"Now," Joe said, wiping away tears from Lizzie's face, "while you're recovering, we're going to take the time to clear up a few other things...set a few other...effects...into motion."

"Like what?"

"Come along. The children and I will show you."

Lizzie and Joe got to their feet, and, along with Jack and Travis, made their way down toward the center of the amphitheater where, clustered around the burning pyre, sat more children.

Waiting.

4

Victor Black watched in livid anger and hatred as the Union forces rammed into their lines.

He was there.

He didn't have a name, but knew he was to finally meet—come face to face with his destiny.

Black shoved aside and slayed others in blue, cutting a swath to the one he knew he must meet on this battlefield. Black saw him—and recognized him—as the man removed his bayonet from one of his own South Carolina comrades. Images of another battlefield—on far-away soil—entered his mind. They wore armor, his opponent wearing that of the Roman army, while he wore barbarian leather. He was wounded, captured, and taken on a long march. Torture, and, finally, death were in his future at the hands of yet two others tied to this man....

Black shook the bewildering images from his mind, images that only further fueled his rage and again focused in on the man he was meant to meet and kill.

Kill!

Black's frustration grew as he tried to get to his target.

There was much confusion, the fighting thick and furious. The noise deafening, the air charged with death, and choked with the smell of black powder and blood. Black tried to reload, but the fighting had become hand to hand, so Black jabbed and butted the enemy with his empty musket instead, used his elbows and knees and fists. Black saw his opponent-to-be still using his bayoneted rifle—when it was knocked from grip. He watched as this man deftly sidestepped the attack, then lunged for his attacker with bare hands, grabbing his opponent by the throat. Black watched him viciously throttle the man until his neck snapped. There was something about this man...an intensity that he knew would have been better used as an ally.

Sensing an opening, Black made his move and charged. His opponent quickly snatched up his rifle and turned toward him. A musket's length apart, the two eyed each other.

Instant, unspoken recognition.

Before Black could react, his opponent in the Irish brigade broke free, having to react to another attacker from behind. The soldier jabbed his rifle rearward into his attacker's stomach and quickly followed through with another jab to his attacker's face, splitting open his head before he collapsed to the bloodied earth. The Yankee was now too far away to lunge after with his musket, so Black reached for one of his knives. He watched as his opponent also shot a hand to a scabbard, withdrawing his own blade. Black's fingers fumbled across his body for...

Where was it?

Bodies rammed into him, and a pistol went off beside his head, sending an intense ringing through his skull. In the flash of an instant, Black's opponent whipped *his* blade at him. Twisting his body, Black tried to deflect the blade with his musket, but failed, and the blade buried itself into his chest. Black steadied himself, grunted, and flung himself forward, his musket held out before him like a pike. Black felt the knife grind into bone, but before he could make contact with his opponent, another Union soldier got in his way and Black's musket ended up hitting and collapsing that man before he could gain ground on his intended victim.

Continually jostled, Black staggered in a painful haze, ears ringing, fumbled for the knife in his chest. Tore it free. Holding the knife out before him, he stared at it. A blade

(*knives…*)

fresh from his attacker's own hand. It felt familiar, somehow *right….*

(*knives*)

Blinking from dripping sweat and beginning to gray out, Black looked up just in time to see the pointy end of a Springfield rifle's bayonet intently forced neatly into his side. As the blade was twisted within him, Black lost consciousness and began the long spiral toward….

Jerking awake, Black found himself sitting at a desk.

"God*damn*." He clutched at his side, grunting in pain and bowed forward. "*Damn* it."

He was alone.

He straightened up, trying to loosen his shoulder and side from the still excruciating pain. These slippages in time had become more and more frequent and annoying. He had to…hadn't he been on his way to interrogate someone? Someone he'd captured?

The time warps were really messing with his head.

Who? Who'd he captured?

He stared blankly into the darkness of his office.

The Man With No Name.

Had he really captured him? The man from his nightmares? That mystery man who'd constantly tormented his waking and sleeping existences near his entire adult life? It seemed too good to be true—

Could he still be dreaming?

Yes…the man had actually walked into his office—and how he'd gotten through all his security was another matter—then simply…

Presented himself.

Offered himself up.

Just like that. Here I am, take me!

After all these years, why so easily give up? It was far too simple.

He had to be missing something.

But Black also had other pressing issues to which he had to attend—like where the hell had that Learjet gone? And after having just wiped out some of the best minds on the planet, there were going to be a lot of pissed off agencies out there.

Repercussions. *Serious* ones.

He'd have to get moving and find things out the old-fashioned way. There were few who could touch him, but if certain agencies decided they wanted him…it'd only be a matter of time.

Perhaps it was time to disappear. Change a few things and find that damned Learjet.

Things were supposed to get easier when you killed off your problems, goddammit.

Chapter Twenty-Nine

1

One way or the other, Victor Black mused, Lizzie Gordon had to go.

He no longer needed her, now that he had this...Man With No Name...and she knew too much about *him*. So, Victor Black decided, he would do what he was good at: he'd kill her before he'd ever met her. He needed to be rid of her; he knew she knew something she was somehow hiding from him, and she was somehow tied to this Man Without A Name without a doubt.

It was time to cut bait and bail.

Maybe now, with this Mystery Man in his custody (and why did *that* feel so strange?), he could continue his work without any further interference—start from a contradictory clean slate, as it were.

Victor Black locked his door, turned down the lights, and sat down behind his desk, focusing on his newest task:

Kill Elizabeth Gordon before ever meeting her.

2

On the morning of his death, Joe Gordon had awoken troubled.

He'd had a most disturbing dream, one in which his wonderful wife had come out to see him at the construction site (as she occasionally did), but had been killed in an industrial accident. An I-beam had swung out of control and struck her, killing her instantly. Joe wasn't much into dreams (except for that one notable exception that'd predicted their meeting each other), in fact, rarely remembered anything about them, and if he did, usually ignored them. But this one was different. It involved his wife, had been nasty, and had been very, very, disturbingly *real.*

After lying in bed for several minutes, staring into the above-bed darkness of their bedroom, and wondering just where the hell he was—as in whether or not he was still dreaming—the dream eventually wore off, and he quietly slipped out from beneath the blankets and downstairs to make coffee and fetch the morning paper. As much as he'd tried to discount—even forget—the dream, as much as he tried to get into his normal morning routine before heading out for work, he just couldn't shake the disturbing images.

Construction site.

Lizzie.

Kiss and talk.

Boom!

As Joe sat down to read the paper, the Metro section fell into his lap, and there, on the first page, in big, bold letters, was:

Woman Killed in Freak Industrial Accident

Scanning the article, his blood ran cold just as his Mr. Coffee began making its gurgling, clicking sounds in the kitchen.

A lady, a passer-by, had walked past an under-construction building, when a section of wall collapsed on her, because a worker on the other side had inadvertently swung his bucket loader into it. What the woman had been doing so close to a construction site was not clear.

Joe opened the Metro section for the rest of the article, but before he found it, his eyes had fallen upon an ad for a funeral parlor.

Schwartz Mortuary.

Shivering from another chill, he threw down the paper and went to the still brewing coffee. He liked his coffee—

Black.

He impatiently scolded the machine for not yet having completed its cycle, nor having yet filled the pot enough for him to pour. He paced the kitchen and grabbed at the spoon he'd laid out beside his coffee mug, but, instead, knocked it off the counter. Bending over to retrieve it, he stood back up—and rammed his head into an open cabinet door above, catching the door on its edge.

He cursed quietly to keep from waking Lizzie and rubbed his head at the point of impact, still uttering restrained expletives. Growling, he quietly slammed shut the cabinet door. As he rubbed at the wound, he looked up to the cabinet door.

He hadn't remembered opening it.

Grinding his knuckles in and around the wound, the pain finally abated.

His coffee ready, Joe snatched the carafe from its warming station, spilling some as he poured it into his cup, then eagerly sipped it before replacing the carafe back into its nook.

Joe went to the La-Z-Boy to resume reading the paper, when his eyes landed on the words "eye beam." Blinking, he looked back down and found he'd mentally combined the words "eye surgery" and "laser beam," from a Lasik surgery article.

He shivered. Finished reading the article and the paper.

Joe took his shower (checked on his head wound and felt curiously lightheaded for a few moments), then left for work. On the way in, he'd had plenty on his mind...mainly, concerned with how to deal with Jeff Skopchek, his most recent problem child, and whether or not they'd complete the job on time. He also wondered about whether or not he and Lizzie should have a child...and when he could ever take off enough time for more than just a couple days, for a decent and proper vacation.

The closer he got to the job site, the more the Jeff Skopchek issue occupied his thoughts. He'd tried to do a friend a favor, but this guy had gone bad...turned into a real mess and had even started to affect his crew and their timeline. And last week—one of many—he'd had yet another accident. He'd backed up a front-end loader he was operating into the structure itself.

(*lady*)

(*bucket loader*)

(*wall*)

As his engineers had to evaluate any possible damage to the structure's integrity (there had been some), that had taken time and effort away from the actual job...and had been yet *another* accident to which Skopchek's name had been associated. As open-minded and willing to work with his employees as he was, not to mention trying to help out a *friend*, Joe felt it was time to let this guy go. He was nothing but trouble. Too many mistakes costing too much time and money. The guy just wasn't all there and was quickly becoming a safety and company liability. Who knew what would happen next? The guy needed to get his life in order, and Joe was going to give him the time to do so—

before something worse happened. He couldn't risk the lives of his crew—nor incur any more delays.

Joe arrived at the job site already spun up, traveling mug of coffee in-hand, and it didn't help matters any that, once again, Jeff Skopchek had arrived late and in a foul mood. Joe couldn't talk to him immediately, but told him he did need to see him. Jeff nodded, didn't say a word, and hopped into the loading crane's cabin. He was supposed to transfer a stack of steel from one location to another, a harmless enough task, Joe'd thought; a child in a hard hat could do it.

It was just about then that—unknown to Joe—Lizzie had pulled up into the parking lot across from the job site, in that small field that also served as a parking lot for the construction workers' vehicles. She sat in her car, smiling, watching him.

Joe approached a small gaggle of workers engaged in chit-chat in-between tasks. He'd said a brief "hello." They talked a little, laughed, until Joe caught sight of one of his foremen he needed to meet with, and excused himself. Unrolling a set of plans, he caught up with the man and they confirmed the day's marching orders. Rolling the sheet back up, Joe tucked it under an arm and headed off to another task, as thoughts of Lizzie and vacation planning once again filled his head. He felt good about life and their place in it. Was glad he had a great life, not one like Jeff Skopchek's messed-up bullshit.

The beep-beep of a backing-up loader brought him back to reality.

Joe again pulled out his plans, looking them over. Once he got rid of Skopchek and put in that other guy who'd quit but wanted back in, they should make up any lost ground. Again rolling up his plans, he looked up and across the field—and saw Lizzie, who'd just gotten out of her car. She waved. He waved back, smiling.

Why was she there...and so early in the morning?

A smile formed on his face...when all time, all sound, all *movement* just...*stopped.*

Joe found himself standing before a guy he'd never met before. Wondered what he was doing on his job site—and without a hard hat. The guy seemed friendly enough, even had his hand extended in a greeting.

"Joe? Joe Gordon?" the man asked.

"That'd be me."

"Nice to meet you!" the Man With No Name said, shaking Joe's hand.

"What's going on? Who are you?" Joe asked, visibly confused.

"There's been a little warp in time."

"A *what?*"

"Joe—can I call you 'Joe'?—I'm here to help put into motion some things we'd planned a looong time ago. Get things kicked off."

As confused as he was, Joe couldn't explain it, but he felt comfortable with this guy, who did seem vaguely familiar....

"I'm listening."

The Man With No Name put his arm around Joe's shoulders and led him away from the job site into the field in which Lizzie stood, also frozen in time.

"What I'm about to tell you is going to sound nothing short of bullshit and science fiction, but if you keep yourself open—which I know you will—you'll remember the words as I speak them. To just jump right in...I'm here to remind you that when you die, you don't really *die*, but instead shift your focus from one focal point to another. Like going from being awake to entering a dream state. Or going from what you were just doing...to what we have here, *now.*"

"Okay...."

The Man With No Name nodded, continuing.

"Not quite convinced, I see."

"Well, come on, what are we talking about here? *Dreams?* If I can't touch, smell, or see it—"

"It don't exist," the Man With No Name finished, again nodding, clasping his hands behind his back. "Understood. Except for your dream about Lizzie, before you met, right?"

"Right—except for that—which, of course, you seem to know about...."

"Well, let me help you remember a couple other things—things that have already come and gone many times, actually. And to remind you you've already remembered and decided upon this. I'm just reminding you—perhaps *reassuring* you, is the better word choice—before we get started, setting the stage, and putting things into motion. I'm the catalyst, if you will—"

"You're kidding, right? I have an apartment building to get up—"

"Yes, you do...but, look, as hard for you as this may be—right now—we have to do it. There's a man out there. After your wife—"

"*Excuse me?*"

"Now, calm down. We are going to keep him from getting her, even though he's already starting to warp events. For instance, why would Lizzie show up, now—so early in the morning? She wasn't up when you got up, was she? Anyway, that's what this is all about. Again, I'm just here to get things going."

The Man With No Name looked away as they continued into the field.

"This guy…he has issues…and is after your wife. He's nasty and operates under some seriously misguided principles. His reasons for this are not important now, but what *is* important is that he thinks your wife knows something about me, is somehow tied to me, and knows too much about *him*—those things, he believes, makes her a serious threat to him and his efforts."

"Is she? And what's so important about you?"

"Not until he started all this. And, as to me, well, that gets into even weirder aspects of all this and is best saved for later. But, he's a nasty government official using his power for his own ends, and I'm trying to stop him."

"That doesn't make any sense."

"It will."

Joe looked at him.

The Man With No Name chuckled. "Look, I did manage to bring you out of your normal time, didn't I? Look around. Things really are at a standstill, aren't they?"

Joe looked to Lizzie…at his crew and construction site—even noticed birds frozen in mid-flight above and around them.

"All these people—even the birds—are all still experiencing normal time. To them, none of this is happening." The Man With No Name examined Joe's expressions. "Even the 'you' back there," the Man With No Name said, motioning back toward the construction site, "is still experiencing normal time, operating at *normal* speed. But here…you're not. It's all real, so, go on…take a good, hard look; all of this *is* real."

Joe looked back from where he'd been *and saw himself still standing way back over at the job site.*

"Holy *shit.*"

The guy was right. His entire world did seem to have come to a sudden and abrupt halt—a standstill—but it wasn't like everything was dead. Though there were no breezes, birds chirping, nor equipment sounds (and he swore he heard faint, incredibly *rich* echoes…), there was something else…a kind of underlying…"excitement"…was the only way he could put it. *Expectation.* But other than that, as was point-

294 | F.P. Dorchak

ed out, indeed, all construction, all movement, all *life* seemed to have stopped—except for them.

Everything else, however, looked normal.

The job site, Lizzie and her car, the town, the passing traffic, surrounding buildings, the trees and birds held motionless in midflight...yet, *they* were the only two moving around.

And *he* was still standing over there at the job site!

Okay, it was pretty odd.

Lizzie would never believe him when he came back and told her about all this. She was the one who always had all the weird experiences, not him, but now he had something to talk about that would knock her

(*block*)

socks off.

And as he thought about it all, he did seem to feel—yes actually *feel*—that other him still back there in 'normal time.'

"Yeah, that's right—that's it!" the Man With No Name said, "I've just split a portion of you off into nontime. You're getting it. Great!

"Ok, this guy," the Man With No Name continued, "his name's Victor Black, thinks your wife knows something about me...that she could lead him *to* me...and to that end—now, please...don't get upset, because we're intercepting him...he plans on torturing her to get what he wants—"

"Oh, come on! How can you know this? How can any of this *be?*"

"Because he's already *done* it—"

"Jesus Christ, you just got done telling me he *plans* on—"

"I did."

"So, if he *plans* on it, how can he already *have done it?*"

"He—"

"You're telling me a man we don't even know—and I barely even know *you*, for that matter—is planning on torturing my wife because he thinks she can take him to you—but you say this really isn't the case until *after* he did this, *does* this—whatever? That it hasn't yet occurred?"

"You're still a little too attached to the emotional aspect of things. Let's try this, instead."

Without another word Lizzie, the job site, the town—all vanished—and Joe was overcome with images blazing across his internal landscape. But they were more than just *images*...

Hadn't he just been standing in that field—he was, *wasn't* he?—it was as if he had one foot in his reality, and the other

* * *

Whisked away into a maelstrom of surreal, bizarre, and fantastic imagery!

Was he still in bed, upstairs at home? Trying to figure out if he was still dreaming? Staring into that dark ceiling?

Or was he now…as he seemed to find himself…blurrily—*dizzyingly*—filling the shoes of untold different people *all at once*…people he seemed to *know*…people he seemed to…*be?*

It was like each of these people were all *him*…different versions of him…a confusing array of faces and lives more than just parading through or across his turned-upside-down mind…he was (*and how could this* be?)…he was experiencing each and every life in its *entirety*…their likes and dislikes…secret thoughts…how they interacted with others…quiet moments as they looked up into the stars at night, or across empty, wind-blown fields (dammit, but he *felt* the winds on his face)…and all the while he knew he was *each and every person*. He was every *one* of them…

…he was a diseased mason positioning a capstone in a Middle Ages castle in Germany…an ancient Egyptian priestess washing her hair before a ceremony for Osiris…a Native American construction worker eating lunch high atop an early 1900s New York City skyscraper still under construction…a navigator aboard a 1600s ship bound for uncharted, north Atlantic waters….

How could he be all these people? How could he be—

A doctor?

Many times a soldier and farmer?

Male *and* female?

Born and died countless times over?

Smelled and tasted and experienced everything between sea and desert and arctic air and grassland across the globe?

And as a child in his current (and what did "current" *mean*, now, anyway?) life, he relived playing with a passed-down set of cherished *Lincoln Logs* that—in another life, he realized—*he'd actually made! The very same* pieces!

Relived his entire current life…all his birthdays…Hallowe'ens…Christmases…playing in the woods…learning the ropes of construction…finding and marrying Lizzie….

So, how could he also be an English sheep herder…a spacecraft engineer….

It only made sense if…

It all came back in a hail of remembrance that bowled him over, and he began to laugh, and laugh, and *howl* into the infinity of life, the universe, and….

Of course! he continued to howl, *what had taken him so long?* This *was why he could be both standing in that field* and *be a miner in 1800's Pennsylvania!*

It all was so powerfully obvious!

Good God, *he could be so* thick *sometimes…*

Joe was back at the construction site, standing in that field, the Man With No Name standing patiently beside him.

"Do we understand each other?" the Man With No Name asked.

Joe nodded, still chuckling to himself, "Yeah, yeah, I got it, good *Lord*, I *got* it."

"It's usually easier to live one life with only one life's worth of data in the old memory bank—for most, anyway. The previous lives usually do end up leaking through, however, but most typically have more than enough to handle in their current focus and choose to ignore any other data. It can be exhausting, I know…."

"Wow."

The Man With No Name went over to one of the nearby motionless birds and gently stroked it.

Joe continued to process. "It's not that…it's just that…*I wanna keep looking in on these other lives*…and it's like, yeah, I've been clobbered with a two-by-four—I *know* it's a two-by-four, but I also know what kind of wood it is, its lineage and genetics, and how it's been manufactured—but I'm still reeling from the actual blow!"

"The 'initial' blow of the revisit stuns a little, don't it?" the Man With No Name said, smiling, "and that's another reason many don't recall their other lives…you do have to concentrate upon the current life."

Joe nodded, still smiling.

"So, to move along, and as I'd alluded to earlier, perception—life—is really nothing but a shift in focus. Since Black is quite adept at this focus-shifting thing—or thinks he is—we have to out-shift him. Lead him where *we* need him to go. There are so many probabilities to what he's trying to do, we had to pick one he'd least expect—something that doesn't give anything away, but still shifts Black's attempt away from Lizzie. There are multiple reasons for why anything is done—"

"Please," Joe said, holding up a hand, "don't go there—I think I'm on the long side of overwhelmed with what I have right now—as fascinating as it all is."

The Man With No Name nodded. "Fair enough."

"But," Joe asked, "if this is all a shift in focus…then, do we really need to change anything—need to do *anything?*"

"Of course you do, and yes. It's perhaps a little difficult to understand—even in your current nontime perspective and with all you've remembered—but there are subtle nuances to all concepts. Though it sounds contradictory, nothing is preordained; there are threads of experience that encompass *all* actions—everything *can* be changed. Just because there are other probabilities doesn't negate the need for personal action.

"It all comes down to a matter of focus.

"If you took one road, but not the other, the naturally curious soul of course wants to know where other roads go…and ends up experiencing *those* roads, as well. But to experience those roads, the individual still has to go *down* them, breathe the air above them, feel the roads beneath his or her feet, and live the passages of apparent time associated with the travel unique to *those* paths, experiencing the moments unique to those emotional points-of-view. But not every personality needs to know this as they take the other paths…because to know the path not taken would color the experience of the path *chosen*. It needs to be experienced in and of itself…though there are other probabilities where consciously knowing such knowledge is desired and needed—"

"Okay," Joe said, again holding up a hand, "I get it. Frankly, my mind's beginning to hurt. So, what do we do now? With Black?"

"You die."

"Why?"

"In actuality, Black had already put his intention into action—has already killed Lizzie—but we don't want him to *realize* that probability—at least not the Black we're dealing with. There are infinite universes and probabilities, and all are highly collaborative efforts on many levels of existence, and this one, the one you chose—where you decided to die for your wife in that life—was the better desired one for the probability that is *you*, standing before me, in this moment. You love manipulating and rearranging things. Look at your current profession—and at many of your other lives' professions—where you love building, creating, and rearranging physical matter. It's who you are, what you do. It was also decided upon, before and after all this hap-

298 | F.P. Dorchak

pened, that I was to kick-start this for you. It was deemed helpful to the other parts of you, in a learning and growing way we also won't get into here, and which are eminently personal to you. Everything we do bleeds through into absolutely every other existence.

"So, what we'd decided upon—*you'd* decided upon—was to focus on what we want in *this* probability...to have Black, as confused and vile as he may or may not be, to think that this is the *only* reality there is for him. For all his adeptness, he still doesn't quite get it nor understand the true nature of reality. If he did, he would be an entirely different personality—and in fact already is, this is just an 'early portion' of his path—and would realize there's no reason for him to do what he's doing.

"*That's* the plan."

"So, what you're saying is that Lizzie has already been killed by him—as much as she's never been killed by him—and since we're in the probability where Black *has* killed her, we're not going to focus on that and choose, in a rather nefarious and covert way—which kinda appeals to me—to fake him out and have him *not* kill her, by *me* taking the fall."

The Man With No Name smiled. "There's a little more to it, but yes. It's all in the details, my friend! By choosing this, your death will cause Black to pick up and focus on all the 'death issues' associated with a person—*you*—dying, which includes initial confusion, the 'what the hell?' energy, et cetera—which is why you also chose to have no memory of this after we part from this moment. It's the only way to throw him off the scent—given current events and focuses, and his juvenile reality changing ability. Of course, as you note, we've already gone through all this, so you do—*now*—know the drill. Though you won't have any memory, quote-unquote—you already do, because of our discussion."

"Man, this gets so convoluted."

"But it makes sense?"

"Goddamn makes my head spin," Joe said, looking out across the field to Lizzie.

"Pardon the pun. But every thought, no matter how fleeting or ill-formed, creates action and probability, creates a need for what's called 'value fulfillment.' All thoughts take shape in some reality, in some form, somewhere. It's immutable. Black just doesn't yet understand the finer print, and we're going to capitalize on that. Later, we'll attack the whole issue—or, rather, *he* will—but this is what is needed now. As long as you remember and forget that, we can move on and save other discussions for later. Just as you are alive and real now, before me, you are also dead in that German castle, that Antietam battlefield, and that ocean bottom in the north Atlantic—well, except for the sharks...."

As the Man With No Name rattled off his deaths, Joe experienced each one again.

"Okay...let's do this."

3

Joe stared out across the field, and paused. The sight and sounds of the construction site—the birds, and passing traffic—all seemed somehow more intense, more *there*. Denser. He looked around, and scratched the back of his head under his hard hat. His earlier injury throbbed.

What was different?

What had he just been doing?

He tapped his set of plans against a blue-jeaned thigh.

He looked back to his crew, heading off in various directions to perform their jobs, and looked back to the field. Why did that empty

(*empty?*)

field seem to stand out to him right now? What was so important?

Shaking his head and smiling (he heard some shouting behind him), he turned and—

Chapter Thirty

1

Victor Black floated in the metaphysical ether.

Kill Elizabeth Gordon before ever meeting her.

She had to go.

Black directed himself to the best opportunity…and came upon a humble, brick building. Inside lay a couple still in bed. Zooming in on the woman (her husband beside her), he found her to be his target. But as he focused in on Lizzie, he picked up on something bothering her husband. He momentarily diverted in on that "something." As Black directed his attention to Joseph Gordon, he was startled to see him staring directly at him. *Through* him, actually.

Of course he couldn't see him; he was merely lying awake in bed, staring up at the ceiling through Black's invisible awareness. Black repositioned off to the side of the bed; watched as Joe got up and out of bed and slipped downstairs to get the paper and make some coffee. As Joe went about his morning routine, Black focused in.

What bothered him?

A dream about Lizzie visiting him at his construction site.

In the dream, Joe talked with his crew when he spotted Lizzie coming over to talk to him. Then, out of nowhere it hits: an I-beam, carelessly swung through the sky. It misses Joe, strikes Lizzie.

Instantly killed her.

Black smiled.

Perfect.

Returning to Joe's present, Black followed him as he banged his head, had breakfast, and left for work…picked up on Joe's continued angst about his dream—and his problem with a member of his construction crew.

Black followed him to the construction site...saw the problem worker as he arrived late...troubled...climbed into the crane's cabin and began moving steel girders...

Black's smile widened. He focused in on changing the picture...brought Lizzie into the scene—just like in Joe's dream—and re-observed the construction site event. Now, Lizzie Gordon *does* pull up into the parking lot...

Good.

Black focused in on the crane and I-beam...willed the girder to swing toward Lizzie and Joe...but, as he did this, he sensed something wasn't right...a *blip*. There was...a momentary *skip* in the image....

He stepped back and reobserved.

Everything *appeared* fine...still on track...but....

Lizzie Gordon, Black focused on, *I-beam kills Lizzie Gordon*.

Black again reviewed his efforts; watched as Lizzie left her car, came up to Joe, and—

Is no longer there.

Her car was gone.

She was gone.

Joe no longer talked to her.

The I-beam was no longer diverted.

Black refocused in on the girder. Observed Joe staring out into the field, confused. Watched him look around, scratch the back of his head under his hard hat...

Damn it!

Refocusing on Lizzie, Black again diverted the girder...

Nothing!

Black watched Joe look back to his crew, back to the field, shake his head and smile, as he returned to work.

Furious, Black went back to the crane. The I-beam soared through the air alright, remained on its original path—but, *there was simply no Lizzie Gordon*.

How could *he?*

He was the only one who could have done this, that Man With No Name—*how could he have* possibly *interfered?* He had that man *contained*...unable to...

Black backed up his perspective and again surveyed the setting. Widened his psychic net. Tried to zero in on who or what was doing this...and detected an ever-so-slight...presence—*disturbance?*—an ener-gy...

Focusing in on this new influence, Black willed the aberration into awareness—and was quickly overcome with an intense, soul-searing sense of dread. A huge, menacing presence that consumed the space around him…hovered…then seeped clean through into the very marrow of his being….

Black held his ground…but the closer he tried to get to the source of the disturbance, the more intense its resistance. He was repelled…as if by a powerful—*angry*—magnet…and felt as if he were drowning within a dark, bottomless ocean…choking on its cloying, dirty waters…and that huge, impossibly strong arms were wrapping around him in a vile, fearsome octopus squeeze…effortlessly pulling him ever deeper into a bottomless abyss of absolute fear…his entire being…the structure of his thoughts, his *soul*…was permeated by this all-pervading horror. Black was no longer concerned with who or what this presence was, nor why it had chosen to interdict him, but had now become so overcome with fear and panic…so consumed and impregnated with it…that the more he tried to push it away, the more intense and horrific this insane drowning octopus-hug had become—

He needed to breathe!

Black tried to back away from the unstoppable entity…closed his psychic vision off from it, and willed himself as far away as possible in both concept and content from…this *thing*. To the opposite end of the universe from it…as outside of Time and Space as he could handle…but the dark, all-pervading entity continued after him…searching, probing, *pulling* him down, down, ever *downward*—

Until it backed off.

Catching his breath, Black decided to reengage and doubled back—but as soon as he began to probe, again felt the all-encompassing black hole of terror once again extend its abysmal tentacles—and quickly withdrew.

Something—or someone—was going to an awful lot of trouble trying to save a woman who continually professed no such knowledge of anything he asked.

He needed to regroup.

Black again began to pull out, this time for good, when—in an evil burst of inspiration—he left an ingenious parting shot. He diverted the I-beam toward *Joe Gordon's* unsuspecting and hard-hatted head.

Targets of opportunity were called that for a reason…

2

Lying on her side and awakening quite groggy, Lizzie brought a hand to her head.

"How are you feeling?" the Man With No Name asked. "Got a bit of a lump there, huh?"

Lizzie winced. She, and the still-unconscious forms of Travis and the former President, were all piled together at the bottom of a large, white tube. The Man With No Name bent down, examining the former President and Travis.

"They'll be fine. They'll come around shortly," he said. "You know where you are?" The Man With No Name stared intently at Lizzie, as he got back to his feet.

Lizzie sat upright. She rubbed her head wound and worked a sore shoulder. She sat back against the cool, hard surface of the enclosure. They were all placed inside a narrow, twelve-by-eighty foot deep enclosure. It was also hard to focus on where they were, because everything was white—

"No—no, no, no—not *again*—" Lizzie said.

The Man With No Name quickly came to her.

"No—it's not what you think," he said, trying to soothe her.

Lizzie's eyes went wide, her body rigid, and perspiration beaded on her skin.

The Man With No Name wrapped his arms around her and hugged her tightly, ssh-ing her.

"No, you're *not* back there…it's *not* what you think."

Lizzie closed her eyes; tried to calm and control her breathing.

"Then…where are we?" she asked, nervously, wiping her forehead and face and clutching her arms inward around herself.

The Man With No Name looked up and around at their confinement.

"Black thinks he's got us stuffed away from the world down inside some abandoned missile silo. Where a Minutemen II intercontinental missile was supposed to be housed."

The Man With No Name got back to his feet, but continued to study her.

"You don't sound convinced," she said. "Where do you think we are?"

304 | F.P. Dorchak

The Man With No Name quietly chuckled. "I think…we're in a far less nasty situation than he would have us believe."

"God, my head is spinning," Lizzie said. "I just can't seem to focus…"

"You'll come around soon enough."

"Why is it so hard? To focus? Things feel *really* weird.…"

"It's because of all you've been through."

The Man With No Name walked about the enclosure, occasionally rapping his knuckles against the curved surface. "He just doesn't get it." The Man With No Name stuffed his hands into his pockets and continued to examine their enclosure. He shook his head, sadly.

"Get what? Why are you being so vague?"

"Because Black himself doesn't even really know what he has here. He thinks it's one thing, but it's—"

"So, what *is* it?," Lizzie asked, still rubbing her head and shoulder. "Why *are* we here?"

The Man With No Name turned to her.

"To answer your second question first—because *I* brought you here—not 'here,' as in this *silo*," he said with a casual wave of a hand, "but 'here' as in *philosophically*." The Man With No Name sighed.

"It's time to put an end to all this."

Both the former President and Travis stirred.

Travis groggily shook his head, reaching out for balance.

Kennedy also tried to regain his balance and looked up. "I feel like I've been on a month-long bendah.…"

The Man With No Name helped everyone to their feet. "Lady and gentlemen…it's time to bring this show to a close…and put things right."

All three eyed the Man With No Name, who, without a word, simply returned their looks.

"No *way*—" Travis said.

"Good *Gawd*—" Kennedy echoed, equally stunned.

Lizzie looked to the three, open-mouthed.

Then each began a slow chuckle, as if just getting a punch-line.

Ring around the rosie,
A pocketful of posies,
Ashes! Ashes!
We all fall down.…

"You've *got* to be kidding," Lizzie finally said.

3

Travis, Kennedy, and Lizzie were all summarily catapulted out of the missile silo and deep into an inner, nonphysical *psychic*scape…hurled across time and space…probabilities and possibilities…to a battlefield, a battlefield that each knew involved the former President and Victor Black. They observed the battle as if watching a movie, but also felt the ground across which the combatants charged…the rush of their charge…the smell of death and black powder…tasted dry mouths and fear—anger—as each zoomed in on the Civil War battlefield personalities of Kennedy and Black. The three focused in on the Black personality, taking on his point of view….

…Black watched in livid anger and hatred as the Union forces rammed into their lines.

He was there.

His as yet unknown foe. They'd met…finally come face to face.

Black shoved aside and killed others in blue uniforms as he cut a bloody path to the one he knew he was destined to meet. Recognized him as he saw him remove his bayonet from one of his own South Carolina comrades. Black's anger flared. Attempted to reload his Enfield, but the fighting had become too close-quartered for use and he jabbed and butted the enemy with it instead, using elbows, knees, and fists. Black saw his target still trying to use his bayoneted rifle—when it was knocked from his grasp; watched as his opponent deftly sidestepped the attack, then lunged for his attacker with his bare hands, viciously throttling another until he snapped the man's neck. Black charged, just as his opponent deftly snatched up his rifle and turned to meet him. A musket's length apart, the two stared at each other.

Instant, unspoken recognition.

Knife to the chest.

Ringing ears.

Bayonetted.

Black was on the ground, a musket's bayonet shoved into his side.

Black grabbed the musket's barrel, but was unable to stop the bayonet's travel. He emitted a long, drawn-out grunt of pain, the blade forced deeper into him—then twisted. In shock and losing consciousness, Black began the long spiral…

Nowhere.

Something happened as he lay on the ground, pinned there like a stuck bug. Something...*morphed*....

...the three saw and felt the unabashed and livid fury that engulfed the soldier that was Black...felt his anger radiate outward across Time and Space...realities...and each of the three experienced that thread and followed it back to...

...Black lifted his bayoneted Enfield before him in reflex...and—to his surprise—the thrown knife *buried itself into the stock of his musket.* Black repositioned his weapon before him like a pike. The knife dislodged. He stood for a fraction of second, confused.

Something wasn't right.

Black refocused and charged his opponent. His target was busy with another of his comrades and twisted away from him in hand-to-hand with this other man. His opponent's back a sudden open and undefended target, Black concentrated his pent-up fury—and lunged. He felt his bayonet sink satisfyingly into unguarded flesh, stopped only by the tip of his musket's barrel. Black saw the man's shoulders arch sharply backward. With a jagged lurch, Black twisted the blade, and in one brutal and savage torso twist, put his whole body into severing the man's spine. As his adversary collapsed before him, Black's musket and bayonet followed him to the ground. As his opponent twisted onto his back, Black freed his weapon from the body and looked into the surprised, glazed and dying eyes of the man he'd called his enemy.

Black's rage suddenly—unaccountably—*softened.*

Something about this was wrong-wrong-wrong...all *wrong*....

For a split second Black saw himself—or was it his dying enemy?—above him, looking down at *him*...as he—~~Black~~—lay dying from a bayonet attack....

Then his enemy did something that completely unnerved him.

He...*smiled.*

His opponent coughed up blood, closed his eyes...*smiled*...then died.

Black blinked and backed up a step.

Humiliated by his own cowardly behavior and jostled back to reality by the continued fighting around him, Black again attacked his now dead foe, forcing others out of his way as he savagely kicked the dead man in the back...the shoulders...the head....

The three found themselves whisked away from the battle...floating and soaring off though infinite silvery, gossamer filaments...*cosmic* filaments...vibrant energetic gridlines that resonated and crisscrossed in and out of an infinite variety of realities...permeating and intersecting each other...*everything*. Each and every filament moved rapidly in and out of each and every other filament, like interlocking fingers. The three flew through the cosmic gridlines and found themselves following multiple lines of consciousnesses...found that the spaces between the filaments were filled with energy...*life*...that the spaces themselves also moved in and out of each other. Or, not so much moved as *existed*...blinked in and out of each other...one moment there, the next, gone—*yet still there*.

Back again.

They experienced the filaments intersecting with each of *them*...became the filaments and spaces themselves...*unbecame* them. These filaments that were (each just knew)...the underlying structure to all of existence...a fifth-dimensional interpretational structure to the energy called *Life*...an infinitely intersecting cosmic gridline that pushed and pulled throughout *all* existences...vibrating...

...shifting, blinking...in and out...*creating* existences...stretching, contracting *energies*....

The three were dizzy with choices...excitement...*probabilities*....

Each experienced...a joyous frustration...picked specific routes to explore, while other portions of their consciousnesses traveled down still *other* routes of exploration....

The trio shot through colorful, multidimensional layers of matter and antimatter, solidity and thought, came upon a nonvisual nexus of multidimensional emotion...multidimensional *concept*. Plunged through mass and nonmass...were outside as well as *within* concepts. Experienced simultaneous dreams, simultaneous existences...experienced the only thing they focused upon—but also experienced multiple layers of concept and reality, as if those were the only things *they* experienced....

It was like drinking from a most delicious fire hose.

Images and events whirled past at implausible speeds, stole their breaths. They felt gently, lovingly guided—directed toward a *particular* concept....

Laughter.

The laughter of *children*....

They diverted toward that laughter.

Experienced...lives and souls and ideas...all formed in a cosmic instant...an instant that caused and brought forth and was formed by these ideas...ideas that had also caused the moments themselves, that had brought *about* the ideas...no time...there was No Time...though they briefly experienced that physical concept...everything...simply *was*...any and all concepts and ideas already fully formed and expressed...in a present that knew no past nor future, only a single, powerful, all-pervading *Now*....

A spacious, past-present-future Present.

The laughter of the children drew them in—they experienced the reality behind this laughter...explored its concepts...existence...*origins*....

Children.

Incalculably *billions* of them.

Their very concept...birth, rebirth, youth, and energy...the gaining of knowledge...wasn't so much about *age*...as about *phases of development*...consciousness...of physical, *conscious* exploration. Concepts and reality were formed...learned...used...tested and refined...

Movement...there was movement of knowledge in the concept of children, of *youth*...a concept inserted into physical reality...a concept untried and untested in initial, physical existence, yet always having existed within it...a concept...initially only thought of...seeking expression...seeking explosive *fulfillment*....

The three found the chosen moment-point of its expression...an archetypal manifestation that served as a design across all existences...an initial physical expression that attracted and selected other concepts to test...nonphysical concepts inserting themselves into physical existence...seeking and fulfilling both physical and nonphysical expression...an energy expression that instantly formed...translated...its nonphysical concept *into* physical expression...*yet had always been expressed*....

This writhing, dynamic energy for this concept became *Children*...they followed one of countless probabilities, and it gathered portions of itself of similar, refined consciousnesses not yet tainted by the created physical, Earthly realities of those already living it...of other portions of its concept...and formed this energy under two charismatic leaders in a time early in the development of another nonphysical energy concept...that of *Adults*...and together explored themselves and the physical world in which they existed...gathered their combined energies...and put their concepts into physical motion....

Formed a crusade...a *Children's Crusade*...another physical expression of a nonphysical energy concept into Earthly existence...that marched across a ravaged and middle-aged (Adult) land during a medieval Holy War...but as the concept explored itself, came into fruition, it discovered it hadn't yet gained the necessary knowledge needed for adequate physical expression...to properly flourish, properly *endure*. Having transmogrified into a physical manifestation, it became immediately couched within the physical constraints...the physical *properties* that not only translated the nonphysical into physical, but also propelled its translated physical models and their properties into *action*...but were not adequately converted...prepared...and the concept quickly lost focus...faltered...began to dissipate...and in doing so, withdrew much of its energy from physical expression....

The children's medieval crusade fell apart.

Focus was lost, many died...were captured...sold into slavery. Murdered and abused. In a land not ready for it...by a concept not properly prepared for physical expression....

The concept had failed.

But the three discovered another thread...one in which this same concept—or a more refined, prepared version of it, with many of its original conceptual energy and expressed physical components—were again preparing for another manifestation...in a different time...with new knowledge gained from other expressions more properly prepared. This new articulation involved...a new breed...a more *particularly suited energy expression*...reinserting themselves into a more appropriate physical time expression...thousands, initially, *millions* eventually...would come from all levels of physically translated concepts of culture...to a time more encouraging to the concept...more *needful* of it. The concept would be noticed as different from the very beginning...would not make the same mistakes...would teach and bring about new paradigms...a New Breed of global, epic transformation that would go beyond the very medium and concepts in which it existed...materialize new schools of thought...new learning. They would be unstoppable.

And this time would not fail.

Chapter Thirty-One

1

Travis, Kennedy, and Lizzie thoughtfully mulled over their Gettysburg battlefield experiences, including the multiple outcomes for the Black and Kennedy soldier personalities.

This wasn't the end of things, was it? they asked the Man With No Name.

No, he answered. *It's more of a beginning, a continuation.*

Why was Black so angry at me? Kennedy asked, as they "returned" to the abandoned missile silo.

"Black was spun up," the Man With No Name said, "by events of the world in which he was to become a part. The concepts of good and evil—while not inherent to Existence itself, with a capital 'E'—became inherent to the *Human* condition, with a capital 'H,' and, therefore, *Black's* makeup. Because of this belief, other indicators and events were also spawned. Black is not unique in this sense. There are many like him, many situations like his. He is but one version of many 'Blacks' and many realities, as you have also just experienced—and of which you are all similarly a part. Mass events take on lives of their own, attract similar events of their own.

"In simpler terms, 'like attracts like.'"

"So…wereah like Black?" Kennedy asked.

"The mechanics of your existences are, but we each choose the lives we live, go where we need and want to go, for our own purposes. Black, unfortunately, the one we all know, here, is what I'd term an 'Angry Soul.'

"All physical matter springs from nonphysical sources—frameworks—dreams," the Man With No Name continued, "the Cosmic Grid you visited—and Black came to be because of specific *en mass* circumstances. Given his creation, he was also granted a desire to *be*—just like anything and anyone else. He hadn't planned on becoming the individual you all know, but that doesn't excuse him from who and what he is. He was actually spun off from another—someone else—and you, Travis," the Man With No Name said, addressing Travis directly, "you and your world changed things as part of *your* business."

"We did?"

No sooner had Travis spoken the words, when the answer formed in his mind.

"You were all given tasks," the Man With No Name said, "tasks you thought were to remotely *view* intelligence data. Since you rarely got feedback or responses from your efforts, you never really knew exactly what you were doing, did you?"

Travis shook his head, his annoyance apparent. "*No.*"

"Though many of your efforts indeed involved intelligence reconnaissance, many also involved highly secret *re*taskings from Black himself, who'd gone—unknown to anyone but himself—into the vaults and safes and swapped out many of the tagged and sealed envelopes with his own taskings...retaskings that actually involved *changing* events in your physical framework. And he did this both physically *and* nonphysically. When you focus on something, you bring it into being...*somewhere.*"

Travis again shook his head. "Just goes to show you, you can never trust anything in covert ops."

The Man With No Name nodded. "That is the very nature of the business. No one really knows who's doing what to whom. Now...were we to follow the threads of Black's anger and hatred...as you all did during that battle experience, but also at various times over Black's life as you know it...you would have seen he cursed our president's soul. Had we followed this further, as I did, we would have found that he'd vowed vengeance upon Mr. Kennedy and his entire family."

"But *why?*" Kennedy asked, "just from that little fight in my study—oh, maybe the appointment interview when I, ah, changed...."

"It's much more pervasive than that, Mr. President. Those were just symptoms of much deeper, underlying issues. Black had been harboring anger against you across *lifetimes*. Again, Gettysburg but one example."

Kennedy nodded.

"You can choose to experience his other instances later, but to summarize, he's angry that you never gave him the time of day."

Kennedy looked to the Man With No Name, puzzled.

"Black's anger is cumulative. He doesn't consciously know why…but, unconsciously does. Earlier I mentioned he was spun off from another—that other, Mr. President, is *you*."

"*Me?*"

"He is what we'll call a 'fragment.' A fragment of *your* personality, one that was never given much attention, energy, nor notice…from *you*. He never quite gained the knowledge or acceptance of himself as his own unique personality, his own unique *existence*. Always felt inferior and in need of competing for your attention. At times, you, or portions of you, *including your current incarnation*, have felt the need to beat him back."

Kennedy shrugged guiltily, grimacing.

The Man With No Name nodded. "Black has been killed many times by versions of yourself, sir, and it is not so much the killing that bothers him, as the way in which Black perceives your careless nonchalance *toward* him. Deep down, you do understand your ties with him…but have never quite accepted it. It's always bothered you…you've always felt him more of a nuisance than the part of you he is and has always striven to be—like the parents who never wanted to be parents, yet still had to feed hungry little mouths or change poopy little diapers when they could have been out on the town. Your personality has always had a rather monumental…sense of self, let's just say. Self-importance would be another way of putting it. Sometimes your personality would let itself get in the way and other times not, but on the whole, averaged out across all your entity's reincarnational personalities, you have taken a rather indignant offense to this little 'poopy diaper' of yours crying out for attention! Why should you have to change his diaper, feed *his* soul. '*Get your own life!*' you'd cry, '*change your own damn diaper, and quit trying to steal* my *thunder*,' you'd admonish. For that reason, Black's anger has accumulated across lifetimes of denial and inattention—both from you and himself. It constantly fed and reinforced itself until it became as foul as it is. It's that simple. You should have been as a parent and a sibling, and you were neither. You each knew and know of each other's presence in each life you've lived, yet you both tended to continue literally beating each other to death, rather than take on the much more important and harder task of reconciliation.

"*This needs to end.*

"You and he both need to resolve your issues, once and for all—

or this will continue. You need to better integrate yourselves. You can never advance until you get beyond this. In fact, you have some lives where you actually become brothers, and later, *husband and wife*—"

"Oh, *Lahd*," Kennedy said, "that ought to be interesting...."

"It is!" the Man With No Name said. "Those lives will have an indescribably rich, incredibly *tremendous* impact upon your soul's growth and will remedy your situations—if you properly handle and deal with each other."

Kennedy momentarily re-experienced threads of Black's anger and the constant re-ignition of his hatred toward him—as well as his own continued indifference and lack of concern. In any way Black could, Kennedy saw, he killed and killed and *killed* Kennedy's various personalities, the soul that was John Fitzgerald Kennedy—and, Kennedy (in turn) returned the favor. It was a neverending vicious cycle.

"No wonder people do the evil they do," Kennedy said. "How do we resolve this?"

"Tackle it head on—but *gently*. You need to take the lead and confront both of your selves—your own interior issues as well as those exteriorized in the form of Black and all his personalities—and to do so *between* lives as well as during them. Make amends...in any way possible. In fact, in your remaining lives—and I'm not telling you anything you haven't already decided upon yourself and already put into action—you actually take the less-dominant roles, to allow him the upper hand. It helps tremendously."

Kennedy nodded. "It can't be rectified in this life?"

The Man With No Name shook his head. "Sadly, no, I'm afraid not—"

"Right, I see—"

"It's actually more than that. As you can see, he's absolutely seething...and each life, whatever its consequences, has to complete to its logical conclusion. Yes, he will continue to curse and rue your very existence and will continue to plot your deaths...but he will, eventually, lose that energy and hatred when you begin to remove *your* indifference and resentment toward him. In fact, sir, there is one very real reality where Black foisted his ills and issues upon *you*," he said, gesturing to Kennedy, "even had you publicly assassinated. Lizzie picked up on it."

Lizzie nodded.

"Wow," Travis said, "it's like the ultimate conspiracy."

The Man With No Name nodded. "It is indeed."

"So, which reality is the real, *baseline* reality?" Travis asked.

"There isn't *one*. All realities are probable versions of each other. It's just that when your point of focus is in any one of them, *it* seems like the one, true reality. I'm trying to show you otherwise. Think differently about any so-called 'rock bed' reality....

"But, back to our story. Once you, Mr. President, and Black begin to work together, he, as you presently know him, will begin to dissipate."

"But all realities *ahr* given free reign," Kennedy said.

"Yes, they are. But again, as you restructure *your* thoughts, *your* feelings toward him, these other realities, though they will always exist, will begin to lose their steam and dissipate from *your* focus. Remove your focus from those probabilities, and the one you *do* focus upon will become the reality that the both of you live within."

2

"...now, actions and events," the Man With No Name continued, "can either exist as physical or *non*physical expressions—but no matter the medium—either one can just as powerfully and easily affect both physical and nonphysical existences."

As the Man With No Name continued to speak, accompanying images played out before each of the three.

"When our Black and Mr. President, here," the Man With No Name said, directing a glance to Kennedy, "began their 'lesson,' *I* came into being. I'll skip the specific mechanics involved and get right to the more salient. In your world, Black had the people under him performing their work, or 'taskings,' as they call it, in changing history—all without their *conscious* knowledge. As each remote viewer did so, each set up such a psychic storm within them that though they didn't consciously know or understand what they were doing, they certainly knew and understood *unconsciously*. Each of them—*you*," the Man With No Name said, looking to Travis, "took on your roles for your own purposes, but other portions of each of you were also involved in this set-up to help Black...see the errors of his ways. Things were getting out of control. Incredible amounts of angst—translated: *energy*—were generated by these nefarious and oftentimes downright evil acts. Each became psychically and metaphysically frustrated, and it was near impossible to break through into your consciousnesses, because Black *knew* what was going on. He had planned for it and was actively blocking any attempts by you and your team to break free of the hold he held on you. Well, 'blocking' is a poor choice of words…let's say, *redirecting*. *He* thought he was blocking your efforts, but what he was really doing was actually only choosing to focus in on the reality *he* wanted. It didn't negate other realities, just blinded himself to them. Anyway, this, unknown to him, gave me all kinds of room to grow. He just didn't know that no matter what you did, once you spun something up, it continued to create as long as there was some kind of energy directed toward it. As I said, no focus, no directed energy and intent, and an event will continue on only as long as that energy it does have is enough to sustain it. Nothing lasts forever in the same form in which it exists, and everything does, eventually, change. Where that energy goes is subject for other discussions.

"So, what does happen is that there are eventual 'bleed throughs' that occur from the nonphysical realms. In addition, Black couldn't possibly plan for everything, as much as he thought he could. Efforts in the nonphysical realms routinely sneak through cracks in realities—which explains, Travis, your Buddy LaRouque in the restaurant, et cetera."

"We were trying to get through to each other," Travis said, mulling it over. "I mean…I kind of figured that was going on, but was so mired by current events I didn't see the deeper meaning…"

"Quite all right. Buddy's good with it. But it gets better. As I stated…*I* came into being. Not that it's a real concern of this instant, but do you all realize—right this moment—that you're not actually…*physical?* Each and every one of you…*is dreaming.*"

The Man With No Name smiled, looking to each person in turn.

"Realize…*that right this moment*…each of you are dreaming. In fact…some of you…are downright—in your terms—*dead.*"

"No *way*—" Travis said.

"Good *Gawd*," Kennedy said.

"You've *got* to be kidding," Lizzie said.

"The dream world is every bit as real as the awake one and in more ways than your race can begin to imagine—we're just not used to being as conscious of it. There are events that we *feel* are real…but, in reality, have never occurred in a physical world, *yet the physical world swears they did.*

"It's like I said…the dream framework is from where the physical world *springs*, so it's not that far of a reach to understand that channels

316 | F.P. Dorchak

overlap—like analog TV or radio reception. Sometimes one channel will bleed over into another. Most might find that annoying or confusing, but I'm saying pay *attention* to those annoying or obtrusive thoughts…try to figure out what they are…where they're coming from, and what they're trying to say, crazed ax-murderer cravings notwithstanding, of course!"

"Okay, so, does that mean—" Lizzie began.

"My dear lady—*all* of you—I am nothing more…*than a figment of your imagination.*"

The Man With No Name disappeared.

Where are you? all three mentally asked.

I am not *and* am *right here!* the Man With No Name said, not yet materializing.

I am everywhere.

The Man With No Name rematerialized, standing behind them. "This is nothing each of you has not already done in your earlier field trip, as it were—it's just that where you are, in one reality, I have never been, nor will ever be, physical—yet I am based upon the concept and even give *it* new meaning, new paradigms, with my existence.

"With all the psychic frustration building around the misguided circumstances our Mr. President and Victor Black created, the rest of you—including you, Lizzie—created a workaround to help correct things. That workaround was *me*. Each of you created me…in the dream world."

"That's why he could never find you!" Travis blurted. "Friggin sneaky!"

"But—you were so real," Kennedy said.

"Oh, I am, Mr. President—just not in the sense you're requiring of me. Events and individuals that exist in the human experience can either be physical or nonphysical. A human personality…or an earthquake. An earthquake is a symptom of underlying phenomenon. It can choose to take effect either as a psychic upheaval or a physical one—or both. It depends upon many factors. For me, it was unconsciously decided among Travis and the others that it would better serve events if I remained disembodied, and I must say I agreed wholeheartedly with the decision," the Man With No Name said, smiling. "After all, to be physical, I would have to have been born into the world, and I much prefer the latitude I currently enjoy to that of being physically constrained!

"And, in order to pull this off, I had to be the most real dream image ever. So I popped in and out of all of your lives as I did and could to better facilitate things. *Confuse* things—"

"Well, you certainly did that," Lizzie said.

"However, in creating me," the Man With No Name continued, "you also spun up parental images—not a huge leap, given your physical existence and concepts—which also played along in further spoofing our Mr. Black. It added yet another level of confusion to Black and our operations."

"But the killing of that family," Lizzie said.

"Yes. Unfortunately, however, they did exist in your physical terms and were murdered. I did my best to interrupt things, but Black kept an extremely close guard on that scenario. He was extremely proud of that operation. They originally began in the nonphysical realms, but accepted the 'expansion' of their roles into physical existence for their own reasons, and the rest, as they say, is history. Again, it further complicated issues for our Mr. Black. However—since all time *is* now, and there *are* a myriad of probabilities, the family does currently exist elsewhere—in other probabilities they were *not* murdered."

"What about Joe?" Lizzie asked.

"As I'm sure you will now experience, Joe was a part of this operation. Like the family about which I just spoke, he also willingly accepted his role."

Lizzie searched out the construction-accident thread.

"What the—"

"It's true," Joe said, standing beside her.

Lizzie threw her arms around him.

"It was all for you," he said, smiling. "It was needed on many levels, and I thought, 'what the hell' *exactly*. There'll be other lives…."

"*Damn* you!"

Joe smirked guiltily.

"What about Mel?" Travis asked.

"Yeah, what about him? How is he? And *who* is he?" Lizzie asked.

"Mel…was a multilayered, nonphysical plant of mine—of me. Mel was my attempt, through my own direct creation, to additionally throw Black off the trail. As I came into being, I threw out different versions of me, so that at least one of us could take root and grow, if others were discovered and 'neutralized,' to borrow the industry-standard term. One who was to become who I was supposed to be, were *I* outed. Mel was a *partially materialized* me, purposely incomplete and confused to further perpetuate the scenario and obfuscate Black should

318 | F.P. Dorchak

he—Mel—be found, which he was. In one very probable reality, 'Mel' was found and hired by The Center—Black—as part of the remote viewer team…part of another covert project known as 'Delphi,' but all in a different probable *dream* world that Black never suspected. That version of me was later hunted down and 'neutralized,' as it were. There are and were others like him elsewhere. Black, like everyone else, also has his nonphysical versions, and it was one of those who 'killed' Mel. This younger version of Mel, however, in being tortured and killed like he was, gave further credence to everything else we'd put into place, including Black's murder of that family a generation earlier. Incidentally, Lizzie, it was through Mel's eye's you were looking when you initially had the dream about that family's murder, and Black 'shot' you in the face. It was through that dream that keyed Black into your *and* Mel's existences. How you became 'important' to him."

"Huh," she said, still looking to Joe.

"Good Gawd, this is all so damned complicated," Kennedy said.

"Perhaps, but it's not quite finished. As I said, Black still has to live out the rest of his life, his energy—which, it turns out, won't be all that long, by your standards. As he correctly surmised, he did piss of the intel community, and the community does hunt him down. We all die as we live.

"And, there is one…more…thing."

"Yes?" Lizzie said, smiling as she remained within her husband's embrace. She and the others heard a suddenly childish chorus of playful laughter.

"My *children!*" Lizzie exclaimed.

"You may not realize this," the Man With No Name continued, "but in your physical reality, you all died when that Learjet crashed. All of you, that is…except one. But since you have all learned from your experiences, you can now focus on other realities. Things *have*, indeed, changed from all this…new realities have been created. New *worlds*. It's time, whenever you're ready, for you to continue on with what each of you has started—to see it to the fruition you all deserve after your last escapade.

"Are we ready?"

Kennedy, Travis, Lizzie, and Joe looked to each other.

"And you'll all be much closer to each other in all of your existences than you could ever have imagined—because of this."

"What about you?" Travis asked the Man With No Name.

"Thanks for asking, but I'll continue to exist like everything else—

as long as there is enough sustainable energy—a need—for me to exist, I will. Believe me, I have plenty I want and need to do! There's so much out there, and I'm looking forward to experiencing as much of it as possible—along with whatever happens when I choose…to alter my state. All time is now, remember that; remember what you've all just experienced. In a very real sense I'll always exist—just as each of *you* will!"

But what about the—

(*children?*) Lizzie mentally finished.

Bless *the children*, the Man With No Name psychically whispered…

And they all disappeared.

3

Ring around the rosie,
A pocketful of posies,
Ashes! Ashes!
We all…
Grow up.

Chapter Thirty-Two

1

Black paced the spartan, low-lit hotel room.

It was only a matter of time.

After thirty years of government service, he'd finally screwed up—*big* time.

Or had he?

The problem was he didn't know whether this was his doing, or that other's. It seemed no matter what he did, he just couldn't shake that guy. That Man With No Name, that burr in his side for nearly as many years.

Nightmare Man.

Black hammered a wall with a clenched fist.

Damn him!

Now, what the hell was he supposed to do? He couldn't go back to The Center nor his apartment. Yet, as pissed and apprehensive as he was, he was also exploding with *euphoria!*

Exhilaration!

What power he'd just wielded!

To do what he'd just done…what no other person in the world could do, or had ever done before…killed all those important, gifted people. People who would, could, and *have* changed the world.

He'd just taken them all out.

Him.

And by doing this, he'd just changed the world himself…and his name would forever go down in the classified annals of history and he'd be remembered and *feared* for that.

Who was the powerful one, now, J-Fucking-K? Mess with me, will you?

You may have the official power, but I pull all the puppet strings—I wield all the real power—in the dark, in the background—where the real work is performed. In all the dirty little places you're too good for, too afraid to tread. I live there. I'm the one who actually dirties his hands and actually gets things done and doesn't just make the ivory tower decisions to get things done. I am the wielder of the

(bayonet)

sword.

He paced the room. Were he a drinking man, he'd already have broken open a bottle, but he wasn't. He had other ways to celebrate. Other *needs*—

There was a light knock at the door.

Black checked the peephole, unlocked, then opened the door.

The attractive, unsmiling woman in her forties, who looked as if she'd been around a block or two, slipped inside without eye contact. Black closed and locked the door behind her.

The woman removed her coat, revealing a tight thigh-high skirt, loose chemise top, and platform, come-fuck-me shoes. Black eyed her like a hungry bear emerging from hibernation. He went to her, grabbed her by her narrow waist, and pulled her into him. Viscously kissing her, drew blood from her lips. The woman didn't resist.

Black reached for her shoulders and began pulling at her chemise blouse.

"Just a minute," the woman said, in a hushed tone, "let *me*...."

Black backed away, eying her like a predator.

The woman intently held Black's gaze and removed her top, revealing a black brassiere.

Black—maintaining eye contact—began undoing his tie and shirt.

Her face blank, the woman crossed her arms, tilted her head, and shifted her weight. She kicked off one platform shoe, then the other. Black finished removing his shirt and lunged for her. The woman forcefully thrust out an arm, a hand to the center of his bare chest. Black stopped, grinning. The woman backed him up against the wall, holding Black's increasingly evil gaze. The woman then backed up a half step and brought both her hands up behind her to undo her brassiere.

Leaning back against the wall, Black closed his eyes and grunted deep, animal growls, while he loosened his belt...

Swift as lightening and out from behind her back, the woman pulled two four-inch razor-sharp blades, which she quickly and professionally spun around in her hands...and drove deep into Black's chest.

Black expelled a surprised puff of air.

In the blink of an eye, she removed the blades, and in another swift and passionate stroke, slit his throat.

Not once, but twice.

Wide-eyed and gagging up blood, Black staggered against the wall.

Before he could further react, the woman fell upon him in a flurry of rage and blades, her face now contorted into a mask of unadulterated, seething *hatred*.

No more rape!

No more humiliation!

No more on-call fuck *receptacle!*

In a hazed frenzy and bathed in his blood, the woman hacked and slashed his face then leaned into him and shouldered him up against the wall, as she repeatedly (and repeatedly) used his groin as a pin cushion.

Bayonet and twist...

Bayonet and twist...

Twice got her knives stuck in his pelvis bone, which required an extra hip check to remove....

When she was done, she pulled away like a cork from a champagne bottle, and what was left of Black dumped to the floor. The woman continued several more impassioned, angry slices through the air, spraying blood across the furniture and far walls before, she, too, collapsed to the floor. On her knees, she supported herself upright, knives still clenched in her fists, gasping for air and still emitting periodic barks of animalistic grunts and growls.

The woman hung her head and wept...

Then abruptly stopped.

Went into a thousand-yard stare.

Slowly came to her feet.

Defiant, bloodied knives hanging to her sides in white-knuckled and clenched fists, she came to her full height and looked to the blood-splattered wall, the mangled body.

Inhaled several gulps of air.

"It's over," she said, inhaling deeply. "*Over*...."

"You all right?" a voice asked through the microphone implant in her ear.

"Fine. I'm...fine."

Her body now trembling, she went to the door, unlocked it, and turned away. Still clutching her bloodied blades, she retreated back away from the door. Again stood before Black, his body slumped at a weird angle at the intersection of the wall and floor.

Stared at him.

Her mouth continued to work for air. Her face remain contorted with disgust and rage.

She spit on him.

Men-in-black stormed the room and immediately set to work.

One came up to the woman and carefully pried the knives from her clenched and bloodied fists. Looked deeply into her eyes. The woman turned slowly to him and gradually came to focus on his eyes.

"*Are you okay?*" the man again asked.

The woman turned back to her handiwork, watching as what was left of Black was unceremoniously crammed into a black body bag. She again spit on him, as he was removed past her. Handing off the knives to another waiting behind him, the man then took the blanket handed him by another and began to wrap the woman within it—when she raised a hand in protest. Holding her head high, she left with another, who'd been motioned over toward her. She was escorted out the door and into an awaiting black van. The van immediately departed before its door was closed.

Black's apartment was sanitized.

It was as if he'd never existed.

2

Lizzie awoke dazed. Every inch of her body throbbed from some kind of full-body pummeling. Fluttering open her eyelids (which even seemed to hurt), she found herself hanging at a weird, canted angle. Something brushed across her face, while something else acrid burned up into her nostrils.

Plane.

Escape.

Crash!

A crash—they'd been going down—Travis and the President and the pilots and the President's bodyguard and her—they'd had an engine failure of some kind, the pilots had said, lost altitude. Lizzie took a quick psychic peek and found several bullets—from Black—had severed fuel lines and punctured electronics—as well as the port engine.

The pilots tried, but what could they do? They did the only thing they could and steered clear of populated areas...tried to keep as low an angle of attack with the ground as possible....

The next series of events had happened fast...they'd lost altitude and had come in hot, a term she'd heard the President use, over the tree tops. Actually heard and felt trees scrape across the bottom of the aircraft—the weirdest sound she'd ever heard, given their situation—past windows, then there was...

Confusion. Explosions. Unconsciousness.

Some very weird dreams.

Now, she hung from an angle that hurt, in a seat that clearly wasn't as secured to the floor as it had been when she'd been strapped into it, with—she saw—deployed oxygen masks dangling before her. And that smell that burned her nostrils was the caustic odor of electrical fires and jet fuel.

Human flesh.

Blinking to clear her vision, she saw the plane listed to its port side, its nose slightly elevated. Smoke was still filling the cabin, but for some reason, hadn't engulfed it. She heard popping and sizzling sounds, but also something else:

Birds.

Looking up, she saw the gaping hole.

To her left, a large section of Learjet had been torn free. She could see birds and trees and sky—

An awakening morning sky.

Lizzie tried to move, but her side hurt—whether from having been banged around or from just having been hanging at this rather uncomfortable angle for who knew how long.

Fumbling with her belt release, fighting bruised and clumsied and cramped hands, and her bodyweight pressed against the buckle, she finally undid it and tumbled out to the sloped floor. She yelped out in pain as she slid down into the slanted bulkhead. She felt like she was in some crazy, burned-out, Fun House. On her way down toward the angled bulkhead, Lizzie passed something "interesting" that briefly registered with her, but she couldn't think clear or fast enough to identify it. After a grunt or two of pain, she took stock in her situation. Yes, she was indeed bruised and battered in a few places, even

(*knives*)

cut—had some drying blood on her face and hands and arms—but apparently nothing serious. She was a little dizzy and disoriented, but felt herself quickly overcoming that.

The worst sensory inputs seemed to be coming from around her.

Lizzie carefully braced herself, trying not to land her hands on anything

(*knives…*)

sharp, charred, or burning, and positioned herself for a better look. She looked for the pilots, but saw no signs of life from the flight deck, which looked quite bashed in, when one of her hands landed on something soft.

The President!

Lizzie quickly scrambled to the former President, who, she now saw, along with his body guard, lay lifeless in a twisted mass among the wreckage. Lizzie tried to move him, but his body behaved in a weird, unnatural way, part of it wedged tightly and unable to move.

Charred.

His back broken.

"Damn it…." Lizzie said.

It was amazing how light he felt, even under all that wreckage. Older people always got lighter. Felt good on the scales, she was sure, but the mechanics of osteoporosis weren't anything to look forward to.

Travis!

Lizzie spun around, looking for her rescuer.

"*Travis!*" she called, "*Trav—*"

He, too, remained in his seat, but both he and his seat had been totally uprooted from the aircraft's deck. He—his legs—were the "interesting thing" she'd slid past on her way down across the floor.

As she looked to him, she saw that he and his seat had not only been ripped from the floor, but were also twisted up in the wreckage. As she forced Travis and his seat back to better examine him, a startled cry escaped her. A large sliver of contorted metal had screwed itself into Travis's chest about where his heart should be. It reminded her of

A bayoneting?

Lizzie bent down and touched him.

He was cold.

Or as cold as one could be among a fiery wreck. Again, she squeamishly reached for him, checking for a pulse…this was a mere formality…as expected, there wasn't one.

"God *damn*, Black!"

Lizzie allowed herself to fall back against the bulkhead, angrily kicking at wreckage and slamming her fists against the enclosure as she slid to the floor. Took in the smell and full scene of destruction. Psychically reaching out, she didn't feel anyone still hanging around.

They'd all quickly departed, and that was good.

Better to move on than stick around the scene of your passing. People died for a reason, and part of that reason *was* to move on. Good for them. But—

Why her?

Why was she to survive? And why had the others who'd rescued her from Black have to die? All these people she didn't even know...had given their lives to save *her*.

Why?

Why had *she* been so worth saving?

Wouldn't she soon be caught anyway, given Black—or whomever—would soon, surely, send rescue aircraft, search teams—

Mommy, the tiny voice whispered, *it'll all be all right. We'll help you. Help you remember....*

Lizzie closed her eyes and was barraged by images flying far too fast to make sense of, especially now. Slowing down the psychic barrage she was able to delineate the images...images of the compound from which she'd just been rescued...but also saw in that very same Blue Ridge Mountain location *other* "centers"...*nongovernment* ones...metaphysical ones...similar, but different...

Schools? Institutes?

For whom?

Us, the ghost-child responded.

Lizzie saw a school of uncommon instruction for a whole new breed of...saint? Psychic?

Humanity?

Saw the person who ran it...a woman who felt...

That's you, *Mommy*, the ghostly child said, giggling.

Me?

You're gonna direct and lead this school...and it will become a new place of learning...enlightenment. It will echo across the planet—consciousness itself—on a scale yet unheard of. We will come...to learn, to grow...become the new breed of humanity...and we call you "mommy" because you'll be like a mother to us when we arrive...and because you've always wanted children....

As Lizzie's heart swelled with emotion, she saw that The JFK Center no longer seemed to *be* there...or was, at one time, but had been...*abandoned?* Saw other versions of institutions...existing in the same location? It didn't make sense.

Different times…different probabilities….

But what of Black?

He's gone, the girl said, her tone changing. *Burned too many bridges. Was a very bad man. We don't have to worry about him anymore.*

"What about…the man…the One With No Name?" Lizzie asked, slowly, stiffly getting to her feet. She leaned against the bulkhead for support. A smiling image of the Man With No Name entered her mind. Yeah, he'll be fine.

Lizzie peered ahead into the still-smoking cabin where, she was sure, were what remained of the pilots entangled in tree branches, electrical wire, twisted metal, and shattered Plexiglas.

You probably don't want to go in there, the girl said. *It's not pretty.*

Okay.

Lizzie again examined herself. She seemed to be in one piece, no worse for the wear, though she did hurt all over and had a slightly banged-up leg. It was hard to straighten up into a fully upright position. Her side still hurt, but she could manage.

You'll be okay, Mommy.

Think so?

Know so. We'll help you find your way home.

I'm gonna need that, since last I remember, my home had up and disappeared…

We'll find you a new one.

Lizzie chuckled—which also hurt.

You should probably get going. Men are on the way. Helicopters. They may not work for Black, but that won't help you much right now.

Lizzie turned to the torn-open bulkhead and looked back one more time to Kennedy and Travis.

"Sorry, gentlemen…but thank you for all you've done. I'm honored. Sorry I have to leave like this—but I'm sure you understand…."

Trying to smile, but wincing instead, she turned back to the bulkhead. Studying her best means of escape, she grunted a little in pain then made her way through the Learjet's open wound. Slowly picking her way through the jagged breach, she landed on soft-and-spongy forest humus, which surprised Lizzie in its actual emotional impact. Crying out, she carefully straightened up and looked around. Curls of smoke, sputtering electrical shorts, and small fires continued to pop and spit sporadically from the wreckage. The sun was just beginning to peek up above and beyond the cover of trees and distant hills. She turned to watch it, wiping away her tears.

A smile formed across her face.

The pilots were fine.

Travis, Kennedy, and Morris, Kennedy's bodyguard—all *fine*.

She knew this.

But the situation…the situation would stick with her forever, and she would miss them—and the others—who died to get her out of there.

Maybe she should start up that school.

What else did she have? She certainly wasn't going back to her old life, that of a phone psychic. It was about time for her to quit mourning, quit worrying about why me—she knew *why me*. Start a new life—a new direction.

A new breed.

Yes, she would establish that school…do something good for *all* of humanity this time, not just unhappy, lonely callers.

She needed to quit hiding from life and put herself out there.

She'd be fine—she knew this, too.

Lizzie looked up ahead, and saw her ghost children. They stood at the edge of the crash site, where the woods were again thick with trees. They smiled, waving for her to hurry.

"I'm coming, I'm *coming!*" she said, making her way toward them. "But, if we're going to be doing this school thing, we'd better get some ground rules straight," she said, as she limped from the wreckage. "No more bossing me around, for starters, and tell me the *whole* story—no more leading me along with all kinds of vague generalities…."

Yes, Mommy, the children said, giggling playfully, as they led Lizzie Gordon through the forest…

And into her new life.